PROMISE OF LOVE

She watched him anxiously as his gaze took her in from the top of her head to the tips of her bare toes. And she saw the way his chest rose and fell unsteadily.

"You're very lovely, Mrs. Ross," he said, his voice sounding huskier than usual. "Have I told you how much I like your hair down like that?"

Automatically, she reached up to touch the long curls that lay on her shoulders. "No, I . . . thank you," she said, feeling stupid and awkward and not the least bit lovely. "Adam?"

He smiled and slipped his hands into the pockets of the robe, as if he didn't have a care in the world. "Yes?"

She had to swallow before she could speak. "You'll have to tell me what to do," she warned quickly.

His smiled widened. "Nothing would please me more."

He came to her, moving silently over the carpet, and she hardly had time to draw a breath when he took her face in his hands and kissed her.

This kiss was different from the one he'd given her in the parlor. This kiss was deep and full of promise, and when he finally lifted his mouth from hers, she was breathless. So was he.

FROM THIS DAY FORWARD

Victoria Thompson

Zebra Books
Kensington Publishing Corp.
http://www.zebrabooks.com

ZEBRA BOOKS are published by

Kensington Publishing Corp.
850 Third Avenue
New York, NY 10022

First Printing: August, 1997
10 9 8 7 6 5 4 3 2 1

Printed in the United States of America

With thanks to Anna Fleck, Director of the Blair County Rape Crisis Program, and all her dedicated volunteers.

One

"Lori."

Adam Ross had called her name, but Lori didn't reply. She didn't reply because she knew this was just a dream. She'd often dreamed that Adam Ross was calling her, and every time she answered him or reached out for him, he faded away, leaving her alone again. So she didn't answer him this time because she didn't want the dream to end.

"Lori."

She could see him clearly. He was standing in a field, waving to her, and then he started running toward her. In her dreams, he didn't need his cane, and he could run as well as any man. His hair looked golden in the bright sunlight, and his smile was so beautiful that it nearly stopped her heart.

She couldn't let the dream end because in another moment he would be with her. Still, this would only happen in her dreams because in real life Adam Ross would never even look at her. Especially now.

"Lori!"

Someone was shaking her awake. *No!* she thought, fighting to hold the dream, but it was too late. Adam was already fading as consciousness returned. Reluctantly, she raised her leaden eyelids and came face to face with the real Adam Ross.

Startled, she cried out in alarm and raised her head, not from her pillow, but from the kitchen table. And she realized several very unsettling things all at once: she'd been sleeping at the kitchen table in the middle of the day, and Adam Ross himself was actually standing over her and looking even more handsome than in her dream. And a lot more concerned.

Dear heaven, what on earth . . . ? she wondered wildly in the instant before the terror took her. *Because if Adam was here, then surely . . .*

She jumped to her feet, desperate to flee, as she glanced frantically around the room for *him*. The bench she'd been sitting on fell over with a crash, and the wooden bowl she'd been holding in her lap thudded to the floor, sending the peas she'd been shelling scattering everywhere. But she hardly noticed any of that in her relief to find that she was alone.

Alone with Adam Ross.

"I'm sorry," he was saying in a voice as deep as a well. "I didn't mean to frighten you."

But he did. The fear rose up again unbidden as it had every day for months and certainly every time a man had come near her. What on earth was he doing here? Instinctively, she backed away and almost went sprawling over the fallen bench.

"Careful," he cautioned as she grabbed the rough edge of the table to steady herself.

He bent to set the bench upright, and even as she automatically recoiled from his nearness, she saw the way he kept his left leg straight as he performed the task. Instantly, she remembered his pain and experienced the rush of affection she always felt for him.

How could she have been afraid? This was Adam, after all. The man she'd known for years. The man she'd admired for as long as she could remember. And the man she'd loved since she had come to understand what love was, even though she knew he would never love her back. Adam, of course, would never hurt her.

He straightened, and she saw he was frowning. "Are you all right, Miss McClintock? Should I get your mother?"

"She's not my mother," Lori said instinctively as she always did when anyone made that mistake.

"I mean your stepmother," he corrected himself. "If you're ill—"

"Of course I'm not ill," she assured him with false brightness, although her hand went to her stomach as if to prove her a liar. Well, that wasn't an illness, was it? "Although you'd have every right to think I was when you find me sound asleep over my chores. I don't know what got into me," she chattered on determinedly, stooping quickly to pick up the bowl she'd dropped and collect as many of the scattered peas as she could, feeling like a complete idiot. "I must have spring fever," she told him, glancing up from where she crouched on the cabin's dirt floor, carefully rescuing the tiny, new peas.

She tried a smile, even though she knew a smile wouldn't distract him from the rest of it. He'd known that she was poor, certainly. Hadn't his slaves been bringing her and Bessie food ever since Pa went off to fight in that stupid war? Didn't he know that she always wore the same dress to church, year after year?

But knowing and seeing were two different things. Now he was seeing where she lived, the dilapidated two-room cabin with its dirt floor and rickety, homemade furniture. The boxes nailed to the walls for storage of their meager belongings. Her ragged, everyday dress that had long since lost whatever color it had once had. Her bare feet, left uncovered so she could save her one pair of shoes for church.

Self-consciously, she ran a hand over her hair, as if smoothing the unruly curls would somehow make up for everything else. Even more self-consciously, she quickly rose to her feet again and set the bowl back on the table. Then she realized she still held a lone pea in her hand and, her face flaming, she tossed it into the bowl with the others.

They couldn't afford to waste even one pea. Then she risked another glance at Adam Ross.

Dear heaven, he was tall. Why hadn't she remembered him being so tall? Or so imposing. He was wearing the dark suit he always wore to church, and the fingers of his left hand curled tightly around the head of his ornately carved cane. He looked every inch the successful planter and as out of place in the McClintock cabin as a pig in school.

What could he want here? Lori swallowed nervously.

"If you're here to see Bessie, she's out in the fields," Lori told him, referring to her stepmother. She wished he wasn't standing quite so close and fought the urge to step back again.

"I'm not here to see Mrs. McClintock," he informed her solemnly. "I came to see you."

"Me?" she asked in surprise, and for one second a spark of hope flickered in her heart. Could he really have come to call on her? Was it possible that he had finally noticed her after all these years? Then, just as quickly, the tiny spark died. Even if he had, it was too late—way too late. "Whatever for?" she asked with more false cheer, desperately concealing the painful emotions roiling within her. "If you want to talk business, you'd best see Bessie. She's the one who—"

"I already saw her," Adam said, his expression even more solemn, if that was possible. "She called on me this morning. She told me about . . . about your situation."

No! It wasn't possible! Shame washed over her like a tidal wave. Shame and humiliation and mortification so thick that she couldn't breathe and she couldn't even see. But that was all right because she certainly didn't want to see the contempt on Adam Ross's face, and she didn't want to draw another breath, either, not if it meant she would live for another moment.

But she wasn't going to be that lucky.

"Miss Lori?" Adam cried, summoning her back. "Are you

all right? You'd better sit down. I can call your mother for you . . ."

"She's not my mother!" Lori repeated through gritted teeth as she fought the nausea that threatened to choke her. How many times had she reminded people of that fact, yet never had she felt the truth of it more than at this moment. Although Bessie had been thoughtlessly unkind to her many times, she had never been cruel, not until now. Bessie had betrayed her, and worse, she had betrayed her to *Adam Ross*. How could she?

"I really think you should sit down," Adam was saying. He reached out to her, perhaps instinctively, perhaps out of concern, but Lori flinched from him as if he were a leper. How could he stand to touch her? How could he stand to *look* at her?

She didn't know, but she did sit, bending her knees out of habit when they bumped up against the bench. She sank down wearily and wrapped her arms around herself since no one else would. The darkness of her own personal horror hadn't quite receded, and she could still see it lurking at the edges of her vision when she finally lifted her gaze to Adam Ross again.

To his credit, he revealed nothing of his disgust for her. His fine features, the result of centuries of good breeding, wore only an expression of deep concern with perhaps a touch of alarm. What could he possibly be alarmed about?

"Can I get you something? Some water perhaps?" he asked solicitously.

For an instant, she pictured him wielding his cane about the cabin as he made his way awkwardly to where the water bucket sat to fetch her a dipperful. Then she shook her head and dropped her gaze again, too ashamed to look at him any longer.

"I didn't come here to judge you, Miss McClintock," he said in what he must have intended to be a kindly voice.

Lori looked up in surprise. *"Judge* me?"

His expression tightened, and she glimpsed a trace of the disgust he was trying so hard to disguise before he was able to control his expression again. The shame twisted in her like a knife, but she managed to hold his gaze.

"I'm here as the head of the Ross family," he explained patiently, as if he thought her too stupid to understand unless he spoke slowly. "When my father died, that left me as . . . well, as the oldest son. Eric and I may be brothers, but I'm still responsible for him and for his . . . his indiscretions."

Indiscretion? Is that what she was? She felt an insane urge to laugh. Instead she said, "So what do you think you can do about *this?*" She could hear the bitterness in her voice and wondered if he could, too.

He shifted uneasily, moving his cane, and she wondered if his leg bothered him. For no reason, she suddenly remembered how he'd come to injure his leg in the first place. That had been Eric's doing, too. They'd both been hurt by him. Terribly hurt. In ways that would never heal.

Tears she couldn't allow herself to shed burned behind her eyes as she forced herself to listen to what Adam Ross was saying.

She thought the color had risen in his face at her question, but he did not flinch. "I'm not certain *what* I can do," he said. "You probably know that Eric has run off to join that bunch of misfits that Rip Ford is getting together to stop the Yankees from invading."

Lori nodded gravely. Everyone knew that the Yankees were, in this year of 1864, finally coming to invade Texas. "Rip" Ford had been a famous Texas Ranger in the old days, and while he had long refused a commission in the Confederate Army, he was more than willing to lead a force of Texans against the "abolitionists, negroes, plundering Mexicans and perfidious renegades" he said were coming to slaughter them all in their beds. After years of avoiding the draft, Eric Ross had answered this call.

"I can try writing to him," Adam continued, "but I'm not

sure where he is, or if he'd get the letter, or even if he did, if he could get back here in time."

Lori didn't want him back here at all. "In time for what?" she asked warily.

Now she had no doubt. Adam Ross's finely constructed face was scarlet. "In time to marry you."

Lori gaped at him. *"Marry* me? Why would he *marry* me?"

"Because." He gestured vaguely with the hand that wasn't holding his cane. "If there's going to be a child . . ."

A *child?* Lori had never thought of the thing growing inside of her as a *child.* It was more like a cancer, something that was going to destroy her, to finish the job that Eric Ross had begun. She never should have told Bessie she was sick. If she hadn't told her, no one ever would have known. Lori could have just killed herself the way she should have done last winter when Eric Ross had shown her just how worthless she really was.

Instead, she had to face his brother, the only man whose opinion really mattered to her, and now Adam knew how worthless she was, too.

"I'm not going to marry him," she told Adam, still incredulous. How could he ever have thought such a thing?

He pressed his well-shaped lips together so tightly that the blood drained out of them, but only for a moment before making himself smile again. "I know you must be angry with him for leaving you, but——"

"Angry!" she spat furiously. "I hope some Yankee blows his brains out!"

As she might have expected from a man like Adam, he was a little shocked by her vehemence, but he was also too well-mannered to react. "As I said, I know you're angry now, and hurt," he continued, just as patient as before, "but you can't let a lover's quarrel prevent you from——"

"Lover's quarrel?" she echoed in outrage, jumping to her

feet and almost knocking the bench over again. "Is that what you think? That we were *lovers?* That I *loved* him?"

"Well," he allowed uneasily, plainly uncomfortable with the subject. "Surely, you had some feelings for him, considering what happened between you . . ."

"What happened between us was that he *forced* me! He held me down and put his hand over my mouth so I couldn't breathe and he . . ."

For a second she was back there, pressed against the cold, hard ground, and she was so certain she was going to die that drawing another breath hadn't even seemed worth the effort. Her throat closed on a sob, and she clamped both her hands over her mouth to hold it back. She couldn't cry in front of Adam Ross, not if she wanted to hold on to what little remained of her dignity. Dear Lord, why hadn't she died that day?

"Miss McClintock, please," Adam Ross begged her, although she wasn't exactly sure what he wanted. Probably he just wanted her not to cry. Pa had never liked to see a woman cry, either. "Should I get your moth . . . your *step*mother? Maybe she could . . ."

But Lori was shaking her head. She didn't want Bessie. She didn't want to see Bessie ever again. This was all Bessie's fault. If she hadn't gone to see Adam Ross, he wouldn't be here now, would he?

Lori drew a steadying breath and lowered her hands. "Don't bother writing to him," she said, as calmly as she could. "Even if he was willing, I'd rather die than marry Eric Ross."

He studied her for a long moment, his eyes as blue as a rain washed sky, as if he was trying to see inside her head. Finally, he said, "I see. I had no idea. Of course, I thought that you and Eric . . . Well, that changes everything, doesn't it?"

Lori blinked in surprise. She wasn't sure what kind of reaction she had expected, but she knew it wasn't this one.

Probably, she had expected him to call her a liar, the way Bessie had done.

"That's what every girl who ever got caught says," Bessie had scoffed. " 'He held me down and had his way.' Ha! I know what you was thinkin'. You was thinkin' 'bout his big house and the silver they got buried so the Yankees don't find it and his mama's jewels and all that land and how this war can't last forever and someday he's gonna be rich again. Set your cap for him, then you spread your legs for him, and now you got a baby in your belly and he's long gone. I figured you for smarter'n that, Lori."

And she *was* smarter than that, only not much smarter, because Eric had tricked her another way. And all because she really loved Adam Ross. What a fool she was!

But when she glanced up at Adam again, suddenly she didn't feel like a fool any longer because of the way Adam was looking at her. He was looking at her as if she was a respectable human being and not the piece of worthless trash she had felt herself to be for these past few months. As she gazed into his beautiful blue eyes, she realized something else, too: *he believed her.* Not only hadn't he called her a liar outright, *he really believed her* when she said that Eric had forced her.

The relief of it sent the blood rushing from her head and for a moment she thought she might actually faint.

She must have looked like she was going to faint, too, because Adam reached out for her and took her arm. This time she didn't shrink from his touch, and she let him ease her back down onto the bench again. His fingers felt so strong on her arm, strong but gentle, too. Adam Ross would never hold a woman down and take her against her will.

She had to blink against tears as she gazed up at his face. He was so good and kind. He bore his own pain with saintly patience and never once complained. And *he believed her.*

* * *

She was lying, of course, Adam thought as he gazed down into her lovely face. Women always lied in this situation. What else could they do? Admit they had surrendered themselves willingly to a man who was not their husband? Admit they had given away the only commodity they had of value, the one thing of worth they could use in the eternal barter between male and female?

Not that he blamed her, of course. What other choice did a girl like this have? What other chance? And, he supposed, glancing around the pathetic dwelling, she would have done most anything for an opportunity to escape this life. Eric must have seemed like the perfect way out.

And Eric, well, many a better man than Eric would have taken what she offered and blessed whatever gods he worshiped for his luck. And Adam, he was ashamed to say, numbered himself among them.

Indeed, how many nights had he awakened sweating and panting from a fevered dream that featured the luscious Lori McClintock? A dream in which his hands were full of her and he had lost himself in her silken depths. A dream in which she saw him as a normal man, in which he *was* a normal man, with two good legs on which to stand.

But he hadn't been that man for many years now, and no woman would ever see him as normal, not even a girl as desperate as Lori McClintock. Except in his dreams.

Right now, of course, she was in his worst nightmare. He cleared his throat. "If you don't want to marry Eric, what do you want?" He had a pretty good idea, of course. She'd want money. Her stepmother had hinted of that this morning. She'd used the words "take care of her," but he knew what that meant, what that *always* meant. Of course, like most people in Texas, he was dead broke, except for a chestful of worthless Confederate script. They'd have no way of knowing that, though, and he wondered at his chances of making them believe it.

He watched her face as she considered his question. God,

she was beautiful. Her raven hair was loose, just the way he'd always imagined it in his dreams, curling riotously down her back and tied away from her face with a piece of rawhide string. Her eyes, the deep, rich color of blueberries, gazed up at him with a puzzled innocence he knew was feigned but which was no less appealing for all of that. Her cheeks were unnaturally pale, but her skin still glowed with the warmth of satin in the afternoon sunlight. And even the shabby, shapeless dress she wore could not conceal the lush, ripe curves beneath. The curves about which Adam had dreamed. The curves which Eric would not have even considered resisting.

Jealousy was like hot bile in Adam's stomach, but he schooled his expression to reveal nothing as he waited for her reply.

Finally, she said, "I don't know."

She was lying again. She had something in mind. He could see that plainly on her expressive face, but for some reason, she didn't want to tell him what it was. He should have been irritated at her games, and he probably would have been if he hadn't seen the tears glistening in her eyes.

Suddenly, his irritation evaporated into pure terror. The one thing he could not bear was a woman's tears. Indeed, given the choice, he would have faced a whole brigade of Yankee guns instead. But of course, his leg had kept him out of the army, so he was doomed to face this instead. "Miss McClintock," he tried, not really knowing what he should say, but knowing he had to say something and quick.

He'd only made it worse, though. He could see that clearly. The tears were now trembling on her thick, dark lashes, and if they started sliding down her face, he didn't know what he would do. "There must be something you need. Something you *want*," he insisted. Everyone wanted *something*, he knew. Please, God, just let it be something he could manage so he could get the hell out of here. Damn Eric, he could cause a disaster when he wasn't even here!

But she only shook her head stiffly, as if she didn't trust herself to speak, and in the next second a single, silver tear slid down her cheek. She wiped it quickly away, but another instantly followed, and then she was weeping in earnest, covering her face with both hands as if ashamed to have him see.

He could have groaned aloud but somehow managed to restrain himself. He also managed to restrain himself from fleeing, which was what his every instinct demanded. His father hadn't raised him to be a coward, however, and if he wouldn't run from Yankee guns, he wouldn't run from a girl's tears either. He would uphold the Ross honor—somehow.

Hovering over her, cursing his cane and his awkwardness and Eric for bringing this down on him and his own helplessness, he reached out instinctively to take her in his arms. Fortunately, he caught himself before he actually touched her and snatched his hand back again. But the strength of his desire to pull her to him and feel her softness against him shook him to his core. For a second, he could almost imagine his father's glare of contempt.

"She's nothing but trash," he would have said, and he would have been right. Poor white trash who had survived only because the Ross family had taken pity on a widow and orphan of the Confederacy. "Pay her off and be done with it!" his father would have advised. Certainly, he never would have offered Eric—not even Eric whom he despised—in marriage to a girl like this. She was a scheming adventuress who deserved nothing from him.

Adam knew all of that even as he carefully lowered himself to the bench beside her and propped his cane against it. With both hands free, he had to curl them into fists to keep from reaching out to her again. As he impotently watched her shoulders shaking as she wept, he couldn't help but notice the perfection of her frame and marvel over the differences between the female form and his own. She was, he quickly realized, naked beneath her thin dress, or nearly so.

The knowledge stopped his breath and sent a strange heat scorching over him. He was near enough that he could catch her scent, a combination of fresh air and sunshine and earthy woman that was both intoxicating and stupefying. Quickly, in an effort to distract himself, he dropped his gaze to the floor, but there he saw her bare feet showing beneath the tattered hem of her dress. They were small and delicate and perfectly formed, just like her hands under the work-roughened skin, and just as he imagined the rest of her to be.

"She isn't worthy of you," his father's voice reminded him inside his head, but the roaring of desire drowned out the words.

Maybe . . . he thought, his mind racing as need overwhelmed logic and reason and good sense. Maybe he could take her as his mistress. He would provide for her and the child in exchange for . . .

In exchange for what? the voice of conscience scoffed. In exchange for allowing him to slake his lust on her? He'd be no better than Eric then. The only difference would be that he'd make her a high-priced whore instead of a cheap one. That wouldn't do much to restore the lost Ross honor, would it?

And what about the child she carried? Eric's child. There could be no doubt of that, since virtually every other man who might have fathered a child on her had left long ago to defend the Southern cause. Only beardless boys and decrepit old men remained in Texas. Oh, yes, and Adam and Eric Ross. Adam who could not fight and Eric who would not, at least until now, when the Southern cause was all but lost.

And if Adam had any shreds of doubt, Eric's parting words to him would have settled the matter. He couldn't recall exactly what he had said, since the words made no real sense to him at the time. Now, of course, he understood exactly what Eric had meant when he'd told Adam that finally Eric had gotten what Adam wanted.

What Adam *still* wanted. He sighed with longing as Lori

McClintock drew a shuddering breath and used the corner of her apron to wipe the tears from her face.

"What is it you're planning to do?" he demanded more gruffly than he'd intended. He was annoyed with himself, after all, not her.

She looked up, startled, as if she hadn't realized he was so close. He couldn't believe it. Her face bore no evidence of the tears she'd just shed except for the dampness of her lashes and the color that had bloomed in her cheeks. Was it possible for a woman to look *more* beautiful when she cried?

"Nothing," she insisted guiltily. "I'm not planning anything at all!"

"Yes, you are," he insisted right back. "You're a poor liar, Miss McClintock. What is it? Are you going to run away? Where do you think you could go and how could you get there? The roads aren't safe, and a woman in your condition—"

"I'm not going to run away!" she snapped, and something flashed in her eyes that might have been a trace of her usual spirit, the fire that had drawn him to her years ago, even before her body had blossomed into womanhood. "I know better than that."

"Then what is it? What is it that you can't tell me? Or maybe you're ashamed to tell me. Is that it?" he accused, welcoming the outrage that had begun to glow in his chest. Perhaps the heat of it could burn away the misplaced lust.

"What *can* I do, Mr. Ross?" she demanded, showing some outrage herself, "except pray to die or—"

She caught herself and turned her face away but not before he saw the terrible bleakness in her dark eyes.

"Or *what?*" he demanded, experiencing a new kind of terror. And when she refused to respond or even look at him, he reached out and grabbed her arms and jerked her around to face him.

She stiffened in fear and her lovely eyes widened with it, but he barely noticed in his quest for the truth. "Or what?"

he repeated. "You aren't planning to do yourself harm, are you? Answer me!"

But her only answer was a terrified gasp as she sat frozen in his grasp like a small animal paralyzed by the gaze of a predator. It took another moment for him to realize *he* was what was frightening her, and he released her at once. Mortified, he jumped to his feet, or tried to, forgetting as always that he couldn't jump anymore and inwardly cursing his clumsiness and the fact that she was there to witness it.

To make matters worse, he bumped his cane and it went clattering to the floor. He stood there helpless before her, unable to walk away without it and unwilling to let her see the contortions he would have to perform to pick it up.

But when he looked at her again, he forgot everything except the fear that still shimmered in her eyes. Honor compelled him to dispel it. "I didn't mean to frighten you," he assured her as calmly as he could, "and I certainly didn't mean to . . . to manhandle you. I beg your pardon, Miss McClintock. I'm just . . . concerned about you." He almost winced at his own choice of words but was gratified at least to see that she looked a little less terrified of him.

"Are you?" she asked so forlornly that he wanted to reach out to her again, but he caught himself just in time. "Why?"

"Because," he began and faltered when he realized he didn't want to tell her the true reason. "Because you . . . Because my brother was the one who . . . and the child . . ." he stammered, at a loss for words to express himself and silently cursing Eric again for getting him into this. How many times had Eric gotten him into something? More than he cared to count, although he had to admit, this was the worst.

"Oh, yes," she replied, bitterly. "The child. The heir to the Ross fortunes and all that. Well, you don't have to worry, I won't be making any claims on you. I won't be making claims on anyone at all."

There it was again, that awful bleakness in her eyes, as if

she were looking death right in the face, and then he knew for certain: she *was* planning to do herself harm.

"Don't!" he cried before he could stop himself.

She stiffened. "I said I wouldn't!" she replied indignantly. "I don't want anything from the Rosses! Nothing at all!"

"No, not that! I know what you're planning, and it isn't the answer! And don't forget, it wouldn't just be your own life you'd be taking. Do you think you have the right to destroy that one, too?"

Her anguish tore at his heart, and he saw beyond a doubt that he had guessed correctly. Her face was white again, her eyes large and terrified in her beautiful face, and she lifted the back of one hand and pressed it to her lips as if to hold back a sob.

He had to do something. Everything that he believed himself to be and ever hoped to become depended upon his ability to sort this out and save this girl and her child from disaster. Perhaps *she* wasn't worthy of his attention, but the child she carried was a Ross. The heir to his family fortunes or whatever remained of them when this blasted war was over. Perhaps the only heir there would ever be.

Certainly, Adam would never have an heir. Eric had ensured that one day long ago when he'd crippled him, and Adam had since resigned himself to the fact that he would never be able to attract a suitable bride. And Eric, if he ever came back at all, could probably be counted upon to resist making a marriage of any kind, even if prodded by a shotgun.

So the only child who might ever succeed them was the bastard that grew inside this girl. His father would never have approved of her. His mother . . . Well, he couldn't be sure what his mother would have done, since he'd been so young when she died, but surely she would have disdained Lori McClintock, too.

But they would both expect Adam to preserve the Ross honor at all costs. And in this case, preserving the Ross honor meant preserving this girl and the child she carried. He could think of only one way to do so.

The idea seemed to come to him full-blown, but he knew he must have been thinking about it all along, ever since he'd walked in here and found her slumped over the table. For a moment he'd been afraid . . . But then he'd seen she was asleep, looking like an angel, all innocence and light.

Well, perhaps not innocence.

"Miss McClintock, you need to be married," he said.

The fear in her eyes flared brighter, and she shook her head vehemently. "I won't marry *him!*" she insisted. "I'll die first!"

He believed her. "Then you must marry me."

He hated the baldness of the words and hated the way he had said them even more, but there was no going back. Besides, a girl in her position would be so grateful for the offer that she couldn't possibly be offended by the tone.

"What?" she asked, her face crinkling in confusion. She obviously couldn't believe her good fortune.

"I said, you must marry *me.*" The words wanted to stick in his throat, but he let his gaze drop to her breasts for an instant to remind him of why he was so willing to make the offer. Then he found it easier to go on. "You are with child, Miss McClintock. The man responsible is gone and might never return. If you bear the child out of wedlock, you face ruin and disgrace. Neither of you will ever be able to hold your heads up. But I am offering you the protection of my name."

She still couldn't believe it. "But why? Why would you . . . ?" She gestured helplessly.

"Because the child you carry is a Ross. We take care of our own, Miss McClintock, and as head of the family, it's my duty to take care of you, too."

It all seemed so clear to him, but she was shaking her head. "I couldn't," she insisted.

Stung, he stiffened, certain she meant she couldn't bear

to tie herself to a cripple. "I realize I must repulse you," he said, feeling the heat of humiliation crawling up his neck. "But I assure you that—"

"Repulse?" she echoed, even more confused now. "What are you talking about?"

His face felt as if it were on fire, but he forced the words past the tightness in his throat. "My leg."

She glanced down at it in apparent surprise, as if she hadn't been thinking of it all along. "Oh, no, that's not what I mean!" she insisted. "I mean, you don't really *want* to marry me, do you?"

He thought he saw something flicker in her eyes, something that might have been hope, but he knew he must have been mistaken. "What I want isn't important," he lied, knowing that while he might not want to *marry* her, he would not object at all to having her in his bed. Eric may have had her first, but Adam would have her forever. The thought sent the heat in his face surging to other, less seemly places. Forcing himself to ignore it, he hurried on. "I have to think of the child, and you have to think of the future. What will become of the two of you if you *don't* marry me? Really, Miss McClintock, I don't see that either of us has a choice in the matter."

There, he thought, watching as the emotions played across her marvelously expressive face. Surely she must understand now and realize she had no choice. Cripple or not, his was the best offer she was likely to get. A girl with nothing who was carrying a bastard child should jump at the chance for security and respectability. After a few moments, the riot of her emotions finally settled into the calm of decision, and she drew a deep breath. He braced himself to receive her effusive gratitude.

"I appreciate what you're trying to do, Mr. Ross," she said, her large eyes infinitely sad, "but I can't let you make a sacrifice like that. It wouldn't be right or fair, and like my pa always said, the McClintocks might not have much, but we've got our honor. My honor won't let me ruin your life, too, Mr. Ross."

Adam gaped at her. "Don't you understand what I'm offering you?" he demanded.

She nodded. "Yes, sir, I do, and it's about the nicest thing anybody ever did for me. You're wanting to make things right, but I can't let you make things right for me by making things wrong for you. That wouldn't be fair, would it?"

Adam couldn't believe this was happening. "Miss McClintock, marrying you wouldn't exactly be a . . . a sacrifice," he tried, wincing at his own understatement.

"Do you love me?" she asked.

What could that possibly matter? "I admire and respect you," he offered. "I'm sure that—"

"Would you be proposing to me if I wasn't in trouble?" she pressed.

Dear God, he hadn't expected an interrogation! "Under the circumstances, I don't see where that makes any difference," he pointed out in exasperation.

"It makes a difference to me. I admire and respect you, too, and I can't ruin your life just to save my own."

"But what about your baby?"

Something like pain tightened her features, but she said, "That's my problem. I'll take care of it."

Adam didn't want her to take care of it. *He* wanted to take care of it. And her. Oh, God, how he wanted to take care of her. In the dark of night, lying in his bed, with her dark hair spread all around and her naked flesh beneath his. And damnit, it was the honorable thing to do!

Unfortunately, he couldn't think of any arguments to make his case, or at least none that he could raise with *her*. Probably, he just needed time to think. Yes, that was it. He needed time, and so did she. Let her stew for a few days. Let her imagine what her life would be like with him and without him. Let her stepmother describe it to her. Meanwhile, he'd come up with some new way to persuade her.

"Well, I can see that you're still upset and . . . and not thinking clearly," he improvised. He hurried on when she would've denied it. "I'll leave my offer open, Miss McClintock, so if you change your mind, don't be afraid to tell me. I can provide a good life for you and for the child. The Ross family fortunes are at a low ebb right now, but as soon as this blasted war is over and we can start shipping cotton again, things will get back the way they were." He glanced around, trying to judge the level of their need. "Can I send you anything? Some flour or—"

"We're fine," she said stiffly, the pride of the impoverished straightening her spine.

"Perhaps you'd like some coffee," he said, naming a delicacy he knew she hadn't seen in years.

Her eyes widened, but she shook her head. "You already do too much," she protested.

"Your father gave his life for the South, Miss McClintock. It's the least I can do to make sure his family doesn't starve. And don't forget, if you change your mind—"

"I won't," she insisted.

He saw the tears gathering in her eyes again and decided he should leave before another storm broke. Then he remembered his cane. So much for graceful exits.

"Would you mind, uh, handing me my, uh . . ." He gestured reluctantly toward the fallen cane.

She glanced down and seemed surprised to see it lying there. "Oh, yes," she said and bent to retrieve it.

She picked it up gingerly, as if she were afraid it might break, but then he decided she probably found it distasteful and didn't want to touch it. She rose and handed it to him, and as he took it, he caught the strangest expression in her eyes. It almost looked like longing, although what she could desire that he hadn't already offered her today, he couldn't imagine.

Self-consciously, he took the cane from her and swung

it down to the floor where it would be out of her direct line of sight.

"If you change your mind, or if you need anything," he repeated, "anything at all, just let me know."

Her lips curved into the sweetest smile he had ever seen, and her eyes glowed with what might have been love if he hadn't known better. "You're about the kindest man I've ever met, Mr. Ross. God will bless you for it."

Adam only hoped that was true, because if God was in a blessing mood, Adam knew exactly what he wanted.

Not trusting himself to say another word, he turned and made his way slowly out of the cabin, fetching his hat from the peg by the door where he had hung it and taking care to limp as little as possible. He'd left his buggy out front, and he untied the reins and climbed stiffly aboard, acutely conscious of her gaze on him, watching every awkward movement. *Damn you, Eric,* he thought as he chucked the horse into motion and lifted a hand in a silent farewell.

She waved back at him, still smiling that sad, sweet smile. It would, he knew, haunt his dreams, as would the rest of her. He'd just have to make sure it didn't haunt *many* dreams before he was finally able to make her see the light.

Who would ever have imagined that he would be so desperate to convince a pregnant, white-trash tart to marry him? And who would ever have dreamed that she'd refuse?

Lori watched Adam Ross drive away, holding her tears until she was sure he was too far away to see them. All she could think about was Bessie's familiar admonition: be careful what you wish for because you might get it.

How many times in her twenty years had she wished for Adam Ross to come calling on her and beg her hand in marriage? How many times had she watched in anguish as he spoke to this young lady or that after church and wondered if this was the one who had finally caught his eye. If this was the one he would finally take to wife and destroy all her youthful fantasies.

But he never had, and the years had gone by, and she had finally grown into a woman pretty enough for him to notice. Except he hadn't. Probably, he'd never even looked at her before today, hadn't even known she was alive until Bessie had gone to him and told her tale of shame.

And finally he had come, and his goodness and kindness had made her feel her shame all the more. Her shame and her unworthiness, and then he'd finally done what she'd prayed he'd do and asked her to marry him. The irony of it was like a stake driven through her heart, and the pain actually doubled her over as she stood in the cabin doorway and watched the buggy disappear into a plume of dust in the distance.

She wanted to die, as she had ever since that awful day late in January, but she knew she wouldn't, not unless she did it to herself. She'd been too afraid before, and now Adam Ross's words came echoing back: *Don't forget, it wouldn't just be your own life you'd be taking. Do you think you have the right to destroy that one, too?*

If she hadn't been able to think of this thing inside of her as a child, Adam Ross did, and if *he* wanted to protect it, how could she do any less? Dear heaven, he wanted to protect it so much that he was willing to sacrifice himself and his every chance of happiness! No wonder she loved him so much.

And she certainly loved him too much to let him marry her.

Sobbing out her anguish, she stumbled back into the house and collapsed back onto the bench, buried her head in her hands, and wept.

She didn't know how long she'd been crying when she heard Bessie returning from the field. Her stepmother was cursing at the old, swaybacked mule that pulled their plow, one of the few animals that had escaped the desperate Confederacy's need for mounts. But even the Confederacy hadn't been *that* desperate, and they had left this particular mule.

Quickly, Lori scrubbed the tears from her face and went to the water bucket and splashed some on to get rid of the redness around her eyes. By the time Bessie tromped into the cabin, Lori was sitting calmly, shelling the peas she'd fallen asleep over earlier.

Arming herself with her own anger at Bessie's betrayal, she looked up and met her stepmother's gaze.

Bessie McClintock was a big woman. Not particularly tall but broad as a beam and just as solid. When she was out in the field with Pa's battered old hat pulled over her eyes and her shabby skirts tied up into makeshift pants, she might've easily been mistaken for a man. Her face was as plain as dirt, as she herself was fond of saying, and her graying brown hair stuck out like straw from beneath the brim of that old hat. She gazed back at Lori through her mud-brown eyes.

"Well, how much did he offer you?" she asked in a voice that could carry half-a-mile.

Lori rose to her feet and favored her stepmother with her nastiest glare. "You had no right to go to him!"

Bessie gave a rude snort. "What else could I do? We can't feed ourselves, and without you to help in the fields, we can't grow half of what we grew last year, either. How we gonna make do for a baby?"

"I'll help in the fields!" Lori insisted.

"How? With your stomach out to here?" she scoffed, making her arms round in front of her. "And what're you gonna do when it's born? Squat down in the field and drop it in the dirt like a darkie?"

Lori wanted to slap her. How could her pa have ever thought this woman could take the place of her dear mother? "We'll manage! We always have, and you know how Pa felt about charity."

"Your pa never had to go hungry. And don't go throwing

his honor up to me. A man with honor don't go running off to some stupid war and leave his family behind to starve."

"He thought he'd only be gone a few months!" Lori reminded her loyally, even though she'd had the same thought more than once herself.

"Yeah, well, he was wrong, wasn't he? And we'd both be dead now if it wasn't for Adam Ross's charity, so don't talk to me about your Pa. I wanna hear what Adam Ross is going to do for us."

"Nothing!" Lori was only too happy to report.

"Nothing?" Bessie echoed furiously. "That no-account hypocrite! That two-bit—"

Lori stopped her before she could start actually swearing. "He offered, but I refused."

"Are you crazy, girl? I know women get funny notions when they're in a family way, but that takes the cake! How much did he offer? I'll take it even if you're too proud!"

"He didn't offer money," Lori told her with satisfaction.

Bessie's eyes narrowed as she studied Lori for a long moment. Lori grew uncomfortable under the scrutiny, but refused to squirm. Lifting her chin defiantly, she met Bessie glare for glare until Bessie finally figured it out, or thought she did.

"He's gonna get that no-account brother of his back here to marry you!" she guessed triumphantly.

"No!" Lori cried in horror. "How could you even think such a thing after what he did to me!"

"What he did to you is what men've been doing to women ever since God put the first two on this earth. A woman just has to get used to it, Lori. I told you before. And even though Eric Ross is about the most worthless piece of horse's backside walking around on two legs and calling hisself a man, he can give you a home and a name for that baby and make sure neither of you goes hungry again. That's about all a woman can ask for nowadays."

"Well, this woman isn't going to ask for it, not from him! I don't care if I do starve!"

"You know what the Good Book says about pride, don't you, Missy?" Bessie warned and walked wearily over to the water bucket and took a long drink from the ladle.

Glad for the reprieve, Lori sat back down at the table and furiously resumed her task with the peas.

But if she thought Bessie was finished, she was mistaken.

"So if he didn't offer to get Eric back here, what did he offer? And don't tell me nothing. I know the Rosses better'n that—Adam Ross at least. He's one of them crazy Southern gentlemen who really thinks he's responsible for taking care of all the evil in the world and protecting all the women and children, too. Since you qualify as both and his kin to boot, I reckon he had to ease his conscience good. How much? And you better tell me or else I'll go and ask him myself—"

"No!" Lori cried, knowing she had lost the battle. She couldn't have Bessie trooping up to Adam Ross's plantation house again. She forced herself to hold Bessie's gaze. "He . . . he offered to marry me himself."

Bessie's jaw dropped in almost comic surprise, but Lori didn't feel like laughing. Bessie did, though, a hoot of joy that fairly shook the rafters. "Hallelujah!" she cried, stomping around in Pa's old boots in a sort of jig. "This is the best news I've heard this year! Do you know what this means, Missy? It means you'll be living in that big house and you'll have servants and clothes and—"

"I told him no," Lori said, stopping Bessie in her tracks.

The woman looked at her as if she'd lost her mind. "What do you mean you told him no?"

"I can't take advantage of him like that! I can't let him sacrifice himself!"

"Sacrifice?" Bessie roared, shaking the timbers again. "What kind of sacrifice do you think it is for a man to take a comely woman to his bed?"

Lori struggled with two conflicting emotions: terror at the

thought of what she hadn't allowed herself to think about before and outrage that Bessie could believe Adam Ross so base. "Adam would never . . . !" she insisted.

"Any man would, and Adam Ross was a man, last I looked, crippled leg or not. What do you think? That he don't get an itch between his legs like everybody else?"

Lori wanted to clamp her hands over her ears so she wouldn't have to hear this slander, but she knew the best way to silence Bessie was to out-argue her. "He wasn't thinking about *that!* He was thinking about . . . about the Ross heir. He wants the . . . the baby," she said, making herself say the word for the first time. "Because it's a Ross. He wants it to have a good home."

"So he'll take you as a brood mare and then turn you out to pasture when you've foaled, is that it?"

Lori had never been so furious in her entire life. *"No! He'll take care of me, too!"*

"He will, if you take care of him in the bed. Use your head, girl! What do you think makes a man get married in the first place?"

"Love!" Lori informed her triumphantly.

But Bessie snorted again. "That's what they call it when they want to get under a woman's skirts." She drew a deep breath and let it out on a long, weary sigh. "Look, what good do you think you'll do by not marrying him? Who are you gonna help?"

"Him! Adam! I can't let him ruin his life!"

"How you think you'll ruin it? He's livin' alone up in that big house, and he prob'ly figures no woman'll look at him because of that leg of his—"

"That's not true!" Lori protested.

"I didn't say it was. I said he thought it."

"How can you know that?"

"He must be almost thirty years old, and he coulda married years ago, but you ever see him court anybody? You ever hear of him even calling on any girl?"

Lori had to admit she hadn't.

"And he's as vain as a girl about that leg. You ever notice how he walks real slow so he don't limp when he thinks anybody's looking? You take my word, he's a proud man, and he ain't about to put hisself in a place where some girl can say no, she don't wanna marry him 'cause he's a cripple. But that don't mean he likes sleeping alone. Then you come along, a girl who can't say no to him because she's desperate. No wonder he wants you, damaged goods or not."

Lori gaped at her, reluctantly remembering how Adam had reacted when she'd refused him. The first thing he'd mentioned was his leg. Bessie was right! But she wasn't going to give her the satisfaction of telling her. "Even if that's true, I can't take advantage of him," she said righteously.

"And just how'll you be taking advantage? You'll be giving him a pretty wife who loves him."

Lori gasped in outrage. "How . . . ? What . . . ? Where did you ever . . . ?"

"It's plain as a wart on a billygoat's nose! Love and smoke can't be hid, girl, and you been in love with Adam Ross since you was in pigtails."

Lori wanted to deny it, but Bessie didn't give her a chance.

"You ever stop to think you'd be doing him a favor? He's all alone, girl. He needs a woman in his life, and you love him. Maybe you even love him more than he deserves. And hell, you might even make him happy. Looks to me like he'll be getting the best of this bargain, whether he knows it or not."

Could Bessie be right about this, too? Dear heaven, Lori wanted her to be, but how could she be sure? "I don't know," she hedged.

"Nobody does, girl. The best you can do is the best you can do, and you ain't likely to get another chance like this. Think about walking into church on a Sunday with that baby big in your stomach and no ring on your finger. Then think about walking in with Adam Ross holding your arm. You don't think you're good enough for him, but look at me and your pa. I know he only married me 'cause he needed somebody to look after you, and he had his high falutin' ideas about honor and such, but we was happy just the same, wasn't we? We was good for each other, and you'll be good for Adam Ross. You'll bring him down a notch or two, and he'll keep you outta the gutter. Seems like a fair trade to me."

Lori let her gaze drop to the bowl of peas in her lap. They blurred into a mass of green as tears filled her eyes as she pictured both scenes in her mind and imagined how her life could be if she accepted Adam's offer. "But how can I face him again?" she asked as the tears began to spill down her cheeks.

"You don't have to," Bessie said. "I'll go see Adam Ross tonight and tell him you changed your mind. Next time you see him'll be your wedding day."

Two

Adam didn't bother to hide his limp as he climbed the porch steps of Elmhurst, the house his father had built over twenty years ago as a monument to his success as a planter. The grounds of Elmhurst were deserted since most of his slaves were in the fields, breaking the earth for the new crop, so there was no one to see if he favored his left leg or not. The buggy ride had caused an ache deep in his thigh, but he ignored it, as he always did. Adam had found that one could endure just about anything if one simply ignored it hard enough.

The house was quiet when he stepped out of the sunlight into the cool dimness of the hallway. The door at the far end, which was actually the front door of the house, stood open to catch the breeze from the river below. Adam paused to inhale the freshness of the air in which mingled the sweetly familiar smells of the house in which he had lived most of his life.

Sensing her presence rather than hearing her, he turned to find his slave Sudie standing in the doorway to the parlor. She held a dust rag in her hand. He had often thought that she could have walked down the street of any Northern city and passed as a white woman, and the impression struck him at this moment more strongly than usual.

Her skin was even fairer than Lori McClintock's, probably because she spent less time in the sun, and her hair, while dark black and quite coarse, was less curly even than his brother Eric's. It was wrapped now in a bandana that was tied in an intricate knot at her forehead to protect it from the dust she stirred up with her cleaning. An apron tied snugly around her waist accentuated the slimness of her figure. She might have been any age from twenty to sixty. She was the nearest thing to a mother he had known in more than twenty years.

"Well, now," she said with just the proper amount of surprise, "you're back mighty quick. Must've took care of your business real fast."

"You know perfectly well where I went and how far away it is," Adam reminded her as she came toward him to take his hat.

"Land sake, how would I know that?" she asked. "You sayin' you think I listen at doors?"

Her indignation was comically overdone, as she well knew. "I don't think you *have* to listen at doors, Sudie. I think you know things because you can read my mind. I first started thinking that when I was a little boy, and you always seemed to know when I'd been up to no good just by looking at me."

She stepped aside to let him pass into the parlor, and she followed him inside. "That wasn't no trick at all, Massa Adam. *Most* times you was up to no good. I just took to givin' you a lickin' once a day just in case."

Adam didn't let her see his smile as he walked to the mahogany sideboard that had been carried to Texas from his mother's home in Georgia almost three decades ago. It smelled of the lemon oil which Sudie had used to polish it. He pulled open one of the doors and brought out a bottle and a glass.

He glanced up in time to see Sudie's quick frown. "Your leg aching you?"

"Some," he said, pouring an inch of the amber liquid into the glass.

"Want me to rub it for you?"

Sudie's hands were magic on those occasions when, out

of patience with his limitations, he rebelliously pushed his body farther than he knew was best and suffered the consequences.

"No, thanks," he said, carrying his glass over to one of the wingbacked chairs that flanked the fieldstone fireplace and sank down into it. He stretched his leg out carefully in front of him, absently rubbing the spot where the minie ball had pierced his flesh so long ago. He managed a smile for Sudie. "It's not bad."

He took a swallow of the liquor, savoring its warmth on his tongue and the way it slid down to his stomach and settled there. In a few minutes, it would seep to his leg, and the pain would be gone.

As he waited, he glanced around the familiar room, aware of its luxury in a way he had never been until he had seen Lori McClintock's cabin. The ornately carved furniture, the luxurious carpet, the heavy draperies with their lace panels. For no reason that he could perceive, the image of her small, bare feet resting on that dirt floor came to him, and he marveled at how so much beauty existed amid such ugliness. And how ironic that amid so much beauty here had grown such ugliness. For an instant, he could almost see Eric's smirking face.

Sudie's voice shattered the image. "I hope you didn't give those people nothin'," she said.

He looked up, a little startled to find she was still there. "I'm sure it's none of your business, Sudie," he said. He was, after all, the master here.

But while Sudie might be a slave, she had still changed his diapers, and she enjoyed a certain freedom with him. "You already do too much for those people."

"That is," he recalled bitterly, "exactly what Miss McClintock said." He could actually see Lori's face, the way it had looked when she'd said it, too. The memory stirred up emotions he didn't want to feel. He took another swallow of whiskey.

"They be dead long time ago, it wasn't for you," she went on as if she hadn't heard. "What for that woman come here anyways? What she need you don't already do for them?"

Adam looked at her in some surprise. Apparently she *hadn't* listened at the door, and here, at least, was one secret she did not know. He intended to keep it that way. Knowing how she felt about Eric . . . Well, no one needed to know Lori carried Eric's child, least of all Sudie. Not yet, anyway.

"Mrs. McClintock wanted my advice on something," he hedged.

"You couldn't give it to her here, in your own house?" Sudie scoffed. "Had to go down there, to that place where they live? I know what it like. My Oscar, he tell me."

Oscar was the man Sudie had taken as her husband after Adam's father's death. Sudie had loved Oscar for as long as Adam could remember, but Chet Ross had never allowed her to take a husband. Adam didn't like to think about why he had denied her. "The McClintock's house is no worse than the cabins in the quarters," he said.

Sudie sniffed in disgust. "The cabins in the quarters is *clean* and the roofs don't leak."

"The McClintock's cabin was perfectly clean, and we've got men here to fix the roofs. They don't."

"Massa Adam, you don't fool me," she said earnestly, taking a step toward him. He noticed absently that she still held his hat in one hand and the dust rag in the other. In her distress, she was crumpling the brim of his hat. "I know what they got at that cabin that we don't got here."

Automatically, Adam pictured Lori's face again, but he ruthlessly banished the thought before Sudie could read it.

Too late. "That girl is trouble, Massa Adam. You mark my words. She trash, and that kind only think about how they can take away something you got."

Adam couldn't help but smile at this new irony. How wrong Sudie was. Adam had offered Lori everything he had to give, and she had still refused him. Dear God, even a penniless girl pregnant with a bastard child wasn't desperate enough to accept a cripple.

All the way back from her house, he'd steeled himself against the truth, not allowing the thought to form in his head, but he could no longer deny it. The pain of it lodged sharply in his chest, as if he'd swallowed a shard of glass, and he swallowed the last of the whiskey in an attempt to dull it.

He held out the empty glass. "I'd like a little more, please," he said, but Sudie merely gave the empty glass a disgusted glance and made no move to take it.

"White trash like that, she do anything," Sudie said urgently. "I know you's lonely, Massa Adam, but don't get caught in that trap! Your mama alive, she tell you the same thing. A few minutes a pleasure and a whole life a misery."

At the moment, Adam would have settled for the few minutes of pleasure, since it didn't appear he was going to get anything else. He only wished Sudie *did* have something to worry about. He decided to change the subject. "Did you ever give Eric that advice?" he asked, knowing full well it hadn't done any good if she had.

At the mention of Eric's name, Sudie's expression instantly softened. And saddened. "I tell him ever since he old enough to put on long pants, but it don't do no good. Least he sow his oats down in the quarters, though. The girls there is willin' enough, and ain't no colored girl gonna show up here wantin' to marry him. You can't blame him none, Massa Adam. You know he can't help the way he is. He really a good boy at heart. He just kinda wild. An' he want some fun in his life. Heaven knows, he ain't seen much ah that. But he settle down when he find a good woman. You see."

Adam doubted he'd ever see anything of the kind since Eric had already found—and bedded—a good woman and hadn't settled a bit. Thinking of Eric, he absently rubbed his leg again, even though the whiskey—or perhaps just the stretching—had already banished the ache.

"You leg achin'?" Sudie asked solicitously.

Adam smiled patiently. "I did ask for a refill," he reminded her, waggling the empty glass.

Her expression radiated disapproval, but she put his hat and the dust rag down on the delicately carved table that his mother had called a "pie crust" table and came over to take his glass. "This stuff ain't no good," she told him, not for the first time or even for the hundredth.

"I'm not my father, Sudie," he reminded her gently.

At the mention of the man who had once ruled this house, Sudie's dark brown eyes narrowed and her expression hardened with remembered hatred. "No, sir, you ain't," she agreed. "Wasn't the whiskey made Massa Chet mean, but it sure did make him worse."

How many times had Sudie risked his father's wrath to hide Eric behind her skirts? But then, how many times had Adam done the same thing, pleading with Chet to spare the boy yet another beating for some small slight, sometimes only imagined. They'd both protected Eric, and look what good it had done.

Sudie's work roughened fingers brushed his as she took the glass from him, and for an instant he pictured the way he'd seen those same fingers stroking Eric's dark curls as she comforted him time and again. While she'd loved Adam dearly, she'd enjoyed a special bond with Eric. For years Adam had assumed this was because she had been Eric's wet nurse. Then he had grown older and learned more of life and realized that Sudie could not have nursed Eric unless she'd had a baby herself. That was when his disjointed memories of the night of Eric's birth had finally made sense.

Just six years old, he'd been confused when his mother took to her bed early one wintery evening, moaning in pain. The weather outside had turned bad as a Blue Norther blew through, drenching the world with an icy rain that froze solid on everything it touched. His father and the slaves had spent that night trying to save the livestock by getting all the ani-

mals to shelter and caring for those that were half-frozen
when they were found.

Meanwhile, Adam's mother had given birth. Adam could
still remember peeking into her room, even though he had
been forbidden to do so, and seeing her on her bed, knees
raised and hands clutching at the headboard as she strained
against some unspeakable agony. Sudie had stood over her,
sponging her forehead and urging her on. Only Sudie had
been sweating, too. Adam remembered because the night had
been so bitterly cold. How could Sudie have been hot? Then
he'd seen her bend nearly double with an agony of her own,
and Adam's terrified young mind had somehow grasped the
knowledge that whatever horror had taken his mother had
also taken Sudie. The two women he loved most in the world
were both dying before his eyes, and he stood helpless.

Then Sudie had straightened from her convulsion and noticed Adam. She'd screamed at him to get out of there, and
even more terrified of her anger, he had fled to the safety
of his own bed where he had spent the night in desperate
prayer. He'd promised God many things in exchange for the
two women's lives, and in the end, only one of those prayers
had been answered.

Sudie handed him the glass she had refilled. Adam looked
at the level with critical eyes. "Kind of stingy, weren't you?"

"I'll rub your leg if it hurts more'n that," she replied tartly.

As he sipped the whiskey, he watched her face. She looked
so serene, no one would ever imagine the horrors she had
endured. He remembered that night again. Hearing a baby
cry, but only one. When his father had come back near dawn
the next morning, he'd been exuberant, rousing Adam to tell
him he had a baby brother. Adam had been jealous. He was
his father's son, and he knew how important that was. Chet
had told him often enough, and Adam didn't think he wanted
his father to have another son, one with whom he would
have to share that distinction.

And he remembered the whispered conversations and the

small bundle smuggled out of the house. Sudie's baby, born dead. Then his mother was so sick for days and days until she died, too. And there they were, the motherless boy and the childless mother. No wonder Sudie had loved Eric so much.

"You expect we get a letter from Massa Eric soon?" she asked hopefully.

"I don't expect we'll *ever* get a letter from him, Sudie," Adam replied frankly. "You should know him better than that."

Sudie looked away, her fingers plucking blindly at her apron while her eyes brightened suspiciously. "I reckon we can't blame him. He don't got as much reason to love this place as you do."

Indeed, he had none at all. Chet Ross had never forgiven his younger son for taking the life of his beloved wife. And Eric had paid a penance so high for that imagined sin that it seemed to have cost him his soul.

When Adam thought of Lori McClintock and her baby, he was sure it had.

Without realizing it, he had drained his glass again, and now he stared into the bottom of it and willed himself not to feel the pain of her rejection. The one time in his life when he'd had the opportunity to finally right a wrong. To cure an injustice. To, by God, *save* someone from needless suffering as he'd never been able to save Eric. And she'd turned him down flat—pretended it was for his own good and sent him packing.

Just who in the hell did she think she was? he wondered in sudden fury. Sudie was right. She was poor white trash of the worst kind. Didn't even worry about what people would say about her bearing a fatherless child. Indeed, she preferred the shame of that to having a cripple touch her and—

"Hello, the house!"

His head came up at the shout that could only have come

from one person. He was out of his chair as fast as his leg would allow, and he rushed into the hall with unseemly—and clumsy—haste.

Bessie McClintock stood on the porch just outside the door, peering in. She looked just as she had this morning only more disreputable because she'd apparently been working in the fields in the meantime. Her stout body smelled of fresh sweat, and she was panting slightly, as if she'd run all the way from her farm.

"Mrs. McClintock," he said by way of greeting. "How nice to see you again so soon." Although he tried not to, he found himself looking past her, out into the yard in a desperate effort to find Lori. She didn't seem to be anywhere in sight, though, and instantly he remembered her implied threat to do away with herself and her child. "Lori?" he asked in alarm. "Is she . . . ?"

"She's fine, or at least she will be, thanks to you," Bessie assured him. Only then did Adam notice she was smiling. She seemed to be missing several of her teeth. "I come to tell you she changed her mind. She'll be mighty honored to marry you after all."

Adam gaped at her, not quite able to believe his senses. If Lori had indeed changed her mind, she hadn't wasted any time about it. What could have prompted her sudden change of heart?

"Oh, and she said to tell you thanks," Bessie added uncertainly, as if aware that Adam expected her to say something else but wasn't sure exactly what.

Adam found his tongue at last. "I can't tell you how relieved I am to hear it, Mrs. McClintock. Please, come inside so we can make the arrangements."

He turned back toward the parlor and only when he saw her in the doorway did he remember Sudie. She was staring at him with eyes full of horror and one hand covering her mouth as if to hold back a cry.

"Sudie," he tried, but she shook her head in silent protest.

Nothing he could say would make this right in her eyes. Nothing except the truth, and perhaps not even that. In any case, he would never find out for sure, because he wasn't going to tell her the truth. "Sudie, will you please excuse us?" he asked as gently as he could. "Mrs. McClintock and I have some business to discuss."

She made a sound that might have been a smothered sob, and then she fled, running down the hall and out the other door as if the hounds of hell were after her. The urge to go after her and comfort her was nearly overwhelming, and Adam had to remind himself he had no comfort to offer. He was going to marry Lori McClintock, no matter how much Sudie might disapprove, and she would have to learn to accept that.

"Your girl don't seem none too pleased by the idea of you getting hitched," Bessie observed with some disapproval of her own.

Adam gave her his best smile and indicated with a wave of his hand that she should proceed him into the parlor. "Fortunately, *my* opinion is the only one that matters, Mrs. McClintock. Is Lori all right?" he added, remembering his initial fears.

"Right as rain," Bessie assured him, plopping herself down into one of the wingback chairs without waiting for an invitation. "Oh, you mean why didn't she come herself," she realized after a moment. "Well, now, can't exactly expect a girl to come running after you, can you? How would that look? But she's willin', make no mistake about that, Mr. Ross. And she'll be a good wife to you. A year from now, *you'll* be the one who thinks he got done the favor."

That, Adam had to admit as he lowered himself into the other chair, was what he was counting on.

"I can't go through with this, Bessie," Lori insisted as she paced around the cabin in her shift. Her wedding clothes, purchased with Adam Ross's money, lay across the table, untouched. "How can I do this to him?"

"How can you do *what* to him?" Bessie asked impatiently as she struggled into her good dress in preparation for the wedding. "Love him? Make him happy? Give him a family? Just which of those things do you think'll be such a curse that you got to spare him?"

Lori blinked at the tears that tried to form in her eyes. Lately, it seemed she was always on the verge of weeping, unless of course she was already weeping. She wondered if that had something to do with her condition or with the sorry state of her conscience. How could what she was doing be right? How could she put her own well-being so far ahead of everything else? "I can't be so selfish!" she insisted.

"What's selfish 'bout wanting to give your baby a name?" Bessie inquired brutally. "You think this is all for you? Talk about selfish! Think about that baby in your belly for once."

"I haven't been thinking about anything else for weeks!" Lori reminded her angrily as she swiped impatiently at the tear that had started down her cheek.

"I mean think about it like it was a person. Like it was a person you loved."

Lori shuddered at the thought and wrapped her arms around herself as if she could somehow protect herself from it. Love? How could she ever feel anything but loathing for this thing inside of her?

"Maybe you can't feel it yet, but after you've carried that baby inside of you for nine months, it's gonna be a part of you," Bessie said as she buttoned the bodice of her dress. "Then it's gonna be a cute, helpless little thing that you'll hold in your arms, and let me tell you, ain't nothin' easier than a baby to love. I know you, Lori, and there ain't no way that soft heart of yours can hold out for long against your own baby. An' it *is* your baby, too, no matter how much you might hate its father. You want that baby growin' up here with nothin', like you did, with other kids makin' fun because he only has rags to wear, only worse because he don't got no father, neither? And how'll you explain to him that he could've been a Ross except you was too proud to take what Adam Ross offered you?"

The pain of Bessie's words had nearly doubled Lori over so that the tears she shed fell straight to the floor where they made small dark spots on the packed earth.

"There now, don't cry," Bessie said, coming over and helping Lori over to one of the benches. "You'll make your eyes all red for the wedding."

Bessie's hands were rough, not smooth the way she remembered her mother's hands being, but they were just as gentle as they brushed the hair away from Lori's face. Bessie might not be her real mother, but she had been a good friend through long, difficult years. She could, she realized as she looked up into Bessie's homely face, even forgive her for going to Adam Ross behind her back. Or at least she could but for one thing.

"How do I know this is the right thing to do?"

"Lori, honey, it's the *only* thing to do. Now hurry up and get your dress on before Adam Ross thinks you changed your mind and left him standing at the altar."

Adam wasn't really standing at the altar. He was standing in his front parlor, or rather pacing in his front parlor. He'd been pacing so long that his leg had started to send up its usual protest, but Adam welcomed the discomfort. At least it provided some distraction.

"Where could they be?" he wondered aloud as he stared out the window in the direction of the road where he still saw no sign of them. "I sent Oscar for them over an hour ago."

"You know how women are, son," Judge Fairweather said from where he sat on the rosewood sofa, his gouty foot resting on a stool. "She's probably still primping. Wants to look her best for her wedding day."

"The judge is right," Reverend Hartsfield agreed heartily. "In all my years, I don't think I've ever had a wedding start on time."

Adam glanced at the two old men whom he had known all his life. The minister was as thin as the judge was stout, and while the sunlight streaming through the windows shone off the judge's bald pate, it gleamed in the minister's thick, snow white hair. Adam wondered what they were truly thinking. They had been his father's friends, and surely they would both share his sense of what was right and proper for Chet Ross's eldest son. Marrying the McClintock girl would not fall into that category, he was certain.

At least they had not tried to dissuade him, as he had feared they might when he had approached them about being present on this day. But they were both men of the world who had seen enough of life to easily guess the real reason behind Adam's choice of a bride and the need for haste. They might think him a fool, but they would never try to stop him from doing the honorable thing by a girl whom he had gotten in trouble. He couldn't help wondering how supportive they would be if they knew it wasn't his own honor he was trying to protect by marrying her.

The sound of a carriage outside drew him to the window again, and he saw that Oscar was pulling the carriage right up to the door. For an instant, he felt relief, and then a brand new set of apprehensions gripped him.

Was he really doing the right thing or was he actually robbing Eric once more of the love and happiness due him? If Eric truly loved this girl, then Adam would be cheating his brother out of her *and* her unborn child—just the way he had cheated Eric out of their father's love for all of his life. But then he forced himself to remember that Eric was no longer the vulnerable young boy whom Adam had been unable to protect. That boy was long since dead, and in his place, inhabiting Eric's body, lived the heartless young man who had stood over Adam as he lay writhing on the ground, his leg shattered, and laughed.

Ruthlessly pushing the memory from his mind, he turned to his companions and said, "They're here."

Not certain of the etiquette of such a situation, Adam decided to meet his bride at the door. Automatically picking up his cane from where he had set it just inside the parlor door, he hurried out. When he stepped outside, he saw that Lori and Bessie had already descended from the carriage, apparently without waiting for Oscar to help them, judging by his disapproving frown, and they were standing uncertainly in the yard.

"Good morning," he said, although he was fairly certain that the day had already passed officially into afternoon.

Lori looked up in surprise, and he was stunned by the shock of reaction he felt at the sight of her. She looked like an angel. A very well-dressed angel.

Bessie's first request of him had been a sum of money which she could use for clothes. "Can't have the girl standing up on her wedding day in rags, now can you?" she'd asked.

Apparently, they had spent the money wisely. Lori's outfit consisted of a fitted jacket and the bell-shaped skirt that virtually every woman wore nowadays. Instead of being the ubiquitous black, however, this one was a lively plaid of reds and blues and greens. The jacket sleeves were belled, and cuffs of lace were visible beneath them.

But it was not the dress alone, although he realized he had never seen Lori so elegantly attired. The dress simply served to emphasize her own natural beauty, which seemed somehow magnified today. Her riotous curls had been drawn up onto her head and fell now in well-disciplined ringlets. Her satiny skin was pale but luminous, as if some inner light made her radiant, and her dark blue eyes glittered with intense emotions. As he crossed the porch and drew closer, taking care not to thump his cane too loudly on the boards and draw attention to it, he recognized at least one of her emotions, a pure, unadulterated terror.

"Lori," he said, and he had to clear his throat. "You look very lovely."

Her full, lush lips quivered a bit before she finally said, "Thank you," so quietly he almost didn't hear it. Were those lips as soft and sweet as they looked? He realized with a jolt of sexual awareness that he would soon be able to find out for himself.

"Come in, come in," he urged too heartily to cover his own unseemly reactions. "Everyone else is already here."

Although Adam would have thought it impossible, Lori grew even more frightened. *"Everyone?"* she echoed in alarm.

"The preacher, of course, and I've asked Judge Fairweather to stand up with me." He didn't think he needed to explain that the men he would normally have asked, men his own age whom he counted as his friends, had long ago gone off to fight the war, some of them never to return. And he and Bessie had agreed that the more private the ceremony, the better, so no other guests had seemed necessary or advisable.

Lori, however, appeared ready to bolt at the news that anyone at all was here to witness the ceremony. She might have, too, but Bessie took her arm and whispered something to her, and Lori straightened her shoulders determinedly and finally began to walk toward him. No one, he realized as he watched her, would ever think of her at this moment as trash.

Lori didn't believe she had ever seen Adam Ross looking so handsome—or so intimidating. Vaguely, she was aware of the hugeness of the house they were approaching, a house she had seen many times during her life but never actually entered. And seeing him here, on its porch, made her more aware than ever of his power and his position. And of her absolute lack of both.

She felt oddly detached from all of this as she carefully

climbed the few steps to the porch, mindful of her stiff, full skirts and the fact that she couldn't see her feet. Her lungs demanded that she take a deep breath, but when she tried, her tightly laced corset prevented her. Why had she allowed Bessie to truss her up like this?

But of course she knew perfectly well why. "That's how fine ladies dress," Bessie had said, and the dressmaker had confirmed it. If Lori wasn't a fine lady, she could at least look like one, so she wouldn't shame Adam on his wedding day. Even if it meant she wouldn't be able to draw a proper breath all day. And although her stomach was tied in knots, at least she didn't have to worry about being sick. She hadn't swallowed a bite of food since midday yesterday.

When she reached the top of the steps, Adam offered her his arm and a smile. She took his arm and tried to return the smile, although her face felt stiff with tension. Feeling as if her head was no longer attached to her body but floating somewhere above it, Lori stepped into the entry hall of the Elmhurst mansion.

She was vaguely aware of rich dark wood and gleaming crystal and floors polished so brightly that she could see her own reflection. Adam ushered her into one of the rooms. It was enormous and had the musty air of a room that was seldom used, and she realized this was the "company" parlor. Two men waited there, and she needed a moment to remember who they were, although she'd known them most of her life.

"Miss Lori, how pretty you look," Judge Fairweather said, bowing over her hand. His smile was warm beneath his thick mustache, and Lori found herself wondering vaguely if he had actually polished his bald head because it was shining so brightly. "I know your father would have wanted the privilege of giving you away. He would have been very proud of you."

Lori wasn't quite so sure, but she thanked the judge and returned the minister's equally effusive greeting. By the time the two men had paid their compliments to Bessie, Lori felt a little calmer, although she still had that strange, detached feeling, as if this were just another of her improbable dreams. Perhaps it was just as well, she reasoned, thinking that if she really believed she was marrying Adam Ross, she might not have the courage to go through with it.

Suddenly, Lori realized an awkward silence had fallen, and everyone seemed to be looking at her expectantly. She had no idea what they expected until Bessie said, "Well, now, what's the hold up? Shouldn't we get started, preacher?"

Reverend Hartsfield jumped guiltily, although Lori was sure he had nothing about which to feel guilty. "Yes, yes, of course," he said, glancing around with an air of confusion. "Shall we stand over by the fireplace?" he asked Lori.

Lori did not believe this was her decision to make, so she glanced at Adam for approval. He was smiling, but she could see the strain behind the smile. His eyes looked almost bleak as he said, "That would be fine," and led Lori over.

They took the places the minister indicated, with Bessie standing to Lori's left and the judge to Adam's right. Reverend Hartsfield cleared his throat to begin, but before he could speak, Adam suddenly stiffened.

For a second, she was afraid he had finally come to his senses and was going to call a halt, but then he said, "I almost forgot," and turned toward the door. "Sudie!" he called.

The woman appeared so suddenly that Lori had the impression she had simply materialized in the doorway. She looked as grave as if she had been summoned to witness a death, and Lori noticed she pretended not to see anyone else in the room except Adam.

"Would you summon the others? We're about to begin," Adam said.

She simply nodded and came in. For a moment Lori thought the woman was blatantly refusing to do her master's bidding, but close on her heels came the rest of the house servants, and she realized they had been waiting just outside, more aware of what was happening in this room than those who were in it.

All of them were dressed in what was obviously their best attire. Some were smiling and others appeared uncertain, while Sudie and the man named Oscar who had fetched Lori and Bessie this morning—a man Lori knew because he was the one who usually brought them the food Adam had sent through the years to keep them from starving—both appeared so solemn they could have been in mourning.

The group amounted to about a dozen or so, and Lori couldn't help feeling uncomfortable in their presence. She had been raised to despise slaves, although she had never quite figured out why. Her father had always spoken against slavery, insisting that the slaves should all be sent back to Africa before they could rise up and murder all the whites in their beds. Of course, the McClintocks had always been too poor to afford slaves themselves, and Lori had often wondered if her father's opinions would have changed if his circumstances had been different.

Then Lori realized in surprise that in a few minutes, *her* circumstances would be different. In marrying Adam Ross, she would become a slave owner, too, and mistress of all these present and several dozen more who were working in the fields. Before she could even begin to understand what that would mean, Reverend Hartsfield began the ceremony.

"Dearly beloved," he said, and Lori felt a whole new set of terrors welling up inside of her. Why hadn't she thought about this longer? Why hadn't she realized that marrying Adam Ross involved more than just the two of them? Why hadn't she considered what her role would be or the fact that she had absolutely no qualifications for becoming mistress of a plantation?

"Join hands."

Adam took her hand in his, making her aware of how icy her own had become. He seemed surprised and wrapped his fingers around hers more securely, as if he could warm them. She looked up into his face and almost felt as if she were seeing him for the very first time.

Standing this close, she could see he had shaved closely. His hair gleamed from the oil he had used to tame it, making it several shades darker than the golden blonde she knew it to be. But his eyes were what she noticed the most. The other day, when he had proposed to her, she'd thought them the color of the Texas sky, but now that sky was cloudy, as if a storm approached. And he was looking at her as if . . . as if he wanted to devour her.

"Miss Lori?" Reverend Hartsfield asked, startling her.

She turned to him in alarm.

"You must say 'I do,' " he explained with a warm smile. Behind her, one of the slaves chuckled quietly, and Judge Fairweather coughed behind his hand.

Her face flaming, Lori quickly said, "I do."

A few moments later, Adam said it, too, promising she knew not what, but very adamant about it.

Then Reverend Hartsfield said, "Miss Lori?" again, and when he was sure he had Lori's attention, he said, "please repeat after me."

Determined not to make another mistake, Lori did as he instructed, pledging to love and honor and obey Adam Ross. For better or for worse. *Wasn't that why she was marrying him, to make things better?* In sickness and in health. *How could she do any less?* Forsaking all others. *Something Lori was only too willing to do.*

From this day forward.

Lori's mind desperately seized on this phrase. Yes, of course, from this day forward. They wouldn't look back, wouldn't dare, because the past could only hurt them. She would only look forward now, toward making a life for herself and for Adam and for the child. *From this day forward.*

When she was finished with her vows, Adam repeated his own, although Lori noticed his voice sounded faint, as if he was afraid to speak out too loudly. Or perhaps he simply didn't mean them. But that wouldn't make any difference, would it? They would be just as married in the end. From this day forward.

Adam's eyes looked so strange. She'd never seem them like that before. They almost looked like . . . But no, Adam wasn't *him*. Adam was different. Adam would never . . .

A ring appeared as if by magic, and Adam slipped it on her finger, making still more promises, something about his worldly goods. She would have taken him with nothing at all, and heaven knew, she had nothing to offer in return—except herself. Which was, she understood instinctively, all that he wanted.

She could see that in his eyes, in his beautiful eyes. She'd seen that look before, in another pair of eyes, just before the lust gave way to fury and the man became a monster.

No! her mind screamed in denial. Adam wasn't like that. Adam would never . . .

But what had Bessie said? All men would. All men *did*. And now she was Adam's wife, and he could do with her what he willed, and she had no doubt of what he willed because she could see it plainly in his beautiful eyes.

Dear God, how could she have been so stupid? How could she have believed him so different, so pure? Why hadn't she listened to Bessie? And what was she going to do now, because Reverend Hartsfield was pronouncing them man and wife, and it was already too late.

"You may kiss the bride," the minister said with a smug smile.

Adam's eyes took on an almost feverish glow as he lowered his face to hers, closer and closer, until it wasn't Adam's face at all anymore but *his* face, closing in, sucking the breath out of her, crushing her beneath his weight until she thought she was going to die.

She gasped or tried to, but her corset wouldn't allow it,

and her head was floating and the room was spinning and the blackness was beckoning, dark and welcoming. Lori gave a small cry before closing her eyes and surrendering to its oblivion.

Three

Adam managed to catch Lori and prevent her from falling to the floor, but he couldn't do any more than hold her since his bad leg would never support him if he tried to lift and carry her.

"Oscar!"

His servant was there in an instant, taking Lori's dead weight and easily lifting her into his strong arms.

Bessie was sputtering in outrage, something about letting a slave touch a white woman, but Adam ignored her.

"Put her down on the sofa," he told Oscar, who obeyed without a word. His chocolate colored face looked as if it were carved from stone, and Adam noticed he didn't so much as glance at the still sputtering Bessie.

"Leave her feet on the floor!" Bessie shrieked when Oscar would have placed Lori on the sofa completely prone. "Don't want none of *them* lookin' up her dress!" she explained at Adam's startled glance, jerking her head in the direction of the servants.

Considering how many petticoats Lori was undoubtedly wearing beneath her gown, Adam wasn't sure what could possibly be visible, but he noticed Oscar obeyed her command. The instant the sofa bore Lori's weight, Oscar released her and stepped quickly away, turning his back lest he be accused of some other imagined impropriety.

"Lori, honey, are you all right?" Bessie demanded, swooping in to kneel beside the unconscious girl. She took one of

Lori's delicate hands in her larger one and began to chafe. "Lord Almighty, she's like ice. Lori, can you hear me?"

If she could, she gave no sign. Her face was chalk white, and Adam hovered over her helplessly, desperate to assist her but not having the slightest idea how to do so.

"Maybe something she ate disagreed with her," Judge Fairweather suggested anxiously, wringing his plump hands. Sweat had beaded on his bald head.

"Can't be somethin' she ate," Bessie snapped impatiently. "She ain't swallowed a bite of food since yesterday."

"That's it, then!" Reverend Hartsfield declared triumphantly. "She needs some sustenance. Some brandy perhaps or—"

"How's she gonna drink brandy when she can't even open her eyes?" Bessie demanded.

Adam knew he should do something. The girl was his responsibility, after all. His wife, in fact. The thought stunned him for an instant, and by the time he'd recovered himself, Sudie was there, waving something under Lori's nose. Smelling salts.

Lori coughed slightly and stirred, and after a few seconds her eyes fluttered open. She looked around in alarm at the faces peering down at her and asked, "What happened?"

Everyone in the room released their breath at the same time in a sigh of relief.

"You fainted, girl," Bessie informed her, laying a hand over her own heart as if to calm it. "That's what happened."

"Oh, dear," Lori said in dismay as she struggled to push herself upright, and Adam didn't think the color that came to her cheeks was an indication of returning health. She glanced around at the circle of faces again with increasing distress.

"Give the poor girl some air," Bessie said, shooing everyone back and giving the group of slaves who still stood gaping an angry glare.

"Mrs. McClintock is right," Adam said quickly, smiling

reassuringly at the servants whose only offense had been wanting to see their master married. "Thank you all for coming, but there's no need for you to keep standing around. You've got a party of your own to go to now, I think."

He'd given all of them and the fieldhands, too, the afternoon off and an ox to roast to celebrate his nuptials. Murmuring their good wishes uncertainly as they passed him, they filed out, and Adam didn't miss the fact that they all stared at Lori as they did so. Well, she couldn't help but be an object of curiosity to them since she would be their new mistress. Unfortunately, falling over in a faint just as their master went to kiss her would not have made a favorable impression on them.

It hadn't made a favorable impression on Adam either, and he hadn't missed the expression of abject terror in her eyes in the instant before she fainted either. The memory galled him, but he couldn't summon up much self-pity, only self-contempt. What had he expected, after all? The girl hadn't exactly been eager to marry him. In fact, if she hadn't been desperate, she wouldn't have even considered it. If the prospect of kissing him frightened her out of her senses, how could he even be surprised?

Oscar and Sudie were the last of the slaves to leave. Oscar paused by the door, waiting for his wife. His expression was still stony, and he refused to even glance at Lori or her stepmother. Sudie was looking at Adam, waiting for his direction.

"Should I put the dinner on the table?" she asked when he offered none.

"Oh, yes, I think . . . that would be a good idea. Miss Lori could probably do with some food."

He thought he detected a slight flinch of distaste on Sudie's face at the mention of his bride, but she merely nodded and left to do his bidding.

"I'm sure a little brandy would be just the thing," Judge Fairweather was insisting as Bessie helped Lori straighten her gown. Adam figured the judge probably wanted a snort himself. He certainly looked as if he could use one.

"Liquor on an empty stomach?" Bessie scoffed. "The girl'll be falling face first in her dinner."

Adam looked at Lori and found himself wondering how anyone as pale and wan as she could also be so breathtakingly beautiful.

"I'm sorry," she said to him. Her hands were clutched tightly together in her lap and her eyes were wide with apprehension, as if she feared his disapproval. Or perhaps she simply feared *him*.

"There's nothing to be sorry about," Adam insisted with as much good cheer as he could muster and deliberately forgetting about the way she had looked at him in that last second before he would have kissed her—as if he were some sort of monster.

"Indeed," Reverend Hartsfield said agreeably. "I've had many a bride faint. It's all the excitement, I think. And young ladies are such fragile creatures and so easily unnerved."

Lori looked at him in amazement, wondering what he would say if she told him how many times she had plowed her father's fields herself and hoed the weeds and picked the crops. *Fragile?*

But then she couldn't deny that she felt that way now. As if she might shatter into a million pieces if Adam Ross so much as touched her.

But he wasn't going to touch her, at least not at the moment. They were going to eat dinner. And then . . . Well, Lori wouldn't think past that, at least not now. Not if she was going to maintain her composure. She would just worry about getting through the meal.

"Shouldn't we at least have a toast while we're waiting?" Judge Fairweather inquired a little too eagerly. Plainly, he wanted a drink rather badly, even though he had to know perfectly well it would only aggravate his gout.

"I reckon that'd be all right," Bessie allowed, "but don't give Lori too much."

"Oh, yes," Reverend Hartsfield agreed. "I think we could all do with a little stimulant. You know what the good book says, 'A little wine for thy stomach's sake.' "

They all looked at Adam, who seemed only then to realize that he was the one who should serve them. "Of course," he said, as if he'd thought of it himself. "I've got a bottle I've been saving for a special occasion."

"Better drink it before the Yankees come and take it," Judge Fairweather advised with a chuckle.

"Oh, young Eric will never allow the Yankees to get this far," Reverend Hartsfield insisted, making Lori's heart stop dead in her chest.

Instinctively, she looked at Adam to see his response, and she noticed he hesitated just a second but then went on walking away as if he hadn't heard a thing. He was moving slowly and not using his cane at all. Lori remembered what Bessie had said about him being so vain, and she realized that he was hardly limping at all.

He stopped before a cabinet, then he opened one of the doors and began to pull out a bottle and glasses for everyone. Moving with the ease of familiarity, he used a corkscrew to open the wine bottle as the conversation continued around them.

"Do you think that rag-tag bunch that Rip Ford gathered up can really protect us from the Union Army?" Judge Fairweather was asking the preacher.

"They're Southerners, aren't they?" Reverend Hartsfield replied loyally. "I've always said one Southerner is better than a hundred Yankees."

"Even if the Southerner is an old man or a child?" Adam asked as he poured the ruby red liquid into the pretty glasses. "And that's all Ford could get, you know. All that was left in Texas, in fact. Boys who haven't yet learned to shave and old men who should be sitting in rocking chairs, dandling their grandchildren on their knees."

"And your brother," the judge reminded him, making Lori's breath catch in her throat again. But she gritted her teeth against the horrible memories. She'd have to get used to hearing people speak of Eric. She was, after all, his sister-in-law now.

Adam was carrying glasses of wine to her and Bessie, still without using his cane. And he was still hardly limping. Somehow she'd thought he couldn't even walk without it, but now she saw he could. It just took more effort.

An effort he was apparently willing to make. He handed her one of the glasses. His mouth was smiling, but his eyes were not. They were troubled. And suspicious. And she didn't know what they saw when they looked at her.

"Thank you," she said, accepting the glass and hating how weak her voice sounded.

"Are you feeling better?" he asked.

He was so kind. "Yes, much. I should've eaten some breakfast. Bessie told me I should, but I just couldn't."

"The excitement," Reverend Hartsfield repeated knowingly.

"Yeah, she was as jumpy as a cat on a hot stove," Bessie confirmed, reaching out to take the other glass from Adam's hand, although he hadn't offered it to her yet.

Adam looked at Bessie in surprise, and Lori was glad to no longer be the center of his attention. Every time he looked at her, she felt the guilt again. He was such an important man, and she was nothing. How could she have allowed him to ruin his own life to protect her?

At least he wasn't looking at her *that way* anymore. As if he wanted to devour her. Probably, he'd never looked at her like that in the first place. She must have imagined it, just like she'd imagined he turned into Eric in that second before she fainted. Adam wasn't like that. He'd never hurt her.

"To Adam Ross and his bride," Judge Fairweather said

when Adam had finished passing around the glasses. "May you always be as happy as you are today."

Lori glanced at him in dismay, but of course he had no idea that this wasn't a happy day for them. And everyone else drank, so Lori lifted the glass to her lips and tasted the sweet wine. Remembering Bessie's warning, she took only a sip, however, and looked up again to see her stepmother was draining her glass.

"That's mighty good stuff," Bessie declared when she'd finished and wiped the back of her hand across her mouth. "You got any more?"

"Of course," Adam said, although she could tell he was surprised by Bessie's boldness. For her own part, Lori was mortified, but she couldn't do anything to change Bessie. Heaven knew, she'd tried often enough without success.

The judge, Lori was relieved to note, accepted a refill as well. The men chatted about the war for a few moments, while Lori stared down into her glass and wished herself some-place—*anyplace*—else but here. Then that slave woman came in, the one who'd been holding the smelling salts under her nose when she woke up. Lori would never forget the look on her face, like *she* was the one who smelled something bad. Like she could hardly stand to be that close to somebody like Lori and was only doing it because it was her duty.

Now Lori noticed that she still refused to look at Lori or Bessie. She spoke only to Adam.

"Dinner's on the table, Massa Adam," she said, looking as proud as if she was the mistress here. Maybe Lori's pa had been right about slaves. Maybe they really were uppity. And dangerous. Lori knew instinctively that this one was a danger to her, although what she could do about it, she had no idea.

"Thank you, Sudie," Adam said and turned to Lori. "Are you feeling well enough to have dinner now?"

Lori didn't think she could swallow a bite of food, not if her life depended on it, but she nodded. "Yes, I'm fine now."

If that wasn't quite the truth, no one needed to know it but her. He offered her his hand, and she took it as she had earlier when they had exchanged vows. His fingers were warm and strong as he assisted her to her feet, and she looked up at him in wonder. This marvelous man was her husband. Although she knew the words were true, she still could not quite grasp the reality of them.

When she was on her feet, he released her hand, and Lori felt bereft for a moment until he offered her his arm. She took it gladly, needing to touch him as much for reassurance as for support. Adam would protect her now. No one would ever hurt her again.

"Shall we?" he said to the others, and to her surprise, Lori saw Judge Fairweather offer Bessie his arm. The two of them followed her and Adam, and Reverend Hartsfield brought up the rear.

Adam was still walking without his cane, and he led her across the entry hall to another room that faced the river. He moved slowly and carefully, and Lori matched her steps to his, not in any hurry herself. The room they entered turned out to be a dining room. The table was the largest Lori had ever seen, and it was covered now with a linen cloth so white it seemed to glow in the bright afternoon sunlight that streamed through the floor-to-ceiling windows. On it sat enough dishes to feed the entire population of the Elmhurst plantation, but they had been arranged into only five place settings. Lori couldn't imagine why anyone thought a person would need so many glasses and plates and pieces of silverware just to eat. How would she ever know which one to use?

Adam had led her over to the chair immediately to the right of the one at the head of the table, and she realized this was to be her seat. Before she could reach for the chair, however, Adam had pulled it out for her, and feeling rather regal, she sat down and allowed him to push it back in.

"Mrs. McClintock, if you will sit here," Adam said, indicating the chair to his left. Judge Fairweather seated Bessie and sat beside her, while Reverend Hartsfield took the chair beside Lori. Adam, of course, sat at the head of the table.

"If you don't mind, I'll do the honors as hostess," Adam said when he had lowered himself into his own chair. He said this to Lori who wondered what he meant. Who ordinarily served as hostess? While she was wondering, Adam picked up a small bell beside his plate and rang it.

Instantly, two slave girls entered through a door at the far end of the room, each carrying a bowl of soup resting on a plate. Lori watched in amazement as the girls set the bowls down in front of her and Bessie, then left to fetch more for the other guests. Each of them used a white linen napkin to hold the plate so that their fingers did not actually touch the plates, and they set the bowls and plates on top of the plates that were already there.

So many plates for just a bowl of soup. And so much fuss for such a simple meal! Somehow she'd imagined the food would be grander here at Elmhurst than what she and Bessie enjoyed, but perhaps Adam was not as prosperous as she had thought. Wouldn't that be a good joke on Bessie, who'd been so sure Lori was making a good match?

Bessie had already picked up a spoon and was slurping her soup rather enthusiastically by the time the serving girls returned with bowls for the judge and the minister. Lori hadn't so much as looked at her spoons, much less tried to decide which one to use. The decision was entirely too daunting, especially when even the delicious aroma of the soup sent her stomach into spasms of rebellion.

Although Lori had been a little embarrassed by the noises Bessie was making, she didn't truly understand Bessie's error until she saw the looks of astonishment on the girls' dark faces when they came back into the room and saw that Bessie was already eating. Their eyes were so wide, Lori thought she could see a rim of white around the dark brown centers. Something was terribly wrong.

As the girls disappeared silently into the nether reaches of the house again, Lori glanced over at Reverend Hartsfield to watch what he would do. If she could see the correct way to eat the soup, she wouldn't make the same mistake Bessie was making. But when she looked at the preacher, she saw he wasn't doing anything at all. And neither was Judge Fairweather. They were simply waiting. And then she understood. They were waiting until everyone else had been served.

"This is mighty good soup," Bessie remarked between slurps. "What's the matter? Ain't you gents hungry?"

Since she didn't pause in her own eating and therefore didn't seem too interested in a reply, no one else apparently felt compelled to give one. For her part, Lori could feel the heat rising in her face and fervently wished she could sink through the floor.

Mercifully, Judge Fairweather said, "The weather's been awfully dry for planting this year, hasn't it?"

"Oh, yes," Adam agreed with what sounded like relief. "Not that it matters. I still have cotton stored from last year that I haven't been able to sell. If we can't drive the Yankees away from the coast by the end of the summer so we can ship our crops, I'm afraid we'll all be ruined whether we get rain or not."

So it was true, Lori realized, as one of the serving girls brought Adam's bowl of soup and set it down with more haste than she had previously used, as if she were trying to help him catch up to his guest. Adam really was poor, just like the McClintocks.

When the girl had withdrawn, Adam said, "Reverend Hartsfield, would you ask the blessing for us, please?"

Bessie looked up in comic surprise and hastily dropped her spoon. It clattered against her bowl, but no one except Lori appeared to notice. Beside her, the preacher rose to his feet and began to pray. He prayed loudly, as if he thought God was far away and wouldn't be able to hear him if he didn't shout. He entreated his Heavenly Father on Adam and

Lori's behalf, begging for them health and prosperity and happiness and the blessing of many children.

Lori thought she heard Bessie snort at the last request, but she wasn't sure. What she *was* sure about was that it had made her own stomach knot even more tightly, something she would have bet was impossible. Thank heaven they were only having soup. Perhaps she would at least be able to swallow a few bites of it so no one would guess how upset she was.

When the minister had finally pronounced his "Amen," Lori waited until he took his seat and from the corner of her eye she watched what he did. He selected the large bowled spoon from the far end of the row of utensils to the right of his plate and began to eat the soup. Before she picked up her own, she glanced over at Adam to make sure he had selected the same one. She didn't want to make a mistake and shame him.

Finally convinced that she had the correct spoon, she picked it up and dipped it into the bowl. Being careful to get only broth and none of the pieces of tender, pink flesh that were floating in it, she ladled it into her mouth so she wouldn't slurp. Even though her senses told her the soup was delicious, her throat clenched in rebellion when she tried to swallow it. How much would she have to force down that throat to give the impression that she had actually eaten? she wondered in dismay. And, of course, she knew she should eat in order to keep from fainting again.

Determinedly, she dipped her spoon again and again until the level in her bowl had gone down noticeably. The men continued to converse around her, about crops and the weather and the Yankee blockade of Texas ports, but Lori made no attempt to follow the conversation. She needed all her concentration to get through the meal without being sick. When she had eaten all she could, she laid her spoon down and sat back to wait for the others to finish.

After a few minutes, she was surprised to notice that she

felt a lot better for having eaten even this little bit. Perhaps, she thought grimly, she would be able to survive the rest of this day.

After what seemed an interminable time, everyone else had finished their soup, too. Adam rang the little bell again, and instantly the serving girls re-appeared to remove their soup bowls. They took not only the bowls but the two plates beneath them, which confirmed Lori's suspicion that this was to be a very simple meal. How disappointed the judge and the preacher must be. While a bowl of soup was more than enough for her and Bessie, Lori imagined they were used to more substantial fare.

"I expect Sudie has outdone herself on this meal," Judge Fairweather said, rubbing his plump hands together as if he expected something. "It isn't every day the master of the house gets married."

"I'm sure she's done her usual best," Adam agreed.

"I can't tell you how many times through the years I tried to buy her from your father," the judge went on.

Lori noticed that even though everyone's plates had been removed, no one was making any move to leave the table. Well, perhaps there was some dessert. Lori hoped it wouldn't be too rich for her to eat.

"That Sudie is a treasure," the judge was saying. "I hope you appreciate her, Mrs. Ross."

Although the judge was looking at Lori, it took her a minute to realize who he meant when he said "Mrs. Ross."

"Oh," Lori said when the truth had finally dawned on her. "Yes, I'm sure I will." She could feel the heat scalding her face, and she couldn't bring herself to even glance at Adam for fear she would read disapproval on his face. Or regret.

"Has your family ever owned slaves before, Mrs. Ross?" the judge asked.

Her face still burning, Lori shook her head. "Never. My pa, he . . . he didn't hold with it."

Bessie made a rude noise. "Couldn't afford it, more likely.

I expect if somebody'd give him a slave, he'd've changed his mind quick enough."

"In any case," the judge went on, tactfully ignoring the reference to Lori's late father, "you will need to establish your authority immediately. Not that I think Adam's slaves are unruly, mind you." He gave Adam a conciliatory smile before turning his attention back to Lori again. "But any servant will take advantage of his master, if given the chance. There's no need to be cruel, of course, but you must be firm. Otherwise they will steal you blind and laugh at you behind your back."

"And remember, Mrs. Ross, that they're like children," Reverend Hartsfield added. "They need your guidance and your protection as well."

Before Lori could respond to either of them—or even think of a response for that matter—the dining room door opened again and the serving girls were back. This time they carried new plates which they set down in front of each of the diners, and before Lori could even begin to wonder what they were for, the girls began to carry in serving platters laden with more food than Lori usually saw in a month.

There was a ham and a roast chicken and fried potatoes and baked sweet potatoes and new peas with tiny onions and fresh salad and pickles and preserves and biscuits and several things Lori didn't even recognize.

What a fool she was to think that Adam Ross would serve the guests at his wedding just a bowl of soup! But why on earth would they prepare so much food for five people? For a moment, she wondered if perhaps Adam had invited more people and they simply hadn't shown up. But the thought was simply too horrible to contemplate, especially when she had to figure out how on earth she was going to do justice to this meal.

In spite of her protests, Lori was compelled to accept at least a sampling of every dish on the table.

"Can't insult the cook," Reverend Hartsfield warned her when she tried to refuse.

Fortunately, the soup had settled her stomach a bit so she was able to eat at least a little of the sumptuous meal. Bessie had the good sense not to remark on the amount and variety of the food, but every now and then she shot Lori a look that spoke eloquently of her amazement. When they got home, Lori would probably be hearing about this meal and the scandalous waste of food for most of the night.

Except, Lori suddenly realized, she wouldn't be going home with Bessie. Not tonight and not ever again. Because now she was Adam's wife. And she lived here—with him.

What little appetite she had fled instantly, and the delicious food on her plate had all the appeal of sawdust. She laid down her fork and reached for the glass of wine one of the serving girls had poured for her. How much of it would she have to drink to drown the hot ball of apprehension that had formed in her stomach? How much to loosen the nerves that had knotted in terror all over her body? Certainly more than was in her glass, and probably more than was in the entire world.

Dear God, how was she ever going to go through with this? How would she ever be able to truly become Adam Ross's wife when the mere thought of allowing a man to touch her turned her blood to ice?

But then, perhaps he didn't want that any more than she did. He wasn't in love with her, after all. He hardly knew her, in fact. And what possible attraction could he feel for a girl like her with no education or breeding or social graces? None at all. In fact, she should consider herself fortunate that he had lowered himself far enough to marry her. What could ever make her believe he wanted any more than that from her?

"Are you all right?" Adam's voice cut into her thoughts. It was so deep and masculine, yet so gentle. "If you're not feeling well, perhaps you'd like to retire," he suggested when she didn't reply.

"No, I'm fine, really," she assured him. She certainly wasn't going to go off to his bedroom, not until she absolutely had to.

As she might have expected, he smiled kindly. "You look awfully pale again. I hope the dinner agrees with you."

"It's wonderful," she assured him. "Everything is . . . wonderful."

"It certainly is," Judge Fairweather agreed. "Don't know when I've had ham this sweet or chicken this tender. It's Sudie, I know. She doesn't do the cooking, mind you," he confided in Lori, "but she runs everything in this house. Adam, you're a lucky man."

"I've always felt fortunate to have her," Adam agreed pleasantly.

Lori wondered if she would feel so fortunate.

"Might be a good idea to figure out what you'll do without her," Bessie advised around a mouthful of food. "Like when the Yankees come and all the darkies run off with 'em."

"Nonsense," the judge insisted. "They'd never run off with the Yankees. Why, we haven't had a single runaway slave in this county since the war started. And the same is true all over the Confederacy. All those prophets of doom who predicted that when the men left their homes for the army, the slaves would revolt, were dead wrong, weren't they?"

"It ain't over yet," Bessie reminded them all. "And we ain't seen a Yankee army in Texas yet, either. Sure, they stayed put 'cause there's a war goin' on and they don't know which side's gonna win, but if the Yankees win—"

The minister and the judge both gasped their outrage at such heresy and cut Bessie off instantly.

"How can you even think such a thing?" the judge demanded.

"The Yankees could never prevail against the best of our manhood!" Reverend Hartsfield insisted.

"They's doin' a pretty good job of prevailin' in most of the South, and now they's knocking on the door in Texas, too," Bessie reminded them. "And if they can't whip us on the battlefield, they'll starve us out before too much longer. Just how long you think we can keep going with all our men off fightin' and nobody stayin' home to grow crops?"

Judge Fairweather made some incoherent noises of outrage and Reverend Hartsfield glared his disapproval, but Adam was the one who silenced her. "I don't think this is appropriate conversation for our wedding day, do you, Lori?"

"No," she quickly agreed, and then realized she had nothing else to suggest as a topic. Surely, a girl with breeding and education, the kind of girl Adam Ross *should* have married, would have known exactly what to say and do. Lori could only sit and listen and think about how terrified she was at the prospect of being Adam Ross's wife. Fortunately, Adam knew how to handle the conversation himself, and he quickly turned it to neighborhood matters and the condition of the church steeple, which had been hit by lightning. Unfortunately, there probably wasn't enough cash money in all of Texas to fix it.

At long last, the servants came in and cleared the table, and then, with a flourish they carried in the wedding cake. Lori didn't think she had ever seen anything so beautiful. So much time and trouble spent just to prepare something that would be eaten in a matter of minutes. In Lori's world, where people barely managed to survive from day to day, no one had the time or the energy to devote to something so frivolous. But this was a different world, like none she had ever known. And now she was a part of that world, too.

Sudie herself had come out to cut the cake. The serving girls, carrying it on a plank, set it at the far end of the long table so it could be properly admired.

"Ah, Sudie, you can be proud of this feast," Judge Fairweather said.

"Thank you, Judge," Sudie said, but Lori noticed she was looking at Adam, as if his approval was all she cared about.

"Everything was delicious," Adam assured her with a smile. The smile was one Lori had never seen before, warm and full of genuine affection, as if he truly cared about this woman. "And that cake is magnificent," he added.

Sudie seemed to grow under the praise, squaring her shoulders and pulling herself up until she actually appeared taller. That was when Lori really understood that she hadn't been mistaken: Adam's praise *was* all she cared about. She hadn't even glanced at Lori, and Lori understood also that her own opinion—and probably the rest of her, too—counted for nothing to this woman.

Stung, Lori could only murmur her thanks when one of the girls brought her a slice of the cake. It was white and tall and looked featherlight. How long since she'd tasted cake of any kind? Not since the Yankees had strangled Texas with their blockade. In fact, not since before her father had left for the war.

Her mouth watered just remembering how the cake would feel on her tongue and how the icing would melt into sugary sweetness. Just the smell alone was intoxicating, stirring memories of birthdays past and Christmases that would never come again.

She didn't realize how long she had been staring at it until Adam asked, "Don't you like cake, Lori?"

"What?" She looked up in confusion and realized everyone was waiting for her to begin. Then she glanced at where Sudie still stood at the end of the table. Her skin, Lori realized, was as white as her own, and only her clothing distinguished her as the servant in this room. But if she felt the inferiority of her position, she gave no sign of it as she met Lori's gaze unflinchingly. If anything, her expression said that she felt herself superior to the woman her master had taken as his wife that day.

You'll need to establish your authority immediately, Judge Fairweather had warned her. But how was she to do so? Lori thought perhaps she would be better served to play to Sudie's vanity.

"I love cake," she told Adam with a forced smile. "I was just thinking that this looks too good to eat."

"Well, don't let that stop you," the judge advised, digging into his own serving with such enthusiasm that no one would have ever guessed he'd already eaten enough that afternoon to keep Lori and Bessie well supplied for a week.

The cake was even more delicious than Lori had imagined it would be. If Sudie was responsible for this and everything else she had tasted today, Adam was indeed lucky to have her. If only Lori had felt lucky, as well.

Finally, the meal was over, and Adam suggested the ladies withdraw to the parlor while the gentlemen enjoyed their brandy and cigars. Bessie probably would have liked a cigar herself, but at least she had the good sense not to say so and embarrass Lori even more completely.

The woman named Sudie led the two of them back to the parlor and saw that they were served coffee.

"Can I get you anything else, Missy?" Sudie asked when the serving girl had withdrawn. Her back was ramrod straight, and Lori could see that it took every ounce of her will to remain civil to Lori and Bessie. Probably, she had never been forced to entertain people of their class in her master's house, and doing so now was taxing her patience to the limit. She still refused to look directly at them. Perhaps, Lori couldn't help thinking, Sudie hoped they would disappear if she refused to acknowledge them.

"No, that's fine. Thank you. And Sudie?" she added when the woman turned as if to go.

She stopped and waited, although every nerve in her body

was radiating her reluctance to obey even the slightest command from the likes of Lori. "Yes'm?"

"I wanted to thank you for . . . for making everything so nice today."

Lori could feel Bessie's outraged glare, but she ignored it and waited for Sudie's response. If she'd been expecting any softening in the woman's attitude, she was disappointed, however.

"I did it for Massa Adam," she said and turned on her heel and left the room before Lori could say anything else.

"Let that be a lesson to you, *Missy*," Bessie said when the doors had closed behind Sudie. "You can't make friends with a darkie. They hate you just 'cause you's white, and that one'd prob'ly slit your throat as soon as look at you."

"Bessie!" Lori exclaimed.

"It's true. Oh, she won't really murder you, but she's likely to think of a hundred little ways to make your life miserable, just the same. Don't you stand for it, though. She gives you any trouble, you have her whipped."

"I couldn't do that!"

"Didn't you hear what the judge said? If they ain't afraid of you, they'll be laughin' behind your back. Can't have that, not if you want to be the mistress here."

Of course, Lori had no wish to be the mistress here. Somehow her youthful fantasies about becoming Adam Ross's wife hadn't included supervising his slaves. She had no idea how to even begin such a task.

Mercifully, Bessie decided she had adequately covered the subject of Adam's slaves and offered Lori no more advice. They drank their coffee in silence for a while.

Then Bessie said, "Well, I reckon I don't have to give you no advice for your wedding night, do I?"

Lori gasped as she felt the heat of humiliation and rage scalding her face. Unfortunately, she didn't have an opportunity to reply because at that moment the parlor doors opened and the gentlemen returned to sit with them.

Adam's gaze, she noticed, sought her immediately as he entered the room. His finely carved lips curved into a smile at the sight of her, and Lori felt her rage at Bessie evaporating in the warmth of that smile. He really was the most handsome man she had ever seen, and it wasn't just his fine clothes. He would, she was certain, have looked just as appealing in overalls and a longjohn shirt, though perhaps not as imposing.

Apprehension prickled along her nerve endings as he approached. "I hope we haven't kept you waiting too long," he said when he stopped in front of her chair. He seemed so tall from where she sat looking up at him, even taller than he usually did. And so blatantly masculine that Lori had difficulty drawing a breath.

In all her youthful fantasies, she had always known exactly what to say and do in Adam's exalted presence. Unfortunately, Adam's *actual* presence seemed to rob her of every sensible thought, leaving her speechless and stupid and feeling every bit the bumpkin that his slave Sudie obviously thought her to be. And which Adam would think her, too, unless she managed to show him otherwise—and soon.

But she didn't manage it that afternoon. Adam chose the seat closest to her, and his gaze kept drifting to her as the five of them sat together in the parlor, as if he expected—or hoped—that she would say something clever. Or at least intelligent. If so, he was disappointed, although Lori had to give him credit, he never appeared to be the least bit disappointed and was unfailingly polite to her through the whole ordeal.

Fortunately, the judge and the minister kept the conversation going with Bessie's occasional assistance until the shadows had begun to grow long outside the tall windows.

"I guess it's time we left the newlyweds alone," the judge said after several hours. His sly smile said he knew why they would want to be alone, too, and Lori felt her apprehension returning.

"I suppose you're right," Reverend Hartsfield agreed. "I'm sure we've long since worn out our welcome."

The two men offered their congratulations to Adam and Lori in turn. When Bessie had made no move to leave, Adam finally said, "I'll have Oscar bring the carriage for you, too, Mrs. McClintock."

Bessie raised her eyebrows in surprise, but she didn't protest. As much as Lori dreaded being alone with Adam, she was equally happy to see Bessie leave.

Bringing the carriage and the gentlemen's horses up took some time, and the men made idle conversation while they all stood on the back porch of the house. Lori could see the slave quarters from here and wondered suddenly where Sudie slept. The thought that she might have a room in the house disturbed her more than she wanted to admit, even to herself.

Finally, the carriage and the horses arrived, everyone said their good-byes again, and this time Bessie also offered Lori her good wishes. Lori even thought she saw a hint of tears in the older woman's eyes when she leaned over to give Lori a quick peck on the cheek. Lori was still too angry with her to forgive her just yet, however, and she offered only the barest acknowledgment of Bessie's farewell.

Finally, she and Adam were alone, and Lori had to fight against the new fears that threatened to overwhelm her.

"I'm sure that's not exactly the kind of wedding you always dreamed about," Adam remarked as they walked back into the house.

He was still not using his cane, and Lori had come to realize that he must only use it in public.

"Everything was very nice, really," she assured him hastily. Once inside the hallway, she stopped, uncertain where to go.

"Perhaps I should give you a tour of the house," he suggested.

That seemed sensible. "I do need to know my way around," she admitted.

"All right, let's start with the back parlor," he said, indicating the door to their right. This was obviously the room he used most. The furniture was comfortable and worn, and bookshelves full of books lined one wall. One of those books lay open, face down, on a table by one of the chairs, and Lori had no trouble at all picturing Adam sitting there reading.

She smiled slightly at the thought and glanced up to find he was watching her closely—too closely. His eyes were like the blue heart of a flame, and Lori actually felt the heat of that flame. Instinctively, she backed up a step.

Her reaction startled him, and when he blinked and looked at her again, she realized she'd only imagined the expression she had seen a moment ago. His gaze was clear and cool and perfectly innocent.

She was acting like an idiot, imagining threats that didn't exist. He was Adam, not Eric. She didn't have to be afraid. "This is a lovely room."

"It's where the family always sat, back when we had a family," he added with just a hint of regret. "Now it's just me. And you, of course."

Lori felt a tremor of reaction at the hint of intimacy, as if someone had grazed a teasing finger down her spine, and she only just managed not to shiver. "Yes," she agreed, wondering how long it would take her to feel as if she belonged here. If she ever truly would.

With that disturbing thought, she led the way to the next room. She didn't allow herself to look at him as he described its use to her, and soon she was able to pretend his nearness didn't disturb her at all. As Adam took her up and down the long hallways, setting a leisurely pace that permitted him to walk with only the slightest trace of a limp, she began to lose track of all the rooms. There was a study and an office and a smaller dining room for every day use and a music room and guest room after guest room. Finally they reached a room whose door Adam made no attempt to open.

"This is Eric's room," he said, as they passed, and Lori

felt her heart shrivel in her chest. For one awful second she imagined the door opening and . . .

But Eric wasn't here, she reminded herself sternly. Eric wasn't anywhere near. He was off fighting a war, and he wasn't coming back for a very long time, maybe not ever. Squelching her automatic wish for that very thing because she knew how sinful it was, she forced her feet to carry her past the closed door of the room she knew she would never enter.

"And this," Adam said when they came to the next closed door, "is my room, or at least it was until today." Something in his tone made her look up, and she realized he had been watching her reaction to Eric's room and didn't quite know what to make of it. Well, what had he expected, that she'd want to see inside?

Then what he'd said about his own room sank in. "This isn't your room anymore?" she asked in confusion.

His smile seemed a trifle skewed, as if it felt awkward on his face. "I thought you'd be more comfortable in the master bedroom. *We'd* be more comfortable, I mean. It's much larger and . . ."

As if he was embarrassed, he turned away quickly and threw open the door at the very end of the long hallway. Lori really was embarrassed, and felt her face burning in reaction. Dear heaven, what had she been thinking? Naturally, Adam would expect to sleep in the same room as his wife. In the same bed. With her.

For an instant, she felt the blood rushing from her head, and she reached out quickly to brace her hand against the wall. Only by force of will did she prevent herself from fainting yet again.

"Lori?"

Adam's voice seemed far away, even though she could see he was standing only a few feet from her. Lori forced herself to smile as the wave of weakness passed and the dark spots dancing before her eyes receded. Drawing as deep a breath as her corset would allow, she put one foot in front of the other and walked past him into the bedroom that they would share.

Her first impression was the one she voiced. "It's beautiful," she whispered in awe.

Indeed, the dark, richly carved cherry wood furniture was polished to a luster. The four-poster bed was draped with a lace canopy and covered with a matching counterpane. Lace curtains hung at the windows beneath heavy damask drapes, and a thick carpet covered the floor. Crystal bottles glittered in the afternoon sun from atop the dressing table. Lori suddenly felt as if she had been transported into a fairy tale.

"The room has been closed since my father died. Sudie and the girls have been working very hard the past few days to get it ready," Adam confided as Lori continued to stare, trying to take it all in at once and discovering something new every second. She detected the faint odors of cedar and rose sachet.

At last her gaze settled on the bed. The enormous bed, built for a man and his wife to share. The bed she and Adam would share that night and every night for the rest of their lives. For some reason, she could hardly breathe.

"You know," Adam was saying, "a man usually gets a kiss at the end of the wedding ceremony, but I missed out on mine."

She looked up at him and was surprised all over again by how tall he was. And how broad. He would be strong, so much stronger than she, and he could take whatever he wanted and she wouldn't be able to stop him—just like she hadn't been able to stop Eric. She tried to draw a breath but couldn't. Something ruthless seemed to be squeezing her.

"Did you . . . ?" She had to swallow and try again. "Did you want a kiss now?" She'd tried to sound playful but didn't think she'd succeeded.

At least he was smiling, although he looked embarrassed again. "Now would be fine."

Whatever was squeezing her tightened its grip, but she swallowed again, forcing down the gorge that tried to rise in her throat. This was *Adam,* she reminded herself frantically, and lifted her face.

No one had ever kissed her, not really, so she wasn't exactly sure what to do, but she closed her eyes so she wouldn't have to see him looming over her and be afraid.

For several heartbeats nothing happened, and then she felt him moving toward her, heard the rustle of his clothes, the uneven step of his injured leg. She braced herself, but still she jumped when he touched her, his hands on her upper arms, holding her so she wouldn't run away. His mouth covered hers, and for an instant everything was fine. Everything was wonderful. His mouth was warm and soft and infinitely sweet, and the kiss was everything she could have wished and more.

But just when it should have been over, his fingers tightened on her arms, and he pulled her to him. Suddenly, she was back there with Eric, and he was forcing her down, his hands cruel as they bruised her flesh and tore at her clothes, and she couldn't breathe and she couldn't move and she couldn't get away and she was going to die!

With a cry, she tore free, ripping herself from his grasp as the terror roared within her. For an instant longer he was still Eric, with Eric's evil grin and Eric's clutching hands, reaching for her. The gorge rose up in her throat again, and she clamped both hands over her mouth and ran.

She'd seen the screen standing in the corner, and although she had no idea what was behind it, it offered the only privacy available. Fortunately, it also concealed a commode chair, and Lori vomited into it, retching painfully again and again until she'd rid her body of every vestige of her marriage feast.

When it was finally over, she sank to her knees and wished fervently to die. How could she ever face Adam Ross again? she wondered as she drew the back of one trembling hand across her mouth. And why on earth would he ever want to even see her? She was disgusting. And thoroughly humiliated.

Why on earth hadn't she taken her own life when she'd had the chance, before Adam Ross even knew she existed?

Then she remembered that he was still out there, on the other side of the screen, and that he'd heard everything. And she began to weep silently, choking back the sobs but unable to stop the tears that coursed down her cheeks.

She didn't know how long she had been weeping when she heard the bedroom door close. Surely, Adam had finally left her alone in her misery. But then someone spoke.

"Missy, you all right?"

Oh, dear God, it was that woman Sudie. Just when she'd thought things couldn't get any worse. She tried to stifle another sob, but Sudie must have heard it or else simply figured out where she was. Suddenly, the slave woman was there, standing over her.

"Lord have mercy," she muttered in disgust.

Lori covered her mouth, but the sobs shook her shoulders, betraying her.

Sudie's hand came down, and Lori instinctively flinched, half-expecting a blow. But Sudie only felt her forehead.

"Don't seem to have no fever," she concluded.

Lori shook her head, wishing she could reassure the woman and send her on her way, but she was afraid to uncover her mouth for fear that she would sob out loud and further humiliate herself.

"Let's get you up from there 'fore you ruin that dress," Sudie said with a resigned sigh, and before Lori could protest, Sudie had her on her feet.

"Come on, I'll get you into bed directly," she continued and would have drawn Lori out from her hiding place, but Lori dug in her heels.

At Sudie's surprised look, she uncovered her mouth at last and managed to whisper, "I don't want him to see me!"

"Massa Adam?" Sudie echoed in surprise. "He gone. You

don't expect no man to stand around while you bein' sick all over the place, do you?"

No, of course not. She should have known. He would have gone for Sudie, who always took care of everything.

Why couldn't she just die?

After Lori had washed out her mouth, Sudie made her sit in the dresser chair, then she went to the door and called for someone named Molly. A dark-skinned girl came running and in a matter of minutes the mess had been removed, a window opened and rosewater sprinkled around to cover the smell.

"We'll get you outta that dress now," Sudie said when they were alone again.

Lori's hand went protectively to her throat, but Sudie didn't notice. She was already moving toward the tall chest of drawers. She opened one and pulled out something white which Lori recognized as the nightdress she had recently purchased for herself with Adam's money. How had it gotten in that drawer?

Then Lori recalled that she had brought with her this morning a small bundle that contained all her belongings. She'd left it in the carriage, but apparently, someone had carried it inside and even unpacked it. Disturbed by this and not even sure why, Lori didn't realize why Sudie had drawn her to her feet again until she started to undress her.

"I can do that myself!" Lori protested weakly.

"I expect you can," Sudie agreed tartly. "Been doin' it yourself all your life, but things is different now. You Massa Adam's wife, and you'll have a maid to do for you. None of the girls is trained yet, 'cause we ain't had a lady to do for here in a long time, but I'll pick one of 'em and teach her what she needs to know. Meantime, you'll have to put up with me."

Even though plainly Sudie was as uncomfortable with this arrangement as she was, Lori realized she had no other choice, since she was still too weak to deal with all the hooks and ties and fasteners of the elaborate outfit. So she stood like a doll while Sudie undressed her, lowering her eyes in shame when she was stripped naked in the instant before Sudie held up the nightdress so she could slip it over her head.

Only when she was covered again, did she dare meet Sudie's gaze, and when she did, she found the slave woman glaring at her with what could only be pure hatred. As if she could tell just by looking at Lori's nakedness just how thoroughly she had been defiled.

"Sit down and I'll brush out your hair," Sudie said.

Lori opened her mouth to protest and realized that to do so would only earn her more of Sudie's contempt. So she sat and allowed the other woman to unpin her hair and brush it out. While Sudie wasn't exactly gentle, she took care not to cause her any pain. But even still, Lori couldn't help the tears that leaked out of her eyes. She only wished they could wash away some of her anguish.

When Sudie had finished with Lori's hair, she laid the silver-backed brush down on the dresser and stepped back. "I'll get you some hot water so you can wash up. And I'll bring your supper on a tray," she said, and then she was gone, closing the door silently behind her.

For the rest of the evening, Lori felt like a cosseted prisoner. A girl brought her water and later her supper, some leftovers from the wedding dinner that she couldn't bring herself to touch. Probably, she should have tried to rest, but the thought of lying down in that bed was simply too terrifying, especially when she was sure Adam would be coming in eventually to join her. She wanted to be standing on her feet when she saw him next. And she would have to explain somehow. She would have to tell him that it was Eric she was afraid of and not him. And somehow she would have to make him understand.

But when she finally heard his knock on the door, she still hadn't figured out how she could do so.

Four

Adam drained his glass and set it down on the table beside him. After summoning Sudie to tend to Lori, he had swiftly retreated to his study where he'd been sitting for hours now, drinking whiskey and pretending to read when all the time he'd been remembering that horrible moment when Lori had wrenched away from him and fled.

He made her sick.

What a fool he was. How could he ever have imagined that any woman, even a woman as desperate as Lori McClintock, would ever be able to endure his touch? Of course, he hadn't expected quite as violent a reaction as he'd gotten today. First, she'd fainted at the prospect of kissing him, and then when he actually did . . .

But it was no more than he deserved, he thought grimly. He'd tried to cheat his fate and take one more thing from his brother. To grasp onto at least a portion of the perfect happiness he'd once hoped to know. To possess a woman's body, if he could never win her heart. But Eric had the last revenge. Too bad he wasn't here to see it.

He looked up to find Sudie standing in the doorway watching him. How long had she been there?

"It's mighty late," she pointed out.

"Yes, I know, and my bride is waiting," he said, managing a smile for Sudie's benefit, although his insides felt as if he had swallowed broken glass. "How is she?"

"I told you before, she fine," Sudie reported, not bothering to hide her disgust. "Prob'ly, she just made a pig out of herself at dinner. I don't expect her kind ever seen so much food all at once."

Adam felt an unfamiliar rush of anger toward her. "That's enough, Sudie," he told her sharply. "I won't have you speaking ill of her. She is my wife, after all."

Sudie stiffened under the rebuke, but she didn't drop her gaze, as most of his slaves would have done. If he never forgot her special position in this household, she was even more aware of it. "Yes, she your wife," Sudie agreed. "And she ain't too sick to do her duty by you, if that's what you was wonderin'."

"Sudie," he said in warning, but she still refused to flinch. "That is what you was wonderin', ain't it?"

Not exactly, although he wasn't about to admit to Sudie that he already knew his bride was not going to be able to do her duty tonight or any other night. Not so long as she was married to a disgusting cripple.

Resignedly, he pushed himself to his feet and marveled that he was still so steady after all the liquor he had consumed. Just his luck that it worked so well on physical pain and didn't even touch the other kind.

"You can go now, Sudie," he said wearily, dismissing her to the cabin she shared with Oscar. "We won't be needing anything else tonight."

She frowned and didn't move except to step back as he approached to allow him into the hallway. He wondered what she was thinking and decided that he didn't want to know. Without a backward glance, he headed in the direction of the master bedroom.

The hall was dark, but he knew the route by heart, having lived in this house for most of his twenty-eight years. He could see the strip of light beneath the bedroom door and knew he'd find his bride still awake. Drawing a deep breath and setting his face into the mask of blankness he usually wore to disguise the pain in his leg, he lifted his hand and knocked.

A moment passed, and then another, and just when he began to wonder, he heard her say, "Come in."

She was standing in the center of the room, clad only in a nightdress. Her hair was loose, flowing around her shoulders in ebony waves, and her breasts were loose beneath the thin gown, soft and full and luscious, and for a few seconds he couldn't seem to get his breath. She was, he was certain, the most beautiful creature he had ever seen. And the most tempting.

Needs he hadn't even known he possessed swirled within him like a hot, dark tide, and he'd actually taken a step toward her before he realized it.

Her frightened gasp stopped him, and he watched in anguish as she wrapped her arms protectively around herself, as if she wished to shrink completely from his sight. He drew a ragged breath and forced himself to speak while he still could.

"This is an unusual situation," he began, reciting by rote the speech he had spent the whole evening preparing and praying the whiskey he had drunk wouldn't affect his memory of it. "For both of us. We . . . we hardly know each other, and therefore . . ." Oh, God, had he really said *therefore?* ". . . we don't feel for each other the feelings that . . . that a newly married couple normally feel."

What a damned liar he was. If he felt those feelings any more, he'd burst into flames. All he could think about was how soft her skin would be if he touched her, if he ran his hands over her throat and her shoulders and her naked breasts and buried his face in her warm, satiny flesh and inhaled her secret scent . . .

"So . . ." He had to clear his throat to continue. "So you needn't worry that I will . . . that I . . ." Although he had sworn not to, he couldn't help glancing at the big bed with its thick feather ticking upon which he had imagined spending this night sampling all the delights Lori McClintock's sweet, young body could provide.

He sensed as much as saw her instant reaction, the rigidity of her body and the widening of her eyes with a kind of terror he could only imagine.

Shame twisted inside of him like a dull knife curving at his soul, and he straightened his shoulders, as if by doing so he could more easily bear the burden of her contempt. "I don't expect anything from you, Lori. I'll continue to sleep in my old room until . . ." Until when? Until he went out of his mind and put a bullet through his brain? ". . . until you feel ready to share this room with me." Whenever that might be. Please, God, let him live to see the day.

Her eyes were still wide, but now he thought she was more surprised than anything. And if she was also relieved, he didn't want to know. "I'll see you in the morning," he said with what he hoped was a friendly smile. In the instant before he turned away, he thought he saw tears glittering in those wide eyes, but he chose not to notice. It was all he could do to leave her standing there unmolested, and he didn't think he would have the strength, to do it if she was crying.

With the last of his will power, he pulled the door tightly closed behind him and walked the short distance down the hall to his old room where he would spend this night alone.

Lori stared at the closed door for a long time. She wanted to weep, but she no longer had the energy. She was simply too exhausted. It was all she could do to comprehend that the thing she had most feared was not going to happen.

Adam Ross was not going to claim his rights as her husband. He was not going to share her bed or use her body for his pleasure. She was not going to have to lie there while he smothered her with his weight and forced his way inside of her, grunting and sweating the way Eric had.

She had been right! He wasn't like Eric, and she didn't

have to be afraid of him. He would never hurt her. He was too good and too kind.

Or else he was simply too disgusted. Because he didn't want the little tramp his brother had used and thrown away. Because she was soiled goods, a brood mare whom he planned to discard after she had foaled.

The pain of it was raw, like a half-healed wound ripped open again. Why was this happening to her? What had she ever done to deserve such suffering? To deserve being married to the only man she would ever love when he could not even stand the sight of her?

The agony of it boiled inside of her, doubling her over, and with what was left of her breath, she damned Eric Ross to hell.

Eric Ross thought he might be in hell. The air was so dry and the dust was so thick, he could hardly breathe as he rode along in the seemingly endless line of ragged soldiers which made up the Cavalry of the West.

When they'd left San Antonio just a few days ago, they'd ridden proudly past the Alamo singing "The Yellow Rose of Texas" as the citizens cheered. Old Rip Ford had ridden at their head wearing his black hat emblazoned with a Confederate States of America emblem, a crimson sword sash and run-down boots. The rest of the troops had been garbed in an odd assortment of whatever clothes they had brought with them and whatever official Confederate uniform parts they had managed to scavenge. Since they weren't officially part of the Confederate Army, they weren't entitled to uniforms, even if the South had had the money to supply them.

Now, of course, every man in the brigade was so covered with dirt, it didn't matter what he was wearing or if he had any sort of uniform at all.

Up ahead, someone called a halt, and the column gradually lumbered to a stop. The men swung down from the horses to "rest their saddles," and some pulled off their bandanas and poured a bit of the precious water from their canteens and swabbed out their horses' mouths. Eric took a long pull from his own canteen, wincing at the brackish taste, then walked over to where several men from his company had gathered in the dubious shade of a scrawny live oak tree.

"Hey, Lieutenant, when do we get to fight some Yankees?" one of them demanded good-naturedly as he approached.

Eric instantly felt some of his fatigue lift at the sound of his new title. As one of the few men in the entire army who was in the prime of his life—almost all the others were either boys fifteen or younger or men approaching their dotage— Eric had quickly been elected an officer. "I expect you'll have to wait 'til you get to the coast, Billy," Eric told the boy who had confided to Eric that he was only thirteen and that he'd never owned a pair of shoes. "But don't worry, there'll be plenty to go around. I expect we'll each kill ourselves an even dozen the first day alone."

The rest of the "men" grinned, some showing missing front teeth.

"How many Yankees you figure you killed already, Lieutenant?" another boy asked.

"I lost count a long time ago," Eric said, squatting down in the dirt beside the tree to bask in their attention. He'd told them he was a wounded Confederate veteran who had only recently been pronounced fit to return to the fighting and had decided to help protect Texas' shore. "In the heat of battle, it's sometimes hard to tell."

"At least a hundred?" a third boy prodded.

"At least," Eric admitted modestly. He glanced around at the boys' faces, soaking up their admiration.

"Tell us again how you was standing right beside Stonewall Jackson when he got shot at Chancellorsville," Billy begged.

"Yeah, tell us," another insisted.

Eric shook his head, as if all the attention embarrassed

him. "Well, now, I was sitting up on my horse beside the General——"

"I thought you said you was standing beside him, holdin' his horse," the boy named Alex protested.

"I was on my horse, and I was holding his horse so it wouldn't bolt from all the noise," Eric corrected in irritation.

"Wasn't the General's horse used to battle noise?" Alex asked. The kid was a jackass.

"He was riding a new horse that day," Eric improvised. Damn, why didn't he just shut up and listen to the story like everybody else? "He was looking through his field glasses. I always figured that's how the Yankees found him. Picked him out from the reflection on the glasses, and the sharpshooter knew just where to aim."

"It's a wonder you didn't get hit, too, sitting up on your horse right next to him," Billy noted, his pimply face slack with awe.

"Well, you know," Eric mused, rubbing his chin thoughtfully, "later on I did find a crease in my saddle horn where a bullet went right by me. I always wondered if that wasn't the same one that hit Ol' Stonewall. If it had just hit me instead, General Lee would still have his good right arm," he added. Lee had said when Jackson died from infection after having his left arm amputated that, while Jackson had lost his left arm, Lee had lost his right one in losing his best general.

The boys were gaping at him in wonder—all but Alex who was frowning. He was going to ask another stupid question, so Eric pushed himself to his feet and said, "Better pee while you got the chance, boys. We'll be heading out again soon."

"Hell," said one of the boys, the dark skinned one that Eric suspected might be a nigger. Sometimes they could be as white as a white man, so you couldn't always tell. "I'm so dry, I ain't had to pee all day."

The other boys chuckled sympathetically. Eric didn't have to pee either, but he walked away from the group and pretended to anyway, just to avoid more questions. He'd have to make sure Alex got shot in the first battle they were in. Eric was getting mighty sick of his questions.

He was getting mighty sick of soldiering, too. Ford had promised them excitement, and they'd been stuck in San Antonio for two stinking months waiting for supplies that never came. Now summer was starting in earnest, and if it didn't rain soon, they'd all choke to death on their own dust before they ever got to *see* a Yankee.

But when they did, Eric would be ready. He'd told so many battlefield stories, he was starting to believe he really had killed a hundred Yankees. He couldn't imagine it would take him long, though. How hard could it be? He'd already shot a man, after all, and that had been damned easy. Fun, even. And this time the old man would be proud, instead of coming after him with a razor strap.

The order to mount came down the line, and Eric sighed and buttoned up his pants. The act reminded him of how restless he'd been feeling, and he tried to remember the last time he'd had a woman. That whore in San Antonio hadn't really counted. The other men had been lined up outside her door, and she'd just wanted him finished and out of there as quick as he could.

He'd wanted to smack her ugly face in, but he figured the men who were waiting wouldn't take too kindly to that. His fingers curled into fists remembering his rage, but he had to open them again to mount his horse. The animal, he noticed, was looking kind of sickly. Maybe he should take its saddle off at the next stop or give it a little water. The dumb thing didn't deserve it, but the prospect of walking to Brownsville didn't appeal to Eric, either.

He could almost hear the old man yelling at him for not taking proper care of the animals. The old man was always yelling at him for something. Sometimes Eric forgot that he couldn't yell at him anymore. He couldn't yell at anyone because he was dead. So now it was Adam's turn to yell at him.

Except Adam didn't yell, Eric remembered with a grim smile as the column shifted into motion again. He pulled his bandana up over his face to filter out the dust and kicked his stupid horse into motion. No, Adam was too much of a gentleman to yell. He just spoke reasonably and told Eric what he thought Eric should do. Adam thought he was so damn superior.

But Eric had gotten the last laugh. He'd gotten Lori McClintock. Oh, Adam had never said he wanted her, but Eric had known. It was plain as day, every time Adam set eyes on her. Tipping his hat so polite while all the time he was figuring out a way to get under her skirt. And she'd been silly for him, too, making moony eyes at him in church every Sunday.

But that was before. Before Eric had changed things. And now pretty little Lori belonged to Eric. He'd told her to wait for him and that he'd marry her when he got back. Hell, he might even do it, too, just to see the look on Adam's face. Yeah, that's what he should do, marry the bitch and move her into the house, right under Adam's nose. Where he'd have to see her every day and know Eric was humping her every night.

The thought was so delicious that Eric was smiling behind his bandana until the dust started sifting into his mouth, and he had to cough and spit to get it out.

Yeah, the last time he'd really had a woman had been Lori McClintock, he realized when he'd stopped spitting. She'd been a fighter. He hadn't had a fighter in a long time. But she wouldn't fight so hard next time. They never did. Next time she'd be as sweet as pie. They always were.

When Lori woke up the next morning, at first she didn't know where she was. Startled, she sat bolt upright and gazed around at the beautiful room. Then she remembered. The strange, new ring on her finger. She was Adam Ross's wife and this was Elmhurst and she was in Adam's bed. Except it wasn't really Adam's bed because Adam was in another bed and likely to stay there.

Lori slumped back against the pillows and closed her eyes against a fresh onslaught of despair. Just when she'd thought her life couldn't get any worse. Just when she'd thought the worst thing in the world had already happened to her.

Well, so much for Bessie's theory that Lori could make Adam happy. He didn't even want her to try. And who could blame him after the way she'd acted yesterday? Getting sick just because he kissed her. Fainting when he tried to kiss her. He would think she was crazy, and perhaps she was. How else would she have gotten married to a man who had no use for her?

She felt the sting of tears behind her eyes, but this morning she refused to surrender to them. Lying in this bed and crying wasn't going to solve anything. If she had any chance at all to make a life for herself here, she was going to have to get up and face him. Face him and that slave Sudie and all the rest of them. And show them she wasn't crazy or stupid or whatever else they might think her.

She threw off the covers and would have jumped out of the bed except the first wave of nausea hit her then. Biting it back, determined not to be sick again, she lay perfectly still until it passed. Then, moving more carefully, she got up and tried to decide what to do next.

Probably, she realized, she should call a slave to help her, but she didn't know how to call a slave and the last thing she wanted was to have Sudie looking at her while she washed and dressed. Fortunately, she hadn't used all the water last night, and although it was now stone cold, she was able to wash up and clean her teeth.

What to wear was her next problem, but her choices were limited. She wasn't going to wear her wedding dress for every day, so she put on the dress that used to be her Sunday best. The once-dark blue calico gown was badly faded and frayed at the hem and cuffs, but it would have to do. Then she put on the new shoes she'd bought with Adam's money. When she was dressed, she went to the dressing table and sat down.

The reflection staring back at her from the mirror startled her. She hadn't expected to look so well today after last night, but except for the circles under her eyes, no one would ever guess anything was amiss. Using the silver-backed brush that Sudie had used last night—she couldn't help wondering if it had belonged to Adam's mother—Lori brushed the tangles from her hair, then pinned it up into a modest bun. Or as modest a bun as she could manage with her reluctant curls.

Satisfied that she looked as well as she could, she pinched some color into her cheeks and bit her lips until they seemed redder. Then she walked over to the bedroom door, drew a deep breath for courage, and threw it open.

She wasn't sure what she'd been expecting, but the hallway was empty. And perfectly still. No one seemed to be in this part of the house at all. Remembering that the halls were in a cross shape and the family dining room was down a different hall, she made her way there, walking quietly so she wouldn't attract the attention of anyone who might be about.

She'd only gone a few steps when her stomach growled, and for the first time she wondered what time it was. Of course she hadn't eaten much last night and had lost all of what she'd eaten earlier, so naturally she was hungry. But the sunlight seemed awfully bright. Probably she'd missed breakfast—by a longshot.

Indeed, when she reached the dining room, it was empty, although she could still smell the aromas of breakfast past. Her stomach growled again. She could go back to her room and wait until noon, but she didn't know how long that would be, and besides, she'd already decided she wasn't going to hide in her room all day. She was the mistress here now, or at least the master's wife. Surely, she could have something to eat if she wanted it.

She walked through the silent dining room and out through the door that led to the covered walkway connecting the house to the outside kitchen. The kitchen door stood open to the morning breeze, and she could hear someone moving around inside. She looked in to find one lone slave woman kneading bread. The yeasty smell made Lori's empty stomach clench.

The woman hadn't noticed Lori's presence, so Lori said, "Good morning."

The small, round woman jumped and looked up in almost comic surprise. "Land sakes, Missy, you give me a fright!"

"I didn't mean to," Lori said quite honestly.

The woman smiled broadly, her large white teeth making a bright slash in her dark brown face. "I expect you's looking for something to eat, since you plumb missed breakfast altogether."

"Did I? I knew I'd overslept, but . . ."

"Yes'm, Massa Adam, he say to let you sleep. I was expectin' to hear the bell anytime now, though. A body can't sleep all day, can she?"

Lori wondered how close she had come to doing just that. And she also wondered why Adam had given orders not to wake her. Probably, she couldn't help thinking, he hadn't wanted to see her this morning.

"Do you . . . uh . . . know where Mr. Ross is?" she asked reluctantly.

"Oh, yes ma'am, I expect he out in the fields. That where he is most mornings. Now what can I get you to eat?" she added, rubbing the bread dough off her hands before wiping them on her apron.

Lori didn't want to be a bother. "A piece of bread would be fine."

The woman clucked her tongue in disapproval. "If Sudie find out I give the mistress just a piece of bread for breakfast on her first mornin' here, she skin me alive. You go on and sit down inside, and I'll fix you up something here in just a minute. You want coffee or tea?"

Until the coffee she'd drunk at her wedding supper yesterday, Lori couldn't remember when she'd tasted either, and she'd never ever had the choice of both. "Tea, I think," she said, thoroughly enjoying the small pleasure of making such a decision. She might learn to like it here, in spite of everything.

"I got some water already hot. It'll be ready in two shakes. Go on now and I'll bring it in to you."

"Thank you," Lori said and turned to go. Then she remembered something and turned back. "Oh, what's your name?"

The woman gave her that broad smile again. "I'm Eliza."

"You're the cook?"

Eliza nodded proudly.

Lori decided to try friendliness to see if it worked better on the cook than it had on the housekeeper. "The dinner yesterday was delicious."

Eliza beamed. "Thank you, ma'am. Sudie, she planned it out, but I did the work. I do believe that cake was the best I've ever made."

"It sure was beautiful," Lori replied. "I don't think I ever saw a cake so pretty."

Eliza just stared, as if she was so unaccustomed to compliments that she didn't know how to respond.

Satisfied that she had at least started to make one friend in this house, Lori turned again and made her way back into the house.

Although this was the family dining room, it was still much finer than anything Lori was used to. The table and chairs were the same dark wood as the furniture in the formal dining room, but these were smaller and less ornate. Lori wasn't exactly sure where she should sit, so she chose to walk around the room, examining everything. The sideboard was covered with a lace runner, and on it sat several large silver serving dishes. They were empty now and sparkling clean, shining as if someone had just polished them. She remembered what Bessie had said about the Ross silver and wondered why this wasn't buried with the rest. She reached out and touched one of the dishes with the tip of her finger, curious to know what real silver felt like. It was cool and smooth and Lori was delighted until she realized she'd left a fingerprint on the polished surface. Glancing frantically around to make sure no one had seen, she quickly wiped it away with the sleeve of her dress. After that, she tucked her hands into her pockets so she wouldn't be tempted to touch anything else.

She was staring at a painting on the wall and marveling at the beautiful scene in which men in red coats rode magnificent horses across an impossibly green landscape when the door opened and a pretty, young serving girl came in.

Lori recognized her instantly as one of the girls who had served the wedding meal yesterday. She had no idea of the proper conduct of a plantation mistress, but she didn't want to be rude, so she said, "Good morning."

" 'Mornin', Missy," the girl said shyly, ducking her head. She carried a tray that held a small teapot and a cup and saucer and some other implements.

She carried the tray to the table and set it down, then looked at Lori expectantly.

"I . . . I wasn't sure where to sit," Lori confessed.

The girl's eyes widened slightly in obvious surprise, but she had the grace not to express that surprise in any other way. Then she glanced around. "I expect here be all right," she said, and began to lay the place for Lori at the seat to the right of the head of the table.

"You ready for me to pour your tea?" the girl asked when she had finished.

Lori's stomach growled again, and embarrassed, she laid a hand over it. "Yes, that would be fine."

She hurried over and took her seat at the table as the girl poured the steaming liquid into the delicate china cup.

How was Lori going to get used to all this luxury? Imagine using such fine china on just an ordinary morning. And being waited on hand and foot, as if she were a princess or something.

"We don't got much sugar, but there's honey and milk," the girl said, setting a bowl and a small pitcher nearby. "I be back in a minute with your breakfast."

Sugar? Lori hadn't known there was any left in Texas at all. And she was so busy marveling over the honey that the girl was gone before Lori remembered to ask her name. Feeling almost guilty, she dipped her spoon into the thick amber honey and scooped some up. Not much. She didn't want to be greedy, but her mouth was watering as she dunked the coated spoon into the tea and stirred it around while the honey slowly dissolved.

By then her stomach was cramping with hunger, and she finally lifted the cup to her lips, savoring the soothing aroma as she took her first sip. This moment, she realized vaguely, was the first true happiness she had known since . . .

But she wouldn't think of that, not now. She didn't want to ruin this, so she ruthlessly pushed the ugly thoughts away and enjoyed her first cup of tea in recent memory.

She had finished it when the girl brought in her food. Eliza had fixed her some scrambled eggs and biscuits for which she'd supplied both butter and jelly and several deliciously golden strips of bacon. Lori ate as much as she could, and she found out the serving girl's name was Esther and that Massa Adam should be back from the fields just any time now and did Missy want him fetched?

Missy most definitely did *not* want him fetched. She wanted to sit here in this elegant room and pretend that her fairy tale had come true for a few more minutes at least.

When she'd finished her breakfast and drunk all the tea in the pot, she realized she didn't have a single thing to do for the rest of the day. What did a plantation mistress do? Surely, she had duties to keep herself occupied even if she did have slaves to do most of the actual work. Did she sew? Did she clean? Or cook? Surely not. Surely the slaves did all those things. And most certainly she did not work in the fields the way Lori and Bessie had to keep food on the table.

Lori looked at her calloused hands resting on the table beside the fine china dishes and quickly closed them into fists and hid them away in her lap. Glancing around self-consciously, she almost laughed out loud when she realized she was completely alone and acting like an idiot.

Deciding she couldn't sit here in the dining room with her dirty dishes any longer, she got up. Her first impulse was to pick up the dishes and carry them out to the kitchen, but then she remembered the dinner yesterday and how the serving girls had taken the dirty dishes away. She didn't want the slaves to be laughing at her behind her back for not knowing how a proper lady should behave, so she left the dishes where they were and went back out into the hall.

At first she couldn't think where to go. Her first impulse was to return to her room, but she wasn't going to hide. Then she remembered that Adam had told her the back parlor was where the family used to sit. She was his family now, as difficult as it was to believe. Fingering the new ring on her finger to remind herself, she headed toward the parlor.

The halls were still quiet, although Lori couldn't imagine why, if all the slaves who had witnessed the wedding yesterday worked here. But if they did, they must be busy elsewhere today. As she moved through the carpeted hallways, she couldn't help thinking how easy it would be to forget a war was raging over most of the rest of the country. Here, in this lovely house where everything was beautiful and clean and designed for comfort, it was hard to believe evil could exist anywhere.

And then she remembered that evil incarnate had grown up right within these walls.

With a shudder, she quickened her steps, as if she could outrun her fears. When she reached the back parlor, she hurried inside and resisted an urge to slam the doors shut behind her.

Once in the room, she was able to get hold of herself. Laying a hand over her pounding heart, she forced herself to take deep breaths and remember that he wasn't here, would *never* be here, not anymore. Adam would protect her now. He was her husband and he would protect her.

After a few moments, when she was calm again, she made herself look around the room, recalling the things she had noticed about it before. How comfortable it was. How welcoming. A place where a family would gather in the evening around the fireplace. The wife would sit and knit while the husband smoked his pipe and the children played at their feet.

At the thought of children, Lori's hand moved from her heart to her stomach. She still felt nothing there. Her body had only changed slightly, and surely no one else could tell yet, at least not through her clothes. And not even Sudie, who had seen her without any clothes at all. But soon everyone would know. And they would count on their fingers and they would understand why Adam Ross had married Lori McClintock, a girl no one had ever seen him speak to in public before. Or they would think they understood. Because no one could ever understand, not really, not if Adam's unselfish gesture was to work.

Adam. What a fool she'd been to dream about him. If she hadn't, if she'd accepted the fact that he would never love her, then none of this would ever have happened. Eric would never have tricked her, and she never would've gotten pregnant and . . . and she never would have married Adam.

Be careful what you wish for.

With a sigh, she forced herself to move, to look, to think of something, anything, else. She stopped before the bookshelves and let her gaze drift over the colorful spines. Some of the books had gold letters on them. Lori recognized the letters, although she didn't know all the words. Some of them were long, and she had barely learned to read in the few years she had attended school. Her mother had insisted she go, but after her death, Papa had needed Lori at home. Since then she hadn't read much. The McClintocks owned no books.

Glancing around to make sure no one was watching her, she lifted her hand and let her fingers drift along the leather spines. They felt soft and rich, and she let her fingers stop at one, a red one with gold letters, and after glancing around self-consciously again, she pulled it from the shelf.

It was thick and heavy in her hand, and she opened it at random, letting the gilt-edged pages fall where they would. The pages were covered with words. Lori had never seen so many words all in one place. What could anyone have to say that they would need so many words?

A noise startled her, and she realized someone was coming up onto the back porch just outside the windows. Guiltily, she slapped the book shut and hastily stuffed it back into its place on the shelf. The footsteps moved across the porch and to the back door which opened into the hall just outside the parlor door. She knew those footsteps, even though she'd heard them only a few times in her life. They were unmistakable. The step and the step-clunk, his cane hitting the boards of the porch.

Her heart began to hammer in her chest as she realized in a moment she would see him framed in the doorway. And he would see her, too. Lori cringed at the thought of how he would react. He must despise her now. But maybe he wouldn't see her. Maybe he would walk on by.

She could see him now. He'd stopped just inside the house, set his cane aside, and pulled off his broad-brimmed hat. After hanging the hat on a hall tree, he drew a handkerchief from his pocket and wiped his forehead and the back of his neck. His face was flushed, although the day wasn't particularly warm, and she knew he must have been standing out in the sun for a long time.

She watched the way he moved, so confident, so sure of himself when his legs were still and he didn't have to worry about his limp. She watched as he ran his long-fingered hand through his hair, hair that looked almost golden today because he hadn't tamed it with oil. It clung damply to his neck and forehead. A butternut coat hung from his broad shoulders, and his shirt was collarless and open at the throat. She'd never seen him dressed so casually, and if he looked elegant in his dress suit, he looked blatantly masculine in his planter's garb.

Lori's heart had slowed and now seemed to be laboring in her chest, and her breath came with difficulty even though she wasn't wearing the hated corset. Why didn't he move? Why didn't he go before he saw her?

She didn't think she had made a sound, but she must have because suddenly he glanced into the room and saw her there. Her heart seemed to stop dead in her chest as she waited for his reaction. But he didn't look angry. For an instant, she even thought he was going to smile, but he didn't, although his expression definitely changed. His eyes seemed bluer somehow, and his face was different, although she could not have said how.

"Good morning," he said.

Lori managed an uncertain smile even if he couldn't. "Is it still morning? I thought I'd slept the day away."

He did smile then. It looked more like relief than happiness, though. And he came into the room, walking slowly so he wouldn't limp. "I told Sudie to let you sleep. You . . . you weren't well last night."

Self-consciously, Lori clasped her hands over her stomach and willed herself not to blush with mortification at the memory. "I'm really sorry about that. I don't know what . . . Well, that's not true. I've been sick like that ever since . . . Well, ever since," she concluded awkwardly, blushing furiously now.

Adam's smile disappeared into a worried frown. "Maybe I should send for the doctor. That can't be normal."

"Oh, it is," she assured him, mortified all over again. Why had she ever mentioned this subject? "Bessie told me. It . . . it's part of it. It'll pass in a month or two."

"Still, we don't want to take any chances. I could have the doctor come and—"

"Come all this way for nothing?" Lori was appalled at such extravagance. "Don't waste your money on me. I'm fine, truly I am."

Adam didn't look convinced. "If you're not better soon, I will. My mother . . ." His beautiful blue eyes clouded for a moment, and Lori suddenly remembered his mother had died shortly after Eric was born. Could she have died in childbirth? No wonder he looked so concerned.

"I'm not going to die," she said before she could stop herself and was sorry she had the moment his eyebrows went up in surprise.

"I'm glad to hear it," he said, a strange undertone in his voice, reminding her of her threat of suicide.

"I mean, you don't need to worry about me," she said, chagrined. Dear heaven, wasn't there a subject she could discuss without humiliating herself? "And for sure, you don't need to send for any doctor."

He didn't reply. He just kept looking at her with those troubled eyes of his. Desperately, she cast about for something new to say. Something safe. "You were out in the fields," she remarked inanely.

"Yes," he said, and she thought he might have been as relieved as she over the change of subject. "I don't have an overseer anymore. He joined the army two years ago, and I haven't been able to find anybody else with all the other men gone off to fight, too. So I do the job myself." He walked over to one of the wingbacked chairs and lowered himself into it. She realized he was tired, and then she saw the way he stretched his left leg out in front of him, using his hands to position it just so, and she wondered if it bothered him. "Some planters use slaves as overseers, but I've found that's hard for the slave. He loses the respect of his fellows, and then he can't ever go back to being just one of them again."

Lori had never thought of such things. She realized she'd never thought of slavery much at all, except in the most general terms.

Adam looked up again, and she saw his gaze sweep over her from head to toe. Acutely aware of how shabby she must look to him, she lifted her hand to her throat as if she could cover the worn dress. "I didn't want to wear my good dress again. The one I wore yesterday, I mean."

He blinked. "What?" he asked in apparent confusion.

"I know what you're thinking. You're thinking this dress . . . Well, it's not what your wi . . ." She caught herself just in time. She didn't want to remind him that she was his wife, not when she knew he couldn't be very happy about it. "It's not what I should be wearing, but I don't really have anything else."

He frowned again. "Then we'll have to do something about that. Can't have the mistress of Elmhurst looking like . . ." He caught *him*self before he could insult her, but Lori knew what he was thinking. Can't have the mistress of Elmhurst looking like poor white trash. She saw the color crawling up his neck, but he managed a smile. "Why don't you sit down, Lori?" He indicated the matching wingbacked chair, the one she had imagined the wife would sit in. Well, like it or not, she was the wife, wasn't she?

Feeling incredibly out of place, she went over and sat down. She wasn't exactly close to him. The width of the fireplace separated them, but still the setting felt intimate, probably because they were alone in this room meant for a family. Lori clasped her hands together in her lap to keep from fidgeting.

After a long moment of awkward silence, Adam said, "Did you sleep well last night?"

"Yes," she replied. Another awkward silence fell as they both remembered they should have been sleeping together last night. Lori dropped her gaze in embarrassment and noticed that Adam was rubbing his thigh with his left hand. The gesture seemed automatic, as if he wasn't even aware of it.

"Have you eaten?" he asked finally.

She looked up to find him watching her. His eyes were so clear and blue, a person could get lost in them. "Yes, Eliza fixed me some breakfast a little while ago."

He nodded, and somehow she understood that he didn't really care if she had eaten or not. He was just trying to get her to talk to him. The knowledge came as a relief because with it came the certainty that at least he didn't despise her quite as much as she had feared. And if he wanted her to talk to him, she had something she needed to say. She drew a fortifying breath.

"Mr. Ross," she began. "I—"

"I think you can call me Adam now, Lori, don't you?" he asked with a small smile.

Instantly, Lori felt the color blossoming in her cheeks, but she refused to acknowledge her embarrassment. "Adam," she said deliberately, calling him by his name for the first time. "I don't know what to do."

For some reason he looked surprised. And oddly hopeful. "What do you mean?" he asked.

"I mean, I don't know what to do with myself," she repeated impatiently. "At home, when I got up in the morning, I cooked breakfast and cleaned the house and did the laundry and baked the bread and mended and worked in the garden and . . . But here, your slaves do all those things. I don't know what I'm supposed to do."

"Oh." He looked surprised. And disappointed. The hand that had been rubbing his leg came up and rubbed his chin.

"Well, now, let's see. It's been a long time since Elmhurst has had a mistress, but I remember my mother being very busy, so I imagine there's a lot of work to be done. Sudie has run the house since my mother died, so she's the one who would know." He smiled with satisfaction and dropped his hand back to his leg again. "Yes, Sudie would know. She'll teach you everything, and I imagine it will be a relief to her not to have that responsibility anymore."

Lori wasn't quite so sure. In fact, she was fairly certain Sudie *wouldn't* be relieved and that she would actually be unhappy to have somebody like Lori McClintock moving in and taking over her house. Just what she needed.

"And Sudie will see about making you some new clothes, too."

Sudie, Sudie, Sudie, Lori thought grimly as she absently watched Adam's left hand working his left thigh again. How could she tell him that Sudie intimidated her? Or that Sudie hated her and would never do anything to make her life here easier?

Adam's hands were so beautiful. His fingers were long and well-made, yet strong and masculine, too. The back of his hand was dusted with golden hair, and Lori found herself wondering if he had hair like that on the rest of him, too.

Startled by the direction of her thoughts, she cast about for something to say to distract herself. "Does your leg hurt?" she asked abruptly.

Instantly, he stopped rubbing his thigh and moved his hand to the arm of the chair, as if embarrassed to be caught. "No, not . . . not really."

"But you were rubbing it," she reminded him, looking at his face again and seeing the truth in his eyes.

"It . . . gets a little stiff sometimes. When I've been walking a lot." He sounded as if the words were being pulled from him, and Lori knew he hated admitting even this little weakness. A man like him would hate being weak. She knew it instinctively.

"You were walking in the fields?" she asked in surprise.

This time the color crawling up his neck was crimson. More weakness to confess. "I can't ride a horse. My leg isn't . . ." He had to take a breath to be able to say the words. "My leg isn't strong enough to mount one, and keeping it bent in the stirrup would be . . . painful for me."

Lori nodded, sharing his pain and remembering what had caused it. "He shot you, didn't he?"

"It was an accident," he said quickly. Too quickly, as if he was so used to making the excuse that he didn't even have to think about it. "He didn't mean it. Eric was only a boy, just twelve years old. He didn't know what he was doing."

His tone was urgent, demanding that she believe him. But she knew Eric now, perhaps better than he did, and she *didn't* believe him. And she had no trouble at all imagining his pain. "Won't it get any better? Your leg, I mean."

His hand was back on his thigh, as if he could conceal his injury from her. "The shot is still in there."

Lori gasped in horror and covered her mouth.

"I was lucky I didn't lose my leg," he explained. "The doctor wanted to cut it off, but my father wouldn't let him." He smiled, but his eyes were bleak. "My father was a stubborn man. That was one of the few times in my life I was grateful that he was."

Lori nodded. How awful for him to have lost his leg. Even a leg that hardly worked was better than none at all. And it was Eric's fault. Everything was Eric's fault. And now Eric's evil had harmed Adam again, this time tying him forever to a woman he could never love.

"I'm sorry," Lori whispered, lowering the hand that covered her mouth.

"It wasn't your fault," Adam reminded her brusquely, obviously still thinking about his leg.

"No, I mean . . . I'll try to be a good wife to you, Adam.

I don't know anything about running a house like this, but I can learn. And I will! I'll work real hard, I promise."

This time his smile was sad. "Will you?" he asked, and she got the feeling he didn't really care what her answer was.

"Sure I will!" she insisted and noticed that he was rubbing his leg again. "Is there something I can do for you? To make your leg better? Something I can get you or . . ." She gestured vaguely.

He didn't reply at once. He was looking at her, studying her, as if he was trying to see inside of her. His expression was so strange that she began to feel oddly warm, as if someone had suddenly lit a fire in the fireplace beside them. Finally, he said, "Sometimes Sudie rubs it for me."

Did he want her to go get Sudie? But that was the last thing *she* wanted. She didn't want the slave woman coming in here and looking at her like she was a bug that had crawled in when nobody was looking. And she didn't want Sudie taking over, coming between her and Adam.

She gazed into Adam's sky blue eyes, looking for the answer, and after a moment it came to her. "Do you want me to . . . to rub your leg for you?"

It wasn't much. It wasn't running his house or making his slaves respect her or having his neighbors accept her as his equal. But it was something. Something a wife would do for her husband.

An emotion she couldn't read flickered across his face, but it was gone before she could name it. She was very afraid it was disgust, but then he said, "Yes, I'd like that."

His voice sounded strange, kind of tight in his chest, and she wondered if he really was disgusted at the thought of her touching him. Maybe he was just being polite.

But he'd told her to do it.

The thought of being that close to him was a little frightening, but she reminded herself that he didn't want her *that* way. Hadn't he said so last night? He wasn't going to hurt her. Biting her lower lip uncertainly, she pushed herself out of her chair and took the few steps over to where he sat.

He looked up at her, and she saw his eyes were as strange as his voice had been. They seemed brighter somehow, as if an unnatural light shone from them.

She felt mesmerized. And very warm. As if the imaginary fire was burning higher. She lifted her skirt and sank to her knees in front of him. His hand still rested on his thigh, and seeing it up close was even more disturbing than seeing it from across the room. She could see every individual golden hair and the way the fingernails curved in perfect little ovals on the ends and how soft the skin looked, not rough and callused like her father's had been.

She glanced up and met his gaze and her breath caught in her throat because being so close to his face was the most disturbing thing of all. He was, she was certain, the most beautiful man alive. The curve of his jaw and the rise of his cheeks and the way his brows, bleached almost white by the sun, arched above the bluest eyes in the world. Forcing herself to breathe, she inhaled his masculine scent, a heady mixture of male musk and sunshine, and for a second she felt lightheaded, as if she might faint again.

"You'll have to show me what to do," she said, oddly breathless.

He looked at her for the longest moment of her life, and then he said, "Give me your hands."

She didn't want him to touch her hands. Her hands that weren't like his at all but rough and callused. But then she remembered the ring she wore on one of those hands, the ring he had put there, and she knew she could refuse him nothing.

She offered her hands, and he took them in his own. His grasp was firm, his palms warm and slightly moist, and for a moment he simply held her hands, as if that was what he'd really wanted all along.

But of course that was silly, and in another moment, he laid her hands down upon his thigh.

Lori had never touched a man's leg before. She'd never willingly touched much of anything of a man's before, and her first thought was how different he was. His muscles were hard where hers were soft. And his leg was so big and so strong, not weak like he'd claimed.

At her touch, he drew in a long, ragged breath through his teeth, and she looked up in alarm. "Am I hurting you?"

He shook his head sharply, but she knew he was lying. His color was high again and a sheen of perspiration had formed on his upper lip.

She would have pulled her hands away, but he was holding them too tightly. "Don't stop," he said hoarsely, and Lori wondered why he was insisting on this torture. "Like this," he added, moving her hands on his leg in a massaging motion.

"Are you sure?" she asked uncertainly, and he nodded very determinedly.

She began to move her hands the way he had shown her, and after a moment, he lifted his away. For a minute or two she concentrated only on her task, working the taut muscles beneath her hands, trying to get them to loosen, but they only seemed to grow more tense. She must be doing something wrong, she was sure of it, and then he said her name.

"Lori." It was only a breath of sound.

She looked up and what she saw in his eyes might have terrified her if she hadn't been so shocked. Desire was a blazing light in the second before he lowered his mouth to hers.

The kiss was gentle and fierce and passionate and sweet, all the things she had ever dreamed a kiss from Adam would be. For one glorious second.

And then Sudie said, "Massa Adam, your dinner ready."

Five

Adam jumped and Lori jerked away from him, nearly falling over in her haste to scramble to her feet. She seemed frightened as she quickly backed away, and Adam cursed silently until he noticed she was looking at Sudie and not at him. Could she be frightened of *Sudie?*

He glanced at the older woman standing just inside the parlor doorway, and he had to admit that, yes, Lori very well could be afraid of her. Sudie could be intimidating when she wanted to be, and apparently, she wanted to be right now. Fortunately, Adam wasn't intimidated. He was simply furious.

"Why didn't you just ring the bell?" he demanded, figuring he already knew the answer.

"I seen you was in here," she replied unrepentantly.

Yes, and she'd also seen he was with Lori. And probably that he was going to kiss her. Damn her. What did she think she could accomplish? They were already married, for God's sake!

Adam wanted to jump to his feet and confront her, but even if his leg had allowed him, he couldn't get up just yet, not until the bulge in his pants receded. He'd have to settle for getting rid of her and worry about the rest later. "Thank you, Sudie," he said through gritted teeth. "You may go now."

"Your dinner get cold, you don't come right away," Sudie warned.

"I'll take my chances," he replied and glared at her until

she finally, after another long moment of defiance, turned and left.

The instant she was gone, he heard Lori release her breath on a long sigh. Fortunately, his fury at Sudie had cured his other problem, so he pushed himself up out of the chair. "Now where were we?" he asked with what he hoped was a reassuring smile.

She looked up at him, her marvelous eyes wide with confusion. They looked almost black in her pale face, and he was struck once more with her beauty. Even that awful dress, the one she'd worn to church every Sunday for as long as he could remember, couldn't mar her perfection. Or conceal it, either.

He'd noticed immediately that she wasn't wearing a corset. In fact, he'd been so distracted by that knowledge, he'd hardly been able to follow the conversation at first. He'd hardly been able to think about anything else at all except her lush, ripe body, the way he'd seen it last night in that flimsy nightdress. The way he'd dreamed about it all night long in his lonely bed.

And then she'd started asking him about his leg. He'd wanted her close. He'd wanted to touch her and smell her. And, by God, he'd wanted to taste her, too. He still did.

He reached for her, but she wrapped her arms protectively around herself and stepped back.

"Your dinner's getting cold," she reminded him.

"The hell with my dinner, Lori. I'm a lot more interested in you at the moment." He instantly regretted his impatience when he saw the fear flicker in her eyes. Damn, this wasn't the way to win her heart. Or any other part of her. He schooled his expression to pleasantness. "I'm not angry at you," he assured her. "I'm angry at Sudie for interrupting us. We've been married almost twenty-four hours now, and I still haven't gotten a real kiss from you."

And he'd been so close this time. So sure she wasn't going to faint or get sick. Damn you, Sudie.

"I didn't think you'd want to," she said. "After last night, I mean."

This time his smile was genuine. And self-mocking. "I'll admit, I was a little discouraged, but that didn't make me stop wanting you, Lori."

Her astonishment was almost comic. "You do?"

"Of course I do. You're a beautiful and desirable woman. Any man would want you."

Alarm flickered in her eyes again, and Adam wanted to bite his tongue. Why in God's name had he reminded her of Eric?

"I want to be a good wife to you, Adam," she said, but the apology in her voice sent despair washing over him.

"But you can't," he guessed. "Because of Eric."

"Because of what he did to me," she confirmed. "I'm afraid . . ."

Of course she was. She'd probably been in love with Eric, damn him to hell. And he'd abandoned her and broken her heart. Leaving her to shame and misery. No wonder she didn't want to trust his brother either.

But she'd said she wanted to be a good wife to him. "Do you think, in time, that you could . . . ?" He wasn't sure exactly how to phrase what he wanted, but he didn't need to say it out loud.

"I'll try. I want to, Adam. I . . . I want to make you happy," she admitted shyly.

God, he could hardly restrain himself from hauling her into his arms. But that wouldn't do. No, that would *never* do. He'd have to be careful. And patient. But by God, if Eric had seduced her, then surely he could, too.

"Well, then, it would make me very happy if you would join me for dinner," he said with a smile.

"But I just ate breakfast," she admitted in dismay.

"You can still sit with me," he pointed out. "You don't have to eat if you're not hungry."

"All right," she agreed with a small smile of her own. She

seemed surprised when he offered her his arm, but after only a slight hesitation, she slipped her hand through it. She looked up in renewed surprise when he laid his other hand over hers, where it rested on his arm, but when he smiled, she smiled back.

How could just having her hand touching him through his clothes feel so sensual? And how could simply resting his hand on hers carry all the excitement of a jolt of lightning?

And how could a woman's smile fill him with such pleasure?

He didn't know and didn't feel compelled to solve the mystery, at least not now, while he was in the midst of enjoying it. She matched her step to his, and if she minded walking slowly—he wasn't about to emphasize his limp— she didn't let it show.

Oh, yes, he would win her. She was vulnerable, her pride lacerated by Eric's cruelty, her heart in tatters. But in a day or two, maybe three at the most, he would have salved her pride and mended her heart. And taken her to his bed. And he would have almost everything that fate had tried to deny him.

Lori couldn't believe it. Adam Ross was looking at her as if he really cared about her. And he wanted her. He'd said so, right out! Of course, the knowledge was as terrifying as it was exciting. But he'd understood how she felt, that she couldn't bring herself to lie with him, not yet, not until . . . Well, until something happened and she was able to forget what Eric had done to her.

How long would that take? It had already been almost three months, and she was still so afraid. But maybe with Adam to help her, maybe she could finally begin to feel normal again, like she was before. Back before anything bad had ever happened to her. Yes, she was sure that with Adam's help she would get through this. And maybe in a month or two, maybe by then she'd be able to let him into her bed.

They reached the dining room, and Adam allowed her to

precede him into the room. She hated letting go of his arm. She'd felt so safe and secure with his hand over hers. But she didn't have to worry, because even without his hand touching hers, she knew she was going to be all right.

Only one place had been laid, at the head of the table.

"Esther!" Adam called when he noticed. He drew Lori to the seat to his right and pulled out the chair for her.

The serving girl pushed open the door and scampered into the room. "Yes, sir, Massa Adam?"

"Lay a place for Miss Lori, will you?" he asked. Lori thought it was odd how he made the question sound like a request when it was really an order.

"Yes, sir, I will. Would've laid one before, but Sudie said—"

"That's all right. Do it now," he interrupted her firmly.

"Yes, sir!" Esther scampered away.

Lori could see that Adam was displeased. She didn't want him mad with poor Esther. "I just ate," she reminded him as he took his own seat. "They probably figured I wouldn't be hungry."

He smiled that smile she loved so much. "You'll have to be patient with Sudie," he said, making her realize he blamed Sudie for the oversight. "She's . . . well, she's been with us a long time. She came here with my parents from Georgia, and before that she grew up with my mother. She was my mother's maid, and she practically raised me, and then she was Eric's wet nurse . . ."

His voice trailed off when he realized he'd mentioned Eric to her, the very last person whose name she ever wanted to hear. But she would have to get used to it. She made herself smile. "That's all right," she assured him.

"Well, after my mother died, she was the only mother we ever knew," he continued when he was certain she had meant her reassurance. "She took my mother's place in . . . in almost every way," he said, and Lori didn't understand why his eyes clouded and he looked away for a moment. But only a moment. When he turned back to her, his smile was in place again. "That's why she takes liberties. Sometimes I think she still thinks of me as a little boy. And she's very protective. She doesn't like to see her boys hurt."

"Does she think I'm going to hurt you?" Lori asked in amazement.

But Adam didn't have a chance to answer, because Esther came rushing back in to set Lori's place.

"This is silly," she said for the girl's benefit. "I couldn't eat a bite!"

"Oh, I imagine she'll find room for Eliza's blueberry pie, won't she, Esther?"

Esther flashed him a grin. "Yes, sir, I reckon she will!" She bustled out and bustled in again almost immediately with two bowls of soup.

Lori realized that it smelled delicious, but she wasn't even tempted to lift the spoon. She enjoyed watching Adam eat, though. In fact, she realized, this was the perfect opportunity to study what he did so she would know herself for the future.

She propped her elbows on the table and rested her chin in her hands.

He glanced at her and grinned. He looked almost boyishly handsome. "Tell me about *your* mother," he said. "Or don't you remember her?"

He could not have asked her anything she would have been more pleased to discuss. "She was a lady," Lori confessed. "Her father owned a business in Philadelphia, and she grew up in a beautiful house."

His eyebrows lifted in surprise, and Lori figured that he didn't believe her.

"I know it's hard to believe, but it's true. I have some of her things. Her family disowned her when she married my father. He was a penniless orphan who worked for her father's business, but he was very handsome, or at least that's what he always told me. He was handsome enough to make my mother fall in love with him, anyway. And they ran away and eloped. He tried farming in Pennsylvania, but something happened. His farm failed, I think. When I was a baby, they came here."

"And settled on my land," Adam said, his lips quirked into a teasing smile.

"Next to your land," Lori corrected him indignantly.

"That's not what *my* father always claimed. He always cursed the McClintocks for stealing part of his land—not that he needed it, mind you," he added at Lori's frown. "And maybe the story isn't even true. Maybe my father just didn't like having somebody settle so close by."

"Somebody who wasn't like him," Lori guessed solemnly. "Somebody who wasn't rich."

"My father was a proud man," Adam conceded. "Too proud, sometimes."

"He always frightened me," Lori confessed. "He seemed so mean."

"He could be," Adam allowed with a troubled frown of his own. "But he was never mean to me," he added hastily. "I was his first born son. He spoiled me rotten."

Adam wasn't spoiled or rotten, not like . . . Suddenly, Lori understood about Eric. All that spoiling hadn't ruined Adam, but it must have destroyed everything good in Eric.

"I guess that's why Sudie had to be strict with you," Lori said. "To undo the damage."

"Did it work?" he asked, as if he really wanted to know.

"I think so," she offered, earning another grin.

Lori couldn't believe she was sitting here at the table with Adam Ross, in his house, chatting and teasing as if they were a courting couple. Of course, they'd gotten a little beyond the courting stage, being married and all, but considering the strange circumstances of their marriage, a little courting was probably in order. And Lori was definitely enjoying it.

As Adam ate the rest of his meal, they talked about their lives on the river, events they remembered and how different their perspectives had been of those events. And by the time

Esther served them their blueberry pie, Lori was more than happy to taste it.

"I thought we might have cake," Lori said as they ate the pie. "You know, from yesterday."

"I imagine the cake is gone by now. All our people would've wanted a slice."

Lori looked up in surprise. "Your slaves ate your wedding cake?"

"Yes." Adam looked puzzled. Plainly, he didn't understand her surprise.

But Lori did, and a hundred things her father had said through the years suddenly came back to her. About how slaves had it better in this world than poor whites. About how nobody was going to look after his children if anything happened to him and nobody was going to feed him and clothe him when he was too old to work for himself. But a slave never had to worry about his kids going hungry or what would happen to him if he got too old and crippled to work anymore. And while Lori and her family hadn't tasted cake in years, Adam's slaves probably had it all the time.

"Lori," he said, laying his hand over hers where it rested on the table. His touch sent a strange warmth surging over her, but before she could even begin to understand why, he said, "Do you begrudge them a little treat?"

"No," she said. It wasn't that.

"Then what is it?"

"I guess I just realized that the reason my father hated slaves so much was because he was jealous of them."

"Jealous? Why on earth would he be jealous of them?"

How could she explain what it had been like for them? To a man who had probably never been cold or hungry in his life? To a man who had never had to wonder what would become of his family if he could no longer work?

"A slave never has to worry," she tried.

"What do you mean?"

Lori frowned as she tried to think of a way to explain. "If

a slave gets sick, somebody takes care of him, because if he dies, his owner loses money. A slave never goes hungry, even if he's sick and can't work, and he always has a place to live. If he dies, his master doesn't turn his children out, and if he lives to be too old to work, his master feeds him for as long as he lives."

Adam smiled and shook his head. "How nice it would be if all that were true. I hope it's true here at Elmhurst, at least, but I know for a fact things are often very different elsewhere. Of course a master takes care of his slaves, but he doesn't necessarily take *good* care of them. Some begrudge the cost of feeding them and give them only enough food to keep them alive. And the slave quarters at some plantations are little more than hovels. Of course, the master wouldn't turn out a slave's children if he died, but he might sell them away from a parent while he was alive, so that he'd never see them again. And I'm sorry to disillusion you about the way elderly slaves are treated, but I've known of masters who put their own mammys out to starve when they got to old to be useful anymore."

"How awful!" Lori exclaimed, horrified.

"I didn't even tell you about the beatings and the . . . the other ways slaves can be abused." Once again, his eyes clouded, as if he had seen too much of such abuse. "At any rate, if your father really was jealous of slaves, all he had to do was remember that he was a free man. He could come and go when he liked and where he liked, he could marry whom he wished—as I gather he did—and take her a thousand miles away to live. Then he could be certain that no one would ever take her or their children away from him." Adam's smile was sad. "I wonder if your father ever realized that he died fighting to protect the very institution of slavery that he hated so much."

"No, he didn't!" Lori insisted. "That's not what the war was about!"

"Perhaps not at first," Adam allowed. "At first, it was for

Southern honor and State's Rights and other high flown ideals. But when Mr. Lincoln issued his Emancipation Proclamation, it became a war about slavery and nothing else."

"But I thought that Proclamation was worthless!" Lori said.

"At the moment it is, since it only actually frees slaves in the states that aren't part of the Union anymore. But if the South loses the war, I'm afraid the Union will take us back in, by force if necessary, and then all our slaves will be free. What will become of us—and of them—then, I have no idea."

Esther came in to clear their plates, and as she did, Lori thought about what Adam had said. How could he run this huge plantation without his slaves. And what would become of the slaves if they were free?

As Esther began to carry the plates away, Adam said, "Esther, would you tell Sudie I'd like to speak to her, please?"

All other thoughts vanished from Lori's head. "Why do you want to talk to her?" she asked uneasily when they were alone again.

"I thought you wanted to know what your duties were," he reminded her gently.

She did, of course, but not if finding out required a visit with Sudie.

Before she could say so, however, the door opened again, and Sudie came in. She wore that same pinched expression she'd been wearing ever since Lori appeared at the wedding yesterday.

"You wanted to see me, Massa?" she said. Her hands were folded tightly at her waist, and her back was ramrod stiff. Not for the first time, Lori thought that if it wasn't for the woman's clothes and the bandana tied around her head, Lori might have taken her for a white woman.

"Yes, Sudie," Adam was saying pleasantly. "Mrs. Ross is going to require some clothes."

Sudie's gaze flicked over to Lori, as if to verify the truth of Adam's claim before returning almost instantly to Adam—as if she couldn't bear to look at her. Lori could feel humiliation stinging in her cheeks.

"I'll see to it," Sudie said without a trace of enthusiasm.

"And of course, Mrs. Ross will be taking over as mistress of the plantation now."

Although Lori could tell Sudie was trying not to reveal any emotion at all, she could not stop the way her eyes widened with shock or the way her face visibly paled.

She seemed to be having a difficult time breathing, too, or at least she couldn't find quite enough breath to speak for a few seconds. Finally, she managed to say, "You want me to give her my keys?"

Lori easily recognized the anguish behind the simple words. And the humiliation. It was so similar to what she herself was feeling. Sudie had been the mistress here in all but name for over twenty years. Now the boy she'd raised was going to give her job to a worthless slip of a girl who'd never even lived in a house with a real floor before.

"I want," Adam said very deliberately and very kindly, "for you to teach her what she will need to know. I'm sure you realize that her background did not prepare her for running a place like Elmhurst."

Sudie did not reply, and she looked so stricken, Lori felt herself softening toward the woman, in spite of everything.

Adam folded his long-fingered hands on the table and leaned forward earnestly. "Sudie, I'm sure you realize that my wife will be expected to possess certain skills. She'll have to entertain my friends and manage the house and the servants and take care of the sick."

Now Lori could feel the blood draining from her own face. How on earth could Adam expect her to do all those things? She would have no idea even where to begin.

But no one was looking at Lori. Sudie was staring at Adam in complete incredulity, and Adam was staring back with perfect complacency.

"And you realize, of course," he went on, as if he hadn't noticed that Sudie looked as if she might faint, ". . . that if my wife *can't* perform the duties expected of her, then it will be an embarrassment to me—and to everyone at Elmhurst. I am depending on you, Sudie, to protect us all from such an embarrassment. I know you will not fail me."

Lori could hardly stand to look at Sudie's face. Her dark eyes were dry, and her lips were tightly closed, but inside, Lori knew she was screaming with pain. Adam had given her the most loathsome task she could imagine, and then he had made it a matter of personal honor that she accept it. Not only accept it, but do it well. To train the girl she despised to usurp her, in order to please the master she loved.

After what seemed an eternity, Sudie drew an uneven breath, and Lori realized the slave woman was trembling, although she was holding herself so stiffly that it was hardly noticeable. "I won't fail you, Massa Adam," she promised softly.

Only then was Lori aware that she'd been holding her own breath, and she let it out in a relieved sigh. Then she realized that she had nothing at all to be relieved about. Because this meant that she would have to learn everything there was to know about running Elmhurst. And she would have to learn it from a slave who hated her.

Apparently, Adam was convinced that he had left Lori in good hands when he returned to the fields after the noon meal. For her part, Lori would have gladly followed him around for the rest of the day. Working in the fields would have been a much more familiar activity to her than keeping a house like Elmhurst.

When Adam had left her standing on the back porch, she turned to find Sudie waiting in the doorway behind her.

"This wasn't my idea," Lori felt obliged to explain.

If Sudie heard her, she gave no sign of it. "I reckon we

best start in the kitchen." She reached into the pocket of her dress and pulled out a large ring with many keys dangling from it. She held it out to Lori.

Lori shook her head and clasped her hands tightly together, refusing the keys and all they implied.

But Sudie rattled them impatiently. "You's Massa Adam's wife now. You's the one should carry these."

She was right, Lori knew, although she would have rather picked up a poisonous snake than those keys. As she took them from Sudie's hand, they clanked. Lori thought they sounded like chains.

Sudie stepped back to allow Lori to enter the house and walk before her. Feeling more awkward than she ever had in her life, Lori led the way to the family dining room and outside to the kitchen.

" 'Afternoon, Miz Lori," Eliza said when Lori entered the kitchen. "You ain't lookin' for something to eat again so soon, is you?" Eliza teased, but her friendly grin vanished when she saw Sudie entering behind her new mistress.

Quickly, Eliza went back to her task. At the sink Esther and another girl were scrubbing the dishes from dinner, and when Sudie glanced at them, they dropped their gazes guiltily and got very busy, too.

"Every week, you meet with Eliza and plan out what meals you want served," Sudie said, making Eliza look up in surprise. "Eliza, she like to make fancy stuff, but Massa Adam, he like his food plain for every day. If they's a party or something, though, he wants to be real fancy."

Lori nodded, wondering how in the world she was going to plan meals. She'd been living on cornbread and beans for so long, she'd almost forgotten what a real meal was supposed to be, and she'd never in her life seen meals like they had at Elmhurst.

But Sudie was talking again, pointing things out to her, things she needed to know. Barrels of flour and cornmeal, bunches of spices hanging upside down from the ceiling to dry. And Lori had to listen. And try to remember.

When they were finished in the kitchen, Sudie directed her out into the yard and took her on a tour of each of several storage buildings. The keys to those buildings were on the ring, and while Sudie showed her what each key was for, Lori knew she'd never be able to keep them straight. One of the buildings was a spring house where perishables were kept cool, even on the hottest summer days. Fresh milk and butter, luxuries Lori hadn't known since they'd had to slaughter their cow for meat almost two years ago.

The smokehouse held huge hams and sides of beef, enough food to feed the entire Confederate Army, Lori thought, although she knew that probably wasn't true. In any case, the Confederate Army was a long way from here.

"Ain't like the old days," Sudie informed her. "This place be so full, can't hardly get anything else in. Now . . ." She shook her head in disgust. "The gov'ment done took almost half a what we slaughtered last fall. Give us nothin' but a handful of worthless script for it, too. What good that stuff gonna do? Won't nobody take it for money no more."

Lori knew exactly what she meant. It was like the Confederate money the state gave her and Bessie as a pension. The thought was generous, but if the paper money was worthless, how much help could it be to them?

There were other sheds and outbuildings, and Lori toured them all, unlocking and locking the doors with the keys Sudie pointed to. There was the henhouse and the hog pen. There was the barn and the stable. And, of course, there were the slave quarters, but Sudie didn't take her there.

"You feelin' all right?" Sudie asked sharply when they had finished in the last of the outbuildings.

"Yes, of course," Lori said, remembering her shameful display last night. "I'm fine. I just . . . last night . . . I . . ."

"Maybe you shouldn't be out in the sun," Sudie said, although her tone didn't sound the least bit concerned. "Lady in your condition needs to take care of herself."

Lori felt the color rising in her face. "What do you mean?" she asked, her mind reeling. It couldn't be! She couldn't know, not yet! No one knew but Adam and Bessie. Surely . . . But Adam had said Sudie was like a mother to him. Would he have told her why he was marrying Lori?

"You know what I mean," Sudie said coldly. "You're breeding."

Lori shook her head in silent denial, although what she was really denying was the truth of Adam's betrayal. "Adam didn't . . . ?"

"If you mean did he tell me, he didn't need to," Sudie informed her smugly. "Why else he marry somebody like you unless he have to?"

But he hadn't *had* to. He'd *wanted* to. But Lori couldn't say that to Sudie. "I think maybe I will go inside," she said instead and started walking toward the house.

But Sudie was right behind her.

"Maybe you think you's gonna have an easy life here," Sudie said so softly that nobody but Lori could have overheard. "Maybe you think you got slaves now to wait on you hand and foot."

Furious now, Lori stopped and turned on her, and Sudie almost collided with her.

"I don't think any such thing, and I don't mind working. I've been working all my life!"

But that wasn't really what Sudie was angry about. "You know the kind of man you got?" she demanded furiously. "You know how good and kind he is? How he took care of his brother and the rest of us here? An' you done tricked him into marryin' a girl who got no right to lick his boots!"

"I didn't trick him!" Lori cried.

"How else a man like him gonna end up with a girl like you? Even the best man in the world gonna take what's offered, and you offered it, didn't you?"

"No!"

" 'Course you did, and Massa Adam, he lonely, and he ain't no match for a girl what's set on trapping herself a rich husband. An' he wasn't thinkin' 'bout anything except what's under your skirt, not what might happen and not how he might end up puttin' a baby in your belly—"

"No, it wasn't like that!" Tears were streaming down Lori's face, but Sudie went on mercilessly.

"Another man would've paid you off, but not Adam Ross. Oh, no, Adam Ross too honorable, and you knowed that, didn't you? That's what you was countin' on, so's he'd marry you and make it all right, but I'm thinkin' you're worse than a sneaky little tramp, 'cause how does he even know it's his baby?"

"It's not!" Lori exclaimed before she could stop herself. Instantly, she clamped both hands over her mouth, but it was too late. The words were out, and Sudie had heard them. Her eyes got wide and spots of color bloomed in her pale cheeks.

"You lying little whore!" she shrieked in triumph, grabbing Lori by the arms and giving her a shake. "I knew it! I knew my Adam wouldn't let hisself get caught by the likes a you! I'll tell him! I'll tell him right now, and he'll throw you out so fast, right back on the dung heap you come from—"

"He already knows!" Lori sobbed. She felt as if her soul were being torn in two, and still Sudie continued to torment her.

"Liar! Why he marry you if he knows that ain't his baby?"

But Lori was sobbing too hard to answer her.

Sudie gave her another shake. "Who is it? Who's the father if it ain't my Adam?"

Through her tears, Lori could see her fury and her scorn. Sudie wouldn't believe her, she knew. If Bessie hadn't believed that Eric had forced her, then surely the woman who had nursed him wouldn't. "I don't know," she sobbed. "I didn't know him. He forced me. I couldn't stop him, and he . . . he held me down, and he . . ."

Lori couldn't say the words, but she didn't have to. Before her eyes, Sudie's anger evaporated into the kind of horror Lori thought no one else but she had ever known.

"Oh, Lord," Sudie wailed with the same anguish that twisted Lori's soul, and she pulled Lori into her arms.

Lori was so stunned that at first she didn't understand what was happening, but gradually, she began to comprehend that Sudie was comforting her. The other woman held her fiercely, protectively, and rocked her against her bosom as she crooned inarticulate words of comfort and patted her back and her shoulders and her hair with hands that had comforted a thousand hurts. What Lori still did not understand was *why,* but she was weeping too hard to even think about that at the moment. All she could do was savor the only solace anyone had offered her since that awful day when her world had come crashing down around her.

Sudie smelled of yeast and sunshine, a soothing combination that made Lori want to pour out the deepest, ugliest secrets of her heart and cleanse herself once and for all. But of course she couldn't do that, so she simply gave herself up to the release she *could* enjoy and blessed whatever gods had given it.

When Lori had cried herself out, she pulled away from Sudie self-consciously, wiping the tears from her face with the back of her hand, and she studied the woman who had been her mortal enemy until only a few moments ago. Sudie's eyes were wet, too, and she made no attempt to wipe them. Lori still had no idea why she had suddenly earned Sudie's sympathy.

When Sudie had determined that Lori was calm enough, she glanced around, as if suddenly noticing that they were standing here in full view of whoever might happen by. Aghast, Lori realized she had made a spectacle of herself.

"Come inside now," Sudie said in a voice Lori had never

heard before. The voice Adam must have heard whenever he'd needed comfort.

Too drained to even think of protesting, Lori let Sudie lead her back to the house. They passed one of the maids who couldn't help but notice Lori had been crying, but Sudie said, "Miz Lori feelin' some poorly. Reckon I kept her out in the sun too long," by way of explanation and continued on until they reached Lori's bedroom.

"Here, you lay yourself down right here," Sudie said, seating Lori on a long piece of upholstered furniture whose purpose Lori hadn't been able to guess until now. Once Sudie had lifted her feet, she realized it was some sort of couch for ladies to lie on when they weren't actually going to bed. Lori had rarely had occasion to lie down during the day and didn't know any women who did, but apparently this was another thing that was different at Elmhurst.

Lori was pleased simply for the opportunity to recline and close her eyes for a few minutes, but after a moment or two, Sudie placed a cool, wet cloth across her forehead.

"There now, you feel better soon. You want some tea or something?"

Although she would never have thought to ask for it, the prospect of tea was heavenly. "Yes, I . . . that would be nice."

Sudie left her alone while she went for the tea, and Lori thought she might have actually dozed for a second or two when she heard the bedroom door open again. She looked up to see Sudie returning with a tray which she set on the dressing table.

Sudie allowed her to sit up on the settee, then served her tea sweetened with wild honey in a fine china cup. Lori thought nothing had ever tasted so delicious.

Sudie had pulled up a small footstool and perched on it at Lori's feet. Lori looked down and was shocked by the kindness she saw in the older woman's face. Once again she could only wonder how she had managed to change the woman's attitude toward her so quickly and completely.

"I . . . thank you for the tea," Lori said uncertainly.

"I didn't know," Sudie said simply. "I didn't have no idea what happened to you. If I did . . . well, I shoulda knowed, shouldn't I? Massa Adam, he just the man to help a girl in trouble, ain't he? Never thinks ah hisself. I always did say he too good for this world."

Lori felt the traitorous tears stinging her eyes again, but she blinked them away as she nodded her agreement. Adam Ross was too good for *any* world.

"How is it for you now?" Sudie asked. "With Massa Adam, I mean? Last night when he come to you?"

This time Lori shook her head, and she could feel the color coming to her cheeks. "He didn't. He . . . he stayed in his own room last night."

Sudie's face lit with understanding. "I shoulda guessed that, too." She shook her own head as if in wonder at the saintliness of her master. "An' I reckon you mighty glad ah that."

"I didn't want to turn him away," Lori protested. The cup in her hands began to rattle dangerously.

"But you glad, just the same," Sudie guessed, taking the cup from her and setting it safely on the floor. "Can't stand the idea of another man touching you."

Lori winced and dropped her gaze, ashamed to have Sudie know how ashamed she was.

"Ain't your fault," Sudie said, surprising Lori with her vehemence. "You can't help you was forced, and you can't help how you feel now."

Lori looked at her in amazement. How could she possibly understand? "It was *all* my fault! If I hadn't been there that day, if I'd been more careful, then . . ."

"Then what? Then he would've got you another day? Or he would've got some other woman. Just 'cause you was there don't mean he had the right to take you, so you can stop thinkin' that right now. Wasn't your fault at all, and wasn't nothin' you coulda done to stop him. Maybe you tried, but it didn't do no good, did it? Just made him hurt you worse."

The tears were sliding down Lori's cheeks now, but she made no move to wipe them away. "How can you know?"

Sudie's expression tightened and her dark eyes grew bleak. "I know 'cause I been there, too."

"You?" Lori asked incredulously. She simply could not imagine this formidable woman at anyone's mercy.

"You think 'cause I's colored, I don't care if a man uses me or not?" she challenged defensively.

"Oh, no, it's not that!" Lori insisted, although she had heard all her life that colored women were different, that they didn't hold to the same moral standards that white women did. "I just . . . you seem so . . . so strong. As if nobody could ever hurt you!"

Sudie shook her head. "A lot you don't know, Missy, but you's learnin', just like I learned. I's strong now, but not then. Then I was like you, all crushed and broken inside and feeling like I wanted to die."

Lori gaped at her, unable to believe she could have known this, too.

"Thing you gotta remember is you can heal. Maybe you never forget what happened, but one day it gets so it ain't so important anymore. That's when you know you'll survive, and that's when you can start workin' on bein' happy again."

Lori had an irrational urge to laugh in scorn. *Happy?* How could she ever be happy? "It'll always be important to me, Sudie," she said bitterly. "Did you forget? I'm carrying around a reminder that'll last for the rest of my life."

Sudie nodded sagely. "You figure you'll hate that baby, don't you?"

"I already do! And what about Adam? How will he feel about it? He'll always know it isn't his."

"No!" Sudie cried, startling Lori again. "My Adam, he never mistreat no young'un, not after what his papa did to his brother!"

"What do you mean?" Lori asked in confusion.

"I mean, Massa Chet, he blame my sweet boy Eric for killin' his mama. Never forgive him, not as long as he live. He hated that chile, and the boy knew it 'fore he even old enough to talk, poor thing. He never hear a kind word his whole life, and Massa Chet, he beat that boy so many times— mostly for no reason at all! If it weren't for Massa Adam, I reckon he mighta killed the boy sooner or later. My Adam, he seen what that do to Eric, how it made him so angry inside. He never be cruel to a chile. You'll see."

But Lori didn't want to see. She didn't want this child at all. She covered her face with both hands as despair washed over her.

"What you thinkin'?" Sudie demanded.

Lori shook her head in silent denial, but Sudie didn't need her words.

"You thinkin' no matter how Massa Adam feel, you'll hate this baby. Well, let me tell you somethin', Missy. That chile can't help who his pappy is. He been done wrong, same as you, and maybe more, 'cause he didn't even get no chance to fight. But you remember something: he's half your'n, too! An' by the time you carry him inside you for nine months, you gonna love him no matter how you got him!"

Just what Bessie had claimed, but Lori knew better. She lowered her hands and glared at Sudie in outrage. "How do you know *what* I'll feel?"

Sudie's dark eyes grew soft with remembered pain. " 'Cause I been where you're at, too."

"You had a baby?" Lori couldn't believe it. Surely, she was making this up! "From the man who forced you?"

But Sudie nodded, and the agony in her eyes convinced Lori as no words could have done. Lori uttered a cry of protest, but Sudie only smiled the most poignant smile Lori had ever seen.

"I loved that chile, more'n I ever loved anyone in this

world," Sudie assured her. " 'Cause he was mine, the only thing I ever owned my whole life."

Lori knew this wasn't true. She remembered what Adam had said about masters who sold their slaves' children away from them, but she wasn't going to argue with Sudie, not now. If she wanted to believe the child had been hers, Lori would let her. "But do you still . . . ? I mean, when you look at him, don't you remember? Don't you . . . ?"

But Sudie was shaking her head. "He gone now, Missy. I don't got him no more. But you gonna keep your chile, and you gonna raise him up to be a fine person, not like that devil who got him on you. Massa Adam, he see to it, and you see to it, too."

Lori had no idea how she could see to anything. "I can't," she protested.

"You can do whatever you set your mind to," Sudie insisted fiercely, taking Lori's trembling hands in hers. "You can't change what already happened to you, but you can make the rest of your life whatever you want it to be."

If only that were true! "How?" Lori asked in despair. "I can't even be a wife to Adam!"

Sudie nodded again, and Lori was beginning to believe she really did understand. "You're afraid."

"Of course I am! Every time I think about it, I . . ." She choked on a sob and had to cover her mouth to hold it inside.

"That'll pass, too," Sudie said. "It takes time, but it'll happen. You'll see. If you want it to, that is."

"Oh, I do! I want to be a good wife to Adam."

"So you can pay him back for what he done for you," Sudie guessed.

"No, because—" But Lori caught herself before she could make any more humiliating confessions. She might never have had a servant before, but she was certain she'd already been much too free with Sudie. "Yes," she corrected herself, straightening her shoulders determinedly. "He deserves a little happiness."

"You want him to be happy?"

"Of course!"

"So he won't be sorry he married you."

Lori was pretty sure he already was, but she said, "Yes."

"Well, then, it'll come in time. Massa Adam, he a good man. He be patient, at least for a while."

Lori winced again. How long was "a while" and what would happen if *she* wasn't ready when it was over? But she *would* be ready. She would have to be. And then she would be a real wife to Adam.

If God gave her the courage.

Six

Be careful what you wish for. Eric Ross could just hear Ol' Sudie's voice issuing that warning as his horse faltered once again in the thick mud of the road. Rain poured down, sluicing over his hat brim to splash down his back. It had been like this for almost ten days now. Eric couldn't even remember what being dry felt like. What he wouldn't give for one of those awful days from last month, choking on dust and rationing water.

Most of the men, he saw, were walking, leading their horses, but Eric wasn't about to go slogging through that mud on foot. His boots were already soaked through. If he put them in that mud, they'd be ruined for good.

When his horse lurched again, he put the spurs to him, jamming them into the animal's sides so he wouldn't get the idea he could quit just because the going was tough. Stupid son of a bitch! He should've taken the bay. The hell with Adam's advice. The bay wouldn't've broken down after only a month on the road.

Adam thought he knew everything. Smart ass son of a bitch, with all that talk about upholding Southern honor and wishing he could fight with Eric. Like hell he did. This was man's work, and Adam wouldn't last a day, even with two good legs.

Eric grinned at the thought of his prissy brother charging through the brush with a gun, chasing down Yankees. Not much honor in that, but Eric had found it a lot more fun than he'd expected. Leading his boys, screaming like banshees as they exploded out of the bush and scared the Yankees shitless.

So far they'd taken two towns like that, two little pissholes he couldn't even remember the names of, something Mexican, but who even cared? The important thing was the Yankees had run off like their tails were on fire. It was true, what he'd always heard, that one good Southerner was worth ten Yankees, and Rip Ford and his men had proven it already.

Soon they'd be at Rio Grande City, and they'd prove it once again.

Up ahead the bedraggled column of soldiers ground to a halt, but not the weary halt of men who had reached the last of their reserves in a losing battle with a relentless nature. Instead, a buzz of excitement went through the unit as a message was passed as quickly as men's voices could carry it. Far up ahead, a cheer rose from the ranks, and Eric stood up in his stirrups to hear what the men in front of him were shouting over the roar of the rain.

"The Yankees are gone!" one of them called.

"Too afraid to fight!"

"Cleared out soon's they heard we was coming!"

Damn! The Yankees had deserted Rio Grande City without a fight! No chance for glory today. No running and screaming and shooting. No dead men in the streets to plunder. Eric swore again.

"How 'bout that, Lieutenant!" one of his boys demanded happily as he rode his pathetic mule over to where Eric sat his blood gelding. It was Billy, the stupid one. "They was so scared, they turned tail and run 'fore we even got close!"

"Yeah," Eric agreed, "reminds me of Second Bull Run when we sent the Yankees scrambling back to Washington."

"I ain't even killed me a Yankee yet," one of the other boys complained. "I never will, neither, if they won't stand still and wait for us!"

The rest of the boys laughed heartily, but Eric could only

manage a small grin. He wanted to fight. He wanted to scream and yell and shoot somebody. And he wanted this goddamned rain to stop.

As the boys chattered around him, their spirits high over a victory so easily won, the order came down the line that they would proceed to the town where they would try to find some dry sleeping quarters. At this news, another cheer rose from the ranks, but not from Eric. He stabbed his spurs into his reluctant horse again and urged it forward in the oozing mud.

Later that night, after Eric and some of his boys had found shelter in a livery stable and managed to dry out some, Eric felt the restlessness return. He'd been trying to drown it with a bottle of whiskey he'd "liberated" for the Confederate cause, but the liquor only seemed to make it worse.

The boys had been taking turns with the bottle, too, and now they were laughing and silly. All except that bastard Alex. He was just sitting in a corner looking sour, like he always did. Hell, the next battle, maybe Eric'd just put a bullet in him himself. If there *was* a next battle. Some of the men were saying the Yankees were gone for good, on their way to Brownsville and their ships. Eric wasn't ready for the fighting to be over, not by a longshot.

Instinctively, he rubbed his crotch, thinking that what he needed right now was a woman. That's what always calmed him down when he got like this. A quick trip to the quarters and a roll in the hay with one of the girls down there. And if he could catch one unawares, when she didn't know he was there, and she was scared and . . .

The blood was pounding in his head and in his groin at the memory. Someone passed him the bottle, and he took a long swig, but the fire of the liquor only fed the flame that burned inside of him.

"You boys interested in a little fun?" he asked.

They perked up immediately, giggling and squirming like

pups around a teat. All except Alex, damn him. Well, he could go to hell. The rest would go with Eric.

"What you got in mind?" one of the others asked.

"Come with me and find out."

A few of them frowned. "I'm sick of the rain," one said.

"It ain't rainin' now," another pointed out.

"Gonna start again, soon," the first one predicted. He was a farmer's boy. Always knew what the weather was going to be, damn him.

"Then stay here," Eric advised. "The rest of us, we're gonna find us some company."

"Company?" the dark one, the one Eric was now sure was a nigger, asked.

"Some *female* company," Eric clarified.

"They got whores in this town?" Billy asked eagerly.

"All women are whores," Eric informed him sagely. "We'll find one, and I'll show you."

Their eyes were wide and trusting, and when Eric got up, the rest of them did, too. All but Alex who sat in his corner and glared. He wouldn't, Eric decided at that moment, live out the week.

"Come on, boys," Eric said. "I'll show you what real men do for a good time."

Adam was pretending to read, but his gaze kept wandering over to where Lori sat opposite him. They were in the back parlor, enjoying the last hours of the day together. She was knitting what appeared to be a sock while he read—or tried to.

She was, he thought for what must have been the thousandth time, the most beautiful woman he had ever seen. He'd always thought her pretty, of course, but he'd never had the leisure to study her before. To linger over her perfections. To savor every feminine curve and line of her luscious body.

To admire every wayward, raven curl and the delightful play of emotion across her face.

If he didn't possess her soon, he was going to go out of his mind.

He'd thought the first few days were the worst. Knowing she was his wife and that she was sleeping just a few feet away. But at least then he'd had the hope that his patience would soon be rewarded. But the days had become weeks, and nothing had changed between them.

Oh, Lori was as sweet as she could be to him and had managed to win the respect—and even the affection—of his servants. She was also running the house on her own now, with just the slightest help from Sudie. She was everything he could hope for in a wife—except for one important thing.

So much for his confidence that he could seduce her as easily as Eric had.

As if she felt his gaze on her, she looked up and smiled. "This rain must be driving you crazy," she guessed. They could both hear it drumming on the roof as it had been for ten days now.

He only wished it was just the rain. "It *is* frustrating not to be able to get out in the fields."

"It's good, though, isn't it? After the drought?"

"Too much of anything isn't good." Or too little.

Her luscious lips drooped into a frown, and she looked down at the knitting that she had stopped momentarily. When she glanced up again, her blueberry eyes were clouded.

"What will happen after the war?"

This was something Adam had not allowed himself to consider. "I expect we'll have peace," he said with a flippant smile.

"I mean what will happen to us. To this place. You said the slaves would be free, and if they are . . ."

"If they are, how can a cripple run a place like this single-handedly?" he finished for her, no longer feeling quite so flippant.

He saw the color come to her cheeks and longed to take those satiny cheeks between his hands. But of course he didn't. If he made one move toward her she would flinch the way she always did when he tried to touch her.

"No, I didn't mean that!" she insisted. "No man could run a place like this alone. You know how small my father's farm is, and he could hardly manage that by himself. For this place, you need fieldhands, lots of them."

She was right, of course, although he didn't like to think about it. Things had been so simple in the old days. He might not have wanted to own slaves, but he'd had no choice. That was the way things were and would always be. Until now.

"Don't worry," he advised her, assuming his role as her protector, a role to which he had been bred. "I expect the slaves won't be any more eager to leave here than I would be to lose them. Where would they go, after all?"

She nodded as if she didn't quite believe him, or perhaps she was simply afraid to. Her life had probably taught her not to place too much faith in the future and to expect the worst because that's what usually happened. Adam was beginning to adopt the same philosophy.

He decided to change the subject to something more pleasant. "Sudie tells me you planned all the meals this week."

Her smile was embarrassed but no less breathtaking for all of that. "She had to help me an awful lot."

"It's a lot to learn, I'm sure. But Sudie *is* being patient with you, isn't she?"

"Oh, yes," Lori assured him. "She's been wonderful."

Why did her voice always remind him of honey? Thick and so, so sweet. "I was worried at first, afraid she wouldn't be able to adjust to the idea that I had taken a wife." There, a little reminder couldn't hurt. She was his *wife,* damnit!

"It was hard for her at first," Lori admitted, and then she frowned again. Damn, he didn't want her to frown. "Adam, what happened to her baby?"

What the . . . ? It took him a minute to figure out what she was talking about. "Sudie?" he asked to clarify.

"Yes, she told me . . . she said she had a baby once, but she doesn't have any children now, does she? What happened?"

Oh, great, the family tragedy. Just what he wanted to explain to her in the moments before they would retire to their beds. Just the thing to get her thinking about sharing one of those beds with him. *Damn.*

"The baby died," he told her resignedly. "The night it was born. The same night Eric was born." Oh, perfect, remind her of his brother, too.

"The same night?" she asked in surprise.

"Yes, there was a terrible ice storm that night. Everyone was out trying to save our livestock, and Sudie and my mother were here alone with me. They helped each other, I guess. At any rate, Sudie's baby died, and a few days later my mother died, too."

"So that's why," she said with a troubled frown. Adam had no idea what she was talking about, but he wasn't going to question her. He didn't want to continue this conversation a moment longer.

But Lori did.

"Do you know who the father was?" She looked embarrassed again, as well she should be to ask him such a question. "The father of Sudie's baby, I mean?" she prodded when he didn't reply.

Adam knew perfectly well, but he said, "No, I don't. One of the slaves, I expect."

"Oscar?" she pressed.

If only life were so simple. "We didn't have Oscar then. He's only been with us about ten years now. And he and Sudie have only been . . . uh . . . married about a year."

Of course they weren't really married. They'd jumped over the broom or something after his father had died. Chet hadn't allowed his slaves to enjoy any form of marriage, especially not Sudie, but Adam saw no harm in it, and of course Eric didn't care.

Lori looked shocked, although Adam couldn't imagine what he might have said to shock her. "A *year?*" she was saying. "So long?"

"A year isn't a very long time," Adam said with forced cheerfulness. But it could be a very long time, indeed, if things didn't improve around here soon.

"No, I mean, it was over twenty years from when . . . when her baby was born until she married."

Adam wasn't sure why that fact should disturb Lori so much, but he had no intention of letting it continue to disturb her.

"I'm afraid we imposed on Sudie for a long time. She had to run this house practically single-handedly. You know how much work that is, and she didn't have anyone to help her the way you do. She just didn't have time to think of herself." That wasn't quite the truth, but close enough. "I intend to make sure the same thing doesn't happen to you, though. I want you to have time to think of yourself. And of me," he added meaningfully.

She must have gotten the meaning because the color came to her face again. She gazed at him with such sweet innocence, it was all he could do not to jump up out of his chair and haul her into his arms.

But such movements never came as easily to him in reality as they did in his imagination, so he settled for saying, "It's getting late. Perhaps we should retire."

"Oh, yes," she murmured, flustered, and started putting her knitting back into the basket that had been his mother's.

While she wasn't looking at him and wouldn't see his awkwardness, he rose from his chair. He waited until she rose, too. Seeing her move was bliss, even though she usually wore a corset now. Her breasts seemed larger than they had before, but perhaps that was only his imagination. Or the way her new dresses fit her, the dresses Sudie had had made for her out of the cloth she'd been hoarding through the long years of the war. He liked this one in particular. Red was definitely her color, even if it was only calico.

He picked up the candle that had been sitting by his chair, and waited while Lori blew out her own. Then he followed her to the door. Out in the hall, the house seemed darker. And quieter. And he and Lori more alone than they had been in the parlor.

She walked slowly, out of deference to his disability, and he imagined that he could smell the scent of roses in her hair. This late in the day, her curls had begun to come loose from the bun into which she pinned them every morning. A few of them trailed along the back of her neck, and Adam had to lock his hand into a fist to keep from reaching up to touch her just there, where the wispy curls lay against her delicate skin.

She glanced up at him and smiled, a fleeting thing that was gone almost as quickly as it had come, a tiny instant that he would treasure. She didn't smile nearly enough. God, he wanted her to smile all the time, to smile for *him*, because he made her so happy. If only she would give him the chance!

The hallway seemed endless, the darkness impenetrable, but at last they reached the door to her room. She opened it, giving him another of those fleeting, heartstoppingly uncertain smiles over her shoulder. He stepped inside the door and held out the candle to light the one that sat on a small table beside the door.

"Thank you," she said. She was smiling again, her face fixed in a pose of calmness, but her hands betrayed her. They were twisting nervously in front of her, as if she knew what was in his mind.

He drew a deep breath and set the candle he was holding down beside the one he had just lit.

"Lori?" he said.

"Yes?"

"I don't believe you kissed me today." He tried to kiss her

every day, at least once. Hoping it would lead to more. So far, it hadn't.

Her eyes widened and her hands stilled, locked tightly together at her waist. "Oh."

He managed not to sigh in dismay. "Would you?" he asked instead.

"Oh, sure," she said, going up on her tiptoes and lifting her face. She was always compliant. But never eager.

Carefully, he lifted his hands and laid them on the points of her shoulders. She felt so soft, so warm, so female.

He lowered his head until he caught her scent, sweet and musky and alluring. Then lower still, until his mouth touched hers. Her lips yielded beneath his, delicate as rose petals, sweeter than the honey of her voice.

Desire roared in him, hot and huge and undeniable, like a beast he could not control. In the next second his arms were around her and her body was against his, her softness crushed against him, enveloping him, and still it wasn't enough, not nearly enough. He forced her lips apart, plunging his tongue into the tender recesses of her mouth, devouring her like a starving man.

He wanted her naked and panting and begging him to take her, but no sooner had he formed the wild vision in his mind than he realized she was struggling, fighting, trying to wrench free.

Instantly, he released her, and she staggered backwards, almost falling as she wrapped her arms around herself and stared at him in absolute terror.

Dear God, what had he ever done to make her *afraid* of him? Disgust he could understand, or indifference, but *fear?*

"Lori?" he asked, still desperate, still needing her more than the air he breathed. He reached out to lure her back to him, but she cringed away.

"I can't!" she cried, her eyes bright with unshed tears. "I'm sorry, but I can't!"

Of course. He'd already known that, hadn't he? She

couldn't bring herself to endure his touch. The pain tore through him like a dull knife ripping open his soul, but he pulled himself up to his full height and managed to salvage what little remained of his pride.

"I'm sorry, too. I didn't mean to . . . to force myself on you."

She flinched again, although he had no idea why. Then, mustering every ounce of his inner strength, he picked up the candle, turned and walked out.

As he made his way down the hall the short distance to his own room, he waited for the sound of her bedroom door slamming shut. He walked slowly, acutely aware that she might well be watching, so he was careful not to limp. When he reached his own door, he turned to see her still standing where he'd left her, hugging herself as if the only true comfort she could find was in her own arms.

I'm sorry, she had said. Perhaps she really was, but not as sorry as he. It was divine judgment on him. What else could explain how perfect this punishment was as retribution for his sins?

Forcing himself to turn away lest he be tempted to go back and take her whether she was willing or not, he opened his door, walked inside and closed it behind him. The click of the latch carried the finality of doom.

Alone in his room, Adam did not seek sleep. Did not even want it. Fatigue was not what had inspired him to come to bed so early. In fact, he wasn't tired at all, and he was certainly much too restless to even lie down.

He stripped off his shirt and washed, but then he began to pace. The walking stirred the pain in his leg, but he welcomed it. A bitter reminder of who and what he was. A man who could never hope for a woman's love and apparently who couldn't even inspire her pity. He walked until his muscles grew too weary, and then he sat in the easy chair and propped his throbbing leg up onto a footstool.

Leaning his head back, he closed his eyes and tried to

think of something, anything, except the girl lying in the next room. Of how she would look—of how he *knew* she would look—in that flimsy nightdress with her ebony hair spilling down her shoulders and a smile of welcome on her beautiful face.

Suddenly, he started awake, not even aware that he had fallen asleep. He had no idea what had roused him. Probably a dream he could not now remember. What time was it? And why wasn't he in bed? His leg would cause him the pangs of hell tomorrow if he didn't give it some rest and—

Then he heard it, a woman's scream.

He lunged to his feet, oblivious to the pain knifing through his thigh. The candle still sat where he'd left it earlier, burned down almost to a nub now. He snatched it up and ran. He didn't even ask himself who had screamed. He simply knew it was Lori.

He ran to her door and realized vaguely that no light shown from beneath it. She would have gone to bed by now and been fast asleep. Could it really have been her scream he heard?

But while he hesitated, he heard her moaning, and he threw the door open.

He wasn't sure what he expected to find, but a quick survey of the room showed that she was alone. Alone and thrashing in the big bed as if she were fighting the demons of hell. He practically threw the stubby candle onto the table, almost knocking it from its holder, and ran for the bed.

"Lori, wake up!" he cried as he pulled the blankets down to free her from their tangle.

Even in the feeble light, he could see her face was twisted with terror, the same terror he had seen earlier only multiplied a thousand times.

"No!" she cried, still fighting, and he saw she was crying in her sleep.

"Wake up!" he commanded, shaking her. "It's just a dream!"

But she was too far away to hear him, deep in some nightmarish hell. He sat down on the bed beside her and grabbed her shoulders, pulling her upright.

"Lori, listen to me!" he practically shouted into her face, and her eyes flew open.

At first they were unfocused, still seeing the dream devils that had tormented her, but then she saw him, and she screamed again.

Startled, he released her at once, and she looked around wildly. "Where is he?" she cried. "Make him go away! Get him out of here!"

"Who?" he demanded. "Who was here?"

"Eric! Make him go away! Don't let him hurt me again!" She was sobbing now, great wracking sobs that seemed torn from her soul.

She was so terrified, that Adam found himself looking around too, almost expecting to find his brother standing nearby, grinning at his consternation. But, of course, no one was there.

"He's not here," Adam assured her. "Lori, Lori, it was just a dream!"

She looked at him then, really seeing him for the first time. "Adam?" she asked in disbelief and drew away from him in renewed terror.

"I heard you scream," he explained hastily, defensively. Dear God, did she think he'd slipped into her room to attack her while she slept? "I came running in here, and you were having a terrible nightmare."

She stared at him, still terrified and not really certain whether to believe him or not.

"What were you dreaming?" he prodded, hoping to get her to realize it hadn't involved him at all.

She glanced around again, taking a quick survey of the room as if to verify that no one else was there. "He was here!" she insisted. "It was just like before! He was holding me down and I couldn't breathe and I tried to scream but nobody heard me!" She turned accusing eyes on him again.

"I heard you," he reminded her, wondering what on earth she meant. Had she had this dream before? "I heard you and I came."

She lifted her hands to cover her mouth as she looked around again, less urgently this time. Her breath was slowing, and he tried not to notice how her breasts rose and fell beneath the thin nightdress. Breasts that were bare except for that shear covering. He swallowed.

"This isn't the first time you've had this dream, then?" he asked.

She shook her head. "I used to have it every night after . . . after it happened." As if aware of his thoughts, she picked up a pillow and hugged it to her breasts.

"After what happened?"

Her eyes widened in astonishment. "You know! After your brother . . . after he forced me!"

Adam blinked in surprise, but she didn't seem to notice.

"I was so scared then, all the time, day and night. I thought he'd come back. I thought he was going to kill me! I couldn't eat and I couldn't sleep, not for days! And when I did sleep, I'd have these terrible dreams, always the same one, over and over. And sometimes I'd have it when I wasn't even asleep. I'd be sweeping the floor or hoeing the garden, and all of a sudden I was back there and it was happening and I couldn't make it stop!"

She lowered her head and began to sob into the pillow while Adam simply stared in disbelief. It couldn't be true, and yet he'd never in his life seen anyone more frightened.

Was it possible? Could Eric really have done this to her?

No sooner did he ask himself the question then he knew the answer. Of course, he could have. Since when had Eric ever hesitated to hurt someone, especially someone as defenseless as Lori McClintock?

Adam could picture exactly how it had been. He'd wooed

her and courted her, maybe even promising marriage, and when she'd been ready to succumb to his charms, expecting a gentle initiation into the rites of love, Eric would have savaged her. How many times had he done the same thing to one of their slave girls? How many times had his overseer complained to Adam about Eric's behavior? And how many times had no one even cared? If anything, that was the one way in which Eric resembled his father, except for the darkness of his hair and eyes. Like father, like son.

But Eric had never harmed a white girl, at least not to Adam's knowledge. Surely, he would have been too afraid of retribution by her family. Except Lori had no family to speak of, certainly no father or brother to defend her honor. No one of whom Eric would have been afraid.

And how his brother would have enjoyed tricking her. Making her believe he really cared for her when all the time he'd been planning to abandon her the instant he had his way. She had been wronged far more than Adam had imagined.

The sound of her weeping tore at his heart, and he wondered how many other nights she had lain here alone, sobbing out her misery.

"It's all right, Lori," he said, surrendering to the almost overwhelming urge to touch her. Although he wanted to do far more, he settled for simply laying his hand on her head and stroking the softness of her raven curls. "No one is ever going to hurt you again."

Lori looked up in surprise, so surprised that a sob actually caught in her throat. Suddenly, she was uncomfortably aware that he was sitting on her bed, clad only in his trousers. His chest was bare and quite broad and liberally covered with the same golden hair that was on his head. He looked so big and so strong and so blatantly masculine—and she was so small and weak and helpless—that she should have been terrified anew. Except he wasn't doing anything to terrify her. In fact, he was promising to protect her. Or at least she thought he was.

"What if he comes back?" she asked unsteadily.

"Who?"

"You know, your . . . your brother."

"He won't. And even if he does, you don't ever have to be afraid again. You're my wife now."

But she wasn't, not really. She drew a deep breath and hugged the pillow more tightly to her breast. "I want to be, Adam, but I'm still afraid."

"Of me?" he asked with a frown.

"No, not you, not . . . exactly. I'm afraid because of what happened to me. I'm afraid of every man."

"It's not just me, then? It's not because of . . . of this?" he added, rubbing his thigh where the old wound still troubled him.

"Oh, no!" she cried, appalled at the very thought. "I never even think about it unless you're rubbing it and I'm wondering if it hurts you."

"Then I don't disgust you?"

"No! How could you even think that?"

But apparently he had no trouble at all thinking that. Bessie had been more than right when she'd said he was ashamed about his leg.

"Are you sure?" he asked.

She wanted to tell him she was more than sure because she loved him too much for anything like that to ever matter. But of course she didn't. "Yes, I'm sure. It's nothing to do with you at all."

He nodded solemnly, as if he didn't quite believe her but was going to pretend he did just the same. "It's because you're afraid, because of what Eric did. Not because you're still in love with him?"

Lori gaped at him. "No! I was never in love with him!" *Because I was in love with you!* she wanted to add, but she bit back the words, still unable to say them.

When she saw the strange expression on his face, she

thought perhaps she should have, and then the moment was lost.

"Lori, I want to share your bed. I want to make love to you. Not tonight," he added when she gasped in renewed alarm. "But soon, as soon as possible. So you must tell me what I have to do to help you get over your fears."

"I don't know! I wish I did," she protested.

"Then let's think about it. You're afraid of being forced, aren't you?" She nodded reluctantly. "Well, then, if I promise not to force you, if I promise not to do anything at all that you don't want me to do, would that help?"

"Yes!" she replied eagerly.

"That won't be enough, though, because that will just keep things between us from getting worse, but it won't improve them, will it?"

No, it wouldn't, because she'd never get over her fears if she couldn't learn to tolerate and eventually welcome a man's touch again. "Maybe if . . ." She hesitated at the boldness of her suggestion. Surely, he would never be willing to agree.

"What?" he insisted.

She drew another deep breath and took a tighter grip on the pillow. "Maybe if I tell you what to do. When to kiss me and how and when to put your arms around me and . . . So it wouldn't be a surprise. So I'd be ready."

To her surprise, he didn't get angry. Instead he looked intrigued, almost amused. "And would you? Tell me when to kiss you, I mean? You wouldn't be too shy? Or too embarrassed?"

She would probably be mortified, but at least she wouldn't be afraid. She was so very, very tired of being afraid. She lifted her chin determinedly. "I want to be a good wife to you, Adam."

He smiled for real at that, and suddenly, she was very aware of how close he was and that they were sitting on the very bed in which he had intended to claim his rights over her on their wedding night. She imagined she could feel the heat of his body, or at least she had begun to feel quite a bit warmer, for no apparent reason.

"All right," he said. "What would you like me to do right now?"

Her first instinct was to tell him to leave, but almost as quickly as the thought formed, she realized she didn't really want that, at least not yet. She'd been so frightened earlier when she'd been dreaming that Eric was back and taking her all over again. And no one had ever comforted her in the night when she'd awakened sweating and trembling and panting in terror. No one had comforted her at all except Sudie that first day in the yard. How she longed for someone to hold her and tell her everything was going to be just fine.

But could she trust him? They were in their marriage bed. She was practically naked and so was he. If she let him touch her, he might not stop. He might go crazy the way Eric did and . . .

"I give you my word as a gentleman, Lori," he said, as if he'd read her thoughts. "I won't do anything except what you allow. But we have to start somewhere."

He was right, they did. "Would you hold me?" she asked, feeling the tears starting again and holding them back with only the greatest effort. "Put your arms around me and tell me everything will be all right."

Some strong emotion flickered across his face, but before she could name it, it was gone again. "Of course," he said, and scooted closer and reached for her.

She knew a second of panic as he loomed over her, but he was so very gentle when he took her in his arms that the panic died almost instantly, and she was able to relax against him. The pillow was still squashed between them, and after a moment he said, "May I?" and removed it. When he pulled her against him, the heat of his body seemed to envelop her in a cocoon of warmth.

Her breasts felt so strange against his chest with only the thin layer of fabric between them. Not bad, just strange, and he felt so hot, like a fire burned inside of him. At first, she didn't know what to do with her hands, but finally she found the courage to put her arms around him in turn and for the first time touched his naked flesh.

For some reason she'd expected him to be rough to the touch—men were tougher than women, weren't they?—but his skin was like heated satin beneath her palms. She was glad that her hands were no longer calloused and red from working in the fields and doing housework. Sudie had given her a cream to soften them, so now they were as smooth as his back.

Curious now, she ran her palms upward, testing the feel of his body, exploring the differences between a man and a woman.

His breath caught, and she froze in alarm, but he whispered, "Don't stop."

His voice sounded a little strained, as if her touch had excited him, and Lori experienced the first flush of feminine power she had ever known. She was exciting him and controlling him at the same time.

He moved his hands, too, but very slowly, so he wouldn't startle her. One of them began to stroke her hair while the other moved in lazy circles on her back. She felt her tension easing as the last, lingering terrors from her dream faded back into the deep shadows of the night, leaving just the two of them clinging to each other.

Her chin rested against his bare shoulder, and after a while, he turned his head and pressed a kiss to her temple. The gesture was so sweet, she had to bite her lip to keep from crying.

"You smell so good," he said into her ear, his warm breath sending delicious shivers up her spine.

"So do you," she replied without thinking, then winced, certain she'd made a fool of herself.

But he chuckled. "Do I? How do I smell?"

"How do *I* smell?" she countered, pulling away a bit so she could see his face in the flickering candlelight.

"Like roses," he replied, amusement glittering in his eyes. That was the rosewater Sudie used to rinse her hair.

"Now how do I smell?" he repeated.

She had no idea how to describe it. She only knew his scent reminded her of her father and how she'd felt when he was alive. "Safe," she said.

"Safe?" Plainly, he didn't think that was a compliment.

She shook her head. "That's not the right word. Good and strong."

"I smell strong?" he teased. "I should've been more careful when I washed up tonight."

"That's not what I mean," she insisted, glad for the darkness that would hide her blush. "I mean you *are* strong, and you make me feel safe."

He reached up and brushed a lock of hair away from her cheek. "You'll always be safe with me, Lori. I swear it."

Because the tears sprang so quickly to her eyes, she ducked her head against his chest so he wouldn't see she was crying. She didn't want to cry, not in Adam's arms. She never wanted him to see her crying again.

"Lori," he said, his hand cradling the back of her head as she tried to stop the tears leaking from her eyes. "Everything is going to be just fine."

As he did every morning, Adam opened his eyes when the first rays of dawn brightened his bedroom. For a moment he was simply aware of a sense of well-being he hadn't known in a long time. He needed another moment to recall exactly why this morning was so different from those of the past few weeks, and then he remembered last night.

Last night when he had held Lori in his arms and felt her breasts against his chest and touched her back and her shoulders and her hair. And held her until she was asleep again, so trusting that she wasn't afraid to be completely in his power. Frustrated desire had throbbed within him like a toothache, and he'd needed every ounce of his strength to leave her there in her bed alone and unmolested. But he *had* left her there because as much as he wanted her, he wanted her *willing*. He wanted her to need him as much as he needed her.

Once he had planned to seduce her, thinking it would be easily accomplished because she was already acquainted with the pleasures of the flesh. Now he planned to seduce her because in doing so he would *teach* her the pleasures of the flesh and thereby bind her to him in a way she had never been bound to his brother. She would be his completely, body and soul.

And he found he wanted her soul almost as much as he wanted her body.

Adam rose and washed and dressed with more than his usual enthusiasm. Only when he was ready to leave his room did he realize what he, as a planter, should have noticed the instant he had opened his eyes this morning: the sun was shining!

He hurried to the window and looked out, not quite able to trust his senses. It was true! The rain was finally over, and today they would be able to work the fields for the first time in over a week. The weeds would be terrible, gone wild from all the rain and choking the delicate seedlings, but his people would save his crop. They would work relentlessly.

Invigorated anew, he made his way out into the hall and stopped as he looked at Lori's door. Should he wake her? He didn't want to miss a moment with her, and there was so much work to do, he probably wouldn't be able to get back to the house again until after sundown tonight.

Before he could decide, her door opened, and there she was, smiling and looking sweet enough to eat.

"Good morning," he said, knowing he must be grinning like a loon, but unable to stop himself.

"Good morning yourself," she replied. "The sun is out!"

"It certainly is, which is why I was going to knock on your door and tell you that you must have breakfast with me, since I probably won't be back again until suppertime."

"Why not?" she asked, coming toward him, her lovely face pinched with distress.

"Because there'll be too much work to do." He offered her his arm. "So if you have any orders for me, you'd better give them now."

"Orders?" she echoed in confusion.

Adam shook his head in mock dismay. "Don't tell me you've forgotten our arrangement already? Or did I dream that I went to your room last night?"

He loved the way the color stained her cheeks when she was embarrassed, but to his delight, she didn't drop her gaze or pretend any maidenly modesty. "I was afraid maybe I'd dreamed it."

"Apparently not, unless we both had the same dream. So what are your wishes this morning, my dear?"

She hesitated only a moment. "I think I would like a kiss."

"What kind of kiss?" he replied.

She blinked in surprise. "What kinds are there?"

God, he adored the way she was staring up at him, so sweet and innocent and gorgeous. "Well, now, let's see." He pretended to consider. "There's the quick little 'good morning' peck, there's the longer 'I'm very happy to see you this morning' kiss, and then there's the 'how could I have lived the entire night without you' kiss. But I warn you, the third one involves a rather enthusiastic embrace."

He actually held his breath as he waited for her to decide, which seemed to take forever. Just when he thought his lungs might burst, she said, "Could we start with the first one and see how it goes?"

He released his breath on a choking laugh that made her laugh, too, and before she could have a second thought, he bent down and touched his lips to hers for the briefest of kisses. To his delight, she actually looked disappointed when he pulled away almost instantly.

"Ready for the second kind?" he asked, still grinning foolishly.

She nodded, and he wasted not a moment. Placing his hands on her shoulders, he covered her mouth with his for a long, lingering, but otherwise chaste kiss.

His heart was pounding as he reluctantly pulled away, and he noticed that her breath seemed to be coming more quickly, too. Was she frightened or . . . ?

They stared at each other for what seemed an eternity, and finally she whispered, "Wasn't there one more?"

With a groan, he pulled her to him, claiming her lips with his open mouth and wrapping his arms around her so tightly he almost imagined he could feel her heart pounding against his. After a few of those heartbeats, she brought her own arms up and wrapped them around his waist. For a second he thought she had actually opened her lips to him, but he was destined never to know for certain.

"Landsakes!"

They both jumped guiltily apart to find Sudie staring at them in shocked surprise from the end of the hall.

"I's sorry, Massa," she exclaimed, backing hastily away. "I didn't . . . I was just comin' to . . . It stopped rainin'!"

Adam swallowed his irritation. Sudie hadn't intentionally interrupted them, after all.

"We know," Lori informed her, blushing prettily.

"You two don't have to . . . I mean, just keep on with what you was doin'. Don't mind me." She scurried away, but Adam knew the moment was lost. And he did have a lot of work waiting for him. Lori would be here when he got back, and when he did . . .

"Shall we go to breakfast?" he asked, offering her is arm again.

She slipped her hand through his crooked elbow and

walked with him down the hall toward the family dining room. Her cheeks were still delightfully pink.

"So, dear wife, which kind of kiss do you like best?" he inquired with a teasing grin.

Lori smiled coyly. "I'm not sure," she replied. "I think I'll have to try them all again before I can decide."

For the first time since he could remember, Adam threw back his head and laughed out loud.

Seven

Adam was whistling as he made his way across the yard toward where the buggy awaited to carry him out to the fields. He had to go carefully, since the ground was still muddy and his cane tended to slip, but nothing could mar his mood this morning. After the most pleasant breakfast he had enjoyed in years, Lori had invited him to kiss her again "the third way," and the taste of her still lingered enticingly on his lips. Maybe he'd come back at noon anyway, no matter how much work there was to do.

"Massa!"

Sudie's urgent cry startled him, and he turned to find her picking her way gingerly around the puddles as she hurried to catch him up.

"Is something wrong?" he asked in alarm, thinking of Lori and wondering what could have possibly happened in the few minutes since he'd left her.

But Sudie grinned at him. "Not if what I saw this mornin' mean what I think it mean," she said.

Adam managed not to grin back. "And what do you think it means?"

"I think it mean you and Miss Lori warmin' up to each other."

"She *is* my wife," Adam reminded her.

Sudie nodded and slowly her grin faded. "Yessir, Massa, she is, an' you been mighty patient with her."

He had indeed. He had practically qualified for sainthood.

"I just wanna warn you to keep goin' slow so's you don't scare her," Sudie continued. "After what happen to her an' all, she still be mighty skittish, even if she think she over it."

Adam stared at her in surprise. He couldn't believe Lori had confided her deepest shame to Sudie, especially not after the way his slave had treated Lori in the beginning. He'd known the two women had made peace but . . . "She told you?" he asked incredulously.

Sudie nodded again. "I don't reckon she could keep what that devil done to her a secret much longer."

This was impossible! Sudie *couldn't* be condemning Eric, not after she'd forgiven every other evil he'd ever committed in his entire life. "She told you who did this to her?" he demanded.

"Oh, no, sir," Sudie hastily assured him. "She really don't know who it was. If you was thinkin' she just kept it a secret from you . . . Well, she didn't know him. Said she never saw him before or since."

Oh, of course, now it all made perfect sense. Sudie had no idea that Eric was the one responsible for all of this. And Adam wasn't going to tell her, either. "I see," he said.

"An' I knows 'bout the baby," she added, answering his other unspoken question. He'd been wondering when she would figure out why he had married Lori in such haste. "Which is why you gots to be extra careful with her. A lady in her condition, well, that make her skittish, too."

Wonderful, just what he wanted to hear. And he didn't want to think about the child at all, not until he absolutely had to. "Thank you for your very considered advice, Sudie," he said, dismissing her. He planted his cane very deliberately as he began to turn away.

"Massa Adam?"

Reluctantly, he stopped and waited for whatever additional wisdom she wanted to impart.

"A baby an easy thing to love, no matter if it yours or not."

Sudie had certainly proven that with her blind devotion to Eric all these years. For his own part, Adam would simply take her word. Not trusting himself to reply, he started toward the buggy again, his pleasant mood ruined.

"Thank you, Missy," the old woman said with a weak smile as Lori finished placing the warm onion poultice on her chest. Lori and Sudie were doing their rounds of the slave quarters, tending to the sick and injured. This woman had the grippe and a terrible cough that the recent wet weather had only aggravated.

"This is what my stepmother always did for me when I had a cough," Lori replied, returning her smile. "I hope it eases you some."

The old woman only nodded, afraid to talk for fear of starting her cough again. Her dark face was sheened with sweat, and Lori was very much afraid she was going to fail in her duty as mistress to save this woman's life. She glanced helplessly at the basket of remedies she and Sudie always carried with them on these calls, and longed to see some miracle there. She didn't.

Sudie touched her arm. "We best go now so Pammy can get some rest," she said softly.

"I'll come back this afternoon to check on you," Lori promised, picking up her basket and turning toward the door. Outside on the beaten path that wound through the slave quarter cabins, she could hear the happy cries of the slave children who played nearby under the watchful eye of the elderly slaves who had grown too old to work in the fields. Pammy had been one of them until illness had felled her. Reluctantly, Lori remembered what Adam had said about how some masters put their old slaves out to starve.

"She's going to die, isn't she?" Lori asked when they were safely away from the cabin and couldn't be overheard.

"Everybody dies, sooner or later," Sudie reminded her. "Look there." She pointed at where two small children were playing in the wet grass. A little while ago, Lori had dosed them with tonic for summer complaint and now they were frolicking as if nothing was ever wrong with them. "You done *some* good today. And don't forget Henry's foot. You saw how much better it looked this mornin'."

Henry had stepped on a thorn and the cut had festered. Fortunately, a tobacco poultice had drawn off the poison, and he would probably be back at work in a few days, as good as new.

Still, she saw the way they looked at her, suspicion in their eyes. She might be Adam's wife, but she had not yet taken her place in their eyes as their mistress. She was beginning to wonder if she ever would.

"You an' Massa Adam seem a lot happier this mornin'," Sudie observed, reminding her that at least one area of her life was improving. It was as close as Sudie would come to inquiring outright into the private business of her master and mistress.

Lori simply smiled politely, not certain exactly how much she should confide in a slave, even one of Sudie's exalted rank.

"How you been feelin' lately?" Sudie went on. "Any more sickness?"

"No, none at all. That seems to have passed," Lori reported with some surprise. She hadn't been thinking about it at all.

Sudie nodded. "Usually does, sooner or later. You feel the baby move yet?"

Lori glanced at her warily. "No," she said and then added, "or at least I don't think so. What does it feel like?"

"Not much at first, just a little flutter, like when you hold a butterfly in your hands."

Instinctively, Lori's hand went to her stomach. "I've felt that! I didn't . . . That's it? That's the baby?"

Sudie nodded, and Lori felt almost faint for a moment as the reality of it swept over her. The thing inside of her was alive! She'd tried not to think about it, tried to pretend it wasn't there, and except for a new tightness in her clothes, she'd managed to ignore the whole subject.

She'd stopped on the path back to the house, and Sudie stopped, too. "You all right, Missy?" she asked with a worried frown.

Was she? She didn't really know, nor was she sure how she felt exactly. Certainly not as disgusted as she had expected to feel at knowing the child lived within her. And as she stood there trying to decide, she felt the tiny flutter deep in her belly again and with it came a sense of wonder so profound that her breath caught in her chest and tears came to her eyes.

"Missy?" Sudie was alarmed now. "Maybe you oughta sit down."

"No, I'm fine, really!" Lori insisted. "I just . . . I felt it move again! Oh, Sudie, I didn't expect to be *excited!*"

" 'Course you is! It's one ah God's miracles, the way he takes even the worst thing in the world and makes it right again."

Things were far from right, of course, but Lori wanted to believe her. She wanted to believe that the child she carried really was innocent and that she might be able to forget someday how she had come to bear it and perhaps even love it the way a mother should. And even, if miracles did happen, that Adam would come to love it, too. But that was too much to hope for right now. For the moment she would be content to know that the hot ball of anger and hate that she had carried for so long was beginning to dissolve. And that today she had known true happiness, if only for a few fleeting moments at a time.

"Now let's get you back to the house," Sudie said, taking

Lori's arm to assist her. "Watch that mud there. Can't have you fallin', not in your condition."

As he had expected, Adam didn't return to the house until after dark that evening. Lori had been sitting in the back parlor, listening for him, and when she heard the rattle of the buggy, she jumped up and ran out onto the porch to meet him.

The buggy and horse were splattered with mud, and when Adam climbed down, she saw he was, too. His boots were caked and his pant legs and coattails were covered. His face was creased with fatigue, too, and he was limping more noticeably than usual, even with his cane, but he was smiling as he made his way across the yard toward her.

"How do the crops look?" she asked, hardly able to keep from bouncing up and down on her toes from the excitement of seeing him again after a long, lonely day without him.

"The vegetables are doing fine, and so is the corn. Some of the cotton was washed away, but we can replant. It's still early enough." He had a streak of mud across his face, and when he pulled off his broad-brimmed hat and wiped his forehead with his sleeve, his hair was wet and matted to his head. She thought he had never looked more handsome, and she had an almost irresistible urge to throw her arms around him.

It must have shown in her face, too, because he held up his hands as if to ward her off. "If you have any orders for me, Mrs. Ross, they'd better wait until I get cleaned up a little. Wouldn't want to mess up that pretty dress."

Her hand went self-consciously to her throat. "Do you really think it's pretty?" It was one of the simple wrappers that one of the slave girls had made for her. She and Sudie had chosen the style because it would adapt to her growing figure.

"Yes," he said, letting his gaze drift lazily over her from

head to feet, "but then maybe that's just because of the lady who's wearing it."

Lori had never received a compliment like that before, and she felt herself flushing with pleasure. If she hadn't already loved Adam Ross, she would have begun loving him in that moment.

"I'll have Oscar take some hot water to your room so you can get cleaned up," she said quickly to get the conversation back on more familiar ground. She stepped aside so he could begin to use the boot scraper to clean off his boots.

He gave the process only half of his attention though, because he kept looking back up at Lori, as if he couldn't bear to go without seeing her for too long at a stretch. For her own part, Lori didn't want to take her eyes off him at all, even though she knew she should be going to find Oscar.

Fortunately, Oscar found them a few minutes later.

"Better get them boots off 'fore you set foot in the house, Massa," he warned. "Sudie have my hide if you get mud on her clean floors!"

"I'd already thought of that," Adam said as he moved to put his heel in the boot jack.

"Don't use that ol' thing," Oscar protested. "That ruin them boots for sure!"

"I don't want you getting all dirty pulling these off," Adam protested right back, and Lori had to admit, it would be a filthy job.

"I can wash my hands easy enough," Oscar pointed out, "but where you gonna get another pair a boots like that with the Yankees makin' sure we don't get nothin' in or out of Texas?"

Without another word, Oscar turned his back and bent over to remove Adam's first boot. He was right, of course, and for the first time in days, Lori remembered the terrible war that raged ever closer to them. How easy it was to forget, except for the inconvenience of getting goods they'd once taken for granted. But of course life at Elmhurst was easier than it had been for her and Bessie because here they had the means to make many of the things that were no longer available.

The skills to do so had almost been forgotten in recent years. Since Texas had grown more populous, ships had begun making regular stops at her ports to deliver the things that Texans had done without or made themselves during the early years. But the war had necessitated a return to self-sufficiency.

"Don't worry about the Yankees, Oscar," Adam was saying. "My brother'll make short work of them, and then we'll be able to get whatever we want, just like in the old days."

At the mention of Eric, Lori felt the blood rushing from her head, and she knew she couldn't stay where she was for another moment. "I'll get some . . . some hot water," she murmured and fled into the house.

She heard Adam calling her name and knew he must realize what he had done, reminding her of Eric when he was the last person on earth she ever wanted to think of again. He'd want to apologize and make it right, but she didn't want to hear that. She didn't want to hear any more about it at all. She found one of the maids in the hall and told her to fetch some hot water to Massa Adam's room right away. Then she hurried off to the kitchen to make sure his supper would be kept warm while he washed.

By the time he returned, washed and wearing fresh clothes with his damp hair combed neatly, Lori had completely recovered herself.

Hearing his step in the hallway as he approached the dining room, she went to meet him. He was walking with his cane, something he rarely did in the house, and she realized his leg must be bothering him.

"Are you in pain?" she asked, but he shook his head.

"Lori, I'm sorry, I wasn't thinking—"

"That's all right," she said with forced brightness, determined not to let any ugliness spoil their evening. "Please, let's not talk about it anymore. Your supper is waiting."

She took his free arm and hugged it tightly, silently telling him she bore him no ill will for his slip of the tongue. He smiled down at her, although his eyes were full of questions. "You look very lovely tonight," he told her, obviously willing to play along with her.

"And you, sir, look much better than you did a few minutes ago," she replied.

"Not much of a compliment," he allowed, smiling for real this time, "but I'll take it."

He allowed her to lead him into the dining room, and he made short work of the simple meal that Esther served to him. For her own part, Lori only picked at her food. She was more interested in watching Adam and studying his every move and every expression. The way his long-fingered hands gripped his fork. The way his lips closed around his food. The way they curved when he smiled and flattened when he frowned. The way his golden hair curled slightly on his neck as it dried. The way the tips of his eyelashes were so light— they were almost invisible. The way his eyes crinkled at the corners and the way they shone when he looked at her.

And what did he see when he did?

Not the ragged girl who had lived in the shack at the edge of his property, at least. She might not be the kind of fine lady he deserved to have as his wife, but at least she wasn't trash anymore. She had shoes on her feet and decent clothes, and if her manners weren't perfect yet, she was making progress. His slaves might not completely respect her, but they did obey her now. And while many of the tasks she would have to master were still a mystery, she had learned most of the important ones. Slowly but surely, she was earning her place in his life, and when she did, when she was the kind of woman he should have married in the first place, perhaps then he would love her the way she loved him.

Adam used his bread to soak up the last of the gravy on

his plate and popped it into his mouth. His hunger satisfied, at least for the moment, he settled back into his chair to sip the remainder of his coffee and to look at his wife.

God, he missed that ragged girl he'd known for so many years. How long had it been since he'd first noticed that she had made the critical transition from girl to woman? When she'd first pinned up her hair and let down her skirts to cover her slender ankles? When her dress no longer hung on her bony frame but clung to newly-rounded feminine curves?

For a second he pictured how she had looked the day he'd gone to see her in that hovel where she lived. Her hair had hung loose, her enticing body had moved freely, unencumbered by corsets or petticoats, and her tiny, perfect feet had been bare. His blood quickened at the memory, even as he stared at the more proper version of the very same woman.

Would he ever possess that girl, the one he had imagined would be the wanton fulfillment of all his fantasies? Even if he stripped away these restrictive clothes and pulled her hair down loose around her naked shoulders, would she become that girl again? Or was she lost forever along with Lori's innocence?

Or perhaps she had never existed at all except in his heated imagination.

Shaking off the disturbing thought, he said, "Shall we retire to the parlor?"

As if she had been anticipating the invitation, she was on her feet in a moment. Adam took slightly longer to get up. His thigh felt like it was on fire, and he had to be careful not to stumble.

He followed her out of the room, distracting himself from the pain in his leg by admiring the curve of her back and the gentle sway of her hips as she walked. As usual, she matched her step to his when she fell in beside him in the hall, apparently taking no notice of how slowly he was moving tonight. It seemed to take forever to get to the other side of the house, but at last they reached the parlor door.

Hating his weakness—and the fact that he couldn't hide
it from her—he sank down into one of the wingbacked chairs
with a weary sigh. Before he knew what she was doing, Lori
had brought over a footstool and set it in front of him. Then,
when he began to lift his foot onto it, she knelt and helped,
taking the weight of his heel in her cupped hands and posi-
tioning it gently on the stool.

He felt the heat of humiliation burning in his cheeks, but
when she looked up, he saw no trace of disgust on her lovely
face. "Can I get you anything?" she asked.

He wanted to say no. He wanted to be the one getting
something—anything—for her. But he said, "Some brandy,
please," because he needed it desperately.

He'd half-expected her to ask where it was, but she went
directly to the cabinet and opened it. She even pulled out the
right kind of glass, the globe-shaped one, and filled it from
the correct bottle. Sudie must have been educating her on
more than just how to plan the meals.

She carried the glass back to him, cradling it with her
hands as if she understood the liquor should be warmed with
body heat before it could be properly enjoyed. Perhaps, he
couldn't help thinking, there were some advantages to having
her become more sophisticated.

"Thank you," he said, making sure to touch her fingers
as he took the glass from her. They felt cool and soft, and
he imagined they trembled slightly.

"Would you like me to rub your leg for you?" she asked,
when he had taken a sip of the brandy.

He was glad she'd waited until he had swallowed. Otherwise, he might have choked. He almost did anyway, although
why he should have been surprised, he didn't know. He'd
shown her how to perform this service for him the very first
day they were married.

"I'd like that very much," he replied. "I'm afraid I was a
little foolish today and did a bit more walking than I should
have."

Wincing inwardly at his understatement—he'd acted like a bloody fool, tromping around in the mud all day like a man with two good legs even when he'd known there'd be hell to pay for it later—he watched as she sank to her knees beside him in a puddle of skirts.

He braced himself for her touch, but he still wasn't prepared for the sensation of her gentle fingers kneading the sensitive skin of his thigh. The pain vibrated through him, quivering like a living thing, while at the same time, pleasure seared him, settling in his groin in a hot pool of desire.

How odd. She was doing exactly the same thing Sudie had always done, kneeling beside him and massaging out the soreness. Why had he never felt these sensations before? This desperate longing? This raving need?

He downed the brandy in long gulps in a futile effort to quench the fire burning inside of him and only succeeded in dulling the distracting agony of his leg. Every other sensation remained unaffected and perhaps it had actually grown more acute.

"Would you like some more?" she asked when she saw his glass was empty.

He did, but he also knew the danger of drinking too much. A man could lose control of himself, and Adam needed *some* control at least. "No, thank you," he said, setting the glass on the table beside him. "What I do need, however, is for you to come up here."

Her fingers froze on his leg. Plainly, she didn't understand.

"Up here," he clarified, patting his right thigh. "So I can hold you. If you will," he added, realizing he had broken their agreement already. What if she refused him? What if . . . ?

But she didn't refuse him. She said, "Of course I will," and rose to her feet and came to him.

He was aware of so many things at once that he could hardly assimilate them. Her scent. Her heat. Her softness. The way her round little bottom settled against his leg. How slender her waist was within the curve of his arm. How fine her skin looked so close up and how her eyes weren't solid blue at all but a dozen different shades of it all blended together.

He could hardly catch his breath for a moment and wondered if perhaps he had drunk too much brandy, after all.

Then she slipped her slender left arm around his neck and all rational thought fled completely.

"I think," she said quite solemnly, "that I would like a kiss."

"You can kiss me, if you want to. You don't even have to ask," he heard the brandy saying.

"I don't?" she asked in surprise, and he smiled because she was the most delightful creature he had ever known.

"Of course you don't. I would never refuse you anything."

It was a rash promise, but he felt no guilt in making it because he honestly believed it to be true.

She seemed to be considering this, or at least she was considering something. Her eyes narrowed and her lips quivered slightly, and then she lifted her right hand and caressed his cheek.

"You'll scratch yourself," he warned, but she only smiled.

"Your beard is soft. I'll bet it's beautiful, too. You should let it grow."

"To hide my ugly face?" he guessed.

"You're not ugly!" she insisted, as he'd hoped she would. "And don't pretend you don't know it! You've got a mirror."

He couldn't seem to stop smiling at her. "How long are you going to make me wait until you kiss me?"

Lori stared into his eyes and saw things there she'd never allowed herself to imagine he might feel for her. Once again, she felt that heady rush of feminine power, and it gave her the courage she needed to lower her face to Adam's and touch her mouth to his.

His lips were warm and soft and yielding, and he tasted of brandy and himself. She had expected him to take over the kiss once she'd started it, but he simply sat, passive, while she sampled his mouth. Emboldened by his submission, she ended the kiss and indulged herself by pressing her lips to his cheek so she could experience the rest of the face she had loved for so very long.

Hesitantly at first, she kissed only his cheeks, but when he did not protest—and indeed, closed his eyes and leaned his head back as if to grant her better access—she continued her tender exploration. His chin, his jaw, his temples, his forehead, even the delicate curve of his eyelids. His breath was coming more quickly when she moved on to his ear where she tasted the fleshy softness of his earlobe, and she could see his pulse racing in his throat.

"Lori?" he said in a strangled voice.

"Yes?" she replied uncertainly, afraid she might have done something wrong.

"I want to touch you."

What did he mean? He was already touching her. His arm was around her and she was sitting in his lap, for heavens' sake. "Where?" she asked stupidly.

"Everywhere," he replied, his voice still rough, but this time with amusement. "But how about if I just start someplace and you tell me when to stop?"

"I . . . all right," she agreed unevenly. Her own pulse was racing now, but whether from excitement or fear, she took no time to decide as she waited for his first move.

As if sensing her wariness, he took his time, settling his arm around her more securely while he brought his other hand up to caress her cheek. His fingers explored her face the way Lori's lips had explored his, delicately and thoroughly, tracing every line and curve and finding sensitive spots she hadn't even dreamed were there. Along her throat and behind her ear and finally her lips themselves. He traced them with his fingertip until they literally tingled with the need to be kissed.

But only when she whispered his name in entreaty did he

end her torment by covering her mouth with his. This time she clung to him with more boldness than she'd ever dared display before, wrapping her arms around his neck to make sure he didn't pull away before she was ready to let him go.

He made no move to go, however. He merely deepened the kiss, coaxing her lips apart with the tip of his tongue until she opened to his gentle invasion. Vaguely, she recalled that she had been frightened the last time he'd tried this, but she wasn't frightened now. She was simply entranced, as if the feel of his mouth on hers had mesmerized her.

His hands were moving on her now, stroking her back and her shoulders and down her arms. Soothing her, gentling her, petting her, until her bones seemed to soften in response. She buried her fingers in the thickness of his hair, holding his face to hers so the kiss would never end, so this pleasure would never end.

His tongue teased hers, daring it to play, and an answering heat swirled inside of her, delicious and dangerous but not frightening—oh, no, because she was still in control, in perfect control. And then his hand closed over her breast.

Her breath caught in surprise and alarm, but he was whispering something against her lips, something to calm her, something about it being all right. It wasn't all right, of course. It was very much *not* all right, but before she could say so, his thumb found her nipple through the layers of her clothing and began to coax it to life.

She gasped again, this time with shock as the most unexpected sensations sizzled over her. She hated it. She loved it. She didn't know what she felt at all, and she felt so many things all at once, she couldn't begin to figure it out.

She'd had no idea that a man's touch could be so magical, not when experience had taught her otherwise. But Adam's hands weren't a violation. Oh, no, they were something else entirely. She wasn't sure she should even be allowing this, but she was so swamped with sensation that she couldn't think how to stop it, either.

Before she knew what he was about, he'd scooped up her legs and draped them over the arm of the chair and leaned her farther back so she was even more helpless. His lips left a trail of fire down her throat and the next thing she knew, his mouth had replaced his fingers at her nipple.

Without Adam's kisses to drug her, Lori's head cleared in a moment, and when she realized what he was doing to her, that she had completely lost control, she cried out in protest. Adam froze at the sound, his mouth still hot on her breast, and in that instant, Lori realized the rasping sound she heard was her own breath, as she struggled to draw it, and the pounding in her head was the labored beating of her own heart.

For a second, neither of them moved, and then Adam lifted his head. His face was flushed, his hair mussed from her hands, and his breath came fast, as if he'd been running, but it was the expression in his eyes that startled her most. The wild, lost look that reminded her so much of *him* that for a second . . .

And then it was gone. With a groan, he lowered his head again, but only to rest it against her breasts, as if he really were as winded as he sounded. She lay perfectly still, hardly daring to breathe for fear she might somehow start him up again and that this time Adam wouldn't be able to stop, just like *he* hadn't been able to stop.

But Adam was merely catching his breath, and when he had, he lifted his head again and smiled at her. It was a naughty, wicked, unrepentant smile that told her he knew what he had done to her and how he'd made her feel, at least for a few moments, and was glad of it.

"That was very nice," he said, making her blink in surprise. "Didn't you think so?" he asked when she didn't reply.

She did, of course, most of it anyway, but she wasn't sure it would be ladylike to admit it. "I was afraid . . . I mean, I didn't think you'd be able to stop," she corrected herself as she struggled to sit upright.

"I didn't want to," he admitted, helping her put her feet back on the floor again so she could sit upright on his knee again.

She looked at him in surprise, not quite sure she believed him. *He* had said he couldn't stop, that no man could, that it was her fault for leading him on. Except that she hadn't, not really. So maybe the rest of it had been a lie, too.

"Don't you believe me?" Adam asked. He seemed amused. "Well, let me assure you, Lori, there is nothing in this world I'd rather do right now than finish what we just started. Why do you find that hard to believe?"

"I don't! I mean, I . . ." She stammered to a halt when his amusement only increased.

"Oh, then you do realize how desirable you are."

"No!" she insisted, blushing furiously in an agony of embarrassment. "I mean, am I? Do you really think so?"

"Of course I think so. I thought I made that pretty clear just now, but if you'd like me to try again . . ." he added suggestively.

"Oh, no, thank you, that's all right," she said hastily, jumping to her feet and out of his arms at last.

She'd expected to feel at least a trace of relief to be free, but instead she felt bereft. And cold. As if all the warmth had suddenly gone out of her life. Then she looked into his eyes again and saw the heat was still there, waiting for her to claim it again.

Part of her wanted to, desperately, a part of her she'd never even suspected existed. But the rest of her was still afraid of what that might mean and the loss of control it would require. So she took a step back to put some distance between herself and temptation.

She cast about for something neutral to say and settled for, "Is your, uh, leg feeling better?"

He grinned, as if he knew exactly what she was doing. "I forgot it was even there," he claimed. "Now other parts of me are aching, but I don't think you'll want to rub them, at least not tonight."

She had no idea what he was talking about and decided she would be wise not to ask. As gracefully as she could, she sat down in the opposite chair and began to fumble in the knitting basket for something to occupy her hands.

"Lori?"

She looked up warily, ready, she hoped for anything.

"What is that short for? Your name, I mean. Is it Laura?"

She managed not to wince. "No," she said, as embarrassed as she always was to admit the truth. "It's Lorelei."

She braced herself for his expression of surprise, the reaction she usually got, unless she received outright laughter at such a ridiculous name. Instead, Adam merely nodded his head, as if he had expected as much. "I should have known. The siren from the sea who lures men to their doom."

"What?"

"Your name. Didn't you know that's what it means?"

She shook her head. She'd always been too humiliated to even consider the possibility it might have a meaning, too.

"The Lorelei was a mythical creature, a beautiful young woman who sat on the rocks by the sea and sang lovely songs. Sailors who hadn't seen a woman in months would be lured by those songs, and their ships would wreck on the rocks."

"How awful!" she cried, more mortified than ever over her parents' fanciful choice of a name for her.

"Perhaps not," Adam disagreed. "I can think of many less pleasant ways to die. And to live, too." His crystal blue eyes darkened, and Lori instantly felt the urge to lighten them again.

"What do you mean?"

For a moment, she was afraid he wouldn't reply, and then he smiled sadly. "I mean it might be worse to hear the Lorelei's song and not even be able to *try* to reach her because something holds you back."

She couldn't imagine what he was talking about, until she noticed he was rubbing his thigh again. Surely, he didn't think . . . But of course he did. He was so proud. He would hate anything that held him back, even if it was only in his imagination.

She should tell him she didn't care, that it didn't matter if his leg was whole or not, that even still he was ten times the man of anyone else she knew. She should tell him that she loved him, that she'd always loved him, and that part of the reason she did was because of his courage.

But while she was trying to find the words, she saw him lean his head back against the chair again and close his eyes and sigh wearily. And after a moment, his hand stilled from rubbing his thigh, and she knew he was asleep. She would tell him, but not tonight. Not when he was so tired. But soon. She would have to tell him soon. And when she did, perhaps she would also find the courage to do what he really wanted and finish what they'd started tonight.

Eric muttered a curse as he rode along, wiping the sweat out of his eyes with his sleeve. Every time he thought it couldn't get any worse, it did. First, there was the choking dust, then drowning rain for days and days, and now the whole world had turned into a simmering swamp. The heat was suffocating, the air thick enough to cut, and not even shade could provide a respite from the miasma.

Not that there even *was* any shade, either, at least not as far as Eric could see, unless you wanted to crawl under some sticker bush. This road seemed to go on forever with nothing in sight. How in the hell they were supposed to scavenge for food when there was nothing out here but . . .

Then he saw it, a solitary cabin sitting in the middle of nowhere. Smoke curled from the chimney, and a few scraps of laundry hung drying on some scrubby bushes.

"Look there, Lieutenant," Billy called, pointing.

"Seems we're in luck, boys," Eric informed his troops. He'd only brought a few of them with him. If they found anything really good, he didn't want to have to share it with everyone.

One of them coughed, and as if that was a cue, several others echoed the sound. It sent Eric's teeth on edge. If there was one thing he hated, it was sickness, and the rain seemed to have made half of Rip Ford's army sick. How anybody could have a cold when it was hot enough to roast meat without lighting a fire, Eric sure as hell didn't know.

"I hope they got a pig," Billy said. He was one of the few who wasn't sick yet. "I sure could use a big plate of pork chops."

"You let me do the talking," Eric warned them. "Your job is to back me in case there's trouble, but there shouldn't be any. The Captain gave me plenty of script to pay for whatever we take."

One of the other boys snorted derisively. "They won't want no script. Everybody knows it's worthless."

That was true, of course, which was why Eric needed armed troops with him. If a farmer wasn't eager to donate his provender to the Confederate cause, they would have to take it by force. In fact, Eric was kind of hoping they would. After the Yankees had fled from Rio Grande City, they'd been stranded for weeks again, waiting for supplies that never came. All this waiting was making him restless again, and he knew just what he needed to calm him down again.

"I wonder do they got any girls at this place," Billy said, inspiring some snickers from the other boys.

Eric grinned. "And what if they do?"

Billy grinned back. "Reckon we could have us a little fun then, like we did the other night."

"Place that small won't have no slaves," another boy said.

"Ain't no rule says she got to be colored, is there?" Billy challenged. "Me, I like white meat better, anyways."

This outrageous remark earned him hoots from the other

boys, and one of them said, "Better look out. You go sniffin' 'round a white girl, you'll likely get yourself shot, Billy."

Billy glared defiantly at the other boys who murmured their agreement, then he looked at Eric. "You said white girls is even better," he reminded him.

Enjoying his role as elder statesman—nobody at Elmhurst had ever sought his opinion about *anything*—Eric frowned the way his old man had always frowned at him whenever he'd considered Eric a fool, which had been most of the time. "They are," Eric agreed, speaking from his vast experience, "but the boys are right, you've got to be careful. No woman's worth a load of buckshot in your backside."

The boys hooted at Billy's embarrassment, and Eric smiled benignly, still savoring the power of his position. These boys would do whatever he told them, whether it be kill a man or hold down a slave girl while they each took a turn with her.

That had been some night, the most fun he'd had since he'd joined up with this godforsaken army. Just enough whiskey to loosen him up and then the girl.

They'd found her sleeping in a shack on the edge of town. Plainly, she belonged to the family in the big house nearby, but Eric didn't think they'd mind too much. It wasn't like they were going to hurt her or anything. She'd screamed at first, until they got a rag stuffed in her mouth, and she'd tried to fight, at least in the beginning. That had been fine with Eric, who had by privilege of rank gone first. But she didn't have much fight in her, so by the time the second or third boy was done with her, she was just laying there crying. Stupid whore. Stupid, stinking whore. What did she have to cry about? Hell, nobody even lifted a hand to her.

And after that, the boys had looked at him differently. They knew he was more than a veteran soldier now. He'd taught them the ways of the world. He'd shown them what life was all about. He was their leader.

The cabin was closed up tight with the shutters drawn when they arrived, although it was obvious somebody was home. Smoke still curled from the stick and daub chimney, and Eric could actually feel the gaze of the residents, whoever they might be. As they approached, Eric heard a dog's frantic barking from inside, but it stopped abruptly as someone hushed the animal.

"They got pigs," Billy pointed out unnecessarily. The stench would have told them, even if they hadn't been able to see the wallow, plain as day. Two fat sows lay in the mud, not even acknowledging their arrival with so much as a flick of an eyelash. This would be a profitable trip.

"Hello, the house!" Eric called. The place was pathetic, practically falling down for want of repair. The shirts drying on the bushes were hardly more than rags.

"What you want?" a voice called from inside. Eric couldn't tell if it belonged to a man or a woman, although if it was a man, Eric was sure he would be too old to be of any danger to them. No other kind of men were left in Texas, and precious few of them now that so many had joined Ford's army,

"We want to buy your pigs," Eric reported.

"They ain't for sale. Now git before I start shootin'!"

That was a danger, of course. Even a helpless old man could kill you with a gun. But they had guns, too, and more of them.

"I've got government script," Eric said in a last effort to be conciliatory. "And I'm prepared to be more than generous."

"Don't make me waste a bullet on you, boy!" the voice called. "I been savin' 'em for the Yanks!"

Eric was studying the situation. The cabin had only one window and that faced the front. The pigs were in the back.

"All right!" Eric said. "You win. We're leaving."

"Lieutenant!" Billy protested, but Eric silenced him with a look.

"Follow me," he commanded his puzzled troops.

"It's just one man," Billy muttered as they turned their horses. "We could take him easy."

"While he picks us off one by one," Eric pointed out.

He led them back down the road until he judged they were out of the line of fire from the window, then he yelled, "Come on!" and kicked his horse into a run and circled back around the house to where the pigs waited.

The boys needed only a second to figure out his intention, and they were right behind him as he charged into the yard.

"You two," Eric yelled, pointing at two of the boys, "set the pigs loose and run them to the road! The rest of you, stand guard!" He pulled his pistol and the others drew whatever weapons they had as their mounts danced excitedly.

The two boys Eric had designated threw open the gate to the wallow and rousted the pigs who began to squeal in panic. Eric fought to control his horse as he kept his gaze fixed on the house, ready to fire at the first sign of trouble. It came from an unlikely source.

"No!" someone behind him screamed, and he glanced over his shoulder to see a small figure darting from the ramshackle barn. "You leave them pigs alone!"

The figure was moving so fast, racing across the yard to head off the escaping pigs, that Eric needed a second to identify it.

"It's a girl!" Billy cried in the same instant Eric himself realized the truth.

A very young girl, to be sure, but a girl, nonetheless. Barefoot and wearing a threadbare gown that hung in tatters around her naked legs, her long black hair streaming out behind her. Recognition sent a pang of longing throbbing through him in the moment before his brain could acknowledge that she wasn't really Lori, but he still yelled, "Catch her!"

Billy needed no further urging, and he kicked his swaybacked mule into a lope and went after her. The other boys shouted their encouragement as Billy gallumped along and the girl deftly zigged and zagged, simultaneously avoiding Billy and herding the pigs toward the thorny underbrush where no horse or mule would follow.

They were all screaming encouragement to the boy who finally managed to capture a handful of black hair and drag the girl to a halt. She was screaming and yelling and calling down every curse heaven could offer as he turned the mule and started walking it back while the girl stumbled and dragged along beside him, still screaming.

"We'll have us some fun now!" Billy shouted triumphantly over her screams. "I get her first, too!"

The boys who had rousted the pigs were running toward him while the other boys were jumping down from their horses, ready for the fun Billy was promising them. Eric had already opened his mouth to shout at them to wait—he was still in charge here—when Billy's head exploded.

Before their eyes could even register the horror of it, they heard the roar of the rifle behind them and then the shouted warning, "Run, Sharon! Run, girl!"

For what seemed like forever, nobody moved. Billy still sat his mule, even with most of his head blown away, and he still held the girl fast by the hair. But in the next second she tore free, leaving a fist full of black hair still clutched tightly in Billy's frozen hand, and she raced for the brush.

Finally, Eric turned to find an old man with one leg, supported by a crude wooden crutch and still aiming the huge, old blunderbuss. "Run, Sharon, run!" he was still shouting, too, and not paying the least bit of attention to any of the men, but only watching to make sure the girl was escaping.

The old bastard! Look what he'd done! In a rage, Eric lifted his pistol and fired. A hole appeared in the old man's forehead, and after another second he crumpled lifeless to the ground.

Satisfied, Eric jerked his horse around again, looking for other enemies, someone else to kill. The girl? Where was she? He didn't want to kill *her* of course, but he'd need her later, after it was all over.

Except that she was gone. Disappeared along with the pigs into the impenetrable thicket of thorns and spines and cactus. "Where's the girl?" he shouted furiously. "Go after her! Find her!"

But the boys weren't paying the slightest attention to him. They were all still staring at Billy, watching in horrified fascination as his mule continued to walk and Billy's half-headed body continued to ride, swaying now, back and forth, growing ever more unsteady until finally, slowly, it slid over to one side and toppled to the ground with a thump.

"Jesus," one of the boys said, and it sounded more like a prayer than a curse.

What the hell was wrong with them? Were they just going to let the girl get away like that?

Eric kicked his horse into a run and raced past where the mule had lumbered to a stop and past where Billy's body lay in a bloody heap and on to the edge of the clearing

"Come out of there, girl!" he shouted furiously, then caught himself. *Use your head!* he told himself, echoing his father's words to him. How many times had the old bastard warned him about going off half-cocked? "Hey, girl!" he tried more calmly. What the hell was her name? Oh, yeah. "Hey, Sharon, come out here! The old man needs you! He's hurt real bad!"

He waited, listening. At first, all he heard was the thundering of his own heart and the roaring of his own blood in his ears.

"Sharon!" he tried again and was rewarded by a rustle in the undergrowth.

She was coming out! His heart thundered even louder as he waited, tracing the noise of a body scraping against the tearing thorns, holding his breath with anticipation. She was a scrawny little thing, but Billy had been right, white girls were always better. Maybe he'd even keep this one, take her with him. She could do their laundry and be the company whore. She'd be a hell of a lot better off than she was here, too, especially with the old man dead.

The movement was getting closer. She was almost here. He jammed his pistol back in its holster and kicked his horse into motion as he hurried to the spot where she would appear. He caught a glimpse of movement, and then she broke free of the brush. Except it wasn't the girl at all, it was one of the pigs. Running free again. Damn it!

"Sharon!" he screamed, trying desperately to peer into the thick undergrowth but seeing nothing. He glanced around frantically and saw the other boys were still standing where they'd been when Billy had toppled over. The frantic pig raced by them unnoticed.

"At least catch the damn pig!" he cried, but none of them gave any indication he had even heard. Kicking the horse again, he rode over to them. "Wake up!" he shouted, leaning from his saddle to cuff first one and then another. "What's the matter, you never seen a dead man before!"

They turned horror-filled eyes on him as they dodged and ducked to avoid his crazed assault.

"You worthless sons of bitches!" he condemned them all, but they didn't seem to even hear the insult. They just kept staring with those huge, blank eyes. "Isn't anybody interested in that piece of tail that got away? Isn't anybody going after her?"

"Billy's *dead!*" one of the boys shouted back, as if that explained everything.

"You've seen men die before," he reminded them furiously, but they only kept staring at him. Worthless sons of bitches. "All right, mount up," he said in disgust. "There's nothing left for us here."

"What about Billy?" another of the boys asked. "What about that old man?"

"Leave them. They're dead, aren't they?"

"We can't leave *Billy!*" several protested.

"Then pack him up and bring him along," Eric said impatiently. "I'll see you sissies back in camp." He put the spurs to his horse again and took off down the road, damning every last one of them to hell.

Eight

"How's things with you and Massa Adam?" Sudie asked as the two women finished up their inventory of the linen closet.

Things were almost as good as they could be. Almost. "How will I know when I'm ready, Sudie?"

Sudie laid down the stack of pillowcases she'd been counting. "Ready to be a wife to him?"

Lori nodded and looked away, unable to meet Sudie's knowing gaze any longer.

"I don't know if you ever will be," Sudie said, stunning her.

"But I have to!" Lori insisted.

"Why?"

"Because . . ." She caught herself before she confessed the deepest of her secrets.

"Because he might turn you out if you don't?"

"No!" Lori cried.

"Then why?"

She shouldn't tell this woman. Sudie was a slave, after all. Lori's servant, not her friend. She could just imagine what Bessie or her father would say if they knew how much she'd confided in her already. Lori pressed her lips together, as if she could hold the truth inside of her by force of will. But Sudie just kept staring at her, willing her to tell with even more force.

"Because," Lori finally admitted, although the words felt

as though they were being ripped from her, "I want him to love me."

Sudie's dark eyes narrowed suspiciously. "That's a mighty hard thing to wish for. Mean, too, unless you love him back."

"I do!" Instantly, Lori covered her mouth, wishing the words back, knowing she had given this woman a power over her that no one had ever possessed: the power of knowing the one thing in the world that could truly hurt her.

But once again, Sudie surprised her. Instead of gloating in her triumph, she threw back her head and clasped her hands to her bosom and whispered, "Praise be!"

Then, just as suddenly, she looked back at Lori, as suspicious as ever. "You really mean it? You love that boy? With all your heart?"

There was no sense in denying it now. "Yes, I do."

"Since when?" Sudie challenged.

"Since always! Or at least since I can remember," she amended at Sudie's frown.

"You don't care he's got a limp?"

"Of course not!" Lori insisted indignantly. "Why does everybody think that's so important?"

Sudie looked at her oddly, as if she was trying to figure something out. "I reckon it's important to him, but if it ain't to you, then it don't matter at all."

"So what's the answer, Sudie?" Lori asked when Sudie offered nothing else. "How can I be a wife to him when I'm still so afraid? How did *you* do it?"

Sudie shook her head, and for a moment Lori thought she wouldn't tell her. Then she said, "I was in love. I didn't think it could ever happen, but it did. Then—well, it wasn't that I wasn't afraid anymore. I was. Sometimes I still am. But . . . you just got to trust him, to believe he won't hurt you."

"I do," Lori said. "I'm *sure* he'd never hurt me."

And if she really did believe that, Lori realized, she no longer had a reason to wait.

* * *

"Would you like some brandy?" Lori asked as they walked into the parlor after supper.

Adam looked down into Lori's lovely face and had to grit his teeth. She was smiling, and her eyes were shining, and he knew exactly what she was thinking and what she wanted. She wanted to sit with him on the sofa, and she wanted to do what they had been doing every evening for almost a week now. She wanted to be kissed. And held. And petted.

Adam wanted that, too, but he wanted more. He wanted everything. And he just didn't think he could take another evening of stopping cold when Lori had had enough and spending the rest of the night enduring the agony of sexual frustration. Not tonight. Not when just looking at her during supper had made him hard.

"Adam?" she said, reminding him she'd asked him a question. Her smile was fading, and the expectant gleam in her eyes had grown puzzled.

"I don't think I'd better drink tonight," he said, choosing the chair instead of the sofa, which they had discovered was much more comfortable for spooning.

She came to him, her expression telling him she had figured out what he had in mind. Or thought she had. But when she tried to sit on his knee, he had to stop her. "Not tonight," he said, his voice strained with the effort of turning her away when he really wanted nothing more than to pull her closer and closer still.

She stepped back instantly, and for a moment he was simply aware of her. Completely aware of her physical presence. Of her full breasts and her shapely waist and her rounded hips. And of the silken flesh that covered all of her, everywhere, beneath the fabric of her dress. The flesh he'd touched here and there, enough to know he would never get enough of touching it, not as long as he lived. And to know he would go out of his mind if he didn't get to touch it all very soon.

Then he saw her face and knew she'd completely misunderstood him.

"I'm sorry," she murmured, stricken by what she must believe to be his rejection of her. Quickly, she turned away and plunked herself down in the opposite chair and began to rummage in the sewing basket for something to do.

"Lori?"

She looked up warily, her eyes large in her delicate face, and she looked so vulnerable, he wanted to reach out to her. Of course, that would be the worst possible thing he could do.

"Lori, it's not that I don't want to . . . to kiss you tonight." Oh, no, not that at all. Not when the mere mention of it had started the heat pooling in his loins. In fact, there was only one thing on earth he wanted to do more. And that was the problem.

Her hurt expression instantly transformed into sympathy as she once again misunderstood him. "Is your leg bothering you? You should have said something! I can—"

"No, my leg isn't bothering me." If only it was. For once the distracting pain would actually be welcome. But telling her what it *wasn't* would not help. He had to tell her what it *was*. Please, God, let him find the words. "But something else is."

"What?" she asked. "Is something wrong with the crops? Something you haven't told me?"

He shook his head impatiently and swore under his breath. "It's . . . it has to do with *us.*"

Her vulnerability returned in a flash, crumpling her perfect face, and something that might have been fear flickered deep in her dark eyes. He hurried on before she could imagine something too horrible.

"Remember when you told me you didn't think I wanted you?"

She nodded slowly, reluctantly.

He closed his eyes and sent up a silent prayer for strength, then said, "Well, the real problem is that I want you *too* much."

When he looked at her again, he saw she still didn't quite understand. Or perhaps she was afraid to.

Damnit, why didn't she *say* something?

He decided to try a different approach. "After we've been kissing all evening, how do you feel?"

She bit her lip, and Adam had to close his eyes for another second. Finally, she said, "I feel very nice. All . . . warm inside."

"So do I," he said, leaning forward urgently. "But I feel other things, too. I feel desire for you, Lori. I want more than just kisses from you. I want to make love to you, in every way. And I want it so much, I'm afraid I'll frighten you. That's why I didn't want you near me tonight. Because I don't trust myself."

The color came to her cheeks, and she dropped her gaze, apparently very interested in the pattern of her skirt all of a sudden.

"Lori, do you understand what I'm saying?"

She didn't answer for a long moment. "You're saying that if I don't let you make . . . make love to me, you'll force me."

"No!" he shouted, startling her, but he didn't bother to regret it. Pushing himself out of his chair, he ignored the way she cringed away from him and began to pace, not even caring that he was limping before her, something he tried never to do. "No, damnit, that's *not* what I'm saying!" he insisted. "I'm saying that I don't *want* to force you or frighten you or alarm you in any way." He ran his fingers through his hair absently as he searched desperately for the proper words. "I want you to give yourself willingly, but you've made me so crazy with wanting you that I don't trust myself to be a gentleman anymore! Can you understand that?"

He was almost afraid to look at her because he didn't

know what he would do if she was crying or something. Instead, he found she was staring up at him unblinkingly.

"And what if I do give myself willingly? Can you trust yourself then?"

"What?" he asked stupidly, unable to believe he'd heard her correctly.

The color came to her cheeks, and he understood just how embarrassed she must be to discuss something like this with him.

"I thought that tonight we should, uh, try to . . . I mean, I want to be your wife, Adam. I think I'm ready. At least, I *want* to be ready."

Adam found it difficult to draw a breath. So many emotions roiled inside of him that he thought he might burst, but he knew he couldn't reveal any of them without great risk. If he had ever needed self-control, tonight was the night. Somehow, he managed a calm smile.

"Well, then, since I'm ready, too, why don't we give it a try?"

Her large eyes grew even larger. "Now?"

He didn't want to mention his concern that she might change her mind if he let her think about it any longer. "We've already been waiting a long time," he pointed out, still pleased to note that none of the burning urgency he felt was evident in his voice. "And if we start now, we'll have all evening to . . . to enjoy ourselves."

Plainly, she couldn't imagine how she would enjoy herself, but she lifted her chin, determined not to flinch. "If that's what you want, then I guess it's all right."

He went to her and took her hand as she rose to her feet. Her eyes were clouded with doubts and fears he didn't want to see. He cupped her chin and lowered his mouth to hers. It took all his will to keep the kiss chaste and brief, but when he pulled away, he had his reward. She smiled at him. A small, uncertain smile, but a smile nonetheless.

Then he thought of the logistics of going to the bedroom

and undressing and . . . "Perhaps I should call Sudie to help you, uh, get ready," he suggested.

Relief flickered across her face. "Yes, I . . . that's a good idea. I . . . I won't take long," she promised.

Adam hoped not. And after that, he wanted to take all night.

Lori stared at her reflection in the mirror and tried to imagine what Adam would be feeling when he saw her. She was bathed and perfumed, and Sudie had brushed her hair until it shone. She wore the delicate nightdress she'd bought for her wedding night and nothing else. She curled her bare toes into the carpet beneath her feet and tried not to wring her hands nervously.

What was she so scared of? This was Adam. The man she loved. The man she'd always dreamed would someday take her as his wife. He wouldn't hurt her. He would never hurt her. Hadn't he promised as much time and again?

Those promises didn't do much to calm her screaming nerves or relax the knots in her stomach or still her pounding heart, though. And she actually yelped in surprise when he knocked on the door.

Feeling like a fool, she laid a hand over her racing heart and turned on the stool to face the door. "Come in," she said before she lost her nerve, then realized that perhaps she should have gotten in bed to wait for him. At least there she could have covered herself. Or would that have been too forward?

Before she could even begin to decide, the door opened and Adam came in. She wasn't sure what she'd expected, but it wasn't this. He was wearing a particularly beautiful robe of some kind of shiny material and apparently nothing else at all. His feet and ankles were bare, which she found oddly more disturbing than the fact that the part of his chest revealed by the vee of his robe was bare, too.

"I sent the servants away," he said, as he closed the door behind him. "We're alone in the house."

For a second, she felt panic as she realized there would be no one to help her. But then she remembered she wouldn't need help tonight. Not to protect her from Adam, not when she didn't want to be protected, not at all. She was sure she didn't.

Slowly, not knowing what else to do, she stood up to face him. The sun had not completely set yet, so she knew she would be as visible to him as he was to her, even though no candles burned.

She watched him anxiously as his gaze took her in from the top of her head to the tips of her bare toes. And she saw the way his chest rose and fell unsteadily.

"You're very lovely, Mrs. Ross," he said, his voice sounding huskier than usual. "Have I told you how much I like your hair down like that?"

Automatically, she reached up to touch the long curls that lay on her shoulders. "No, I . . . thank you," she said, feeling stupid and awkward and not the least bit lovely. "Adam?"

He smiled and slipped his hands into the pockets of the robe, as if he didn't have a care in the world. "Yes?"

She had to swallow before she could speak. "You'll have to tell me what to do," she warned quickly.

His smile widened. "Nothing would please me more."

She hardly had time to register the words when he added, "Stay right where you are."

He came to her, moving silently over the carpet, and she hardly had time to draw a breath when he took her face in his hands and kissed her.

This kiss was different from the one he'd given her in the parlor. This kiss was deep and full of promise, and when he finally lifted his mouth from hers, she was breathless. So was he.

"You'll tell me if I do anything to frighten you," he said, and she nodded obediently, making him smile again. "God, you're so beautiful," he marveled, trailing his hands down the length of her hair.

When he reached her shoulders, he slid his palms along her bare arms, sending delicious shivers racing over her. Then he caught her hands and drew her with him. She realized instantly that he was taking her to the bed, and instinctively she hesitated. His gaze was questioning as it met hers, his blue eyes so crystal clear they almost took her breath.

Trust him, she could hear Sudie begging her, and she forced her feet to move again, to follow wherever he would lead.

When they reached the bed, he helped her climb the step stool up to the high feather mattress. Sudie had turned the covers down for them, and Lori moved to the middle of the bed. Not certain she should lie down just yet, she sat up and pulled her knees primly to her chest as she waited for him to instruct her.

But he didn't, not at first. Instead, he sat on the edge of the bed and began to arrange the pillows at the head into one heap. "Sit here," he said when he'd finished, indicating she should take her place propped up in the center of the ornately carved headboard.

As gracefully as possible, she slid over and leaned back against the pillows, feeling awkward and silly again and more than a little nervous. She tensed when Adam moved toward her, but he said, "I'm just going to kiss you for a while, exactly the way I've been doing the past few nights. All you have to do is kiss me back," he added with a grin.

That wouldn't be too difficult. She liked kissing Adam. Of course, she usually did so with more clothes on than this and not in a bed, but she wouldn't think about that, not now. Now she would think about Adam's mouth on hers and how delicious he was and how warm he made her feel inside where she had thought she would always be cold.

He lingered over her mouth, drinking her in with long, slow kisses that fogged her mind so that soon she thought of nothing but him and his hands and his lips. His hands were like magic, stroking her arms and her shoulders and her throat until she wanted to purr under his touch. When his lips moved lower, she arched like a cat, offering him unrestricted access to her neck which he covered with sweet, wet kisses.

When his hand came up to cup her breast, she started slightly, but only for a second. She'd grown used to him touching her there, and the sensations were even more pleasant with only a single layer of clothing separating him from her.

Her body seemed to come alive beneath his caresses. Nerve endings tingled and her blood raced in her veins and a strange heat enveloped her as he teased her nipple erect.

"Lori?" he whispered against the pounding pulse at the base of her throat. "I want to unbutton your gown."

Vaguely, she wondered why, but she said, "All right," because she didn't want him to stop kissing her.

His hands were quick and deft, making short work of the tiny buttons, and when he was finished, she was glad she had consented because he pressed his mouth to the spot between her breasts where her heart pounded out a tattoo of need. She sighed, thinking nothing could be sweeter until he slipped his hand beneath the fabric and caressed her naked breast.

"Oh!" she said, or thought she did, but perhaps the sound was lost in the moan that escaped her lips in the next second. Her breasts had grown tender and more sensitive in the past few weeks, and Adam's touch aroused sensations Lori hadn't even known she could feel. Soon his mouth followed his hands, licking and suckling and stirring feelings within her that had no name. As if a silken cord stretched from her breast to her core, she felt an answering spasm deep inside as he teased and tugged. Need hollowed out a space inside of her that burned with wanting, so she felt no fear when his hands moved lower, skimming her hips, caressing her thighs.

"Lori?" he said again. "Open your eyes."

She did, not even aware that she had closed them. Adam lay beside her now, one hand beneath her head, the other resting intimately on her hip. He looked so handsome, her breath caught in her throat, and he was so close that for a moment . . .

"It's me, Lori," he told her. "You don't have to be afraid."

"I'm not," she lied, although it was only a little lie. She wasn't *very* afraid.

"I want to give you pleasure," he said. "But you have to help."

She had no idea what he was talking about. He'd already given her more pleasure than she'd ever expected. "How?" she asked.

Her question seemed to please him because he smiled. "I want you to open your legs for me."

Only then did she realize that her legs were clenched tightly together in silent defense against the invasion she most feared. If she opened them, she would be completely vulnerable to him.

But if she didn't, she would never be his wife.

"Please, Lori," he whispered, and for the first time she recognized that his need was even greater than her own. He craved her trust as much as he craved her body. How could she deny him?

Slowly, she opened to him, aware of the terror she held at bay only with the greatest of effort and aware of the wonder in his eyes as he witnessed her surrender.

She tried not to think about what he was doing, tried not to feel for fear she would feel pain, but his will was stronger than hers, and she could not fight him for long. His hands moved below with even more skill than they had moved above, pushing aside her nightdress and playing her body as if it were a fine instrument from which only he could coax exquisite music.

Heat swirled in her, centering in her loins, and when at last he cupped her *there,* she gasped at the odd relief she felt that he had finally captured her desire.

"Yes, oh, yes," he crooned to her, as if she had done something miraculous when all she had done was allow *him* to do something miraculous.

This was it, then, the pleasure he had wanted to give her. Except it wasn't, not at all, as she soon discovered.

"What . . . ?" she asked as his fingers began to explore her most secret places.

"Shhh," he said, soothing her, except his voice could not undo what his hands were doing, and they were not soothing her at all. Strange sensations coursed through her, churning up a restlessness she had never known and a need that could never be met.

Her breath came faster and faster, and for one second she wondered vaguely what any of this had to do with becoming Adam's wife. Then just as quickly the thought was gone, washed away on a tide of desire so fierce and undeniable that nothing could stand before it.

She cried out as the spasms of release shook her, quaking loose the moorings of her very soul in the wake of a pleasure purer than any she had ever imagined she could feel. As if from afar she heard Adam's voice, urging her on, praising her beauty and her courage, until the last of the shudders died away, leaving her spent and sated and thoroughly confused.

"What . . . happened?" she managed to ask, but Adam only smiled again.

The smile was smug and masculine, and Lori might have resented it, if he hadn't made her feel so wonderful.

He kissed her gently, reminding her that there was more, so much more, the part she hadn't wanted to think about.

"Keep your eyes open," he warned her. "Look at me. You don't have to be afraid."

But she was, so very afraid, because she knew what was coming and how it would hurt. Except he'd promised never to hurt her so why was he doing this? *Why?*

He rose over her and suddenly she couldn't breathe. She looked up at the ceiling, not closing her eyes but still not looking at him so she wouldn't have to see what he was doing.

Then she felt the prodding, that terrible thing, and she went rigid with terror.

"Lori!" he said sharply, making her look at him, making her see that it was Adam. "It's all right, Lori," he said, his voice husky again. "It's all right."

And it was because then somehow he was inside of her, and it didn't hurt at all, not at all! Eyes wide with amazement, she watched his face as he sank into her depths. He almost seemed to be the one in pain, and he drew in his breath with a hiss. But she knew it wasn't pain he felt. Oh, no, only pleasure so acute he could hardly bear the joy of it. Pleasure such as he had given her, and now she was giving back to him.

Her last remaining fears evaporated in the heat of that knowledge. She had power. She had control. And she had the chance to show Adam how very much she loved him.

His robe had fallen open, and she reached up to touch his bare chest. His skin was warm, almost feverish, and satiny smooth beneath the blanket of silky hair. Under her palms she could feel his heart pounding just the way hers had been pounding a few minutes ago.

He breathed her name, and she smiled at the reverence in his voice. "Tell me what to do," she begged, wanting to know some secret that would bind him to her forever.

He'd been braced above her on his arms, and now he lowered himself until their bellies were touching and he rested his weight on his elbows.

"Just stay right where you are," he advised her unsteadily, touching his forehead to hers.

As if she could do anything else, she thought with a small laugh, and he gasped in response.

"What's wrong?" she asked in alarm.

"Nothing," he assured her hoarsely. "It's just . . . when you laughed, I . . . felt it . . . down there. Oh, God, Lori, you're so . . ."

She never knew what he intended to say, because the words were lost on a groan as he began to move inside of her. He buried his face in the curve of her neck, and his breath rasped in her ear, sending delicious chills racing over her. She clung to him, holding him tightly while he strove and strove for his own release. Once or twice she felt a flash of panic as his weight bore down on her, but she refused to surrender to it, and mercifully soon, he groaned again and shuddered and went still, and it was over.

For a few long moments he lay on her, sobbing for breath as the last of his shudders died away, but when Lori could stand his weight no longer, when she began to feel she was suffocating again, she stirred uncomfortably. He rolled away instantly, but if she had thought to be free of him, she was mistaken. He pulled her into his arms and held her against his pounding heart while he fought to catch his breath.

Her first instinct was to break away from him, but then she remembered this was Adam, the man she loved. The man she'd prayed would one day want to hold her in his arms. She inhaled his musky scent and forced herself to relax into his embrace, savoring the sweet sensation of, for once in her life, actually being cherished.

The room was almost dark now, so she could hardly see his face when he reached down and tipped her chin up so he could look at her.

"Are you all right? Did I frighten you?"

"No," she said, almost truthfully. He hadn't frightened her very much. "I'm fine."

"Only fine?" he asked, his smile showing white in the shadows. "Didn't you enjoy it just a little?"

She certainly had and more than a little. She didn't think it would be ladylike to say how much, though. "Yes, I did," she admitted shyly, glad for the darkness that would hide her blush. "I didn't expect . . . well, I didn't expect anything at all."

He settled her more comfortably in the crook of his arm and brushed the hair back from her face. "That was only the beginning, Lori. It will get even better from now on."

Lori couldn't imagine how it could get *better,* but she had no intention of asking him to explain. Quite suddenly, she realized that she was lying in bed with Adam Ross and that he had just possessed her body the way he had always possessed her heart. And she was nearly naked and he was virtually so. His robe was completely open, and if she just looked down, she would see . . . Except she wasn't going to look down. It was all she could do to come to terms with his bare chest right there under her hand. For a second, she couldn't seem to get her breath, and then he was talking again, just as if they were sitting in the parlor and everything was completely proper.

"I'll have Sudie move my things in here in the morning," he was saying, and for a moment she wondered in alarm where *she* would be sleeping. And then she realized he meant that he would be sleeping here with her, just as if they were a real married couple. Which they were now.

She would be sharing her bed with Adam Ross, just the way she would be sharing the rest of her life with him. She was his wife, really and truly. The one thing in the world she had always wanted.

No sooner had the thought formed in her head then she remembered Bessie's warning: *Be careful what you wish for.* But even memories of Bessie couldn't mar the perfection of this moment when she knew that all her dreams were coming true. Nothing would ever hurt her again because she had

Adam to keep her safe. Holding that knowledge very close to her heart, she snuggled up to her husband and surrendered to the oblivion of sleep.

Adam woke her the next morning with kisses.

"Good morning, Mrs. Ross," he told her when at last she realized she wasn't dreaming and opened her eyes.

"Good morning," she replied, her voice still rusty from sleep.

Adam was smiling, and he looked so handsome, even with his cheeks covered with morning stubble and his hair tousled, Lori couldn't seem to stop looking at him.

"Do you know what day it is?" he asked her.

Her brain wasn't quite functioning yet, so she needed a few seconds to remember. "Sunday?"

"The preacher is here this week, and I thought you might like to go to church." Most of the area ministers had long since joined the Confederate Army, too, so those who remained were spread pretty thin and had to ride a large circuit, making regular services few and far between. "We do have something to be thankful for this morning, don't we?"

Oh, yes, she thought, gazing up at his beautiful face.

"And I haven't had a chance to show off my new bride yet, either," he added.

Plainly, he was looking forward to the prospect, although Lori wasn't quite so enthusiastic. There would be questions. People would want to know why Adam Ross had so unexpectedly married a girl he'd never looked at twice. But at least she didn't have to worry that anyone would ask those questions aloud of her and Adam. And later, when people found out she was pregnant and counted on their fingers, they would know, or at least they would think that they did.

"Well, then, I guess we'd better get up and get ready, hadn't we?" she said, trying to match his cheerful mood. She was Adam Ross's wife now. If she was still afraid, down deep inside, she wouldn't let anyone know, not even him.

His smile told her he was pleased with her answer, but he said, "In just a minute. First I have to do this." And he leaned over and kissed her long and hard, the way a man kissed his wife in the privacy of his bedroom.

Lori's body responded instinctively, and almost of their own accord, her arms slipped around his neck to hold him close for as long as the kiss lasted. Vaguely, she realized that the shoulders she caressed were warm and completely bare, and when he finally, breathlessly, pulled away, she saw that his robe was gone and he was naked. Dear heavens, had he been that way all night?

"Maybe we shouldn't go to church after all," he mused, still staring down at her face and now with such longing that her heart lurched in her chest. "Maybe we should just stay right here for the rest of the day so I can show you what I meant when I said it can only get better between us, Lori."

She gaped at him, shocked speechless at such a suggestion. Surely, he couldn't mean it!

And then he chuckled, telling her he *didn't* mean it at all. "The look on your face!" he marveled and bent down to drop a last kiss on the end of her nose. "Now we'd better get moving or we'll be late, and I think we've given everyone enough cause for gossip already, haven't we?"

Before she could even register what he'd said, he turned away and threw off the covers and climbed out of the bed, and she saw that he *was* naked. Completely. She caught a glimpse of his broad back and tightly rounded buttocks in the second before she slammed her eyes shut.

She heard him moving around and wondered frantically what she should do. She had no desire to see any more of him, but she couldn't just lie here with her eyes shut all morning, either.

She didn't have to wonder long.

"Oh, no, you don't. You're not going back to sleep," he

scolded, and before she could protest, he flung the covers off of her.

With a yelp of outrage, she bolted up, scrambling to pull her nightdress down to cover herself and realizing in the process that the front was still unbuttoned and providing no concealment at all! Frantically grabbing it shut around her, she threw him a furious glare before she remembered she shouldn't be looking at him at all.

Fortunately, she saw that he had found his robe and now was belting it around him.

"You'd better get yourself out of that bed before I change my mind and climb back in it with you," he warned with a wicked grin, and Lori needed no further encouragement.

She scrambled out of the bed, nearly falling when she missed the step stool and blushing furiously in embarrassment. Righting herself quickly, she glanced over to see if he'd noticed her clumsiness and found to her mortification that he was watching her every move with great interest.

Then she remembered her unbuttoned bodice and snatched it closed again.

"I'd better go get dressed while I still can," he said, still grinning, and when he was gone, Lori grabbed the bedpost and sagged against it, trying desperately to get control of her rioting emotions.

Dear heavens, she was Adam's wife now, really and truly. She'd given herself to him and somehow she'd pleased him and miraculously, he had pleased her, too, more than she'd ever dreamed possible. Everything, she saw in the light of day, was going to be all right.

The door opened and Sudie came in. Her expression was worried until she saw Lori standing by the end of the bed, still holding the front of her nightdress closed with one hand. Lori gave her the biggest smile her face could hold, and Sudie released her breath in a long sigh.

"Praise be," she said. "Now let's get you ready for church."

* * *

Being "late" for church did not involve missing the beginning of the service, but rather missing the visiting that went on in the hour *before* the service. If you weren't there, as they said, people would be talking about you, so most folks tried to be there.

Since church services had become so irregular in the past few years, such gatherings had taken on even greater importance because it occurred so seldom.

Lori found her apprehension growing as their buggy approached the church. She and Adam would surely be the main topic of conversation on this, the first worship service since their unexpected wedding. Indeed, she could see every head turning in their direction, and she imagined all conversation would have stopped.

Clenching her gloved hands tightly together in her lap, she prayed for strength as Adam drew the buggy to a stop at the end of the long row of wagons already parked near the church.

When he had set the brake, Adam glanced at her and shook his head. "Smile, Mrs. Ross, or people will think I've been abusing you!"

That made her smile in spite of herself. Adam could never abuse anyone. The mere thought was ridiculous.

He climbed down carefully from the buggy, ever mindful of his leg, and then reached up to help her down as well. Lori was wearing her wedding dress, and she would need every ounce of confidence that came from knowing she looked her best.

As she straightened her skirts, she imagined she heard the whispered reaction to her dress making its way through the crowd. The women—especially the *young* women—would be envious. What with the privations the war had caused, she couldn't remember the last time someone had worn a new dress to church.

"Don't forget to smile," Adam whispered as he offered her his arm, and she had no trouble smiling for him. He was, she was certain, the most wonderful husband anyone had ever had.

Adam set the pace, wielding his cane with a flourish, so they walked slowly, giving everyone a chance to observe them. Lori wondered who would be the first to speak to them and was relieved to see it would be Reverend Hartsfield who hurried out of the crowd to greet them.

"Good morning, Adam," he said, shaking Adam's hand, then turned to Lori. "You're looking very well this morning, Mrs. Ross."

"Thank you," she said, hating the flush she knew was rising in her cheeks. Why had he made a reference to her health? Was that what everyone had been talking about this morning, her delicate condition?

He turned to the crowd, all of whom were staring at them now, and said, "Here they are, the newlyweds!"

There was some forced laughter, and then Lori saw Bessie making her way through the crowd toward them. She was wearing her "good" dress, the one that was so old the black had faded to green in spots, and a bonnet that had long since lost its shape, but she looked beautiful to Lori, who knew that she, at least, would be kind to them.

"My, my, don't you look fine," Bessie exclaimed, taking Lori's hands in hers. She glanced up at Adam. "You must be takin' good care of her, Mr. Ross."

"I've certainly been trying to," Adam admitted.

"Come on and show everybody your ring," Bessie told Lori, and brooking no refusal, she drew Lori with her as they headed for a group of ladies standing near the church steps.

Lori glanced back longingly at Adam, but he was smiling his approval. He would expect her to mingle with the other women, not cling to his arm for protection. She managed to smile back, then turned her attention to where Bessie was leading her.

The crowd in the church yard was almost entirely female, and the males, except for Adam, were either elderly or very young, virtually the only kind of men left in Texas. People stood in clusters, divided by ancient and unspoken rules according to social rank. When Lori recognized the women in the group toward which Bessie was leading her, she almost stopped dead in her tracks.

Bessie wasn't taking her to the women with whom they usually conversed on Sunday morning, the other poor widows whose husbands had owned tiny farms and had left them penniless when they went off to war. Oh, no, she was taking her to the group of planters' wives and daughters. Some of these women were widows, too, and many of them might be a lot poorer than they'd been before the war, but they were still the most important people in the county—people who, until today, had never had more than a nod for Lori McClintock.

But now, of course, she was Lori Ross.

"Lori," one of the women said, "what a surprise! We had no idea that Adam Ross was courting you." Her mouth was smiling, but her eyes were cold.

Lori glanced around the circle of familiar faces, faces she had seen at every church service she had ever attended, and saw no trace of friendliness in any of them. She lifted her chin in defiance, determined not to betray the slightest hint of shame. If nothing else, she owed it to Adam not to flinch before them. "Didn't you?" she replied with an insincere smile of her own.

"What a clever girl you are," Sally Smythe cooed through gritted teeth. "To steal the last bachelor in the county out from under our noses!" Sally, Lori knew, was two years older than she, and under ordinary circumstances would have been considered, at age twenty-two, a hopeless old maid. With all the men off fighting the war, however, most young women remained unmarried, and considering how few of those men would be returning home, they might well die that way, too. No wonder Sally was angry.

"I don't think I *stole* him," Lori insisted.

"No, indeed," Bessie confirmed. "Why, he come to the house begging me for her hand. Wasn't any of Lori's doin' at all."

Lori wanted to tell Bessie to shut her mouth and keep it shut, she was only making things worse, but of course she couldn't say a word.

"We're all a little disappointed that we weren't invited to the wedding," Mrs. Price said with feigned regret. She was a tall, slender woman whose face was creased with lines that showed she seldom smiled. "Nobody has parties anymore, and I'm sure we would have been happy for an excuse to get together."

"Adam wanted a private ceremony," Lori said. "But we've been talking about having a party real soon." That wasn't really a lie. Adam had mentioned the idea once or twice, she was sure.

"That would be lovely," the first woman said. She was Mrs. Simmons, a plump woman with five unmarried daughters, and her sour expression told Lori that celebrating another woman's wedding wouldn't be lovely at all.

"That's a new dress, isn't it?" one of the younger women said with thinly disguised bitterness.

Lori looked down self-consciously, as if she had to remind herself of what she was wearing. "Oh, yes," she confirmed.

"Mr. Ross had it made up special for her," Bessie was only too happy to report. "Nothing would do him but she had to have new clothes for the wedding."

Lori managed not to wince.

"I wonder where he got the cloth," Mrs. Simmons said, not bothering to hide the envy in her voice. "I haven't seen anything so fine in Texas in years."

"That girl of his probably had it squirreled away," Mrs.

Price said with a sniff. "What's her name? The one who practically runs his place?" she asked Lori.

"Sudie," Lori said, although she would have liked to pretend she didn't know what they were talking about. For some reason she felt disloyal mentioning Sudie's name to these women.

"That's right," Mrs. Price agreed. "I've told Mr. Price a dozen times, if we had a girl like that, I'd never have to turn my hand!" Mr. Price, of course, was off fighting with Hood's Texas Brigade and had been for four years.

"Must be nice for you now, Lori," Sally said with an evil grin. "With Adam's slaves, you don't have to do your own work anymore. Wonder what your father would've said to that. He was an abolitionist, wasn't he?"

"My father died fighting for the Confederacy, as you know perfectly well," Lori replied, truly angry now. These people might be Adam's friends, but he wouldn't expect her to stand here and be insulted. She had half a mind to—

"Of course he did, dear," Sally's mother interjected quickly, giving her daughter a warning look. "Where's your breeding, Sally? If you aren't careful, Lori won't ever invite you to Elmhurst again!"

Plainly, Sally hadn't considered this possibility, and her eyes grew large with alarm as she did.

"You haven't shown us your ring," another of the younger women said in an obvious attempt to placate Lori.

"Oh, yes, do let us see," Mrs. Smythe agreed quickly.

Slowly, deliberately, Lori pulled off the glove she had bought with Adam's money and held out her hand for them to see. Only when she looked down herself did she realize how changed she was in just a month. The hand that had been red and rough and callused was now smooth and white, a lady's hand. Her clothes were different, too, marking her as one of the elite. No one who saw her this morning would mistake her for white trash.

She only wished the knowledge gave her more comfort.

Suddenly, all the women seemed determined to make Lori feel welcome in their company and include her in their conversation. Their talk swirled around her, although she replied to their remarks with only a word or two. Mrs. Smythe's warning about being excluded from Elmhurst must have frightened all of them into choosing to overlook how much they might resent the fact that somebody like Lori had captured one of their own.

Finally, Bessie poked her in the ribs with her elbow and leaned over to whisper, "Be civil!"

Lori glared at her, but she also knew Bessie was right. She had nothing to gain by being rude back to these women. In fact, she should be enjoying the novelty of having them try to make friends with her, especially knowing how much it must gall them to do so.

For a few moments she did just that, managing to reply politely to inquiries and even asking a question or two of her own to move things along.

Then, suddenly, Sally asked, "Have you heard anything from Eric?"

Stunned, Lori gaped at her, unable to believe even she could be so cruel. But to her surprise, she saw not a trace of smugness on Sally's face.

"Has he written Adam any letters?" she pressed eagerly. "Do you know when he's coming home?"

Lori's head was spinning, and she needed another minute to realize that Sally was merely interested in hearing about Eric. She had no idea what he had done to Lori, or how Lori felt about him.

"Oh, yes," Mrs. Price agreed. "We haven't heard anything in so long from those boys. When I think that they are all that stands between us and the Yankees, I can hardly keep from weeping."

"Has there been any word?" Mrs. Simmons asked after a moment, when Lori didn't reply.

"No," she said thickly, wishing she didn't feel so faint. "We . . . we haven't heard a thing."

"Oh, I'm sure he's just fine," Mrs. Smythe assured her, patting Lori's arm. Obviously, she had misinterpreted Lori's reaction as concern for Eric's safety.

"Yes, indeed," Mrs. Price agreed. "We can't afford to lose any more of our young men, can we? Who will our girls marry?"

"Not Adam Ross," Sally observed acidly. "He's already taken. But at least Elmhurst still has one bachelor left."

Mercifully, the church bell began to ring at that moment and the group of women began to disperse, most to find children or friends and a few to find husbands. Counting herself among the lucky ones, Lori looked around and was relieved to see Adam coming for her.

He'd been discussing something, probably politics, with a group of elderly men.

"How's things between you two?" Bessie inquired in a whisper while the two of them waited for Adam's slow approach.

Silently grateful that Bessie hadn't asked her question even a day earlier, Lori was happy to report, "Just fine."

"He treats you good?"

"Yes, better than good."

"And what about them slaves? They give you any trouble?"

"Not at all," Lori said.

Bessie made a rude noise. "I been expectin' a invite to Sunday dinner. Guess you're too good for the likes of me now."

Lori's conscience tweaked her. She'd been afraid to have Bessie in her new home until now for fear she would sense that things weren't as they should be between her and Adam. Knowing Bessie, she would have asked a lot of questions Lori didn't want to answer and offered a lot of advice Lori didn't want to hear. Now she no longer needed to worry about that. "Will you have dinner with us today?"

"About time," Bessie grumbled.

Adam had reached them, and he offered Lori his arm. "Good morning, Mrs. McClintock," he said to Bessie.

" 'Mornin' to you, too. Lori here was just tellin' me you been treatin' her real good."

Mortified, Lori glanced up at Adam and was even more mortified to find him smiling knowingly back down at her. "Has she now?" he remarked suggestively. "I'm glad to know she's pleased."

Lori's cheeks began to burn, and she knew she was blushing furiously.

"And while it's probably of no concern to you," he went on, thoroughly enjoying Lori's embarrassment, "Lori has been treating me very well, too. Very well indeed," he added softly, for Lori's ears alone.

Lori felt the oddest little tremble in her stomach, and her knees suddenly seemed to be made of jelly.

"Stop looking at me like that or I'm going to kiss you right here in front of God and everybody," Adam warned her in a whisper.

Obediently, Lori looked away, acutely aware of how very much she *wanted* him to kiss her. Was it possible? Was she beginning to actually feel physical desire for Adam? And if so, did that mean she was finally over her fears?

No sooner had the question formed in her mind than Judge Fairweather approached.

"Good morning, Mrs. Ross, Mrs. McClintock. And how are you ladies this fine morning?"

Grateful for the distraction, Lori returned his greeting.

They were almost to the church steps, and the judge fell in step beside them. "Say, Adam, I forgot to ask you earlier. Have you heard anything from that brother of yours?"

Nine

"What's wrong?" Adam asked her as they lay in the dark that night. He'd been kissing her for a long time, kissing and caressing her and trying to elicit at least a ghost of the response she had given him last night. She'd tried, she really had, and she'd prayed he wouldn't notice that she hadn't been able to succeed. But of course he had.

"Nothing's wrong," she insisted as she lay in his arms. "I'm just . . . tired."

"Don't lie to me, Lori. You've been upset ever since we got home from church this afternoon. Did someone say something to you? Something about our marriage?"

"No, not at all," she insisted quite truthfully. That wasn't why she was upset.

"Was it Bessie, then? I thought you wanted her to come to dinner—"

"I did. No, it wasn't anything. I told you, I'm just tired."

"It was Mrs. Price, wasn't it?" Her arms were still around his neck, and she could feel his whole body stiffen with outrage beneath the fabric of his nightshirt. "I saw her talking to you. That old biddy, she has a tongue like an adder. What did she say to you, Lori? I'll call on her tomorrow and demand that she—"

"No, Adam, she didn't say anything to me." She reached up and stroked his face, trying to calm him. "It wasn't that, I swear it."

"Then what is it? And I want the truth. I can't protect you if I don't know what's wrong," he warned.

Protect her. How beautiful those words sounded. And how silly she was being to keep the truth from him. For too long she'd felt so defenseless, and now here was Adam practically begging her to let him help her. He would understand if she could only bring herself to tell him about it.

"It was all that talk about . . . about your brother today," she admitted at last. She still couldn't bring herself to actually say his name.

She could instantly feel the change in him, as if something that had been tightly coiled inside of him had suddenly grown tighter. "Eric?"

"Yes, everyone kept asking if we'd heard from him and how he was and . . . it was so awful!"

"He is my brother, Lori," he reminded her. His voice was strained, so she knew he understood how difficult it was for her to talk about his brother. "You have to expect people will speak of him to you."

"I know but . . . You understand, don't you? Why it hurts me to hear his name and to pretend that . . . that nothing's wrong?"

"Nothing *is* wrong," he insisted impatiently. "You're my wife now, and what happened with you and Eric is over and done with."

How could he say that? How could he even think it? Even if Lori could someday forget how Eric had violated her, there was still the child she carried. What Eric had done would haunt them both for as long as they lived.

"It's not over!" she said. "It will *never* be over!"

Something that felt very much like anger quivered through him, although why *he* should be angry, Lori had no idea. "It won't be over if you refuse to forget about Eric," he said and pushed himself away from her.

Hating the darkness that hid his expression from her, she

reached out to him in desperation. "I'm trying, Adam! I really am, but it's so hard to forget something like that!"

She touched his shoulder and found it as stiff and unyielding as his words. How could this be happening? How could Adam be angry with her? She'd thought he understood.

And then she realized what was wrong. He was hurt because she hadn't been able to respond to his lovemaking. She knew how much it had meant to him when she'd finally been able to give herself to him, and now he must be feeling terribly rejected.

"Adam, I'm sorry," she tried, changing her touch to a caress on his shoulder. "I . . . if you want to . . . to make love . . . it's all right." She could give him that much, at least.

She heard him draw in a deep breath and let it out in a long sigh. "I wouldn't dream of taking advantage of you like that, Lori. You said you were tired. Go to sleep."

With that he rolled over, turning his back and, in the process, shrugging off her hand. Stung, she lay there for a long time, blinking at the tears that kept gathering in her eyes and refusing to give in to the comfort of weeping. Only when she was sure Adam was asleep did she allow herself to shift into a more comfortable position. She was certain she wouldn't be able to sleep. The pain of Adam's rejection was too great, and the reminders of Eric too fresh. But her body's needs overcame her mind's turmoil, and she slipped more quickly into oblivion than she would have suspected was possible.

Adam felt her roll over, and since every nerve in his body was attuned to her, he knew the instant when her breathing changed, signaling her surrender to sleep. He lay there alone in the dark, and cursed himself for being a fool.

Well, what had he expected? Had he really thought that one night of lovemaking could make her forget that she had loved his brother? And more than that, make her forget his crippled leg and love him instead? Had he truly believed that by simply possessing her body he could win her heart as well? He was worse than a fool; he was well and truly insane.

And when he allowed himself to feel the frustrated aching in his loins, he cursed himself all over again for being too proud to take the one thing she *had* offered him. Was he striving for sainthood? First he'd waited weeks to consummate his marriage, and now he was denying himself the one comfort his bride was prepared to give him, just because he knew how distasteful she must find his attentions.

Oh, she'd denied it. She'd even convinced him she welcomed his caresses. But what was she supposed to do? He was her husband, after all. The man who had offered her protection when she was desperate. Her one hope. She couldn't exactly show him her true feelings, could she? Not unless she wanted to risk being thrown out on her own again. So, of course, she'd pretended affection for him. And Adam had been only too willing to let her pretend.

And, he had to admit to his own shame, he would be willing to again. Tonight he'd managed to be noble, but that had only been an act. He wasn't noble at all, not where Lori was concerned. She might be nothing more than a silly chit whom his brother had seduced and abandoned, and she most certainly would never be the soulmate he had once imagined he would find to share his life, but she could more than fill his bed.

Unable to resist another moment, he rolled over to face her. She lay on her back, and while he couldn't make out her features in the dark, he already knew them by heart. The gentle sound of her breathing seemed to fill his head, and every beat of his heart sent an answering throb to his loins. Dear God, even her scent was intoxicating, an erotic mixture of roses and female musk that made him dizzy and made him ache.

He lay like that for a long time, like a man obsessed, which he was. And just as he was about to despair of his own sanity, she whimpered in her sleep. She was crying! Remembering the time she'd awakened him screaming from a nightmare she couldn't escape, he instinctively reached for her.

That was almost his undoing. She felt so soft, so feminine that desire roared in him like a caged beast. But then he felt her shoulders shaking and knew that she was weeping in earnest now. The nobility he had earlier denied saved him. While his body screamed for physical release, his honor prevailed, allowing him to cradle her gently in his arms and press chaste kisses into the thickness of her ebony hair.

By the time she had quieted, by the time she again lay peacefully sleeping in his arms, he knew he was lost. But he also knew that, by God, somehow, someday, she would be as lost as he.

Lori awoke the next morning with a certainty that something was terribly wrong. Still groggy with sleep, she needed a moment to figure out why, and then she remembered what had happened last night, the way Adam had rejected her. In the next instant, she realized that she was alone in the bed. Alarmed, she came completely awake in a moment and sat upright only to find she was alone in the room, too.

When had he left her? Had he gone back to his old bed as soon as she had fallen asleep? But that was ridiculous. Why would he do a thing like that? And when she glanced around, she saw his nightshirt hanging from a peg on the wall, and then she noticed that the room was bright with morning sunshine, and she sank back against her pillows in relief. She had merely overslept. Angry with her or not, Adam had spent the night here and gotten up at his usual time, leaving her to sleep.

But, she realized with renewed alarm, that wasn't particularly good news, either. Every other morning he had been eager to share breakfast with her. Because he enjoyed her company, he had said. This morning he hadn't wanted her company, however. The knowledge was like a lead weight in her chest as she threw back the covers and climbed out of the big bed.

Trying in vain to judge how late she had slept, she moved slowly to the washbasin to begin her morning routine. There was no reason to hurry. If Adam didn't want to see her, nothing else was important.

She dressed carefully, perversely wanting to look her best, even though she knew nothing mattered anymore. When she was ready and could think of nothing else to keep her here, she reluctantly opened the bedroom door and stepped into the hall. Expecting to see no one, she almost cried out in surprise when she saw Adam striding toward her.

"Oh, good, you're awake," he said, smiling at her as if nothing untoward had ever passed between them. "I didn't want to leave without seeing you, but you were sleeping so soundly this morning, I didn't have the heart to wake you."

"I'm sorry," she said quickly, thinking he must be criticizing her for lying abed when she had work to do. "I don't know what's wrong with me."

"You were tired last night, remember?" he said with one of the smiles she'd never thought she'd see again.

Her cheeks burned at the reminder. Why on earth was he being so nice to her? "I wasn't *that* tired!" she protested guiltily.

But he took her hands in his and gazed down at her with eyes that held not the slightest hint of reproach. "Just be sure you aren't that tired tonight," he said, and lifted each of her hands to his lips by turn and kissed them.

Nearly breathless with surprise, she said, "I won't, I promise!"

And then he kissed her mouth. "I'll hold you to that, Mrs. Ross," he said when he was done.

He tucked her hand in his arm and led her back through the house to the rear door where Oscar had the buggy waiting to take him to the fields.

Lori was still speechless with amazement as she stood waving while he drove away.

And as the days stretched into weeks, her confusion only increased. The night she'd thought marked the end of her relationship with Adam might never have happened. He treated her with every kindness and courtesy during the day, and almost every night he made slow, sweet love to her until she cried out her pleasure.

If sometimes memories of Eric's attack made her want to recoil from him, if sometimes she resented the fact that the instrument of his pleasure was the same one that Eric had used to inflict pain, she never let him know it. And if, on those occasions, she was slow to respond and even certain she never would again, Adam was ever patient with her, coaxing her until her responses were no longer hers to control, until Adam was the only driving force in her life.

After only a few short weeks of such tender wooing, Lori understood that while she had already given Adam her heart years before, her soul no longer belonged to her, either, but had somehow passed into his keeping. She was obsessed with him, and his happiness became the only thing she considered important anymore.

"What are you making?" he asked one evening. They were in the parlor, as they usually were after supper, and Lori was taking advantage of the lingering daylight to do some embroidery.

He'd laid a possessive hand on her shoulder as he stood over her chair, and his touch had galvanized her because she knew what it meant. It meant that he was so anxious to make love to her later that he couldn't stop himself from touching her now. Her body responded instinctively, as he had trained it to do with his relentless tenderness, and Lori savored the golden glow of her own desire.

"It's a wrapper for the baby," she said without thinking, gazing up at him lovingly.

Instantly, the spark of desire died in his eyes, and the hand on her shoulder stilled in its caress.

She wanted to snatch the words back. By unspoken agreement, they never mentioned the child. Lori knew he must have noticed the changes in her body. He had spent so many nights exploring every inch of it that surely he was just as aware as she of the way her stomach had rounded. But to say the word "baby" aloud, to acknowledge the child's existence, was something they had never yet done. Until this moment.

"It's . . . very nice," he said and moved away, going to the sideboard where he kept the liquor.

Her first impulse was to stuff the small garment back into the sewing basket, out of sight, and to begin chattering cheerfully about something inconsequential, so they could both pretend that everything was fine again. Adam, she was certain, would be perfectly willing to assist her in that pretense, but sooner or later they were going to have to come to terms with the fact that there would, in a few short months, be a baby in this house. If she let this opportunity pass, heaven only knew when she might have another.

Very carefully, she stuck the needle into the cloth and laid the tiny garment in her lap. "Adam?"

She didn't need to look at him to know what he was doing. She could hear the clink of the neck of the bottle touching the rim of the glass and the splash of the liquor as it poured. She also knew he wasn't medicating the pain in his leg.

"Yes, my dear?" he replied with forced pleasantry.

When he turned to face her, glass in hand, he was smiling, but she knew him well enough now to recognize the falseness of that smile.

"I thought I was going to hate this baby," she told him, forcing herself not to look away, to see his reaction and not to cringe from it.

His smile vanished, but she was glad to see it go. She

wanted no pretense tonight. "Did you?" he asked noncommittally.

"After what happened . . . well, I guess you remember that I wanted to die. Until you came along, that is," she added quickly.

He stood where he was, perfectly still, holding the glass in one hand and not even raising it to his lips. She waited, willing him to say something, anything. After what seemed a lifetime, he nodded once.

Understanding that was all the encouragement she was going to get, she took a deep breath and hurried on. "I'll always be grateful to you, Adam." She thought he winced slightly, but knew she must have been mistaken. "Without you, I don't know what would have become of me . . . of us. If you hadn't married me . . ." She caught herself. That's not what she wanted to say to him. "Anyway, like I said, I expected I would hate the baby, but . . . Well, Sudie told me I wouldn't. Bessie did, too. They said I'd even come to love it in time. I didn't believe them then, but now that I've felt it move . . ." Instinctively, she placed her hand over the small mound of her stomach and felt the feeble fluttering that told her the child knew she was thinking about it.

She drew a deep breath to control the conflicting emotions swirling inside of her. "Now that I've felt it move," she repeated determinedly, "I can't hate it. Maybe I don't love it yet, but . . ."

She looked up at Adam again, silently begging him to understand. But she saw no sign of that. His face was as cold and still as marble.

"We have to think about the future," she went on relentlessly, knowing she had to say these things now, because if she didn't, she might never again find the courage to do so. "Pretty soon people will start to notice. They'll know there's a baby—maybe they already do or at least they've guessed, but now they'll start talking about it. To us," she clarified. "And they're going to think you're the father."

His lips stretched into the most ghastly grin she had ever seen on his face. "I certainly hope they will."

Responding to an overwhelming urge to go to him, knowing only that she had to reassure him in some way, she laid aside the wrapper and rose to her feet, but he stopped her with a gesture.

"Lori, if you're worried that I'll tell someone the truth—"

"No! Of course not!"

"Then what *are* you worried about?" he asked with obvious reluctance. He did not want to have this conversation.

How could she put it into words that he would understand? "We never talk about the baby. I get the feeling that you . . . that you want to pretend it doesn't exist."

"Of course I do," he admitted, shocking her. "I want to pretend that you married me because you wanted *me*. I want to pretend that I was the first man—the *only* man—who has ever had you."

"But you are!" she said. Only when she saw his surprise did she realize what she had said. "You're the only man I ever gave myself to," she corrected herself. "The only man I ever wanted."

"Really?" he asked, but he looked more suspicious than convinced.

"You must know I want you, Adam," she insisted, moving toward him at last. "I didn't think I had any secrets from you anymore."

He smiled then, a sad thing that made her heart ache because she had no idea what could have hurt him so deeply. "I'm sure you have a lot of secrets from me, Lori."

She did of course, the one secret she hadn't yet found the courage to share with him, the truth about her love for him. Still she shook her head in silent denial, but Adam finally seemed to remember the glass he held and lifted it to his lips, using that as an excuse to turn away from her.

Once again, Lori wondered what kind of pain he was trying to ease.

"Adam," she said when he had lowered the glass again. "What's the matter?"

He looked at her then, and his blue eyes were as cold as crystal. "I'm trying to figure out what you're trying to tell me, Lori, but I'm not sure I really want to know."

She'd known this would be hard, but she'd never dreamed just *how* hard it would be. "Sudie once told me that you'd never be mean to a child, that you'd never blame it for . . . for things that weren't its fault . . . the way your father did."

He stiffened at that, probably thinking about Eric, but Lori didn't want to think about Eric, so she hurried on.

"She said you'd be a good . . . a good father to my baby. Adam, I didn't want this baby, but it's coming whether I want it to or not. Whether *we* want it to or not. You told me you would take care of it because it's the Ross heir, and I let you because I needed someone to take care of me, too. But now . . ."

He waited, standing so still that Lori realized he wasn't even breathing. Finally, when she didn't go on, he prodded her. "Now?"

Oh, dear Lord, how could she say this? How could she ask such a thing of him? But then, how could she not?

"Now that I've really started to feel like . . . like I'm your wife—not just a girl you felt sorry for," she added when she saw his frown. "Now I want us to be a family. I want you to be a . . . a father to my baby. Because I don't want this child to turn out like . . . like his real father did."

Adam closed his eyes, and she thought she saw a tremor pass over him. For a moment she was afraid, more afraid than she had ever been, even when she thought Eric was going to take her life. But then Adam opened his eyes, and all the coldness was gone.

"I swear to you, Lori, that will never happen." He lifted his arm, reaching for her, and she came to him then, slipping her arms around his waist. She felt so good, so perfect, in his arms that for a moment he couldn't get his breath. Twisting quickly, he set his half-empty glass back on the sideboard so he would have both hands free to hold her.

But even that was not enough. There was still too much between them, clothes and corsets and uncertainties that could only be alleviated when he was inside of her. But the thought reminded him once again that he was not the only man who had known her intimately. He might be the only man to whom she had responded, but he was not the only man she had known. And he was most certainly not the man who had put a baby in her belly.

A baby he had just sworn to protect. And a baby he knew in his heart he would always resent as a reminder of who had come before him—and why. Because he now knew Lori well enough to be certain she would never have even considered surrendering to Eric unless she had loved him.

The knowledge was like a knife in his heart, a knife that twisted every time he realized that she did not love him the same way. Oh, she'd surrendered to him, but only because she was his wife and it was her duty. And she had responded to him because he had given her no other choice. But he didn't know how to make her love him, and he was beginning to fear he never would. Maybe if she'd never loved Eric . . .

But she *had* loved him. The bitterness of it was like gall, and he kissed Lori fiercely, needing her sweetness to counteract it.

She responded as she always did, opening her lips to him, granting him access to the depths of her mouth, just as she granted him access to the depths of her body. At the taste of her, his own body tightened with the desire that having her only seemed to intensify.

When they were both breathless and he had to break the kiss, he rested his forehead on hers, still holding her tightly.

"You know," he said, managing a grin, "I just realized that my leg is bothering me."

He loved the way her beautiful face instantly creased into

a worried frown. "Why didn't you say something! Come and sit down . . ."

"No," he said, still grinning down into her eyes. "I think I need to *lie* down. In bed. With my devoted wife by my side to comfort me."

He also loved the way the color came to her cheeks as if she were still a virgin, instead of a woman who had known two men.

"And just what kind of comfort will you be needing?" she asked, smiling shyly in spite of her blush.

"The kind only you can provide," he informed her, releasing her just enough so they could walk side by side toward the door.

She went willingly, but she pretended reluctance with another frown. "Maybe I should call Sudie," she teased. "She has a lot more experience than I do."

"Not with the kind of comfort I'll require," he assured her.

He couldn't even wait until they were undressed, and he made love to her with most of their clothes still on, struggling and cursing and laughing as they fought with ties and buttons and pieces of fabric that insisted on being in the wrong place at the wrong time. But at last they came together, and Adam lost himself in her silken heat.

For a few blissful moments no one else existed except the two of them and the exquisite pleasure they gave each other. When Adam heard her cry of joy and felt her release rippling around him, he tried to hold back, needing to savor this one perfect moment when she belonged only to him. But his body betrayed him and within seconds he, too, convulsed with his own completion.

When it was over and they were both satisfied, Adam rolled off of her, wanting nothing more than to cradle her in his arms and revel in his possession of her for the rest of the night.

"You're mine," he whispered against the softness of her

hair, needing desperately to hear her confirm it. But once again his body betrayed him, and before she could respond—if she *did* respond—he fell asleep.

Lori was so happy. She hadn't been happy since the day she'd learned her father had been killed in a battle so unimportant it didn't even have a name. Not until today, at least. Because today she'd found out that Adam loved her.

Well, he hadn't said so, not in so many words, but she knew he did. Why else would he have sent her a note and asked her to meet him? She'd thought her heart would burst this morning after church when he'd smiled at her. Oh, he'd smiled at her before. She'd known him practically all her life, after all, but this morning had been different. This morning he had looked right at her, and the smile had made his blue eyes glow.

She'd been so thrilled by this special attention that for once she'd forgotten to be ashamed of her faded dress and her worn bonnet and for the first time in her life she'd actually felt pretty. And then his brother had handed her the note.

"Adam asked me to give you this," he'd said, slipping the piece of paper discreetly into her hand as he walked by her in the churchyard.

His smile had been so knowing, Lori had blushed furiously and imagined that everyone there must have guessed her secret. But when she'd looked around, she realized no one had even noticed the exchange. No one was looking at her at all.

Her heart pounding with apprehension and anticipation, she'd hurried away, out of sight behind the church and opened the note.

"My dearest Lori," it began, and Lori flushed with pleasure each time she recalled how he had addressed her. "I'm sure you must have noticed my great admiration for you. For years I have been satisfied to admire you from afar, but I believe the time has come to tell you in person just how much you mean to me. You will make me the happiest man alive if you will meet me by the oak tree that marks the boundary of our properties at three o'clock this afternoon. Until then, I remain your devoted servant, Adam Ross."

Lori had read the note so many times, she knew it by heart now. She'd had plenty of time for that, since she'd been waiting by the oak for at least an hour. She and Bessie had no clock, so she had no way of knowing when it was three o'clock exactly, and she hadn't wanted to be late.

After the longest wait of her life, at last she saw him. He was riding a horse, coming quickly over the fields, and her heart began to thunder with excitement. He couldn't wait to get to her! He was as eager as she! She could hardly breathe, and for a moment she was afraid she would faint, but somehow she remembered to draw some air into her lungs, and soon the feeling passed again.

She wasn't sure exactly when she realized something was wrong. She should have known immediately, of course, because Adam never rode horseback. What had she thought, that his love for her had worked a miracle and healed his leg? But she hadn't been thinking at all. She'd been stupid, so stupid, such a silly stupid girl.

Then he was close enough and she could see for herself. She didn't have to remember about his leg or anything else, because she could see it wasn't Adam at all. She should have known *then* at least, but she hadn't, not then, because she was so stupid. And because he was smiling. And so handsome. Not as handsome as Adam, of course, but handsome just the same. All the girls said so and would have even if he *hadn't* been practically the last bachelor left in Texas.

But handsome is as handsome does, as Bessie was so fond of reminding her, and by that rule, Eric Ross wasn't handsome at all. He'd lied and cheated and bribed his way out of serving in the army. Everybody knew it. Everybody knew he was a coward and a traitor to the Southern cause. And he was mean. She'd heard stories about how cruel he could be, and how he had a temper that no man wanted to test. How he could be so different from his brother, nobody could understand, but he was.

Why hadn't she remembered that then? Why hadn't she run away?

But she'd stood there like a lovesick fool, trying to figure out why *he* had come instead of Adam. Something must have happened to Adam, she'd decided. Was he sick or hurt? Her heart went still with terror at the very thought. That must be it. Something terrible had happened, and he had sent his brother to tell her. No, he had sent his brother to *fetch* her because he needed her. She was sure that must be it, because nothing less would have kept him from their rendezvous. But, she soon discovered, nothing terrible had happened at all. At least not yet.

He'd ridden up to her, his smile still wide, so happy, as if she'd come to meet *him*. If something had happened to Adam, his brother didn't seem too upset.

"You came," he said, climbing down from his horse. He left the reins trailing, so the animal wouldn't wander, and came toward her.

"Where's Adam? Is something wrong?" she asked. Her heart was still pounding, but now it was with fear.

"You don't have to pretend," he said. "We both know why you're here."

She had no idea what he was talking about, but before she could figure it out, he was reaching for her. She backed away in alarm.

"Where's Adam?" she repeated desperately.

"How the hell should I know?" he replied impatiently.

"But wasn't he . . . ? The note . . ."

"I've been watching you for a long time, Lori," he told her, smiling again. He seemed very pleased about something. "I might not've noticed you except I saw Adam making cow's eyes at you, and then I realized you were all grown up all of a sudden."

She was so confused. What was he talking about? And where was Adam?

"And I saw the way you looked at me this morning when I gave you that note," he continued, apparently oblivious to her distress. "I knew a girl as pretty as you wouldn't have any use for a cripple, not when you could have a real man."

He reached for her again, and this time she wasn't quick enough. He caught her by the arms. She gasped in shock and tried to pull away, but he tightened his grip, making her cry out in pain.

"Let me go!" she cried. "You're hurting me!"

"Then stop fighting," he replied, holding her even tighter. "I don't want to hurt you. I want to have some fun. You want to have some fun, too, don't you, Lori?"

She shook her head frantically and continued to struggle, but he didn't seem to notice.

"Yes, you do. You just don't know it yet, but I'll show you I'm twice the man my brother is. I'll make you forget Adam Ross even exists!"

She fought him as best she could, but she was no match for him, and finally he slapped her so hard that stars danced before her eyes. Stunned, she could not resist when he forced her backward to the ground. He held her wrists over her head with one hand while he did whatever he wished with the other, touching her breasts while she squirmed futilely and tried to get away, but his weight pinned her in place. He was crushing her and all she could do was scream until he slapped her again.

The pain exploded in her head, and before she could even gasp, he clamped a hand over her mouth, shutting off her air. This time black spots clouded her vision, and he was just a blur above her through the tears that had filled her eyes. She was going to die, she knew it. He was going to kill her.

"Don't make me hurt you, Lori," he was saying, his voice

faint, as if he was very far away even though his breath was hot in her face.

The darkness was closing in on her as she felt her life slipping away, and just when she was sure she would die, he lifted his hand. Desperately, she gasped air into her burning lungs. She was so intent on simply breathing again that she didn't realize what he was doing until she felt the cold air on her legs.

"No!" she cried or tried to, but the protest was lost in a cry of agony as he forced himself inside of her. The pain seared through her, threatening to tear her apart, and once more she knew she was going to die. She couldn't breathe and she couldn't see and he was crushing her and killing her, grunting in her face like an animal while her life slipped away in a crimson tide of agony.

"You're mine now, Lori," he'd said. "I'll come back for you, Lori. Wait for me, Lori. Lori. Lori . . ."

"Lori! Lori, wake up! Lori!"

He was still holding her, and Lori fought back, clawing and kicking and struggling with every ounce of her strength until he pulled her upright and shook her, making her open her eyes.

"Lori, wake up! You're having a nightmare!"

She saw him then. It was Adam. *Adam,* not the other one, not the one who had hurt her. Adam who had promised to keep her safe.

She collapsed against him, sobbing out her terror while he held her fast against his heart.

"My God," he was saying, "what on earth were you dreaming?"

But she couldn't tell him, couldn't speak at all because she was sobbing too hard. She'd thought she was over it. She hadn't had a nightmare like that in weeks, not since she and Adam had really become husband and wife.

It had all seemed so real, too, as if she was really there with Eric and it was happening all over again. And he was promising to come back for her because she belonged to him now.

But Eric *wasn't* coming back, she told herself fiercely. And even if he did, Adam would protect her. Eric would never hurt her again.

She clung to Adam and wept away her terrors until she was too exhausted to weep anymore. Only when she lay spent against his chest, silent except for the occasional hiccup, did she realize dawn had broken. Soon it would be time to get up and start a new day. Instinctively, she tightened her grip on Adam, not wanting to let him go ever.

"What in God's name were you dreaming about?" he asked her again, pushing her away slightly so he could gaze down into her face. He looked so dear with his hair mussed from sleep and the day's growth of golden whiskers stubbling his chin and the worried frown creasing his handsome face that she wanted to weep all over again. She certainly didn't want to tell him about her terrible dream.

He smiled slightly when she did not respond. "Surely, you don't believe that old superstition that if you tell a dream it'll come true," he said, trying to tease her.

"It already came true," she told him wearily. "I dreamed about *him,* about when he attacked me." She shuddered at the memory, and feeling her reaction, Adam tightened his arms around her.

"It's all right," he assured her, brushing the hair away from her damp cheeks. "It's over now and it won't ever happen again."

And it wouldn't. Adam would see to that, because he had no intention of ever sharing Lori with any other man. And as alarmed as he had been to see her in the throes of the nightmare just now, he also knew a sense of triumph. Lori might have once loved Eric, but if this dream was any indication, his brother had hurt her in ways Adam was only beginning to understand.

Perhaps there was more hope than he had realized. Perhaps

Eric's violence really *had* destroyed Lori's tender feelings for him, or at least damaged them. If that were true . . . Well, if that were true, Adam would be a fool not to damage them even more, wouldn't he?

"Lori," he said, still stroking her lovely face. "I wasn't completely honest with you about something."

He saw the fear spark instantly in her beautiful dark blue eyes, and he hastened to relieve it.

"What I told you about Eric, about him shooting me, that wasn't true. Or at least not completely true," he amended quickly. "He did shoot me, but it wasn't an accident. That's what I told my father and everyone else, but that's not how it happened."

Her eyes grew wide as the horror of the truth dawned on her. "He shot you on purpose?" she asked incredulously.

"He was lying in wait for me. I think . . ." His voice broke on the words he'd never spoken aloud to anyone because he had never, until this moment, wanted to admit they were true. "I think he intended to kill me."

She cried out, an incoherent sound that was part sob and part protest that yet spoke eloquently of her outrage and horror. After a moment, she managed only one word, "Why?"

He felt something inside of him, that terrible secret fear, ease with a swiftness that was almost painful. *She hadn't defended Eric!* She hadn't even considered the possibility that Adam might be wrong.

"He hated me," Adam told her baldly. "I told you how my father blamed him for killing our mother. He made Eric suffer every day of his life. I tried to protect him, and Sudie did, too, but we couldn't, not when my father was so determined to punish him. And after a while, Eric seemed determined to suffer. He almost went out of his way to provoke my father, as if he believed a beating was better than simply being ignored."

"But why would he hate *you?*" she asked. "You tried to

protect him! If he wanted to hurt anyone, I'd think he'd want to hurt your father."

"I've been trying to figure that out for over ten years now. The only reason I can come up with doesn't make any sense to me, but it's the only one that makes any sense at all. I think he must have believed somehow that if I was gone, our father would love him instead, that Eric could take my place."

"That's crazy!" she insisted.

"He was only a child, barely twelve years old. But you should have seen his face that day. The ball went in my leg and knocked me down. I was lying there in the dirt, bleeding and writhing in pain, and he stood over me and laughed."

"He *laughed?*" Lori echoed in horror.

"I never told anyone that," he confessed. "If I had, my father would have killed him. As it was, he almost did anyway, even though I swore it was an accident."

"Why did you protect him? Why didn't you tell the truth? He didn't deserve your help!"

"He didn't deserve a lot of what had happened to him, either. It wasn't his fault that our mother died, and he was as much my father's son as I was. I felt guilty because I was loved and he wasn't, and so I'd been protecting him—or trying to—all of his life. But I can see now I made a mistake. If I'd told the truth then . . . well, maybe he wouldn't have hurt you, too."

"Oh, Adam," she said, and tears filled her eyes again as she gazed up at him adoringly. Perhaps she didn't love *him* yet, but she loved Eric less now.

His conscience pricked him just a bit. Once again, he was taking the love that should have been Eric's, just as he was taking Eric's woman and Eric's child. But if his motives were selfish, they were also just, because Eric had forfeited any claim to Lori and her love when he had abused her so cruelly.

"But if he hadn't hurt me," she said, as if she could read his thoughts, "then you and I wouldn't be together now."

Her smile was so sweet that Adam could almost imagine

the emotion shining in her eyes was love instead of merely gratitude. Longing throbbed painfully in his chest, the desire for what he needed so desperately and feared he might never have.

"Do you think us being together now was worth the pain?" he asked to torture himself, knowing perfectly well she couldn't lie about that, not even to please him.

But to his amazement, her smile never wavered. "It was worth almost anything," she assured him.

That was when Adam understood the true depths of his own obsession, because he was so eager to accept her lie.

Eric wanted to go home. Nobody was likely to care if he did, of course. It wasn't as if he was in the real army or anything. But he couldn't go home, because if he did, everyone back there would know he'd run away. That would pretty much ruin whatever respect he'd gained from joining up with this godforsaken bunch in the first place.

He should've joined the regular army. He could see that now. At least he would've gotten some glory and seen some real fighting. The regular army had uniforms and guns and ammunition, too. None of that had seemed very important before, when he was back home in the comfort of Elmhurst. Why, he'd thought then, should he risk his neck to fight in a war to protect a cause he didn't give a damn about? Southern honor? He'd seen enough Southern honor to know it wasn't worth protecting, and it for damn sure wasn't worth dying for.

But that was before he started getting all those funny looks from people who thought he was a coward or worse. Who thought he ought to join all their sons and fathers and husbands in the fighting. What the hell did they expect? He'd already paid some poor son of a bitch to take his place, and what good would it do if he went himself? One man wasn't going to make a difference one way or the other.

But then he began to realize that if he *didn't* go he might suffer more than he would if he did. He began to realize that the men who had fought and died for the South were now saints, and the ones who had fought and lived would be heroes. But the ones who hadn't fought at all would be outcasts, despised by one and all.

Eric had had enough of being despised by his father. He didn't want to have to face it from everybody else, too. So when the call had come from Rip Ford to protect Texas from the Yankee invasion, he'd ridden to join them.

Glory. Honor. Respect. That was all he'd wanted. Instead, he'd gotten dust and mud and wormy rations and a bunch of snot-nosed kids who didn't know their asses from their elbows.

That was Eric's last thought when he heard someone banging on a pan to rouse the men from their fitful sleep. Eric threw off his blanket in disgust and rose stiffly from the hard ground. The scarlet sky, he saw at once, boded ill. A red dawn meant more rain and more mud, and then the steaming heat that would follow.

Eric would have killed a man for a cup of real coffee, but this army hadn't seen real coffee in weeks. He settled for "borrowing" some of the putrid brew that one of his "men" had made from scorched mesquite beans. At least it was hot.

"When are we going to see some more Yankees?" one of his snot-nosed "men" asked crossly.

"Pretty soon," another reported. "I heard they wasn't far from here."

The talk swirled around him, but Eric didn't deign to join in. The boys weren't as much fun now that Billy was gone. And they looked at Eric differently, too, like they thought it was his fault Billy'd gotten himself killed or something. The hell with them. Eric didn't care what a bunch of kids thought, anyway.

He was chewing on a piece of hardtack when the orders came down. They were going to attack the Yankees who were camped at a nearby ranch on the banks of the Rio Grande. Captain Dunn would lead them, and Colonel Showalter's men would go with them. Hell, Showalter might even be sober, since it was so early in the morning.

Eric felt his blood begin to stir, the first time he'd felt anything like excitement in weeks. By the time they were mounted up, a slow rain had already begun to fall.

"We'll drive them damn Yankees into the sea!" Dunn shouted as the order came to ride. The old ranger sure got worked up, but Eric was pretty worked up himself.

Half-expecting the Yankees to be gone by the time they got there, the men rode hell-bent up to the ranch only to discover they were still there. Shouts and Rebel yells filled the morning air as they charged straight into the Yankee ranks.

As the drizzle became a sodden downpour, men fought hand to hand, screaming and bleeding and dying and charging onward. Using the sword he'd taken off a dead Yankee several weeks back, Eric slashed his way into the melee.

Swinging furiously at a blue jacket, he felt the shock up to his shoulder when the blade struck bone. The man's howl of agony filled Eric's head as the man's blood spurted hotly in his face. The sensation was nothing he'd ever experienced before, and he felt a rush of joy that was so much like sex that he actually clutched his crotch with his free hand for a moment. And then another Yankee charged him, and Eric cut him down with one swift blow. More screams, more blood, and Eric was lost in the lustful frenzy of death and destruction.

The Rebels were unstoppable, and beneath their assault, the Yankee line shattered. As Confederate reinforcements arrived, the Blue Coats broke and ran. The Rebels reloaded empty muskets and fired after them, cutting them down in their tracks. A handful managed to reach the river and swim to safety in Mexico. A few more were captured, but most fell in ignominious death on the muddy banks of the Rio Grande.

Eric got himself a new pair of boots from a dead Yankee corporal, and some tobacco from a dead captain. And they all had coffee and real meat that night from the supplies the Yankees had left behind. There were guns, too, and horses and wagons. The Cavalry of the West wasn't quite so pitiful anymore.

And neither was Eric.

"Did you boys see me out there today?" he asked as he approached them that evening. They were sitting around a campfire the evening after the battle. "I near cut a Yankee's arm clean off!"

They watched him warily as he took his seat among them. They were, he was gratified to notice, looking at the blood-stains on his tunic.

"It was just like at Antietam," he continued now that he had their attention. "Guns were a waste of time. A man couldn't get his rifle reloaded because the Yankees were right on top of us before we knew it. It was all fists and bayonets. I always swore I'd get myself a sword before I went hand-to-hand again."

The boys were staring at him, with admiration he was sure. He rubbed one of the bloodstains just to remind them of what he had done that day.

"I finally got to kill me a Yankee," one of them said suddenly, trying to draw their attention to himself. "Shot him when he was running into the river."

"You'll get a lot more chances," Eric said, drawing them back. "We've got them cornered now. They've got the sea to their backs, so they'll have to stand and fight at Brownsville."

He glanced around at the circle of faces and saw exactly what he'd wanted to see. They held him in awe again. They'd forgotten about Billy, and he was once more their leader.

He reached into his pocket for the tobacco pouch he'd taken from the Yankee. "Anybody want a smoke?" he asked generously.

As the boys passed the pouch and stuffed the tobacco into the crude pipes they'd fashioned or brought from home, Eric smiled.

"Too bad there ain't no women around here," he said, rubbing his crotch as he savored the memories of the battle. "But wait 'til we get to Brownsville. That's where we'll have us some real fun."

Ten

"You feelin' poorly this mornin', Missy?" Sudie asked Lori when she had gone back into the house that morning after seeing Adam off for the day.

Instinctively, Lori touched her head which still ached from the awful dream she'd had just before dawn this morning.

"No, I'm fine," she lied automatically, then just as quickly realized how foolish she was being to try to conceal the truth from the one person who might be able to offer her comfort. "I just . . . I had a bad dream last night."

Sudie stopped in the middle of the hall, and her worried frown instantly became sympathetic. "About him? About that man what attacked you?"

Lori nodded, not wanting to even think about it but knowing she had to if she ever hoped to be normal again. "I dreamed I was back there, that it was happening all over again."

Sudie nodded her understanding. "I reckon you was mighty scared."

"I was sure I was going to die. Just like I was then. Oh, Sudie, I thought I was over it!"

"You never be over it," Sudie told her but hurried on at Lori's cry of protest. "That don't mean you can't be lots better, though, and one way you can is to change your dreams."

"What?" Lori asked, certain she had heard wrong.

"Change your dreams. Like last night. I reckon you dreamed it just like it happened, right?"

Lori nodded reluctantly.

"Then next time it happens, you change it."

"I can't change my dreams!" she insisted.

"Yes, you can," Sudie insisted right back. "You start with figurin' out what you wish happened instead of what really did."

"I wish I'd gotten away from him!"

"Is that all? Don't you want to hurt him back, too? Make him sorry he ever touched you?"

Of course she did, although she'd never admitted it, not even to herself. She nodded reluctantly.

"Then that's what you think about. You picture it in your mind, how you want to fight him and hurt him before he can hurt you."

"I couldn't do that! I don't want to think about him at all!"

Sudie shrugged, as if it was all the same to her. "Suit yourself, only you'll keep havin' them dreams, and they'll get worse, maybe even worse than it really was."

Lori felt herself grow cold at the very thought. How could it possibly be any worse? And how would she survive a dream like that? "But how can I change the dream? How can I make it come out different?"

"Do like I said. You picture in your mind how you want things to happen. Don't be afraid, neither. You be just as mean to him as he deserves. Keep doin' that, and next time you have the dream, it'll come out different."

Before Lori could weigh the truth of that promise, she felt a strange sensation low in her side that could only have been a kick.

She cried out in surprise and laid a hand on her abdomen.

"Somethin' wrong?" Sudie asked in alarm.

Lori smiled to reassure her. "No, I . . . I think the baby just kicked me."

Sudie nodded wisely. "He tryin' to tell you I's right."

"Sudie . . ." Lori said, warning her she wouldn't listen to any more tall tales.

"You think he can't hear when we talk? You'll see when he born. He know your voice and Massa Adam's, too."

"Adam's? How?"

" 'Cause he hear it all the time, that how," Sudie assured her. She started down the hall again, a silent signal that they should be getting to work, and Lori fell in step beside her. "You think of a name yet?" she asked casually after a moment.

"A name for what?" Lori asked absently, still intrigued by the possibility that her child could hear her when she spoke.

"For the baby," Sudie said, surprising her all over again.

"I . . . no." She hadn't even considered such a thing.

"Better talk it over with Massa Adam," Sudie suggested. "Can't go callin' that young'un 'hey you' when it gets here."

Lori tried to smile, but the prospect of discussing the baby with Adam was still entirely too daunting, even after their talk last night when he'd assured her he would be a real father to her child.

That night as she and Adam sat in the parlor, Adam read silently and Lori stared blindly at her knitting, doing the intricate stitches by instinct rather than by conscious thought. Her conscious thought was miles away, under the big oak tree where she'd thought to meet Adam and where she'd met his brother instead.

What would she have wanted to happen instead? The question seemed easy enough until she considered it. She wanted it to have never happened at all. She wanted to have ignored the letter Eric had given her. She wanted to have been smart enough to know he was tricking her. But she knew Sudie would tell her that wasn't enough. She couldn't pretend the attack had never happened. She'd already tried that, and it hadn't worked.

No, she had to go to the oak tree again in her mind, and this time she had to change what occurred there. As her fingers worked the knitting needles, her mind drifted, plotting and planning.

She was waiting when he came, but she wasn't frightened, oh, no. She was strong and she was brave. She wasn't afraid of anything, not even *him*. He'd lied to her, and that made her angry. He'd tried to trick her because he thought she was stupid and weak, but she wasn't stupid and she wasn't weak.

He got off his horse and came toward her, smiling that evil smile, but she wasn't fooled, oh, no. She wasn't fooled at all! She knew him for the liar that he was. She stood up to him and laughed in his face.

But now *he* was angry! He reached out and grabbed her. He was strong, so much stronger than she . . . But no, she was strong, too. She could fight him. She wrenched away. She slapped his face! Yes, yes, she slapped his face. She slapped him hard, and he cried out in outrage.

But that wasn't enough because a slap wouldn't stop him. He came for her again, lunging and grabbing with his hands that were so strong and so relentless. And this time she fought him better because she was stronger, too. She punched him and kicked him and made him howl with pain, and when he tried to force her to the ground, she wrenched away. She was free! She was getting away!

Was that enough? Was it enough to run? No! He had a horse! He could catch her even if she ran like the wind, so she didn't run at all. Oh, no, she turned and faced him down because . . . because she had a gun! Yes, that was it! She had a pistol, that old hog leg pistol her father had left for her and Bessie to protect themselves! She lifted it with both hands, pointing it right at his face, and she saw his eyes grow large with terror and—

"Lori?" Adam's voice startled her back to reality, and she

was surprised to see he was staring at her with a worried frown. "Is something wrong?"

With difficulty, she banished the fading remnants of the too-vivid image. "No, what could be wrong?" she asked with what she hoped was a normal voice.

He didn't look reassured. "You were . . . I don't know. Making noises or something."

"I was?" Oh, dear. Had she said anything aloud? Would he be able to guess what she had been thinking about?

But he was smiling now, a puzzled little grin that told her he was simply intrigued and trying to figure something out. "I hate to say you were grunting—that sounds so unlady-like—but I can't think what else to call it."

"I was . . . thinking," she excused herself, trying valiantly not to blush.

"It must have been hard work," he pointed out in amusement.

If he only knew!

"What were you thinking *about?*" he added.

Frantically, she cast about for a topic that might have distressed her. "I . . . uh . . . I've been trying to think of a name for the baby."

Instantly all trace of amusement vanished from his face. "Oh."

She'd been right, this *was* a topic he didn't want to discuss. In spite of his promise to be a father to the child, he still wasn't thrilled about its existence. She hurried on. "I was wondering if you . . . if you have any preferences? On names, I mean."

"I haven't really given the matter a lot of thought," he said in a carefully neutral voice. "I'm sure whatever you choose will be fine."

He was being polite. And tolerant. And generous. She hated it when he was like that. She wanted him to be happy and enthusiastic, although she knew she was foolish to even dream of such a thing. Tolerance was probably the most she had any right to expect.

"I was thinking . . ." she said, forcing herself to go on when every instinct warned her to let the subject drop. "If it's a boy, I'd like to name him Matthew, after my father—if that's all right."

"It's your baby, Lori," he reminded her, still the model of courtesy. "You can call it whatever you wish."

His words were like a whip lash across her heart. It's *your* baby, Lori, not *mine,* was the unmistakable implication.

Her pain must have shown on her face, because he frowned. "Lori? What is it?"

"Nothing." Resolutely, she turned her attention back to her knitting.

But Adam wasn't fooled. She could feel him watching her, trying to figure out what was wrong and why. He hadn't hurt her on purpose, after all, and now he was trying to figure out what he had done and how he could make amends. If she had loved him for no other reason, she would have loved him for that, and the knowledge helped soften the sting of his earlier reminder. Still she was surprised when he spoke again.

"And what if it's a girl?"

She looked up in surprise. "What?"

"I said, what if the baby is a girl? Surely, you won't name her Matthew, too." His smile was tentative as he tested her mood. Was she angry? Hurt? Or simply annoyed?

All her anger, hurt and annoyance evaporated in gratitude, and she returned his smile. "I thought I'd name a girl after my mother . . . Faith."

"That's a lovely name. Faith McClintock Ross."

As if the baby had heard the name and wished to offer an opinion, it kicked Lori in the side in almost the same place it had kicked her this morning. "Oh!"

"What's wrong?" Adam asked in alarm, just as Sudie had done.

Lori shook her head as she absently rubbed the spot of the kick. "The baby moved," she said, feeling the wonder of it all over again. As the child grew larger and more active, her own enthusiasm grew, too.

"It *moved?*" Adam echoed incredulously. Lori nodded. "And you could feel it?"

Lori nodded again.

"But it's so small," Adam argued, still unable to believe.

Lori touched the swell of her stomach. "It's getting bigger," she reminded him with a self-conscious smile. Beneath her hand she felt the familiar fluttering as the child shifted inside her. "There it is again."

"What does it feel like?" he asked, laying aside his book and leaning forward in his chair.

He was interested, she realized, and felt a tingle of excitement at the knowledge. She rewarded him with a smile. "Sometimes it feels like an angry butterfly, and sometimes it feels like an angry mule."

His eyes widened in surprise, and he leaned forward even farther. "Does it hurt you?" His beautiful face was creased with a concern that warmed her heart.

"Oh, no," she assured him, and then an idea occurred to her. It was bold, perhaps too bold, but wasn't she growing stronger and braver every day? She decided to take the chance. "You can probably feel it, too. Would you like to try?"

This time his eyes widened in shock. *"How?"*

"I think, if you put your hand on here . . ." She laid her hand on her stomach again to show him how. ". . . then you could feel it."

As she had suspected, he needed no second invitation to touch her. In an instant he was beside her, down on his good knee, offering her his hand.

She took his hand in both of hers, surprised as always at how warm his flesh felt beneath her fingers. Even kneeling beside her, he seemed huge and formidable and so strong she knew he could easily overpower her. Yet he had never used his strength to hurt her. In fact, he had taken great pains *not* to hurt her. He was a gentleman in the truest sense of the word, a *gentle man.*

Only when she laid his hand on the mound of her stomach did she realize she had been holding her breath. His palm was large and hot against her stomach, almost covering it. The warmth seeped into her, stirring her blood and settling in her loins. She glanced up at him to see if he had sensed her reaction, but he wasn't looking at her face at all. He was staring intently at his hand, as if he expected to see something as well as feel it.

His eyes were so blue, they took her breath, and she used this moment when he was so close but not looking back to study him. She loved his face. The sun had darkened his skin to the color of oak, making his hair look even blonder in contrast. The tips of his eyelashes were blonde, too, and could only be seen up close like this. She adored the line of his nose and the way his finely shaped nostrils flared slightly when he took in her scent. The way his eyes crinkled at the corners. And the curve of his mouth, so straight and unyielding except when he was kissing her and it became soft and tender.

She traced the curve of his ear with her gaze, learning it and loving it, as she loved everything about him. And she inhaled his masculine scent, growing more intoxicated by it with every passing second.

For what seemed an eternity, neither of them moved, and Adam hardly even seemed to breathe, so intent was he. But perversely, the child lay perfectly still, and finally, Adam lifted his gaze to her face.

"I don't—" he began, and as if it had been startled by the sudden sound after the long silence, the baby jumped.

"Did you feel that?" Lori asked breathlessly.

Plainly, he had. His expression was total amazement.

"That's it? That was the baby?" he asked in a near whisper. As if he was afraid the child would overhear.

"I think he jumped when he heard your voice," Lori told him in delight.

This was more than Adam could accept. "That's impossible," he insisted aloud, and this time the baby kicked, striking Adam in the heel of his hand.

"My God, what was that?"

"That was the angry mule," Lori told him with a smile.

His wonderful mouth stretched into a wondrous grin. "It's almost like he did hear me."

"Sudie said he can," Lori was happy to report. "She said that when he's born, he'll know our voices, mine and yours, too."

Adam shook his head, not certain whether to believe her or not, but he didn't move his hand. As if the child could feel the warmth of that touch, he stirred again, almost the way a cat curves itself under a human hand for a caress.

"My God," Adam murmured again, and when his gaze lifted to hers again, his eyes were full of awe. "It's really alive. I don't think I truly believed that before." Then his eyes narrowed. "How soon . . . I mean, when will it come? I just realized I don't have any idea."

"The middle of September, I think, although Sudie says babies come when they want, so it could be two weeks either way."

"So soon?" They had less than three months to wait. He glanced down at the knitting that still lay in her lap. "And you've got enough clothes for it? Everything you need?"

"I will, yes."

"How about a bed? I think there's a cradle in the attic—"

"Sudie said she'd get it down."

Adam frowned thoughtfully. "We'll have to find a wet nurse. Several of the girls have babies. I'll have Sudie send them up, and you can pick the one you like best."

Lori frowned, too. "Adam, I . . ."

His gaze met hers, and for a moment all she could think of was how much she loved him.

"What is it?" he prodded when she didn't continue.

"I . . . I think I'd like to nurse the baby myself . . . at least at first," she added at his frown of disapproval.

"Lori," he said gently. "The master's wife doesn't nurse her own children. You'll have too much to do, too many responsibilities."

He was right, of course. Only poor white trash nursed their own children, and probably he was thinking that very thing. And Lori should have been glad for the opportunity to turn the child she'd never wanted in the first place over to someone else. But she wasn't. Oddly enough, she found herself possessive of it instead. Probably that was guilt because she *hadn't* wanted it. Or penance to make up for wishing it dead. But whatever the reason, she knew she couldn't turn the child over to a slave.

A slave! Why hadn't she thought of that before! "But what if we lose the war," she reminded him. "What if the Yankees free all our slaves, and they run away?"

Adam shook his head and gave her a tolerant smile. "I told you before, that won't happen. Even if they were free, where would they go? You don't have to worry about that, at least. I'll tell Sudie to find you a good mammy."

She wanted to argue with him but decided it was too soon for that. She'd made her point, and now she'd have almost three months to drive it home and convince him that she was right. That should, she judged, be long enough.

Adam stayed just where he was for a few more minutes, but he waited in vain for more movement from the baby. "He must be asleep," Lori finally decided.

Adam grinned with renewed wonder. "It's hard to imagine he sleeps and wakes up in there."

"Don't forget he also kicks," Lori reminded him, returning his grin.

His gaze met hers, and suddenly the warmth in his eyes

became heat of a very different sort. The hand on her stomach which had been as impersonal as a handshake had begun to caress her.

The instant she was certain of his intention, she felt the instinctive resistance tighten within her, the resentment that he was going to take possession of her body. Why did she still feel that resentment? This was *Adam,* not his brother. Adam who had never hurt her and never would. She was a fool to let that other one come between them. Ruthlessly, she squelched those feelings and concentrated on responding to him as his hand moved in ever-widening circles.

And then she remembered something very important.

"Adam," she began, "Sudie said . . ." Her breath caught as his fingers grazed the apex of her thighs through the fabric of her skirts.

"What did Sudie say?" he asked, knowing full well what he was doing to her and taking great pleasure in the knowledge.

"She said that the . . . the last two months we can't . . ."

"Can't what?" he prodded, but he kissed her then so she couldn't answer him right away. When he was finished kissing her, she'd almost forgotten what she'd been about to say.

Almost.

"She said," Lori continued breathlessly and determinedly, "that for the last two months we can't make love."

She saw the consternation flicker across his beloved features, but then he grinned again. "Well, then, since that's not for a few weeks yet, I think we should take advantage of every opportunity remaining to us."

He pushed himself to his feet, taking great care so he wouldn't stumble or appear clumsy before her. Then he offered her his hand and drew her to her feet.

"How is it possible," he asked, cupping her face in both his hands, "that you're even more beautiful now than when I married you?"

Dear heavens, he thought she was *beautiful!* Her heart

seemed to swell in her chest as a dozen different emotions warred within her for preeminence. What had she ever done to deserve such happiness? And how could she ever repay it? Without thinking, she offered him the one thing she had yet to give him. "Oh, Adam, I love you so much!"

She'd expected surprise, but not the flicker of pain she saw deep in his eyes. He smiled, but the expression did not reach those eyes.

"Do you now?" he asked as if he didn't believe her, but he didn't wait for her reply. "Whatever have I done to deserve such a tribute? Oh, I know," he said, pretending he had just discovered the answer. "And if you'll come along with me to our bedroom, Mrs. Ross, I'll be only too happy to do it again."

Lori made her mouth smile, but she knew her expression of joy was as strained as his and equally as false. Because she had just discovered a very frightening thing about her husband: that no matter how much she might truly love Adam, he didn't believe that she did.

Why he should doubt her, she had no idea, just as she had no idea how to convince him of the truth.

Fight and wait. Fight and wait. If Eric had only known what war was really like. After their victory at the Las Rucias ranch house, the Cavalry of the West had been kicking their heels for almost a month, sweating and sweltering in the mid-summer heat, but now they were finally moving toward Brownsville. Surely, this would be the end. They'd slaughter the Yankees and drive them into the sea, just like they'd driven them into the river the last time. At Las Rucias, only eight Union cavalrymen had escaped, and this time there'd be no river to cross to safety.

All around him, boys and old men were coughing and swaying in their saddles. Some of them had swamp fever, others dysentery or worse. Old Rip Ford himself hadn't been able to climb into his saddle this morning without help, but once astride, he'd stayed put. If he could ride, his men would do no less.

Eric reached into his coat and took a quick nip from the flask he'd concealed there. He figured the whiskey he'd managed to buy or steal was what had protected him so far from the various diseases that were plaguing this army, so a little fortification was always in order.

As he glanced up and down the line of grim, gray and ragged men, he grinned. They sure as hell didn't look very dangerous, but God help any Yankees who got in their way.

A while back, they'd had a brief, screaming battle and driven the Union screening forces back to the Brownsville city limits. Having outrun their supply line—again!—they'd had to wait almost two weeks for it to catch up, sitting on their side of the river across from the city. At first they'd been surprised to see civilians coming toward them, wading through the river carrying white flags. Traders, they'd thought at first, until the men arrived. But they were citizens, the ones who'd been too old for the regular army and had remained behind. One of them had actually fought at San Jacinto almost thirty years ago. And they were all volunteering to fight with Ford.

Rip Ford had earned his nickname years earlier as a Texas Ranger. His job then had been to compile the lists of the Rangers killed in the line of duty. At the end of each list, he'd written "Rest in Peace." But as the lists got longer, he began to abbreviate the sentiment "RIP."

Showalter's troops were at the front of the line, marching on foot, and the line halted while they did a quick reconnaissance of the town.

"What's taking so damn long?" one of his boys wanted to know as they stood around, resting their saddles.

Several of them had sunk wearily to the ground and a few were even lying flat, their faces flushed and damp with fever. Eric wanted to kick them. What did they think they were doing, getting sick just when they were facing the final showdown?

"It's awful quiet, Lieutenant," another of the boys pointed out. "What do you think that means?"

"It means we've got those Yankees scared shitless," Eric was glad to report. "I remember at Antietam—"

"I hope to hell they ain't run off," the first boy said, cutting Eric off before he could manufacture a story for them. "I never even got to fire my gun the other day. How can I kill Yankees if I never shoot my gun?"

Eric glared at them, but they didn't seem to notice. And certainly, they didn't care that he was annoyed with them. Then he remembered the purchase he'd made last night from one of Showalter's men, a sure fire way to get their attention and keep it.

"Hey, you boys want to see some pictures?" he asked.

"What kind of pictures?" a boy wanted to know. Plainly, he wasn't too interested.

"Pictures of women," he reported, gratified to see them all look at him now. Even the sick ones perked up, pushing up on their elbows.

"Let's see," the boy challenged, as if he didn't believe Eric had such pictures. The son of a bitch.

"What have you got to trade?" Eric challenged back.

"How do we know these pictures is worth a trade?"

Eric grinned. "Because the women in these pictures don't have no clothes on."

The pictures had cost him a bottle of whiskey, but they'd been worth it. Just the expressions on the boys' faces was enough. "Line up now. Hurry, or we'll be moving again and you'll miss your chance."

The boys began digging in their pockets for something that might be considered worthy of trade, and a few enterprising ones came forward immediately.

"Oh, they's *drawed,*" the first boy in line complained of the erotic sketches.

"What'd you expect, a tintype of a real naked woman?" the second one scolded. "If you don't want your turn, get out of the way!"

As the boys crowded around, jostling for position, Eric smiled benignly. "Soon's we get to Brownsville, we'll find us a real woman," he promised. "Then you boys won't need pictures anymore."

Eric had expected a cheer or at least some grins, but instead he only received several startled looks, and most of the boys wouldn't even look at him at all. What the hell was wrong with them?

Before he could figure it out, the word came down the line: the Yankees were gone from Brownsville. They'd fled across the river to Brazos Island, a barren strip of sand that nobody in his right mind would want to fight for, leaving behind a trail of scattered equipment leading toward the coast from Fort Brown.

The men moaned in disappointment.

"Look at it this way, boys," Eric advised them. "At least you won't be tuckered out from fighting when we find that woman."

But he got no knowing grins in reply. In fact, all the boys studiously avoided looking at him. Alex was the only one who would meet his eye. The little bastard actually glared at him. "We won't be goin' with you this time, Lieutenant."

Eric glanced around in fury. "You gonna let this sissy speak for the lot of you?" he demanded.

A long moment passed during which Eric felt his remaining power over them draining away.

Finally, Alex said, "I reckon they are, Lieutenant. If'n you want a woman, you'll have to find one on your own."

Lori was so happy. She hadn't been happy since the day she'd learned her father had been killed in a battle so unimportant that it didn't even have a name. Not until today, at least. Because today she'd found out that Adam loved her.

He'd sent her a letter.

"My dearest Lori," it began, and Lori flushed with pleasure each time she recalled how he had addressed her. "I'm sure you must have noticed my great admiration for you. For years I have been satisfied to admire you from afar, but I believe the time has come to tell you in person just how much you mean to me. You will make me the happiest man alive if you will meet me by the oak tree that marks the boundary of our properties at three o'clock this afternoon. Until then, I remain your devoted servant, Adam Ross."

Now she was waiting for him, waiting for him to come to her, and then she saw him. He was riding a horse, coming quickly over the fields, and her heart began to thunder with excitement. He couldn't wait to get to her! He was as eager as she! She could hardly breathe, and for a moment she was afraid she would faint, but she wasn't going to faint because she was too strong for that. Oh, no, she wasn't going to faint ever again.

She wasn't sure exactly when she realized something was wrong. She should have known immediately, of course, because Adam never rode horseback. And because she knew Adam would never have sent her a note. He would have told her himself if he wanted to meet her. In fact, he would have called on her at her house. He would have asked Bessie for permission, and he would have come to visit. She knew that because she wasn't a foolish, silly girl. She was smart and she was brave, and she wasn't afraid when she realized the man riding toward her was Eric Ross instead.

He climbed down from his horse, and he was smiling, an evil kind of smile that made Lori furious because he thought he was going to hurt her. But he couldn't hurt her. Didn't he know that?

"You're mine," he told her, reaching for her, but she batted his hands away.

"Don't touch me!" she cried and began to hit him. She slapped and punched and kicked and then she had a stick and she began to beat him with it. He cowered before her, screaming in terror, trying to cover his head as she beat him to his knees.

"Don't hurt me!" he begged her over and over. "Please don't hurt me!"

But she kept hitting him and kicking him, feeling the blows vibrate through her body, then lifting her stick to strike another one.

And then he was laughing, just the way Adam had said he'd laughed that terrible day when he'd crippled his brother. He was looking up at her and laughing and no matter how many times she hit him, he just kept laughing. And that was when she remembered the gun, and then it was in her hand. Cold and heavy, and he just kept laughing because he didn't think she would shoot him, but she would, she knew she would because she was stronger than he was and she would win.

She lifted the pistol, holding it tightly in both hands. She aimed for his head, using the site as her father had taught her, centering it on his forehead, and then the gun exploded in her hands. But there wasn't any smoke, not any at all, so she could see that she'd shot him all right, but not in the head. She'd shot him in the leg, and he was rolling on the ground, bleeding and screaming and writhing in agony.

And Lori looked down at him, and she laughed.

She woke herself laughing, a strangled sound deep in her throat because she was really asleep and startled herself before she could actually laugh out loud. She opened her eyes to the first gray light of morning and an amazing sense of triumph.

The dream was ridiculous, of course. She could never hurt anyone the way she had hurt Eric in the dream, and she could certainly never shoot anyone. Where on earth had that come from? Revenge for Adam, she supposed, thrown in on top of her own. Revenge for both of them. It was so sweet, she only wished she could share it with her husband. He was sleeping beside her, one arm thrown over her as if to hold her in place. She could wake him up and . . .

But he didn't like for her to speak of Eric. And he wouldn't understand, anyway. Nobody would understand, except maybe Sudie. Lori would have to tell her all about the dream first thing. Each time she'd had it, she'd managed to make it end more satisfactorily. Sudie would want to know she'd finally managed to shoot Eric.

No, she corrected herself instantly. Not Eric. Sudie must never know he was the one who had attacked her. But she'd want to know Lori had shot her rapist, if only in her dream.

Her relief was almost palpable as she snuggled more closely against Adam. The room was sweltering hot already, so the day promised to be another scorcher, but she still longed for the closeness. She and Adam hadn't been able to make love for several weeks now, and in spite of all the times she had resented his taking possession of her body, now she found she missed the sense of intimacy she experienced only when he was inside of her.

Had she once longed for this respite, thinking she would relish having her body to herself once more? How foolish she'd been, because her body still belonged to another. It had merely passed from her husband's possession to her child's. The last time she and Adam had made love, they had almost given up in frustration because her bulk had nearly made the act impossible. Now she was even more huge and so awkward that even getting up out of a chair was a day's work.

The heat hadn't helped, either. Her hands and feet were so swollen, she couldn't wear shoes, and she'd had to remove her wedding ring. She'd tried not to look at herself in the mirror, but she didn't need to see her reflection to know she looked like a cow. How Adam could stand the sight of her, she had no idea, but at least he still sought her out in the dark of night, pulling her close to him and holding her there.

As she felt his arm tighten around her in sleep, tears came to her eyes, tears of joy and gratitude for the wonderful man who had married her. She'd had no idea anyone could be so good and so kind and so unselfish. Perhaps, she prayed, someday she would be worthy of him.

That bastard Showalter was drunk again. All the men were whispering about how he'd let a Union wagon train escape because he'd been too drunk to understand what was happening and give the orders to attack.

Well, what did they expect a man to do? Eric wondered bitterly. Another month and more had gone by since they'd raised the stars and bars over Brownsville, and not a Yankee in sight. Old Rip Ford had stood upright that day just long enough to see the flag raised, and then he'd fallen over in a dead faint. For days he'd lain in bed, too sick with the fever to even sign his name to orders, but he'd had to remain in charge because his senior lieutenant colonel—Showalter— and his chief of staff were both too drunk to take command.

Eric would've been drunk, too, if he could've gotten his hands on enough whiskey at any one time to do the job. Unfortunately, that and everything else was in very short supply. Ford had scattered his forces over the countryside, so they could find forage for their animals, since most of the grass was burned browned by now, so late in the summer. And in the countryside, whiskey and women were as scarce as grass.

To make matters worse, the Mexicans were getting into the fracas. Eric didn't understand and couldn't have cared less about the political situation south of the border, but for some reason one side or the other of the ongoing revolution down there had decided to fight for the Yanks. Probably had something to do with Showalter's troops taking potshots at the Mexicans from their position on Palmito Hill overlooking the river southeast of Brownsville.

Eric couldn't be bothered with figuring it all out. The only thing he knew was that word had come down that he and his men would be riding to reinforce Showalter just in case of trouble. About time, too.

Some of the boys in his company were too sick to sit a horse, so they'd been left behind. Eric was happy to note that Alex, the nasty little bastard, was one of them. Maybe he'd die this time. Eric kept forgetting to shoot him whenever they were in a fight.

They hadn't ridden very far when the sound of big guns shattered the morning stillness. Up ahead they could see the billows of smoke from the Mexican side of the river that told them artillery had opened up on the Confederate troops at Palmito Hill.

Putting the spurs to their horses, they broke into a run, racing to support Showalter and his troops. But they were still several miles from the hill when they saw the troops racing back toward them, running in panic from the attack. It was a hell of a mess, and only afterward did they find out the reason for the panic and retreat: Showalter had been too drunk to command. Again.

George Giddings relieved Showalter on the spot and replaced him with Major Kavanaugh. They managed to stop the retreat and form a defensive line several miles from the hill. But it was too late. Palmito Hill now belonged to the Yankees, and they would control all traffic to and from Mexico.

The Cavalry of the West braced for an attack, but none came. The rain began again and fell so heavily that the Yankees couldn't exploit their victory.

And as he sat in the rain, huddled under a sodden blanket, Eric began to shiver with the fever he had, up until now, managed to avoid. Swearing, he took a pull on his pocket flask, only to find it empty.

* * *

Lori paused in her inventory of the kitchen, putting both hands in the small of her back and stretching to relieve the ache that had settled there. Her back had been aching for weeks, but this was the worst it had ever been.

"I tol' you," Eliza said from where she was kneading bread at the counter. "That baby done dropped."

Several other of the slave women, including Sudie, had made the same observation. She hadn't been sure what it meant, and she still wasn't.

After glancing around to make sure they were alone, she asked, "What does that mean?"

Eliza grinned, showing where she had recently lost a tooth. "It mean that baby be born real soon now."

Dear heaven, Lori hoped so! She no longer cared that it had been less than six months since her marriage. That people would talk and count on their fingers and cluck their tongues. She just wanted to be able to roll over in bed and get up out of a chair and walk across the room again. And she wanted to feel like a woman instead of a cow. And she wanted Adam to look at her without frowning.

And, although she hadn't admitted this to anyone, she wanted to hold her baby in her arms.

Sudie had been right. She no longer hated the child or even resented it. Her feelings had progressed from those to pity to actual affection. The child, as Sudie had told her time and again, couldn't help who his father was or how it had been conceived. He deserved a chance in this life, and he would have one or Lori would die trying to give him one.

How much help Adam would be, she had no way of judging. He'd promised to be a father to the baby and to make sure he didn't grow up bitter and angry the way Eric had. He'd even begun to express an interest in the child. But would he ever be able to look at it without remembering it wasn't his? Or without remembering how it had come to be?

The muscles in her back tightened again, making Lori wince and forcing her to stretch again.

"You lookin' a might poorly, Missy," Eliza observed with a worried frown. "Maybe you best go lay yourself down for a while. I'll fetch Sudie to see you to your room."

"That's all right," Lori insisted with a smile when the spasm had passed and she could speak again. "I don't need help getting to my room!"

But she'd taken no more than a few steps when she felt a rush of warm liquid running down her legs. "Oh, my!" she cried in humiliation. What was happening to her? How could she have lost control when she hadn't even been aware of an urge to relieve herself?

"What's the matter?" Eliza asked in alarm, and then she saw the puddle forming at Lori's feet. "Oh, Lordy, Lordy!" the girl cried and began screaming for Sudie.

"What's wrong? What's happening?" Lori demanded, nearly frantic and certain from Eliza's reaction that it must be something terrible.

But Eliza only smiled again. "I reckon your water done broke, Missy. That baby be here before night!"

Eleven

Adam was examining a cotton boll and trying to judge the yield per acre he would get from this field when a young boy came running up to him.

"What is it, Jeremiah?" he asked the panting, sweating child who usually worked in the house.

The boy needed a second to catch his breath, and Adam waited patiently, wondering what on earth could have been so important to send him running on a sweltering day like this. The only thing he could think of was Lori . . .

Dear God, what was wrong with him? "Is it Miss Lori?" he demanded of the boy who nodded vigorously.

"Sudie," he managed to gasp. "She sendin' the buggy . . ."

But Adam wasn't going to wait for the buggy. He began to run himself, or at least to move as quickly as his bad leg and the rough ground allowed him to.

It was the baby, it must be. She'd said the middle of September but two weeks either way, and this was only a week short of the middle of the month. So it had to be the baby. Unless . . .

Dear God, don't let anything be wrong with Lori! he prayed frantically as another thought occurred to him, one he hadn't even let himself consider until this moment. *Please let her be all right!*

Visions of his mother suddenly appeared in his head, visions of her lying on her deathbed, too delirious to even know she'd had a baby, too weak to even squeeze Adam's hand as he stood beside her bed, begging her to get better.

He stumbled and almost fell, catching himself just in time. Up ahead he could see the buggy rattling toward him, but he didn't stop. He kept on going, oblivious of the searing pain in his leg, oblivious of everything except his desperate need to make sure Lori was all right.

Somehow, he finally reached the buggy, but Oscar wouldn't let him drive. He practically hauled Adam onto the seat, then he whipped the horse into a run again.

"Is she all right?" Adam demanded of Oscar as he clung to the handstrap to keep from being flung out.

"The baby comin'," Oscar reported with a grin, and Adam sagged back against the seat in relief. At least for a moment. Because no sooner had he felt that relief than he remembered that his mother had come through Eric's birth just fine. It was only later that she'd sickened and died.

"Can't you hurry?" Adam cried.

"Sudie say ain't no hurry," Oscar informed him. "First babies usually takes they time."

Adam didn't care. He grabbed the whip out of Oscar's hand and snapped it over the horse's back just the same.

After what seemed an interminable time, they finally arrived at the house. Adam jumped out of the buggy before it was completely stopped, nearly falling in the process. Ignoring Oscar's cry of alarm and the searing pain in his leg, he staggered into the house, bellowing for Sudie.

One of the maids, he didn't even notice which one, met him in the hallway.

"Sudie say you should wait in the parlor, Massa," she reported, but he brushed her aside and kept going, down the hall and through the house until he reached his bedroom door.

The door was closed tightly, but Adam threw it open, not certain what he expected to see. What he did see nearly stopped his heart.

Lori was on the bed, her hands tied to the headboard, her body hunched, and her beautiful face contorted in agony. Several slave women hovered over her, but none of them was doing a damn thing for her!

"Lori!" he cried, knowing he had to do something but not certain exactly what that might be.

The slave women all turned to face him, although Lori hadn't seemed to hear him at all.

"What you doin' in here, Massa?" Sudie demanded, closing on him with that look that used to mean he was going to get a licking. "Didn't Effie tell you to stay in the parlor?"

"What's going on? What's the matter with her?" Adam demanded right back, terrified to see that Lori's face was scarlet and sweating. Did she have a fever already?

"She havin' a baby, and she don't want no man around watchin' her do it!" Sudie scolded him. "Now you get yourself out of here right now! Didn't I teach you better manners than to go where you ain't wanted?"

"Get him out of here!" Lori's voice cried in near hysteria. "I don't want him to see me like this!"

" 'Course you don't, sugar," Sudie soothed, then turned back to Adam with an ugly glare. "Come on, right now!"

Grabbing his arm, she hustled him back out into the hall and slammed the door shut behind them.

"What's the matter with you?" she asked, glaring up at him as if he were still ten years old. "Don't you know a birthin' ain't no place for a man?"

"She's in pain," Adam told her indignantly. "Why aren't you doing something for her?"

" 'Course she in pain. She havin' a baby, and we doin' everything we can," Sudie insisted. "Now you just get yourself back to the parlor and sit yourself down to wait. That's about all you can do right now."

"I'll send for the doctor," Adam decided, knowing he couldn't just sit idly by.

"What for you do that?" Sudie scoffed. "By the time he

get here, it be all over. I already done sent for her stepmother.
Ain't nothin' no doctor can do that we can't do just as good."

She was probably right, but still . . . "Is she going to be
all right, Sudie?" he asked as the terror gripped his heart,
turning it cold as ice.

Sudie looked at him curiously, as if she'd just discovered
something very interesting about him. "I can't make no
promises, Massa. I just do what I can."

With that, she turned and went back inside, leaving him
standing there gaping. And still completely terrified.

What was he going to do if something happened to Lori?
How could he survive? And why in God's name would he
even want to?

Lori could no longer remember anything except the pain.
It came and it went but it was the only thing left in her life.
She couldn't remember what had come before or even why
she was here, suffering the torments of hell, and she was
much too exhausted to even try.

The pain was starting again, coming on her in a wave that
started as a tightening and ended in agony. Bessie was on
one side of her and Sudie on the other. They were saying
things to her, but she couldn't understand them and didn't
have the strength to figure out what they were telling her to
do. She only had strength for the pain and living through it
until the next few moments, however brief, when it was gone
again.

"You doin' real good, Missy," Sudie told her as she gasped
for breath. She mopped Lori's face with a cool rag that felt
wonderful against her super-heated skin. Her nightdress
clung wetly, soaked with her sweat. "I can see the head now."

"Look at all that hair," Bessie exclaimed.

"Once more now, Missy. Give us a push for all you're
worth!"

Lori would have cursed her, if she'd had the strength. She'd already been pushing for all she was worth for hours now. This was never going to end, not ever. She was going to die in agony.

Then the pain came again, swelling up inside of her on a crimson tide that seemed to envelop her. Vaguely, she could hear Bessie and Sudie urging her on as she strained against it.

"Get a blanket!" Sudie cried in the blissful seconds when the pain subsided, but before Lori was ready, it came again. Only this time when she pushed she felt release as the tiny body slipped from her.

"Looky here, Missy!" Sudie cried, lifting the small creature up for her to see. "You got yourself a boy!"

Only when he noticed that the room was dark did Adam realize how much time had passed since he had been summoned from the fields. Checking his watch, he calculated how long he'd been waiting without any word at all about Lori.

His dinner sat on a tray nearby, untouched and forgotten, and he'd sent Effie away when she'd tried to bring him supper, too. How much longer could this go on?

Not for the first time he considered storming back down the hall and demanding to know what was happening. Only when he remembered how Lori had screamed for him to leave the room did he hesitate.

For hours he had tortured himself with visions of her in pain, sick and pale with the life draining out of her. What would he do if she died? How would he go on?

He had no idea, and that terrified him. When had this happened to him? When had Lori become the most important thing in his life?

Because she was. He may only have realized it now that he was in danger of losing her, but he understood the truth of it as he had never understood anything else before. It didn't make any sense, of course. She was nothing—not educated, not cultured, not even truly beautiful, and certainly not the kind of woman worthy of being his life's partner. But somehow none of that mattered anymore. Because she *was* his life's partner and the woman he wanted beside him until the day he died. Not just in his bed, either, but beside him to share every joy and sorrow that he would have to face in his allotted three-score-years-and-ten.

He no longer cared that she had loved Eric and had wanted his brother instead of him. He no longer cared that Eric had known her first or even that she carried Eric's child. He could forgive her everything. He could forgive her *anything* if only she would live.

He paced around the parlor, savoring the pain in his leg, grateful for the distraction from the pain in his heart and the desperate fear in his soul. Finally the sound of a footstep in the hall caught his attention. He was halfway to the parlor door when Sudie appeared in the doorway.

"How is she?" he demanded before Sudie could open her mouth.

"She just fine," Sudie assured him with a smile. "Her and the baby *both* fine."

But Adam didn't care about the baby, just so long as it was born and Lori's suffering was over.

"Are you sure? She's really all right?"

"I's sure," Sudie said with a grin.

"Can I see her now?" He couldn't trust anything except his own eyes.

"I expect you can," Sudie began, but he didn't wait to hear what else she might have to tell him. He had already brushed past her and was heading down the hall.

The bedroom door stood ajar, and as eager as he was, he felt himself hesitate. What if she still didn't want him to see her? What if Sudie had been lying to him? What if she was ill or dying? What if . . . ?

The door swung open, and Bessie stood there, grinning up at him. "You go on in, Mr. Ross," she told him.

Figuring that was all the invitation he needed, he stepped into the room, his gaze immediately finding Lori in the big bed they had shared these past few months.

He'd braced himself for just about anything, but he found her sitting propped up against the pillows and looking fresh and radiant and more beautiful than he had even remembered. Her hair had been brushed back from her face and was tied with a ribbon, and she wore a frilly nightdress. Her face was no longer red or sweating or contorted in agony. She might simply have been taking an afternoon rest. And then she smiled at him.

The smile was tentative, as if she feared his reaction, but Adam didn't bother to wonder why she might. He was simply too relieved and grateful to see her alive and apparently well. He hurried over to the bed, not even bothering to disguise his limp. He opened his mouth to speak but found his throat was too tight to release any words just yet, so he contented himself with simply looking at her.

Vaguely, he was aware that Bessie had left, closing the door behind her, but he didn't even spare her a glance.

"Adam," Lori said, and he was amazed at how normal her voice sounded. "This is Matthew."

Only then did he notice the bundle she held in her arms and which she had tilted up so he could see.

He glanced down and was surprised to see a tiny face nestled in the blanket. It was small and red and hideously ugly and crowned with a thick black fuzz of hair.

"Matthew?" he repeated stupidly, trying to comprehend what that meant. "It's a boy," he decided.

To his additional amazement, the tiny eyes snapped open at the sound of his voice and looked straight at him.

"Look," Lori exclaimed happily. "He *does* recognize your voice!"

Adam was still sure that was impossible—probably the

child was just responding to the deepness of Adam's voice—but he still couldn't seem to tear his gaze away from the child's. Its eyes were so blue and were staring at him raptly, as if he couldn't get enough of looking at Adam.

"Sit down," Lori invited, patting the bed beside her with her free hand.

"Are you sure? I don't want to . . . to cause you any discomfort." He spoke to Lori but kept looking at the baby who kept looking right back at him.

"Of course I'm sure," Lori said, and Adam very carefully hoisted himself up onto the high mattress beside her. He turned to face her, pulling his bad leg up with both hands.

He wanted to hold her. He wanted to pull her into his arms and crush her to him and never let her go. But he also didn't want to hurt her. And there was the baby to consider, too. He glanced back down to find it was still staring at him hungrily.

"Why is he looking at me?" Adam asked.

"Because he knows . . ." Lori hesitated a moment, but when he glanced up at her she hurried on. "Because he knows you're his father." Her mouth was smiling, but her eyes were shadowed, as if she were asking him a question and wasn't sure of the answer.

But she should have been. Hadn't he repeatedly assured her he would treat the child as if it were his own? But of course that had been before, back when the child was merely a possibility. Now it was a reality, lying in Lori's arms. And she was waiting for him to accept that reality.

He somehow managed a smile, even though he felt the old twinges of jealousy over all that had happened in the past. But hadn't he sworn none of that would matter if Lori survived? Hadn't he bargained with God for her life using promises of his own? Promises that he would forgive and forget it all? And here was Lori, alive and apparently well, at least for the moment, so he had a debt to repay.

He dropped his gaze to the child again. "He's awfully small," he observed, unable to think of anything kinder.

Lori laughed with apparent relief. "That's how babies come," she told him happily. "But he'll grow. Isn't he beautiful?"

Beautiful was not the word Adam would have chosen. He pretended to consider the question, instinctively reaching out to push the blanket back from the child's face to get a closer look while he tried in vain to think of an appropriate reply. In the process, his finger brushed the child's tiny hand, and instantly, the five even tinier fingers closed around his much larger one in a surprisingly fierce grip.

Adam gasped in surprise, and oddly, he felt the sting of tears behind his eyes, although why having a baby grab his finger should make him want to weep, he had no idea. Perhaps it was just a reaction from being so worried for so long and now being so relieved. But the child didn't let go of his finger, and he also kept staring at Adam, as if he expected something from him.

Perhaps he did. Perhaps he understood in a way Adam would never understand just who Adam was to him. Perhaps he was trying in some primitive way to reach out to him. To win his heart. To make Adam accept him. Because if he didn't . . .

A vision of a laughing twelve-year-old Eric standing over him as he writhed in agony flashed across Adam's mind, and he knew he could never allow this child to become like Eric.

"I think he wants you to hold him," Lori said, and Adam didn't bother to question the logic of her assumption. Probably *she* wanted Adam to hold him, in hopes of fostering some sort of bond between them. In any case, he did not resist when she placed the child in the crook of his arm.

The baby still held his finger tightly, as if he was afraid to let go, and his large blue eyes continued to stare. When he blinked, he reminded Adam of an owl, wise and old beyond his years. Did babies know when they weren't wanted?

When their very existence was a trial to be borne rather than a joy to be experienced? Could they sense to whom they must apply for acceptance? If so, then this child was a master of the art.

As he stared down into the baby's huge blue eyes, he felt something inside of him growing oddly warm. And when he realized how very small the baby truly was—dear God, he hardly filled Adam's arm and surely he weighed no more than a loaf of bread!—and how strongly his fingers were still gripping Adam's, he was well and truly lost.

"Hello, Matthew," he heard himself say, even though he knew the child couldn't possibly understand him.

To his astonishment, the baby opened his mouth, and for one brief second, Adam actually thought he was going to reply! But the opening grew larger and in the next second, Adam realized the baby was simply yawning.

"Oh, look," Lori said fondly. "He's sleepy. He should be. He worked hard today."

Unable to tear his gaze from the child's face—why did he look so much like an old man when he was so very young?—Adam watched as the large blue eyes grew heavy and then, finally, slid closed. In a few more seconds, the grip on his finger loosened, and he knew the child was asleep.

Even still, Adam couldn't tear his gaze away from the little face. The wonder of it—how something so small could be alive—and the enormity of the obligation he had toward this tiny being were nearly overwhelming.

For a few seconds, Adam couldn't seem to get his breath, and once again he felt the sting of tears. He blinked furiously against it, and only when he had successfully mastered it did he dare to look up at Lori, only to discover that *she* was crying.

"Oh, Adam," she said, as the tears ran down her perfect cheeks.

"Oh, my God, what is it? What's wrong?" he demanded in instant terror. "Sudie said . . . but she was lying, wasn't she? I should have sent for the doctor! He'd be here by now—"

"Adam, what on earth are you talking about?" Lori asked as she wiped the tears from her face with the edge of the sheet that covered her legs.

"Sudie said you were all right! She said you were both fine, but you're not, are you? Something's wrong! You're sick, aren't you? Tell me, Lori! I have to know the truth!"

But she was shaking her head. "I'm not sick, and the baby isn't, either. I'm tired, of course," she admitted with an embarrassed smile. "I don't think I ever worked that hard in my life, but . . ."

"You'll never work again, either," Adam promised rashly. "You'll never have to turn your hand. We have plenty of slaves here to do whatever needs to be done, and Sudie can run the house. She always has before, and there's no reason you have to exert yourself."

Lori's smile was puzzled. "I'm not *that* tired, Adam. Sudie said I'd be up and around in two weeks, as good as new."

"And we'll get a wet nurse for the baby," he insisted as if he hadn't heard her. "I know you don't want one, but that can't be good for you, taking care of a baby when you're so weak—"

"I'm not *weak*, just tired!" she insisted right back. "And as soon as I get a good night's sleep, I'll be fine!"

"And I don't care what Sudie says, I'll send for the doctor just to be sure there's nothing wrong. Sometimes it takes a few days to . . . Well, you can't be too careful."

Lori's confusion gave way to understanding as she finally figured out what he was talking about. "Like your mother, you mean."

"You aren't going to die, Lori," he said, and although he had meant the words as a command, they came out as a plea.

Her tears were flowing again, and Adam felt the moisture in his own eyes and was powerless to stop it this time.

"Of course I won't die, Adam," she said, laying a hand

on his cheek. Her fingers felt cool in spite of the heat, and he turned his face into her palm and kissed it.

With a little cry, she came to him then, sliding across the bed and wrapping him and the baby he still held in her arms.

She was crying, sobbing really, against his shoulder, although he couldn't figure out why she should be weeping. And he was trying *not* to weep, because he didn't want to appear unmanly and because he didn't want her to suspect how very much she had come to mean to him.

He cradled her with his free arm, marveling at how slender she suddenly was. It had been so long, he'd almost forgotten what she really felt like in his arms. It hadn't been so very long since he'd kissed her, but he'd forgotten how wonderful she tasted too, even tinged with the salt of her tears. He covered her mouth with his, determined to lose himself in her once and for all. But he never got the chance.

"Now, now, none of that just yet," Bessie scolded.

Adam jumped guiltily, although why he should feel guilty for kissing his own wife, he had no idea.

"Lori needs her rest now," Bessie reminded him. He looked over to see she was carrying a tray of food, then realized Lori would have missed her supper, too.

Reluctantly, he allowed Lori to straighten away from him, although she clung to his hand with both of hers. When he looked at her, she wasn't crying anymore. Instead she was smiling as she lifted his hand to her lips and kissed the back of it.

"Thank you, Adam," she whispered as Bessie carried the tray around to the other side of the bed.

"For what?" he asked.

Her smile grew radiant, and for the first time Adam could almost believe that she really did love him. "For being the man that you are."

* * *

Eric huddled under his blankets, shivering so hard his teeth were chattering in spite of the sweltering heat. Damn them. Damn them all! Damn Rip Ford and his goddamned army and the Yankees and the Rebs and the Mexicans—every last stinking one of them. And especially damn those people back home who made out that he was some kind of coward because he hadn't gone off like a damn fool to fight in this damn stupid war! Who in the hell were *they* to judge?

Eric wasn't a coward! Hadn't he stood up to the old man every day of his life? Hadn't he taken everything the old man could give him and gone back for more? Eric wasn't afraid of *anything!*

Somebody was coming around with a bucket of water, offering it to the men who were lying here, shaking with fever. If he'd been able to get up, Eric would have gone over and wrested the ladle away from that stupid bastard. He couldn't get up, though, so he had to wait until the stupid bastard came to him. Offering him a ladle that was only half-full.

Eric dashed the water in the boy's ugly face. "What the hell's the matter with you?" Eric demanded hoarsely. "Can't you even fill a dipper?"

"What the hell's the matter with you?" the boy replied angrily. "Can't you drink what I give you?"

Before Eric could guess his intent, the boy was moving on to the next man. "Come back here, you son of a bitch! I want a drink!"

"People in hell want water, too," the boy told him with an evil grin, wiping the water from his face with his forearm.

Eric cursed him with every curse he knew until the chills took him again and his teeth started chattering so hard he could no longer speak.

Damn him. Damn them all. He curled himself into a ball, trying vainly for a warmth he couldn't find. If only he was home. If he was at Elmhurst, Sudie would take care of him. Sudie would bring him water and soup and she would feed it to him with a spoon. She would sponge him off when he was hot and she would heat stones and wrap them in flannel and put them in his bed when he was chilled. Sudie would never let him suffer like this, he thought, as the chill passed and the fever returned with a vengeance, forcing him to throw off the blanket he'd been so frantically clutching just moments ago.

Water! He needed water! But when he tried to call for it, he could only make an incoherent croak. Damn that boy, he'd kill him when he was able. He'd kill them all.

He closed his eyes, and Sudie was there. She was smiling down at him and sponging his head with a cool rag. He tried to say her name, but as he watched, her face changed and her hair changed and everything changed and she wasn't Sudie anymore. She was Lori McClintock.

Lori McClintock with her dark curls and her lush breasts and her white thighs. Lori McClintock, the sweetest little piece he'd ever had. And now Lori was sponging his fevered brow and smiling down at him and Eric was reaching up, reaching and reaching and he almost had her, but then she was gone, evaporating into a fever haze.

Damn it, Lori, come back! But she didn't come back. She couldn't, because she wasn't here. And Eric wasn't going to be here much longer, either. Because as soon as he was able to sit a horse, he was getting the hell out of here. He was going back home. To Elmhurst. And to Lori McClintock.

Lori couldn't believe she was so happy. As she sat in the rocking chair, her child suckling greedily at her breast, she considered how wonderful her new life was and tried to decide what on earth she had ever done to deserve such joy.

She looked up when the bedroom door opened and smiled when she saw Adam come in. He returned her smile, although he was trying to look stern and disapproving when he saw what she was doing.

"It's been over six weeks," Adam reminded her, closing the door behind him.

"I know, you told me that yesterday, and the day before," she said. She'd finally gotten Adam to agree to let her nurse the baby herself for a few weeks. Wisely, she hadn't specified how *many* weeks.

"Sudie's getting mad at me. Says I can't control my own wife. Are you going to shame me in front of my servants?" he asked in mock consternation.

"I just want to have him all to myself a little longer," Lori argued. "If I give him to a wet nurse—"

"You can see him whenever you want," Adam reminded her. "He'll still be your son."

He came over to her and took the hand she offered him and kissed the lips she lifted to him. Every day she thought she couldn't love him any more than she already did, and every day she found out she could.

"Enjoying your dinner, Matt?" he asked, grabbing one of the baby's bare feet and giving it an affectionate tweak.

The baby opened his eyes to acknowledge his father but never faltered in his avid sucking.

"Would you like to share, young man?" he asked, and before Lori realized what he was doing, he leaned over and planted a kiss on the smooth slope of her bare breast.

"Adam!" Lori scolded, scandalized.

"You can't blame me for taking what I can," he informed her unrepentantly. "Do you know how long it's been?"

She knew exactly, and blushed at the reminder. She'd grown comfortable with celibacy or thought she had until the past few days. Last night she'd even dreamed . . . Well, it was too embarrassing even to remember, and she felt the color coming to her cheeks.

"Oh, look, Matt, your mama's blushing! I hope it's with shame for making her poor husband live like a monk."

Lori didn't know what a monk was, but she could guess he didn't have a wife to satisfy his needs. But she had a secret, one she wasn't quite ready to share with Adam. After her dream last night, she'd discussed the matter with Sudie, who had given her permission to welcome her husband back into her bed again.

At the very thought, she felt a familiar warmth settle into the pit of her stomach. Perhaps she should tell Adam now, give him something to look forward to, something to make him happy.

But he was already happy, if the expression of adoration on his face was any indication.

"I think somebody's asleep and doesn't want to admit it," he observed, and she looked down to find the baby was still sucking but only faintly and out of instinct. His tiny body was limp in sleep. Feeling a rush of love, she stroked his silky cheek before removing her nipple from his mouth.

She heard Adam's sharp intake of breath at the sight of it, and she waited an extra few seconds before covering herself again, just so he could enjoy the sight of her.

Only when she had pulled her bodice back over her nakedness did she venture a glance up at Adam, and she was pleased to see the unmistakable glow of desire in his eyes. He still wanted her, perhaps more than ever.

Once again, she had the urge to tell him, and once more she hesitated. No, it would be more fun to make him wait, to tease him all evening with kisses and caresses and then, when he was nearly wild with trying to hold himself back, she would tell him. Yes, that's what she would do.

"Would you put him in his cradle?" she asked, lifting the child to him.

"I don't know if I can handle him anymore," he teased as he took the baby from her. "He's getting as fat as a suckling pig. Sudie said she thinks you're giving cream."

"Sudie should mind her own business," Lori said, half-seriously. She knew Sudie was only doing what she thought was best, and she thought it best that the mistress of the house have a wet nurse for her baby.

She would have to give in soon, though, she knew. Adam wouldn't like sharing his bed with a damp, squalling baby, even one of whom he was as fond as he appeared to be of Matthew.

He cradled the baby in the crook of one arm and gazed down at him affectionately. "How many chins do you think he has now?" he asked with mock seriousness. "I'm afraid I've lost count."

"He's not that fat!" Lori protested as she buttoned her bodice.

"Your mama isn't exactly unbiased in her judgment," he told the sleeping baby as he carried him to his cradle. With amazing tenderness, he bent over and laid the child in the cradle, then covered him with a thin blanket. Summer was officially over, and while the air was still warm, no one wanted to take a chance on Matthew catching a chill.

When the baby was covered, Adam ran his hand over the baby's small body, smoothing the blanket, or at least that's what she thought he was doing until she realized he was actually caressing the baby. Gently. Tenderly. Lovingly. The way a father would caress his child. His *own* child. Lori fought the urge to weep with joy.

Finally, he straightened again, and when he turned back to face her, his expression was troubled.

"Is something wrong?" she asked, getting up and going to him as her joy instantly turned to alarm.

He smiled or tried to. "No, not *wrong*," he assured her, glancing down at the baby again. "It's just . . . I didn't expect to feel this way. About the baby, I mean."

"And how do you feel?" she asked warily, not really certain she wanted to know *exactly* how he felt about the baby.

His grin was sheepish. "I feel like his father."

"You *are* his father, Adam," Lori assured him as her heart swelled with joy and gratitude. "In every way that matters! You're the only father he'll ever know."

And he was, because Eric wasn't coming back. He was never coming back. Hadn't Adam promised her that?

"You told me once that you wanted us to be a family," Adam reminded her. "I think we are one. At least, I feel like we are."

"Oh, Adam!" Lori cried and wrapped her arms around him, pulling him close. He felt so blessedly familiar, so strong and warm and wonderful, and she loved him more than life itself. She'd tried telling him before, but he hadn't seemed to believe her then. Perhaps now . . .

She looked up at him. "I love you so much, Adam," she said, praying the truth of it showed on her face. Praying he would believe her.

He cupped her face in both his hands, as if she were infinitely precious to him, and he said, "I love you, too."

Tears sprang to her eyes, tears of a happiness so great, she didn't think her body could contain it. With a cry of joy, she kissed him, wishing she could show him in every way how much she loved him.

And then she remembered that she could.

Instantly, her kiss became more carnal as she surrendered to the desires she had been feeling for days—desires she hadn't really believed herself capable of feeling after what Eric had done to her. But that was over now, all over, as if it had never happened, as if Adam was the only man who had ever touched her. Adam had made everything right again, and she would reward him with the passion he had created in her.

But before she could, Adam pulled away, gasping for breath and half-laughing but pulling away, nevertheless. "I'm not a saint, Lori. I can't take much more of this in my present condition," he warned her. "Another kiss like that, and I won't be able to stop."

"You don't have to. You don't have to stop, I mean. Sudie said it was all right if we . . . make love," she admitted, suddenly shy.

Adam's astonishment was almost comic. "Are you sure? Why didn't you tell me?"

"I just did," she reminded him happily, and kissed him again so she wouldn't have to talk about it anymore.

This time when they broke the kiss, they were both gasping. "I don't think I can wait until tonight," he told her hoarsely.

"Then don't," she suggested breathlessly.

He glanced uncertainly at the baby, as if trying to decide what to do about him.

"He'll sleep for hours," she said.

That was all the encouragement Adam needed. "I won't need *hours,* I'm afraid," he said ruefully as he led her to the bed.

He was already unbuttoning his shirt, and Lori quickly unhooked her bodice. The next few minutes were a flurry of clumsily shed clothing that reminded Lori of another time when Adam had been too eager to wait until they were completely undressed. They didn't wait this time, either, and when Adam tumbled her onto the bed, she was still wearing her chemise and stockings and Adam had managed only to completely shed his trousers and shoes.

Their kisses were frantic, their caresses desperate, as they re-learned each other's bodies after months of denial. Desire was a maelstrom of sensations swirling in her, roaring in her ears and scorching her nerve endings and raging in her loins.

By the time he touched her *there,* in her secret spot, she was already wet and aching and too far gone to endure much more. She pulled him to her, needing to feel him inside of her, needing to know that he was as lost as she. So she did what she had never done before and touched him back, wrapping her fingers around his hot, hard shaft.

She had never even been able to consider touching the part of him that was a symbol to her of ugliness and pain, and she'd expected to feel repulsed. But she wasn't repulsed. Instead, she marveled at how smooth it was and how powerful, and when he gasped in reaction, she reveled in the knowledge that she was even more powerful.

She guided him to her before he had any right to believe she would be ready. But she *was* ready, ready and willing and nearly frantic with wanting him. Still he entered her slowly, easing past her lingering soreness to fill the aching void desire had created within her.

She clung to him for a long moment as they simply savored the sensation of being one again, but then the passion flared between them, and all thoughts of tenderness vanished. Their bodies responded instinctively, moving to the ancient rhythms as naturally as if they'd never been apart. Thrusting, striving, clinging, panting, they drove each other to the brink of ecstasy and then fell together into the swirling abyss of release.

They lay in each other's arms for a long time after the exquisite spasms had ceased. Adam shifted his weight so he wasn't crushing her, but he stayed inside of her as long as he could, until he finally grew limp. Even then, he didn't release her but held her to his heart as if he would never let her go.

The last thing she remembered before she slipped into the oblivion of sleep was his whispered confession, "I love you, Lori." The most beautiful words she had ever heard.

Lori awoke with a start and for a moment had no idea what was she doing in bed, half-dressed, in the middle of the afternoon.

And then she remembered. She remembered Adam and how they had made love and how wonderful it had been and how he'd said he loved her. Adam loved her! And he loved Matthew, too. How wrong she had been to think her life was perfect before! But now it was, without a doubt. She was the luckiest woman in the world.

She glanced around and realized with disappointment

that Adam was gone. Of course he was. He couldn't lie abed in the middle of the day. But he'd let her sleep. He'd even covered her up before he left, she noticed with a rush of affection.

But she shouldn't be lying abed in the middle of the day, either! What would the servants think? With a rush of energy—when had she last felt this good?—she threw off the blanket and went to check on the baby. After determining that he was still sleeping soundly, she began to collect the clothes that she and Adam had scattered in their haste.

When she was washed and dressed and certain that no trace of her afternoon of passion remained in her appearance—except perhaps for the glow in her cheeks—she checked the baby one last time and slipped out into the hall, closing the door softly behind her.

Where was Adam? she wondered with a rush of longing. She wanted to see him and touch him and hear his confession of love one more time. She wanted to tell him everything, how she had loved him all her life, how she had dreamed that someday she might be his wife, without ever having any hope that those dreams could come true. And she wanted to tell him how good he was for loving her back and for loving her child and claiming it as his own. While she might never be worthy of such devotion, she would do everything in her power to repay it.

As she walked down the hall, she listened for the sounds of the house, the clues that would tell her where everyone was and what they were doing. But the place was oddly silent, as if everyone were out doing something else. Adam was probably out, too. He might be supervising some chore or other or even lending a hand. There was always so much to do after the harvest to ensure none of the bounty was lost.

She reached the center of the house where the hall to the bedrooms crossed with the hall to the front and back doors. Automatically, she glanced down toward the back door which was the one everyone used. She'd expected to see no one or perhaps a servant. What she saw instead stopped her heart with terror.

A man stood there. A man in ragged clothes with a bushy beard and long, scraggly hair and a shapeless hat. He stood in the open doorway and with the sunlight behind him, she couldn't see his face, but she knew he was someone who shouldn't be here, in her house, in *Adam's* house.

"What are you doing here? What do you want?" she demanded, wondering where everyone was, knowing someone must be near, even though she couldn't hear anyone. Surely, if she screamed, help would be here in moments. And then the man spoke, and Lori's throat closed with terror, and she couldn't scream at all.

"Lori?" he said in surprise, peering at her through the dimness of the hall. "Lori McClintock, is that you?"

That voice! She knew that voice! She'd heard it in a hundred nightmares! And this must be a nightmare, too. She hadn't really awakened just now. She was still asleep and dreaming of the one man she feared most in the world. And now he was coming toward her, and just like in her nightmares, she couldn't move, couldn't run, couldn't even scream!

"Well, now, don't you look fine," he was saying, looking her over as he closed the distance between them with strange, shuffling steps. "What a nice coming home present, to find you waiting right here for me, all fresh and sweet and good enough to eat."

Now she could see his face, his hideous face, half-covered with a filthy beard, and his eyes all rheumy and gleaming wildly and his awful hands, reaching for her, ready to pull her down and—

Someone was screaming, someone far away, and Lori was glad because it had stopped him. Whoever was screaming had stopped him in his tracks, and he was looking at her so strangely, and she remembered then that she was strong now and she didn't have to be afraid of him, so of course he was looking at her strangely.

Then she heard someone running. People were coming. Adam and the slaves would be coming. They would come and they would help her and they would take him away, far, far away, where she would never have to see him again.

And just as they arrived, all shouting at once—"What's going on?" "What is it?" "Who's there?"—Eric fell, crumpling in a heap before her, like a rag doll that could no longer stand alone.

"Oh, dear Lord, Missy!" Sudie cried, taking Lori in her arms as Oscar knelt to look at Eric. "Don't be scared! Oscar, he take that fella out right now! He won't hurt you none! He prob'ly just lookin' for some food! Hush, now, hush!"

Only when Sudie placed her hand over Lori's mouth and the screaming stopped did Lori realize *she* was the one who had been screaming. She wasn't powerless after all! She really *was* strong, and she'd screamed and they'd all come to help her.

The rest of the maids were spilling out of other rooms and rushing in from the kitchen to see what the commotion was about. And then Adam was there, taking her from Sudie and enfolding her in his arms. "What on earth is going on?" he asked before he noticed the man lying on the floor.

"Some tramp come in the house," Sudie told him. "Done scared Miss Lori half to death!"

Some tramp? Was that right? Could Lori have been mistaken?

But Oscar had rolled the man over, and now he looked up at where they all stood above him.

"This here's Massa Eric," he told them in amazement.

Everyone gasped in surprise, and Adam's arms tightened protectively around her, so she knew that he understood and that he would keep her safe.

"Eric?" Sudie echoed in surprise. "My Eric? He come home!" With a cry of joy, she fell to her knees beside him.

"We got to get him into bed! He burnin' up with fever! Oscar, take him right now!"

Oscar had no trouble at all lifting Eric onto his shoulder, and no one seemed to hear Lori's cry of protest as Oscar carried him past her down the hall toward his bedroom.

"Adam!" she cried in supplication, looking up at him, unable to believe he was going to let them bring Eric into the house!

But Adam just looked down at her and said, "It's all right, Lori. There's nothing to be afraid of now. It's just Eric."

That was the moment when Lori realized the beautiful life she'd thought she had was really as fragile as a bubble. It had seemed so perfect, but Adam had just destroyed it with a word.

Twelve

Adam watched Oscar carrying Eric away, trailing Sudie in their wake. She was giving nearly-hysterical instructions to the other maids to fetch hot water and rags and other things she thought she might need to tend to Eric.

Dear God, he hadn't even recognized his own brother! Eric did indeed look like the tramp Lori had taken him for. No wonder she had been so terrified! She was still trembling in his arms. He looked down to find her staring up at him, her eyes still wide with horror.

"You said you'd protect me!" she said. It sounded like an accusation.

"I will," he assured her, figuring she was even more upset than Sudie.

"You said he wouldn't come back!"

What on earth was she talking about? "Who?"

"Eric!" she cried, and he noticed with alarm that her face was ashen.

"I said I didn't *think* he'd be back," he reminded her gently.

"You can't let him stay here! You promised!" she insisted.

So that was it! Now everything made sense. And Adam was gratified to see how reluctant she was to share her home with his brother. If he'd thought she still harbored any tender feelings for Eric, her reaction at this moment would have allayed those fears. "Of course he won't stay here. When he finds out we're married, he won't *want* to stay here!"

"Then why did Oscar take him back to his room? I want him out of here, Adam!"

Her eyes were too bright, her face too pale, and he was very much afraid she was going to faint. He tightened his grip on her arms just in case. "Lori," he said, speaking slowly because she was obviously too upset to understand reason, "Eric is sick. He can't go anywhere at the moment."

"He's not *that* sick! You didn't hear what he said to me! He thinks I'm here for *him!* Adam, you have to send him away! *Please!*" She was gripping the front of his shirt with both hands, nearly frantic, and he had no idea how to calm her.

"You don't have to be afraid of him anymore, Lori," he reminded her. "You're my wife. You're completely safe!"

But she shook her head, her eyes still terrible with a fear he now understood was completely irrational. Before he could reassure her further, however, they both heard the baby crying.

With one last desperate look, she broke away from him and ran down the hall toward the sound. He noticed she swerved to give Eric's door the widest possible berth, as if she was afraid he would come darting out to grab her, and then she continued to flee until she reached their bedroom door and disappeared inside.

Good God, he thought, running a hand through his hair. He'd known Eric had hurt Lori, but that was months ago. She should have forgotten all about it by now. Certainly, she was entitled to be bitter because Eric had gotten her with child and left her destitute and alone in her disgrace. But that was in the past, and she wasn't destitute or alone or disgraced any longer. She was his *wife,* for God's sake. And what he had seen on her face just now had been far more than bitterness. She seemed to be actually *afraid* of Eric, and she also didn't seem willing to take Adam's word that she had nothing to be afraid of.

But perhaps she was just reacting to the fright she'd gotten when she'd thought he was a stranger who had invaded their home. Yes, that must be it. What else could account for her panic? Nothing in Adam's experience, surely.

Sudie stuck her head out of Eric's door. "Massa Adam, he askin' for you!"

Still shaking his head in confusion, Adam made his way to his brother's room.

Lori closed the door tightly behind her and wished desperately that it had a lock. She wouldn't feel safe even then, but she did need a lock, at least. Casting about for something, *anything,* to serve the purpose, she settled on grabbing one of the ladder-backed chairs and wedging it under the doorknob.

Only when she was satisfied that the door was secure did she turn her attention to the baby who was now screaming in his cradle.

"There now, sweetheart, don't cry," she crooned, although she noticed her voice was still shaking and her hands, when she picked him up, where unsteady.

The baby was wet, so Lori forced herself to change his diaper and his wrapper, crooning to him all the while, although he continued to scream with hunger through the entire operation. By the time she'd managed to re-dress him, she felt a little calmer. She settled them both into the rocking chair and opened her bodice, although she couldn't help a glance at the door, just to make sure it was still secure. The thought of Eric coming in and seeing her . . .

But that was ridiculous. Eric was too ill to be going anywhere, wasn't he? Matthew stiffened furiously in her arms, unable to understand why she wasn't offering him her breast. Quickly, guiltily, she opened her bodice and silenced him in an instant.

As the baby began to suckle, Lori's gaze shifted back to the door. For an instant she imagined the knob began to turn, and her heart seemed to stop dead in her chest. But in the next instant she realized she was being an idiot. The knob hadn't moved. The chair was secure. She was safe— for the moment.

But the baby released her nipple and began to howl in protest again. What was wrong? Had Eric's arrival soured her milk? But then she realized that her milk wasn't flowing. She was too tense, too terrified.

Drawing a deep breath, she forced herself to relax and guided Matthew's mouth back to her nipple again. Closing her eyes, she leaned her head back and began to rock, willing her milk to flow and her fears to subside. She couldn't let Eric terrify her anymore. What had become of the strong Lori she had been these past few months? What had become of her courage?

They were still there, she knew. She simply had to summon them again. She simply had to gird herself so she would be able to go out of this room and face whatever must be faced.

Because surely Adam wasn't going to allow him to stay. Perhaps a day or two, until he was able to travel. And then he would throw him out. She could stand this for a day or two, especially if it meant she would be sure, once and for all, that Eric Ross would never bother her again.

As she rocked and rocked and cradled her child, she began to feel the terror and the tension drain out of her. She would be all right. Everything would be fine. Adam loved her. He would keep her safe.

Adam looked down at his brother and shook his head. No wonder Lori had been so terrified at the sight of him. Adam wasn't sure even *he* would have recognized Eric under the scraggly beard and the filth.

Sudie had already stripped off his clothes, and one of the maids had taken them out to burn them. Still his unwashed body stank abominably, and Adam could actually see the lice in his hair and beard.

"This is what a soldier looks like, brother," Eric said. His voice was cracked and hoarse, and his eyes glittered from the fever that flushed his face.

"Were you wounded?" Adam asked, although he'd seen no sign of bandages.

"Not likely," Eric said with a ghost of his usual grin. "Hardly ever got to fight. I got the fever. Half of the army's got the fever, even Ol' Rip Ford himself."

"I can't believe they sent you home, sick as you are!" Adam said. He'd been protecting Eric all his life, and the outrage he felt on his brother's behalf was the same he had always felt.

"Oh, they didn't *send* me—I sent myself. If I'd stayed there, I would've died," he added defensively at Adam's frown of disapproval. Eric glanced at Sudie who was wringing out a cloth in a bucket of steaming water that one of the girls had just carried in. "I knew if I came home, though, Sudie'd save me, won't you, Sudie?"

Sudie looked up and smiled, a sad smile given only to reassure Eric and which did not reach the concern in her eyes. "I shore will, Massa Eric. You done the right thing comin' home. This where you belong." Using the rag, she began to bathe the dirt from Eric's face.

"Did you desert, Eric?" Adam pressed him.

Eric winced at the baldness of the question—or perhaps he was just wincing from the heat of Sudie's wash water. "I wouldn't call it that. The Cavalry of the West isn't the regular army, you know. I doubt anybody cares that I'm gone, if they even know that I am."

"Don't they let soldiers take baths?" Sudie shook her head in disgust as she examined the rag she'd been using on Eric.

"I've been sick for weeks," Eric excused himself. His too bright gaze found Adam again. "Funny how this fever works.

I keep thinking I see Lori McClintock. I thought I saw her just now, in the back hall."

Adam felt Sudie's quick glance, but he ignored it. "You did," he said.

To his surprise, Eric grinned. "I asked her to wait for me, but I never figured she'd wait *here*. That was mighty nice of you, brother, to take her in for me. How'd she convince you?"

He'd asked her to wait for him? Lori had never told him that! Adam felt the old jealousy scalding through him, raising all his old fears. If she hadn't waited for Eric, why did Adam think she would be any more faithful to *him?* Of course, she'd been desperate when Eric had left her, and she'd had no other choice but to accept Adam's offer. But she wasn't desperate now. And Eric was back. Eric was the father of her child, and he still wanted her. And Eric wasn't a cripple.

But Eric wasn't going to *get* her back. "Lori is my wife now, Eric."

Eric's forehead creased as he tried to comprehend this outrageous statement. "What?"

"Lori and I were married in April. She's my wife. That's why she lives here. She lives here with me."

He waited, not certain what to expect. He could feel Sudie's gaze, but he continued to ignore it, keeping his gaze on his brother's face. Would Sudie guess the truth now? But no, she still believed Matthew's father was some stranger. She wouldn't guess the truth. No one would, not now, not ever.

Adam saw the anger flicker over Eric's face, but to his surprise, he controlled it, and to his amazement, Eric actually grinned. "You *married* that little whore?"

"Watch your mouth, Eric," Adam warned him furiously. "Lori is my wife!"

"Then you're a fool! You didn't have to *marry* her—she spread her legs for me without a wedding ring on her finger!"

Adam had never felt such rage, and he'd actually made a

move toward Eric when Sudie stopped him with a cry. Only then did he realize his hands were curled into fists, ready to pound the life out of his brother to silence his filthy mouth.

But he couldn't hit a man as sick as Eric, not a man who might be on his death bed, and certainly not his own brother, no matter what the provocation. "Stop it, Eric!"

But Eric laughed, a terrible, hollow sound that raised the hairs on Adam's arms.

"And just how long do you think she'll stay with you, big brother?" he scoffed. "Now that the real men are coming back home? She promised she'd wait for *me,* and you see how long *that* lasted! Well, don't worry, I wouldn't have her now, not if you *paid* me to take her off your hands. Unlike you, I'm not willing to take another man's leavings!"

Adam lunged for him then, and he didn't know what he might have done if Sudie hadn't thrown herself between them, grabbing Adam and holding him back.

"It the fever talkin'!" she insisted, clinging to his shirt when he would have thrown her aside. "He don't know what he sayin'!"

If only Adam could have believed that! But he knew if he stayed in this room another moment, he would murder Eric where he lay, so he fled, tearing out of the bedroom and down the hall.

He was out of the house before he knew where he was going, and then he realized he needed to be with Lori. She'd said she loved him, and she'd *made* love with him only a few hours ago. Surely, that wasn't a lie. No matter what had happened before, she belonged to him now, didn't she?

He had to find out.

For a long time after the baby had finished nursing, Lori continued to rock him, unwilling to be parted from him, needing to feel his warm little body in her arms. He lay quietly, watching her face as if he found it as fascinating as she found his. Did he look like Eric? She was sure he didn't. His pale blue eyes were already darkening, as Sudie had predicted they would, but Lori was sure they would remain blue like hers and not turn brown like Eric's. And his face looked like hers. Everyone said so, although how they could tell, she had no idea. He just looked like himself to her, like a fat little baby. The most beautiful baby in the world.

A noise startled her, and she realized with instant terror that someone was trying to open the door.

"Who's there!" she called in alarm, half rising from the rocking chair, although she wasn't certain if she intended to fight or flee.

"Lori? What's wrong with the door? Why won't it open?" Adam called out in irritation.

Lori gasped out her relief. "Just a minute!" She carried Matthew over to his cradle and laid him down, then hurried to open the door, fastening her bodice up as she went.

When she had pulled the chair out from under the knob, she opened the door to find Adam standing there, frowning in consternation.

Lori spared him only a glance before instinctively looking past him for any sign of Eric. But the hallway behind him was empty, and Eric's bedroom door was closed. Sighing with a second wave of relief, she stood aside for Adam to enter.

"Did you have something pushed against the door?" he asked her.

"The chair," she said, gesturing vaguely at it while she closed the door carefully behind him and wondered if she should put it back in place again, just in case. But no, Adam was here. She was safe, at least for the moment.

"Why did you barricade the door if you were just going to let me in?" he demanded.

Did he think she'd barricaded it against *him?* "To keep your brother out!"

He didn't look as if he believed her, but he said, "Eric

isn't going anywhere for a while, so you won't be needing that chair again. And he assured me that he won't be bothering you at all, in any case."

"He *talked* to you about me?" Lori asked, horrified. The mere thought of Eric mentioning her name made her feel somehow violated.

"Yes," Adam said, and he looked as if the admission pained him. "He thought . . . he thought you were waiting here for him to get home."

Lori felt the gorge rising in her throat, and she had to swallow to keep it down. "Why in God's name would he think a thing like that? You told him, didn't you? You told him we're married?"

Adam nodded, and once again he looked pained. "He was a little surprised since you'd promised to wait for him."

"What?" Lori couldn't believe this was happening! It must be another nightmare, one she couldn't seem to awaken from. "I never promised him *anything!* He *attacked* me! Why would I promise to *wait* for him?"

Adam looked so strange, as if he were in physical agony, although that couldn't be true. He wasn't even limping. "It's all right, Lori," he assured her, as if she were the one in pain. "I know you loved Eric. I know you wanted to marry *him* and not me, and I know you thought that if you gave yourself to him, he'd marry you."

Lori cried in protest at the horrid lies, but he took her arms in a reassuring grasp.

"I don't care about any of that, Lori, not anymore," he told her urgently. "I love you, and I'll forgive you anything."

"Forgive?" she echoed incredulously, certain now this wasn't really happening. It was simply too awful. This couldn't really be Adam saying these terrible things to her. Not Adam, the man she loved. The man who claimed to love her, too!

"I don't care if you were with another man first or how you felt about him, just as long as you'll stay with me now.

If you'll stay with me, Lori, we'll never speak of this again. It'll be as if none of it ever happened."

Lori thought she must be losing her mind. "I never loved *him!*" she insisted, desperate to make him believe her. "It was you! It was always you, from the time I was old enough to love anyone at all!"

Another spasm of what might have been pain twisted his face, and he said, "You don't have to lie anymore, Lori. I told you, none of that matters."

"But it *does* matter!" she cried, nearly frantic with frustration.

Before he could reply, however, they heard shouting in the hall, and Sudie's voice rose above it.

"Massa Adam, come quick!"

Adam glanced impatiently over his shoulder in the direction of the summons, then turned back to Lori. "As soon as he's well enough, I'll tell him he has to leave," he promised. "You'll never have to see him again."

He took her mouth in a kiss that seemed intended to stake a claim on her. Then he was gone, hurrying away to answer Sudie's summons.

Without thinking, Lori snatched up the chair and wedged it under the knob again, although whom she was trying to keep out this time, she could not have said. Instinctively, she wiped the back of her hand across her mouth, trying to erase the taste of him on her lips.

How dare he *forgive* her when she'd done nothing wrong? Nothing at all except love Adam. That had been her first and only mistake, giving her heart to a man who, she now understood, was not the good, wise and gentle man she'd imagined him to be. In fact, she hadn't known him at all, which meant that she hadn't really loved him at all. She'd only loved some imaginary ideal. An ideal that the real Adam had just shattered.

She felt as if her heart had been ripped from her chest, and she actually had to double over from the pain of it. How

could this have happened? How could she have been so
wrong about him?

But maybe there was still hope! Maybe Sudie could explain it to him. *She* understood! She could tell Adam the
truth and make him understand, too! If there was any part
of him half as good as she had believed him to be, Sudie
could tell him what Eric had done and . . .

Then she remembered. Sudie didn't *know* it was Eric.
Sudie thought Lori's rapist had been some stranger, someone she didn't even know. And if she'd been afraid to tell
Sudie the truth before, she was even more afraid to tell
her now that Eric was here. She'd seen the way Sudie's
face had lit up when she'd recognized the ragged man as
her "baby." Oh, no, Sudie would never take Lori's side
against him.

So Lori had nothing and no one to turn to. And if she'd
been afraid to stay here before because *Eric* was here, she
was even more desperate to escape now because *Adam* was
here. Adam whose betrayal hurt far more than Eric's violation ever had.

Knowing only that she had to get away, she began gathering her things, blindly pulling her clothes from the wardrobe and throwing them on the bed. Only when she'd made
a pile of them did she stop to think and realize that she
needed something in which to carry them. And she'd need
to take Matthew's things, too. And him. She could tie him
in a sling across her chest the way she'd seen the slave women
carrying their children. She'd need a sheet for that, and another to make a bundle of their belongings. But she wasn't
going out into the hall to the linen closet to fetch them. Instead, she ripped the comforter off the bed she had shared
with Adam and stripped off those sheets.

She didn't bother to wonder why she felt compelled to
hurry. She knew that if Adam caught her, he would try to
stop her, and she couldn't take that chance.

When she had gathered everything, she was amazed to

see how many possessions she had accumulated in her short stay here. How many things Adam's wealth had supplied her. She'd felt unworthy of his generosity before, but now she simply didn't *want* anything from him.

In the end, she hung her new dresses back in the wardrobe and took only the ragged things she'd owned when she'd come here. Except for the dress she was wearing, which she would send back later since she couldn't afford the time to change just now, she took nothing of his. For Matthew, she had no choice because everything he owned was Adam's, but she figured he owed the child that much. When she had finished packing and had the bundle tied securely, she picked up the baby from his cradle.

He smiled at her in delight, flailing his little arms as if sensing her excitement, and she couldn't help smiling back at him. Poor little angel, what would become of him now? What could she offer him? Nothing of material value, certainly, but she now understood that the luxuries of Elmhurst were worthless without trust and honor. Those were things that had no price and which even the penniless McClintocks had in abundance. For a moment, she simply cradled him to her, burying her face in the sweet curve of his neck and inhaling his delicious baby scent.

Tears pooled in her eyes, but she refused to let them fall. She didn't have time for that now. Later perhaps, when she was safely away from here, but not now, not yet. Quickly, awkwardly, she tied the baby to her chest with the sheet, and when she was satisfied he was secure, she picked up her bundle and went to the window.

Outside she could see that the yard was deserted. The fieldhands would still be busy about their tasks, and the house servants were no doubt scurrying around, answering Sudie's every beck and call for tending Eric.

Satisfied that she would be unobserved, she raised the window and began the laborious climb over the low sill to the ground below.

* * *

Eric was delirious with fever. It had taken both Adam and Oscar to hold him down while Sudie tied his hands and feet to the bedposts so he wouldn't harm himself or anyone else as he thrashed around.

"If only we had some ice," Sudie lamented. In the old days, before the war, ships had carried ice down from the north every spring and they'd stored it in the spring house, even through the heat of summer. They could have packed Eric's fevered body in it and lowered his temperature. But no one had seen northern ice for more than four years now.

"I'll keep the girls coming with fresh spring water," Oscar told her. "That's about the coldest thing we got."

Sudie nodded absently and sent the maid for more rags.

When she was gone, Adam and Sudie were alone in the room with Eric. He was still filthy except in the places Sudie had managed to wash before the fever took him, and he was muttering curses in the depths of a fever dream.

Adam tried to feel pity for him. He'd felt pity for his brother all his life, and it seemed the natural reaction now, considering how seriously ill he was at the moment. Still, Adam could not forget that Eric had called Lori a whore or that he'd taken advantage of her innocence in the first place to satisfy his own lust. Or that he'd abandoned her when she'd needed him most. Eric may not have had the same advantages as his older brother in his life, but Adam couldn't forgive him his deliberate cruelty toward the woman he loved.

"It's his baby, ain't it?" Sudie asked, startling Adam from his angry thoughts.

"What?"

"Matthew. He Massa Eric's chile, ain't he?"

Adam stiffened in surprise as his mind raced, searching for something to say. "Don't be ridiculous," was all he could manage.

Sudie snorted in derision. "I ain't the one bein' ridiculous."

"Matthew is *my* child," Adam insisted, as much to remind himself as to convince Sudie.

"No, he ain't, and we both know it." Her expression hardened. "That little liar! She tell me she was *forced*. She tell me it some stranger she never seen before or since!"

Of course she had, and then Adam remembered her wild claim that she had always loved him. It seemed there was no end to Lori's deceptions.

"She had to tell me *somethin'*, I expect. I knowed right off it weren't yours," Sudie reported furiously.

"How could you have been so sure?" Adam asked.

" 'Cause you never laid a hand on that girl until after you was married, is how. You ain't that kind a man."

"But Eric is," Adam said bitterly, glancing at the figure still writhing on the bed.

"He can't help hisself!" Sudie defended him. "He just want somebody to love him, and how he gonna say no when some trashy girl sets her cap for him and don't care what she gots to do to catch him?"

She was right, of course. Eric would not have hesitated an instant in taking what Lori offered.

But that was in the past. "Lori is my wife now," he reminded Sudie. "He won't be able to stay here, not after he's recovered."

Sudie's eyes grew wide with alarm. "You can't turn him out! This his home as much as yours!"

"He can't live here with me and Lori," Adam pointed out.

"Then put *her* out!" Sudie cried.

"Are you crazy?" he nearly shouted.

"You can keep the baby!" she insisted, nearly hysterical. "We get a wet nurse for him, he be just fine! You ain't gonna let some poor trash girl come between you and your own brother, are you?"

She'd grabbed his arm, as if to compel him to see reason,

but he shook her off. "Stop it, Sudie! I don't care what you think of Lori. She's still my wife, and she'll *stay* my wife."

Adam never learned how Sudie might have responded because Eric began to shout, screaming at some invisible demons, and he managed to rip loose the bonds on one of his hands.

He nearly knocked Sudie over before Adam could get him restrained again, and by then Oscar and the maid had returned from their errands. Adam stood back, watching as Sudie lovingly tended the man in whom only she had ever been able to see any good.

Had he once felt gratitude to Eric for ruining Lori and thus forcing her to marry him? It was hard to remember a time when he would have considered any of this a blessing. Perhaps if he could believe that Lori truly loved him . . . but even that claim was suspect now in light of all her other lies.

But regardless of how she felt about him, he still loved her—more than life itself. And enough, he was afraid, so that he was willing to throw his own brother out of his home in order to make her happy.

Leaving Eric to Sudie's care, he stepped into the hall. His gaze went to the bedroom door behind which Lori had earlier sought refuge. She'd seemed genuinely frightened of Eric, but probably she was just afraid that he would turn Adam against her.

He needed to talk to her, to touch her and hold her and remind himself of why he was doing all this. But he didn't trust himself just yet. He was still too angry from his argument with Sudie. Later, when he was calmer, he would go back to Lori. He would let her tell him she loved him again, and he would pretend to believe her. If he pretended hard enough, perhaps he really would begin to believe her.

But even if he didn't, he thought bitterly, it wouldn't matter.

* * *

Lori ran until she couldn't breathe anymore and a stitch in her side brought her to a staggering halt. But when she looked back, she saw no sign of pursuit. No one, it seemed, had witnessed her escape and no one was coming after her.

Still, as she leaned against a tree on the bank of the river, sobbing for breath, she felt the fear curling in her stomach. The fear that Eric would come after her and catch her and . . . But of course that was ridiculous. The only one she really needed to fear right now was Adam. Because she knew he wouldn't let her go without a fight. And because, after the things he had said to her, she couldn't go back with him, not ever, not even if Eric Ross was dead.

The rawness of the pain brought tears to her eyes, and she didn't bother to wipe them away when they began to fall. There was no one to see, after all. No one except Matthew and he'd fallen asleep, lulled by the warmth of her body and the motion of her running.

Setting down her bundle, she wrapped her arms around the child that slept against her breast, cherishing his small body.

"I love you, little one," she whispered brokenly against his downy head as her tears continued to fall.

Her chest still felt empty, as if she had no heart left, and when she remembered why, what Adam had said to her and what it had meant—that he had never believed her at all!— her silent tears became wrenching sobs.

But she couldn't stand here weeping, not when Adam might discover at any moment that she was gone and come after her. Somehow she scooped up her bundle again and staggered on, her body still so wracked with sobs that each step was an effort and she could hardly see where she was going. But somehow she kept on, following the path more by instinct than by sight as she sought the only refuge remaining to her.

* * *

"Massa Adam?"

Adam looked up from where he had been pretending to add the plantation accounts to find the maid Effie standing in the doorway to his office.

"Yes?"

"Supper's ready, Massa, but . . ."

"But what?" he asked, suddenly noticing the way she was wringing her hands nervously. Was something wrong? Had Eric . . . ?

"I knock on Missy's door to tell her, but she don't answer."

"Maybe she's asleep or something. Just open the door and—"

"I try, Massa, but the door don't open. Feel like somethin' pushing up again' it, and—"

Adam didn't wait to hear the rest. He brushed past her and headed down the long hallway to where his bedroom door loomed huge and impenetrable.

Lori had pushed that damn chair against the door again, that was all. And she'd fallen asleep, so she didn't hear the maid knock. That's all it was. Nothing to be concerned about. No reason whatsoever for apprehension to be tying his stomach into a knot.

He reached the door and tried the knob and found the door wedged tight as it had been before.

"Lori?" he called, rattling the knob.

No response.

"Lori, wake up!" he called louder and pounded on the door.

Still no response.

"Lori, can you hear me?" he shouted to the solid wood panel and briefly considered throwing his weight against it and breaking it down.

But he wasn't yet that desperate, although the apprehension in his stomach had now become a hot ball of fear when he remembered the threats she'd once made to harm herself. But surely she wasn't *that* upset now, not when he'd already promised her he'd send Eric away and do whatever she wanted.

He glanced over his shoulder to see that Effie had followed him down the hall and now stood by, still wringing her hands. He saw that his shouting had also brought Sudie to the door of Eric's room to see what was going on.

"I done tol' you—" Effie began, but he cut her off.

"Go outside to the bedroom windows and see what you can see. If one of them is open . . ."

But she was already running to do his bidding.

"What's the matter?" Sudie asked, coming toward him, her hands locked tightly together at her waist, as if afraid of what they might do if she let them go.

"Nothing," Adam said with a forced smile, wishing he really believed that. "Effie couldn't rouse Lori, so I've sent her out to climb in a window."

"Why don't you just open the door?' she asked with a frown.

Somehow he held onto his smile. "Because Lori has a chair wedged under the knob and it won't open."

"What for she do a fool thing like that?" Sudie asked in amazement.

What for indeed. "I think . . . she was afraid." Only when he said the words did the truth of them really hit him. She *must* have been afraid to have blocked the door like that! But why?

"Afraid of what?" Sudie asked.

What had she told him? "She said . . . she was afraid of Eric."

Sudie snorted in disgust. "He can't get outta his bed. Why for she be afraid of him?"

Before Adam could think of an answer, they heard footsteps on the other side of the door. Finally! Lori had heard them and was opening the door. They heard the sound of the chair being removed, and then the wooden panel swung inward to reveal . . . Effie.

"The window was open, so I come on in," she began, but Adam pushed past her, his frantic gaze scanning the room. The bed had been stripped, the bedclothes lying on the floor in a heap, but there was no sign of Lori.

"Where is she?" he demanded of the girl who cringed away from his fury.

"I don't know!" she cried in terror. "She just gone. And the baby, he gone, too!"

By the time she reached the cabin, Lori could hardly stand. She wasn't sobbing anymore because she was too weak for that, but the tears still streamed from her eyes, and she was still staggering as fast as she could, terrified that Eric and the other demons were after her.

She burst through the cabin door to discover Bessie bent over a pot that hung on the fire, stirring.

"Lord have mercy!" Bessie cried when she had looked up in surprise and identified her visitor. "What's the matter? Oh, dear God, it ain't the Yankees, is it? Have they come? Did they burn Elmhurst to the ground?"

But Lori couldn't answer because she was still crying too hard and because she couldn't catch her breath and because her legs would no longer hold her upright and the room was spinning.

"Sit, sit!" Bessie commanded, grabbing Lori just before she fell and easing her down onto one of the benches that she'd pulled from under the kitchen table. "Are you hurt? Is the baby all right?"

Lori didn't know whether to shake or nod her head, so she managed to gasp, "Fine," while Bessie proceeded to unwrap the sling that held the baby against her so she could see for herself.

Matthew awoke instantly, and he wasn't at all happy about being disturbed. She wondered if he could be hungry again, but decided that it was too soon. He was just angry.

"There, now, what's all the fuss about?" Bessie wanted to know, cradling the baby in her arms and rocking him instinctively.

He gave another plaintive wail and then settled down, allowing himself to be placated by the rocking and the attention.

Lori managed to reach up with trembling hands and wipe the tears from her face as her breathing slowly returned to normal. She was aware of Bessie's troubled gaze and the questions she would be asking again in a moment. She drew a deep breath and answered them before Bessie could press her.

"I left him."

"Who? Adam?" Bessie asked in amazement.

"Eric came home," she said. "He deserted from the army. He's sick with a fever."

"So you left *Adam?*" Bessie asked incredulously. Of course she wouldn't understand. She never understood anything.

"Adam said . . ." she began, and her voice cracked as the pain of his betrayal washed over her again. She drew a breath and tried once more. "He said he *forgave* me! Like he thought I did something wrong!"

"*Adam* forgave you?" Bessie clarified, clearly confused.

Lori nodded.

"Then what's the matter? Good Lord, girl, if he ain't gonna hold the past against you, what you got to be worried about?"

"I shouldn't have come here!" Lori cried in despair, jumping to her feet. "I should've known you'd be like this. You never believed me, either! Give me my baby!"

"Only if you're goin' back to Elmhurst," Bessie warned her, holding the child away.

"Not as long as I live!"

"Where you think you gonna go then? It's comin' on night! You gonna sleep out with a young'un? Go to some neighbor and explain how you left your husband 'cause he took his sick brother in?"

"Give me my baby!" Lori screamed, lunging for her. Or trying to, but Bessie clamped a strong hand on her shoulder and pushed her back down again, and she was too weak to resist. And she was crying again, tears she was afraid would never stop because they could never wash away the pain of Adam's betrayal.

"You sit right down there and rest. I'll fix you some supper and then we can talk about what you're gonna do."

As if she had a choice, Lori thought miserably, and laid her head down on her arms on the table and wept.

"All her clothes are still here," Adam pointed out to Sudie who, like Adam and Effie, was searching the room frantically for some clue as to what had happened to Lori and the baby.

Sudie came over and glanced in the wardrobe. Then she pulled open the top drawer of the dresser and rummaged through it. "All the clothes *you* give her is here," she said. "What she brung with her is gone."

"What does that mean?" Adam demanded.

"That mean *she* gone, too."

Effie moaned in distress.

"Hush up!" Sudie snapped. "You go see if Massa Eric need anything."

The girl seemed only too glad to escape.

"Where could she have gone?" Adam asked desperately the moment they were alone. "And why?"

"It don't matter, do it?" Sudie asked in return, her eyes shining brightly. "You free, Massa! That girl done tricked you into marryin' her, but now you's free!"

Adam grabbed her by the arms, wanting to shake her but somehow managing to restrain himself. "But I don't *want* to be free!"

Sudie refused to understand. "She be glad to give you the

baby, that's what you want! A girl like that, she take money and be gone before you know—"

This time he did shake her, once, making her head snap back and silencing her. "Don't you understand?" he asked her furiously. "I don't care what she's done or why! I just want *her!* I want her back here safe and sound, and I'll do anything to *get* her back. Anything at all!"

"Even kill your own brother?" she asked, her face white as the truth of his words sank in. "That's what you do," she hurried on when he would have protested, "if'n you throw him out, sick as he is!"

"I told you he could stay until he's well!"

But Sudie shook her head and tears filled her eyes.

Adam released her at once, shocked speechless at the sight of those tears. He could never remember seeing Sudie cry, not once, not in his whole life.

"She can't have gotten far," he said gruffly. "I'll send some of the men out to look for her. And when she comes back," he added, lifting a finger in warning, "you'll treat her with all the respect due my wife."

Sudie lifted her chin, refusing to cower before him. "Yes, Massa," she said, letting him hear all her fury and disgust.

Too angry to deal with her another second and too anxious to find Lori to delay, he turned and hurried out of the room.

He had just reached the bedroom door when she said, "What if she won't come back?"

He didn't even acknowledge the question because he didn't know the answer.

Thirteen

"I wish you'd eat somethin'," Bessie fussed as she turned down her bed for Lori.

"I just can't, not tonight." Lori had tried, but she couldn't even bring herself to swallow anything more solid than the cup of tea Bessie had finally forced on her when she'd been unable to eat the beans and fatback she'd fixed for supper.

"You don't eat, your milk'll dry up, and then you'll *have* to go back to Elmhurst to get yourself a wet nurse!"

Bessie, of course, felt certain that Lori would be returning to Elmhurst the instant she came to her senses, which in Bessie's estimation should happen at any moment.

Lori glanced down at the baby in her arms and knew a moment's regret for what he would miss if she never went back. But only a moment's. She couldn't trade her self-respect for material things.

"Here you go," Bessie said when she had finished turning the covers back on the big bed she and Lori's father had shared. "I'll be up in the loft if you need anything."

"I hate to put you out of your bed," Lori said guiltily. "I should sleep up there."

"You can't carry that baby up the ladder to the loft, so you two'll sleep here tonight, and we'll worry about the rest of it later." The implication was clear: she didn't expect Lori to be here long enough to have to worry about it at all.

Night had fallen, and Bessie picked up the lone candle and began to carry it into the other room. "Leave the door open a crack. I'll wait out there with the light until you're tucked in."

Lori nodded. Once she'd been used to getting undressed in the dark because candles were so dear. Life at Elmhurst had spoiled her.

Bessie had just stepped into the front room when they heard the sound of an approaching rider.

Lori's heart seemed to stop beating as terror gripped her. *He was coming for her!* She didn't even bother to wonder who *he* was. She only knew she didn't want him to find her.

"Don't tell him I'm here," she begged Bessie in an urgent whisper.

The rider carried a torch, and its light cast eerie shadows through the shuttered windows. Lori instinctively shrank from them.

"You want his slaves turnin' over every rock in the county lookin' for you all night long?" Bessie scoffed. " 'Course I'll tell him you're here. That don't mean you got to go back if you don't want to, though. You just stay right where you are. I'll take care of everything."

Lori laid the baby on the bed and took up a post by the bedroom door which Bessie had left just ajar so she could hear what was going on.

She heard a man's voice yell, "Hello, the house!" and her terror abated somewhat. It was just Oscar. What had she expected, that one of the mighty Ross brothers would come traipsing after her himself?

The front door opened, and Bessie called back, "What you want?"

" 'Scuse me for botherin' you, Miz McClintock, but Miz Lori, she gone missin', and Massa Adam, he was wonderin' did you know—"

"She's here," Bessie told him sharply, taking great pains to let him hear her annoyance. "And you tell your *massa* that if he wants his wife back, he'll have to come fetch her

himself, not send some darkie after her like she was a runaway dog!"

Lori winced. The last thing she wanted was for Adam to
come after her, but she couldn't help appreciating Bessie's
grit. What had ever made her think her stepmother would
turn her over to the Rosses if she didn't want to go?

"Oh, yes, ma'am," Oscar said quickly. "I tell him that
directly. He be mighty relieved to know she all right. He was
nearly distracted, what with worrying 'bout her and all."

Bessie sniffed in derision. "Maybe if he'd worried about
her before now, she'd still be up there and not down here
with me. You tell him *that* while you're at it. And you tell
him not to bother comin' down here tonight, either. Miz
Lori's just retired for the night, and she's too wore out to
have any visitors."

"I don't know, Miz McClintock," Oscar said. "He mighty
anxious to see her—"

"Then you tell him *I'm* mighty nervous, what with all
those Yankees tryin' to invade Texas, and if I hear somethin'
outside in the middle of the night, I might just shoot first
and ask questions later. He don't mind a butt full of buckshot,
you tell him to come on down. Otherwise, mornin'll be soon
enough."

With that Bessie slammed the cabin door. They both
waited another minute, Lori literally holding her breath to
see what Oscar would do. But all he did was turn his horse
and ride away.

Releasing her breath on a relieved sigh, she sagged against
the doorframe. Bessie was beside her in an instant, pushing
the door back open again.

"You all right?"

"You shouldn't have said Adam could come down here,"
she scolded. "I don't want to see him!"

Bessie was unrepentant. "You might change your mind in
the mornin', and you don't want to be the one goes crawlin'
back, now do you? Better if he comes and begs you. And if

you still don't want to see him tomorrow," she added when Lori would have protested, "then I'll send him packin', just like I did his slave. Now get some rest. Everything always looks worse when you're tired. You might feel completely different in the light of day."

Bessie pulled the door nearly closed again, leaving only enough space for the candlelight to illuminate the room so Lori could see to get undressed and into bed.

Bessie meant well, she knew, but a night's sleep wasn't going to change anything. And she wasn't going back with Adam until he finally believed her and begged *her* forgiveness. Which, she reluctantly admitted, wasn't likely to happen, not tomorrow and not any other day, either. The awful knowledge was like a lead weight on her heart.

When she'd stripped off her dress—the one she was going to send back to Elmhurst, she slid into bed in her chemise, tucking Matthew in beside her. She offered him her breast, and he began to suckle greedily, even though he wasn't really hungry. It was as if he needed the comfort as much as she needed him close to her. Her body ached both from weariness and grief, and when she closed her eyes, she was instantly asleep.

"Hitch up my buggy, Oscar," Adam said the instant he'd heard the news that Lori had—as Sudie had guessed—taken refuge with her stepmother.

"That ain't all she told me, Massa," Oscar said, holding up his beefy hands as if to stop Adam from rushing out the door.

"Is something wrong with her?" he asked in sudden alarm. "Is she hurt? Is she—?"

"No, sir, she fine, or at least I expect she is. Miz McClintock didn't rightly say. What she *did* say is that they don't want you goin' down there tonight. Miz McClintock say she shoot you if you come."

"What?"

"I don't think she was teasin', either, Massa." Oscar's broad face was grim, and Adam was *certain* that he, at least, wasn't teasing.

"What am I supposed to do then?" Adam demanded in outrage. "Just leave her there?"

" 'Til mornin', at least," Oscar confirmed.

"She just playin' with you," Sudie said from where she'd been listening in the doorway of Adam's office. "She run away so's you'll go chasin' after her. Then she pretend she don't wanna come back, and you promise her whatever she wants to get her to come. I reckon we both know what she wants, too, don't we?"

Adam was so furious that he wanted to smash something. "This isn't a *game,* Sudie. I already told her I'd send Eric away."

"Then she want somethin' else. More clothes maybe or—"

"Then why did she leave the ones she already has behind?" Adam challenged.

"I don't know!" Sudie cried, as frustrated as Adam. "All I know is she want somethin', and she ain't comin' back 'til she gets it!"

Adam distractedly ran his hand through his hair.

"You still want me to hitch up the buggy, Massa?" Oscar asked after a moment.

Adam weighed his desire to see Lori with Bessie's desire to shoot him and decided that discretion really was the better part of valor. Besides, what would he accomplish if they were both exhausted and upset? "No, I'll . . . wait until morning. That's all, Oscar. You can go on to bed. You, too, Sudie."

"I's sittin' up with Massa Eric," Sudie reminded him. Adam didn't like the righteous tone in her voice.

"How is he?" he asked guiltily. He should only have wondered because the sooner Eric was well, the sooner he could leave. But Eric was still his brother, and his old habit of needing to take care of him was hard to break.

"He was sleepin' fine when I left him just now, but the fever comes and goes. I reckon it'll be back right soon."

He wanted to ask her when Eric would be well again, but he figured she wouldn't tell him, or at least that she wouldn't tell him the truth, even if she knew it. His concern was too suspect.

"Call me if you need me," he told her and bid them both good night.

But when they were gone, he didn't even consider retiring to his bedroom. Since the baby's birth, he'd been sleeping in his old room, but tonight he was to have returned to the master bedroom where he would have again shared Lori's bed. He wasn't ready to face either of those places when he knew Lori was no longer even in the house, so he probably wouldn't sleep at all tonight.

How could he, in any case, when all he could think about was how in the hell he was going to get Lori back?

He could force her, of course. That was his right as her husband. He could carry her back bodily if necessary and lock her up to keep her here. Except that hardly seemed the way to win her heart, and her heart was what Adam wanted even more than her physical presence.

But perhaps Sudie was right. Maybe all she wanted was some new clothes or some other finery. It didn't seem likely, though, since Lori had never really expressed a desire for more of anything, but Adam couldn't help hoping it would be that simple. Money was tight, but he'd spend whatever he had to if that would make her happy.

If. The problem was, of course, that he had no idea what would make her happy, because he had no idea why she had left in the first place. Good God, he'd already promised her that he'd send Eric away, and he'd told her that he'd forgiven her for everything she'd done. And he hadn't even mentioned the lies she'd told. What else could he do? What else could she *want* him to do?

Damnit, he wanted to wring her neck for causing him so much trouble!

Except that if he really *did* wring her neck, he'd no longer be able to make love to her, which was what he *really* wanted to do. He wanted to hold her and kiss her and stroke her until she was desperate for him, as desperate for him as he was for her. He wanted to sink into her velvet depths until they were both lost, until she clung to him with arms and legs and threw back her head and cried out her release. And until she told him again, true or not, that she loved him.

Yes, that was what he wanted, and that was what he would have. No matter what price he had to pay. No matter what price his *brother* had to pay. Had he once prided himself on the Ross family honor? Had he once believed that marrying Lori was nothing more than a fulfillment of his obligation to the family name? Well, now he knew that he had no more honor than the McClintocks and the rest of their breed. He would do whatever he had to in order to get Lori back.

It was dark, so dark, and Lori was running. She was trying desperately to get away, but the night was so dark and she couldn't see where she was. Couldn't see who was after her, either, but she knew he was there. She could hear him in the blackness, his pounding footsteps and his labored breath, wheezing in his throat as he ran and ran, closer and closer. And Lori ran and ran, but she couldn't run fast enough because her legs were so heavy. Heavy, so heavy she could hardly lift them, but he was getting closer, and she had to get away. She couldn't let him catch her. She couldn't let him put his hands on her and hold her down and spread her legs and force himself inside of her. She wasn't going to endure that, not ever, ever again, not if she had to die to prevent it.

But he was coming closer and closer and she couldn't run any faster and she couldn't get away and she couldn't breathe and she couldn't see and he was coming, he was coming! She tried to scream but her throat seemed frozen. She opened her mouth and tried and tried but no sound came out, and he was there, right behind her. She could hear his breath like a roaring in her ears, and she could feel it, hot and scalding, on the back of her neck, and she opened her mouth again and his hand came out of the darkness and grabbed her and she screamed for dear life.

She awoke with a jolt that shook the whole bed. Beside her Matthew jumped in surprise and began to whimper as Lori sobbed desperately for breath. She felt as if she really had been running for her life and realized her whole body was trembling and damp with perspiration.

As she reached over instinctively to soothe Matthew back to sleep, she heard the thump of feet on the floor in the other room as someone jumped down from the ladder to the loft.

"Lori?" Bessie cried through the darkness. "Dear Lord, girl, are you all right?"

The bedroom door flew open, and there stood Bessie, clutching a flickering candle, her hair sticking up every which way, her threadbare gown rumpled from sleep and her eyes wide with terror.

"What in God's name was you screamin' about?"

Dear heaven, she must have actually screamed aloud! "I . . . it was a nightmare," she said, still breathless from the terror of it.

"Must've been some nightmare!" Bessie exclaimed, hurrying over to the bed. She held the candle up so she could see Lori's face better, and she gasped. "Was you cryin' in your sleep?"

Lori reached up and was surprised to find her cheeks wet with tears. With unsteady hands, she quickly wiped them away.

"Good God, you're shaking! And you're white as a ghost! What on earth was you dreaming?"

Lori shook her head. She didn't want to talk about it.

But Bessie wasn't going to give up. "Was it Adam? Did he do something—?"

"No," Lori said before Bessie could imagine things were worse than they were. "I was dreaming . . . He was after me. He was going to force himself on me again." Before she could stop them, the tears flooded her eyes and filled her throat. "I'll die before I let him touch me again!" she choked out, covering her face with both hands as the sobs began to shake her.

"There, now, don't cry," Bessie soothed, setting the candle down on the crate that served as a bedside table and taking a seat beside Lori on the bed. "You don't gotta stay with him if he mistreats you, even if he is your husband!"

Lori sobbed harder in frustration. "Not Adam!" she managed to say. "His . . . the other one!"

"Eric?" Bessie guessed uncertainly, and suddenly Lori's anger overrode her despair.

"Of course Eric!" she cried shrilly. "He's the one who attacked me! I told you and told you, but you never believed me! Nobody ever believed me, not even Adam!"

The truth of that pierced her heart, and the pain of it tore a new sob from her. She tried to turn away from Bessie, but Bessie caught her anyway, taking her in her arms to offer the comfort she had denied months ago when Lori had thought the pain of it would kill her.

Time hadn't eased that pain, but Bessie's arms helped. She held Lori and crooned meaningless phrases and rocked her as if she were the baby instead of Matthew who, oblivious to his mother's crisis, had fallen asleep again.

For a long time Lori simply wept against Bessie's shoulder, sobbing out the pain of Eric's attack and Adam's betrayal. Only when she was too exhausted to weep anymore and her sobs had died away was she able to realize what had happened.

She pulled away and looked at Bessie in amazement. "You believe me?" she marveled, her voice still hoarse from weeping. "You believe Eric attacked me!"

" 'Course I do," Bessie replied indignantly.

But Lori wasn't going to let her off so easily. "You never did before," she reminded her.

Bessie had the grace to look chagrined. "I reckon I didn't. Didn't *want* to believe it," she added at Lori's frown. "I mean, why would a man like Eric Ross *need* to force a girl? He's got his pick of slave girls in his own quarters, and heaven knows, there's enough white girls who'd be willing, if they thought he'd look at them twice."

"And you thought I was one of them!"

"You wouldn't've been the first poor girl who believed a rich man's lies," Bessie said. "And then it didn't matter *how* you got yourself in trouble. The important thing was getting you out."

Lori lay back down on the bed and covered her eyes with her arm as despair washed over her again. "You did a good job on that," she reminded Bessie bitterly.

Bessie crossed her arms over her ample bosom. "You was grateful at the time, if you remember. Now, you gonna tell me why you up and left Adam Ross? The real reason and not just 'cause you're afraid of Eric attackin' you again."

Lori sighed wearily. "He said he forgives me."

"For what?"

With the remembered pain, she felt a fresh onslaught of tears, but she fought it, determined not to weep over the Ross brothers anymore. "For having an affair with his brother," she said, instantly angry once more. "I thought he believed me! I thought he believed that I hadn't loved Eric or let him court me, or believed his lies or let him seduce me! I thought he understood and that was why . . ."

She had to stop when her voice broke and once more she

fought the tears. When she could speak again, she said, "But he didn't understand at all, and he doesn't even believe I'm afraid of Eric. He thinks I just hate him or something for jilting me, and that's why I want him out of the house. And then he said he *forgives* me for everything! As if *I* was the one who did something wrong!"

"Hush, now. Hush!" Bessie begged when Lori began to cry again. "You're making me sorry I didn't let Adam Ross come down here tonight so I *could've* put a load of buckshot in him!"

That picture drew a choking laugh from Lori in spite of her tears and saved her from surrendering to them completely. "What am I going to do, Bessie?" she asked, feeling herself sinking into despair again. "How can I live with him when I know what he thinks of me?"

Bessie shook her head. "Ain't something you gotta decide this minute. Like I said before, things always look better in the morning. You get some sleep now or try to," she added at Lori's skeptical frown. "You got a baby to take care of, and you need your rest. We'll talk about this tomorrow, and maybe when Mr. Adam Ross shows up here . . . Well, you never know. Maybe he'll come to his senses, after all."

When Bessie had gone, leaving her alone in the dark again, Lori snuggled up to Matthew, grateful for the warmth of his little body that seemed to be the only thing that could touch the chill in her soul.

How could she ever have thought she loved Adam Ross? How could she ever have thought she knew who and what he was? But, she had to admit to herself as she lay there holding her son, even though he wasn't the man she'd believed him to be, even though he had hurt her beyond bearing, and even though she was afraid she could never trust him again, in spite of all of that, she did still love him. More than life itself.

* * *

As he drove his buggy into the yard of the McClintock cabin, Adam had to squeeze his hands into tight fists around the reins to keep them from trembling. He couldn't remember ever feeling so apprehensive about any encounter in his entire life. Why he should be, he had no idea. Lori was his wife, after all. She and her child belonged to him in every possible way. Surely, she understood that, just as she must understand how much she owed him.

Hadn't he taken care of her when she had been desperate and alone? Hadn't he given her the protection of his name and accepted her child as his own? Hadn't he forgiven her sins that any other man would have condemned her for? And in spite of all of that, by God, hadn't he even fallen in love with her?

And now, here he was, humbling himself even more to go crawling to her to beg her to come back and humiliate him even more. Because he knew, after only one night alone and no matter what kind of woman she might be, that without her, his life would not be worth living.

Except for a plume of smoke ascending lazily from the chimney, the cabin seemed deserted. For a moment, he wondered if he was too early, if perhaps they weren't even awake yet. But the smoke told him that someone was up, and he figured that if Lori wasn't quite prepared to see him, he would have the upper hand.

After setting the brake and tying off the reins, Adam climbed out of the buggy, taking care not to stumble. For a minute, he considered whether or not to take his cane, and finally decided against it. No sense in reminding her of his disability, not when his whole purpose in coming was to convince her that she was powerless against his will.

He didn't call out a greeting, figuring they had most certainly heard him drive up, and indeed, he had not even reached the door when it opened. Bessie McClintock stood there, looking every bit as formidable as Adam wished to.

"Good morning," he said, making himself smile.

She didn't smile back. "What do you want?"

Adam bit back the sarcastic reply that came instantly to his mind, refusing to rise to her bait. "I would like to see my wife," he said, reminding her—and Lori, who could no doubt hear every word—that she *was* his wife.

"What if she don't wanna see you?" Bessie challenged.

Adam felt the heat of his instant anger flooding his face, but before he could reply, he heard Lori's voice say, "It's all right, Bessie. Let him in."

With obvious reluctance, Bessie stepped back and allowed him to enter the small cabin. The smell of bacon was strong and the heat of the fire oppressive, or perhaps it was just nerves that caused Adam to feel suddenly very warm.

His eager gaze found her instantly in the interior dimness. She was standing stiffly by the table, and she was just as beautiful as he remembered or perhaps even more so because she wore her old, ragged dress and her hair was loose around her shoulders, just the way it had been the first day he'd come here. He felt a rush of tenderness that left him weak. Then he saw that her hands were locked together at her waist, which told him that she was as apprehensive about this meeting as he was, and his strength returned.

"How are you?" he asked, realizing the remark came from genuine concern rather than just ingrained politeness.

For a moment, he was afraid she wasn't going to answer him. She lifted her chin, as if defying him, but at last she said, "We're fine *now.*"

He winced inwardly at the implication that she could only be fine when she was away from him, but he refused to let her see his reaction.

A noise drew his attention, and he saw that a basket sat on the table and that Matthew lay in that basket. He was smiling and gurgling, kicking his feet and waving his hands in excitement, and Adam realized he was happy to see the man he believed to be his father. He felt another rush of tenderness for the child he had come to love as much as he loved Lori, and he had to close his hands into fists to keep from reaching for the baby.

But he couldn't stop himself from speaking. "Good morning, young man." Matthew replied with a happy coo that made Adam's heart clench painfully in his chest, and only then did Adam understand that Matthew was just as important to his happiness as Lori.

When he looked back at her, he thought her eyes seemed suspiciously bright, as if she, too, understood the bond that had developed between Adam and her baby. But if she did, she chose to ignore it. "Will you just say what you came to say?" she asked, sounding almost desperate.

Adam had been planning his arguments all night, but now he wasn't exactly sure where to begin. Of one thing he was certain, however, and that was that he didn't want to begin in front of Bessie.

He glanced back at her over his shoulder. "Would you mind leaving us alone, Mrs. McClintock?"

She made a rude noise, but she said, "Lori, you holler if you need me."

Adam felt another flash of anger at the implication that Lori might need protection from him, but he swallowed it down. He couldn't allow himself to be distracted now, not at this most important moment. When Bessie was gone, leaving the front door open behind her—all the better to hear Lori's cries for help, he thought bitterly—he turned back to Lori.

Instantly, he was struck again by how beautiful she looked. And by how awful. Her face was pale, her eyes shadowed by dark circles that told him she had slept as little as he had last night. And he realized with annoyance *why* she was wearing the faded, threadbare gown. Damnit, did she hate him so much, she wouldn't even wear the clothes he had provided for her?

"Lori, this is insane!" he blurted in exasperation. "I want you to come home with me right now!" Not at all what he had planned to say. And, he saw instantly, exactly the wrong thing.

"Why?" she challenged. Her face was no longer pale. Two spots of vivid color had blossomed in her cheeks.

"Because you're my wife. Because you belong at Elmhurst with me, you and Matthew both. Eric won't bother you. You won't even have to see him, and as soon as he's well enough to travel, I'll send him away. I already told you that."

But it wasn't enough. He could see that in her expression, in the way her dark blue eyes looked bleak and unyielding. Then, as if she didn't trust herself to speak, she shook her head.

"I don't know what more you want from me, Lori!" he cried. "I don't know what else I can do! Good God, I've told you I'll send my own brother away, throw him out of his own home just to please you! I've given you everything you ever wanted!"

"And you've forgiven me," she reminded him with what sounded oddly like bitterness.

"Yes, I have! How many other men would have done as much? How many other men would have married you and given your child a name?"

"Not many," she admitted. "I thought you were a saint for doing it."

Adam should have felt gratified, except she didn't sound exactly grateful. "What do you want from me, Lori?"

This time there was no mistake. Her eyes did fill with tears. "I want you to be the man I thought you were."

"I can't be a saint!"

But she shook her head. That wasn't what she meant. "You still don't understand, do you? You don't have any idea why I left."

"How could I? You didn't pay me the courtesy of telling me," he reminded her angrily.

"I did tell you. You just didn't listen."

He drew a deep breath to keep from grabbing her and

shaking her. Sudie had been right, she *was* playing with him, and it was a game at which he had no skill at all. With the greatest effort, he managed to control his fury. "Then perhaps you will do me the favor of telling me again. I promise I'll listen this time."

She was crying now. Not out loud. Silently. He cursed inwardly as the tears ran slowly down her cheeks unheeded. God, he hated it when she cried.

"I never loved Eric," she told him. "I never looked at him twice. You were the one I loved, the only one. But he tricked me, and he got me alone, and he forced me." Her voice caught, and for a moment he thought she wouldn't be able to go on, but somehow she did. "He held me down and hurt me until I thought I was going to die. Afterward, I was so ashamed. I felt stupid and like it was my fault somehow. I tried to pretend it never happened, tried to act like everything was the same as always, but there was . . . Matthew, and I couldn't do that anymore.

"Then you found out and offered to marry me. I didn't want to ruin your life, but Bessie reminded me of how much I loved you, and she made me think maybe I could make you happy. I wanted to, Adam, I wanted to so much!"

"You did, Lori!" he assured her. He reached for her, certain he had won, but she stiffened in alarm and jumped back, out of his reach.

"Did I?" she challenged, and she sounded almost angry. "I'm so glad! I'm so glad I was finally able to be a wife to you, Adam, even though the thought of any man touching me again made my skin crawl. And I'm glad you didn't seem to mind when I woke up screaming from nightmares that your brother was attacking me again. In fact, you hardly seemed to notice. Just like you didn't really notice how terrified I was when he came back yesterday. And just like you didn't seem to notice when I begged you to send him away. He attacked me, Adam! How could you imagine that I could stay in the same house with him for one minute? And how

ould you say you *forgive* me when *he's* the only one who
d anything wrong?"

"Lori," he began, not knowing what to say, not even sure
e understood, but certain that if he could take her in his
ms, everything would be fine again, just the way it had
een before.

But when he reached for her again, she screamed, *"Don't
ouch me!"*

"Lori, please, listen to me," he tried, desperate to calm
er.

But her cry had summoned Bessie who came bursting into
he house.

"Get out of here!" Bessie demanded, snatching an aging
hotgun down from where it hung on the wall. "Get out of
ere right now, while you still can!"

Surely, she wouldn't really shoot him, and he didn't have
he time to argue with her at the moment. "Lori," he tried
gain, but Lori shook her head.

"I can't talk about this anymore, Adam. Not now. You told
he you forgive me, but I can't forgive you, not until you at
east understand what you've done to me."

"All I did was love you, Lori," he insisted desperately.
And make you my wife and give you a home."

"And turn a piece of poor white trash into a lady," Bessie
dded angrily.

Lori's eyes widened, as if she had just realized something.
"That's it, isn't it, Adam?" she said. "You made me a fine
ady, so I'd look good when you took me out in public, or
when you had guests over, but you still think of me as trash,
lon't you? The little tramp your brother used and threw away.
A girl who'll do anything to get what she wants."

Adam shook his head in silent denial, even though he
knew she was right. He *had* thought that, but . . .

"Go home, Adam," Lori said wearily. "Go back to your
big house and your plantation and your slaves and your fam-
ly honor."

"I can't leave you here!" he protested.

"What's the matter, Mr. Ross?" Bessie scoffed. "Yo afraid of what your slaves'll think if you come back withou your wife?"

He felt the heat in his face, but he refused to acknowledg Bessie's barb. "I can force you to come home," he reminde Lori, playing his last card. "It's my legal right."

"Yes," she said quietly, as if she had finally found peace "You can take me against my will, and then you'll be jus like your brother."

Stung, he actually recoiled from her, and when he saw th look in her eyes, the steely gleam of triumph, he knew h had lost her.

With one last longing glance at the baby who was stil watching them in fascination, as if aware of how importan their conversation was, Adam turned on his heel and strod out as quickly as he could, not even bothering to disguis his limp. What did it matter if she saw it now? She coul not despise him any more than she did. Or any more tha he despised himself.

Lori and Bessie stood there, frozen in place, until they heard the buggy pulling away. That was when it hit her: Adan was gone—really gone.

"For a minute there, I thought I was gonna have to shoo him," Bessie observed, lowering the shotgun at last.

That was when Lori's legs gave out.

"Lori!"

Bessie was at her side in a moment, helping her up, seating her on the bench at the table.

"I told you to eat some breakfast," Bessie reminded her worriedly. "How long since you ate anything?"

"I don't remember," Lori said as she drew deep breaths in an attempt to ward off the overwhelming urge to faint.

"At least you can take a little bread. I'll put some bacon rease on it and—"

"No!" Lori gasped, trying not to gag at the thought. "No, lease, I just couldn't, not yet."

"You best lay down then, before you fall down," Bessie dvised her, still frowning with concern. "I'll keep an eye n little Matt," she added when she saw Lori glance at him. "He'll be getting hungry soon."

"I'll bring him in when he starts to fuss. You don't look ke you got much sleep at all last night. You could probably se a nap."

Lori would have argued if her head hadn't been aching uite so much. She probably should lie down for a while. nd then she might feel like eating something. She knew Bessie was right. She might not want to, but she had to think f Matthew, and if her milk dried up . . .

"Maybe just for a little while," she said finally and rose nsteadily to her feet.

How much longer could this go on? Adam wondered as e paced around his office. Two days had past since Lori ad sent him away with his tail tucked between his legs. Two ays during which he had gone over and over in his mind he things she had said to him.

Was it possible? Could he have been so very wrong about er? And if he had been, how could he ever expect her to orgive him?

Sudie had been silently triumphant when he had returned o the house alone, but she'd had the good sense not to say word to him. He'd spent the remaining time trying to keep imself too busy to think about Lori but instead thinking bout her almost constantly.

All that thinking hadn't done him much good, however. Ie still had no idea what to do, at least as long as Eric was till in the house. Maybe when he was gone . . .

But it might be weeks until he was well enough to eve sit a horse. And even then, how could he get Eric to leave In spite of his promises to Lori, Eric had as much right t live here as Adam did, and Adam had no idea how to con vince him it was in his best interests to give up the only li he had ever known, a life of ease and comparative luxur and start over anew someplace else. And he would *have* t convince Eric it was in his own best interest, because Eri had never been interested in anyone else's.

As he sat at his desk, staring blindly at the account book he'd opened before him and subsequently ignored, Adar heard a knock at the door and looked up to see Sudie standin in the doorway.

"Is something wrong? Is Eric . . . ?"

"He sleepin' just fine. The fever ain't bothered him a day, and he doin' a lot better now. Even sat up and took som solid food."

Adam nodded. "That's good." He should feel glad that hi brother was so much better, but he couldn't help remember ing that the longer he was sick, the longer Adam could dela dealing with him.

But Sudie was looking at him oddly, and instead of leavin now that she had given him her report, she came into th room and stopped in front of his desk, frowning down a him. "You look like you was drug through a knothole back wards," she declared.

Self-consciously, Adam smoothed a hand over his hair although he knew she wasn't referring to his grooming. "I'v had a lot on my mind," he excused himself.

"Esther said you ain't been eatin', and I can see by lookin at you that you ain't been sleepin' either. If you're worried about that girl—"

"She's not *that girl*," Adam snapped. "She's still my wife whether you like it or not."

"Looks like you're the only one remembers that," Sudie observed caustically.

"I'm sure Lori remembers it, too."

"Then why ain't she here where she belongs?" Sudie anted to know. "Or is she just waitin' for whatever you romised when you went to see her the other day?"

"I didn't promise her anything," Adam was happy to inorm her. "And if it makes you happy, she didn't ask me to. he only wanted . . ."

He caught himself just in time. Some things even Sudie idn't have a right to know.

"So she did want somethin'," Sudie said with satisfaction. And you're ashamed to tell me."

Shame, of course, had nothing to do with it. But perhaps e had been wrong not to tell Sudie at least *some* of what ori had said.

Adam leaned back in his chair and gazed at Sudie reflecvely for a moment. "What did she tell you happened to er? Why she had Matthew, I mean."

Sudie grimaced with distaste. "She say some stranger orced her. Some man she never seen before."

"And you believed her?"

She was loathe to admit it, but she nodded once.

"Why?"

She considered for a moment, as if she was trying to remember, then she frowned again. "She tricked me. She acted ust like . . ."

"Just like what?" he prodded when she hesitated.

"Like she'd been forced," she admitted with obvious reuctance.

"And how is that?"

Sudie didn't want to tell him, because unspoken between hem lay the knowledge of how she herself had come to this understanding. The ugly family secret that they never, ever discussed.

But finally she said, "She acted afraid and sad and she claimed she had nightmares about it—"

"She did," Adam said. "One night she woke up screaming." He remembered other nights, too, when he'd held her while she trembled in the aftermath of a dream she would never describe to him. "And she could hardly stand for me to touch her at first. Is that part of it, too?"

Sudie's expression tightened, as if she were steadying herself against her own feelings. "Maybe she just don't like you to touch her, Massa Adam," she said cruelly.

Adam winced but he didn't back down. "She liked it fine once I convinced her I wasn't going to hurt her," he said. "But she was still afraid of something. You could see that, couldn't you? That's why you believed her."

"Maybe she *was* forced, then," Sudie admitted grudgingly. "Maybe some stranger did it, and she blamed Massa Eric so's she could get money from you for the baby."

"Why does it have to be a stranger?" Adam asked, watching her closely. "Why couldn't it have been Eric, after all?"

"He never do a thing like that!" Sudie insisted too quickly. "What for he waste his time with a trashy girl like that? He gots his pick of every girl in the county!"

"And every girl in the quarters, too," Adam said blandly, almost hating the way he knew the words would hurt Sudie.

"He don't force them girls!" she cried desperately. "He not that way! He never do them things, not like—"

She caught herself just in time, but Adam knew what she was going to say.

"Not like his father," he finished for her. "But he is like him, isn't he? So much so that he forced himself on every slave girl he could get his hands on. I know you tried to pretend you didn't know, but it's true, Sudie."

"Only colored girls!" Sudie cried. "He never bothered no white ones, though!"

"None that we know of—except maybe Lori."

"She lyin'! I tol' you! She just out for what she can get!"

"Did you see how frightened she was when Eric showed up here the other day? She was screaming so loud, I thought someone was murdering her."

"She thought he was a tramp, somebody who'd wandered
 and—"

"Then why did she lock herself in her room after she knew
was him? Why did she run away?"

Those were the questions that had haunted him for days,
uestions that had caused him to doubt everything he had
ver believed about himself. Questions to which he desper-
tely needed answers.

But plainly Sudie did not have those answers. "I don't
now what go through her mind," she huffed. "I only know
at my boy never laid a hand on her!"

"Do you?" Adam challenged her. "How can you be so
ure?"

Once again her expression tightened, but she wasn't about
 back down either. "Well, maybe he did lay a hand on her.
aid so hisself, didn't he? But he never forced her."

"Sudie," he began impatiently, but she cut him off.

"He never forced her!" she insisted, and fled before he
ould reply.

Adam hardly slept that night. Instead he just kept thinking
r trying to, trying to figure out how he could have made
uch a colossal mess of his life. Morning brought no relief
ince he hadn't come up with any answers, or at least none
hat helped him any. He was sitting in his office, having once
gain failed to do justice to the delicious breakfast that had
een laid before him, when he heard someone knocking at
he back door.

It was early for visitors, too early for anyone, really, which
vas why Adam was sure it must be Lori. She'd come back
o him! She'd realized what a terrible mistake she'd made
nd . . .

"I'll get it," he told the maid who came hurrying down
he hall. He fairly ran to the door, ignoring the protesting
ain that shot through his leg.

But when he threw open the door, he found not Lori, bu[t]
Bessie, standing on his doorstep.

"Mrs. McClintock, what—?"

"It's Lori, Mr. Ross. She's dying."

Fourteen

Instinctively, Adam's gaze swept the yard, looking for Lori. "Where is she?" he demanded.

"I left her at the house."

Adam started outside, ready to call for Oscar to fetch his buggy, but Bessie grabbed his arm. "She ain't gonna die this minute. Why don't you hear me out before you go running off half-cocked?"

Adam wanted to argue—every instinct demanded that he go to Lori immediately—but Bessie hadn't let go of his arm and didn't seem inclined to, unless he listened to her first.

"All right," he reluctantly agreed, prepared to give her only a minute to say her peace.

But she glanced down the hall to where the maid still stood, listening to every word.

"Let's step into the parlor," he said, giving the girl a speaking glance that sent her scurrying away.

Bessie proceeded him into the parlor, and he carefully closed the doors behind them. "What do you mean, Lori is dying?" he asked as he turned to face her.

"I mean she ain't had anything to eat since she come to my place."

Adam was outraged. "If you needed food, why didn't you tell me? I'll have Oscar—"

"I got plenty of food," Bessie said impatiently. "Your people keep me supplied just fine. It's just that Lori can't eat none of it. She's too upset."

Was it possible? Could Lori be missing him as much as he was missing her? "What do you mean?"

"I mean she cries all day, or nearly so. I mean she can't sleep most nights, and when she does sleep, she wakes up screaming from dreams of that son of a bitch brother of yours coming after her. I ain't never seen nobody so scared in all my life, Mr. Ross. She's took to sleeping with the shotgun beside her bed."

"Dear God," Adam breathed.

"You say you love her," Bessie said, and Adam was alarmed to see her eyes growing red-rimmed and suspiciously moist, as if she were about to weep herself. "If you do, then you gotta do something, 'cause I don't know how much longer she can stand this. If she don't start eating soon, she'll lose her milk, too, and the baby will get sick and—"

"What can I do?"

"I reckon you can shoot that no-good brother of yours, but I don't reckon you will. Short of that, I just don't know."

"I can go see her," he offered. Indeed, every nerve in his body was commanding him to do just that, but Bessie shook her head.

"Unless you can tell her your brother's gone, I don't expect she wants to see you. At least, that's what she says."

"Eric's still too sick to even get out of bed," he said, absently rubbing the bridge of his nose against the ache behind his eyes. "How about if I send a girl down to nurse the baby? At least that will keep him from getting sick, and maybe if Lori doesn't have to worry about him—"

"I don't know if she'll be too happy to give up her baby," Bessie said with a frown, "but I'll do what I can to convince her it's for the best."

"Maybe Sudie knows some remedy that will calm her down and help her eat," Adam said. He turned and threw open the parlor doors, ready to call for Sudie, but the instant he opened the doors, he came face to face with her.

She'd been standing just outside the room, although how

long she'd been there or what she'd heard, Adam had no idea. For a long second, they stared at each other in surprise, and then Adam said, "Mrs. McClintock says Miss Lori is ill. She's not able to eat or sleep, and when she does sleep, she has terrible nightmares. The kind of nightmares she used to have when she first came here," he added, lest there be any mistake. "Mrs. McClintock thinks she's frightened. Of Eric."

Sudie was stricken. Her face had gone starkly pale, and she shook her head as if to deny his words.

But Adam felt no pity for her. "If she doesn't eat soon, she'll die. Is there something you can give her? Something that will help her eat? And sleep?"

Her eyes were enormous in her fragile face, and her gaze darted to Bessie. "She's afraid?" she asked, as if to confirm the unthinkable.

"I ain't never seen nobody so scared," Bessie assured her.

"She wakes up screaming," Adam said brutally. "She's afraid he'll come after her again." He thought he saw a tremor pass through her. "She didn't lie," Adam whispered for Sudie's ears alone.

Sudie's eyes filled with tears, and she refused to look at Adam, but she said, "I'll fix something for her. And I'll get one of the girls to go down and nurse the baby."

In a moment she was gone, hurrying away to do his bidding. Adam stared at her back as she fled, silently cursing her and himself. How could he have been so blind? How could he have been such a fool?

"I'd like to see her," he told Bessie, turning back to her at last.

Bessie drew a deep breath and let it out in a long sigh. "Better let me ask her first. Don't want to upset her any more, do we?"

Adam agreed reluctantly. "You'll send me word? Right away?"

"Right away."

"I'll have Oscar hitch up a wagon to take you and the nurse back. Just, uh, have a seat. Can I get you anything?"

Bessie shook her head, but Adam said, "I'll send in some coffee. Please, sit down. I'll be right back."

A short time later, the wagon left, carrying Oscar and Bessie and the nurse and a bottle of tonic that Sudie had prepared for Lori.

Adam watched them go, feeling as alone as he had ever been in his life.

Eric leaned against the window frame and watched the wagon driving away. What in the hell was that old bat doing here? And why in the hell was Adam having one of their darkies—no, *two* of their darkies!—take her home?

Then he remembered that the old bat was Lori McClintock's mother or something. And that sweet little Lori McClintock was now living *here,* with Adam.

Or had he imagined all that? It seemed too fantastic to be anything more than a fever dream, but Eric hadn't been as far gone as he'd been pretending to be these past few days. He'd heard a lot more than anybody thought, and he was pretty sure Adam really had married Lori. And he was also sure that even though they were married, all was not quite well.

Eric smiled, rubbing a hand over his nearly-shaved head and smoothly shaved cheeks. Sudie had been pretty brutal in removing most of his body hair, and Eric hadn't really minded, since the lice had gone with it. Still, he'd have to keep his hat on for a few weeks, until he was presentable again.

Smiling at the thought, he heard the bedroom door open and turned to see Sudie coming in.

"What you doin' outta bed?" she demanded, outraged.

"Jesus, Sudie," Eric cried, clamping both hands over his privates and scurrying back to his bed. Only when he was safely under the covers again and saw the expression on Sudie's face did he realize his mistake.

"You're actin' kinda spry for somebody knockin' on death's door," she observed.

Well, how long had he expected to be able to fool her? She'd always been the only one who could see through him. He gave her one of his grins, the one that usually softened her up, no matter what he'd done. "Maybe I just like havin' you wait on me, Sudie. Reminds me of when I was a little boy. You were always the only one who cared about me."

But this time she didn't soften. In fact, he thought she stiffened slightly, as if in silent resistance to his charm. He felt a faint stirring of alarm. If Sudie wasn't on his side anymore . . . But that was ridiculous. He'd always been able to get around her before. He was just out of practice.

He reached out a hand to her. "You're about the only woman I know who gets prettier as she gets older, Sudie. How do you do it?"

As he had expected, she smiled, although it wasn't the smile he was used to. This one was harder than the one he remembered, but maybe she'd grown hard while he was away. But she took his hand in both of hers. Her palms were rough and callused, just the same as he remembered, and he found that comforting.

"You always did like pretty womens," she observed.

"But you're my favorite," he swore. The only one who had ever truly cared about him.

"I didn't know you was courtin' Miss Lori 'fore you left," she said, and her smile vanished.

Bitch! What business of hers was it? But of course he didn't say that. She was still his only true ally in this house.

"I wouldn't call it *courting* exactly," he said, loathe to have even a slave think he'd ever been seriously interested in that little whore.

Still holding his hand in one of hers, she reached over with her other one and stroked his forehead. "But you said she promise to wait for you. She must've thought you was gonna marry her."

He frowned, remembering how he'd thought the same thing, at least once or twice. The memory of sweet little Lori had been a comfort to a lonely soldier. But she'd forgotten *him* the minute he was out of sight!

"It was always Adam with her, wasn't it?" he said, not realizing he'd spoken aloud until Sudie replied.

"Why'd she take up with you then if she wanted your brother?"

Stupid bitch! All women were stupid bitches, no matter what color they were! "Because she's a lying little whore, that's why! Always making eyes at Adam, but when I wanted to meet her, she came, didn't she?"

"You met her some place?"

Eric gave her a disgusted glance. "You don't think I went calling on her, do you? A Ross, going to see a piece of trash like that? Of course I met her some place!"

"I bet she was easy to trick," Sudie said, and when he looked up at her, he saw the admiration in her eyes.

He grinned, basking in it. "So easy, I almost felt guilty!"

"How'd you do it?" she asked, leaning forward eagerly, still holding his hand and stroking his face, just the way she'd always done when he was a little boy.

"I gave her a note," he admitted, almost chuckling with the recollection of how easy it had been.

"You must've said some pretty things to make her forget about Adam," she guessed.

But he had been much more clever than that! "She thought the note *was* from Adam," he bragged. "She thought *he* was the one who wanted to meet her!"

Sudie's eyes widened with surprise and, he sensed instantly, disapproval.

"What kind of a girl would meet a man alone?" he demanded in his own defense. "I told you, she's just a cheap little whore. And when I showed up instead of Adam, she didn't mind a bit! She was just as happy to spread her legs for me, wasn't she?"

"Was she?" Sudie asked, still frowning.

"What did she tell you?" he asked, suddenly suspicious.

"That you forced her," Sudie said.

"Lying little bitch!" he fairly shouted, bolting upright on the bed. "I never forced a woman in my life! Oh, she put up a little fuss—they always do so they can claim they're ladies—but she wanted it. She wanted it more than I did! And when it was over, it was *me* she loved, not Adam! And she said she'd wait for me, that lying bitch."

"There now, don't get worked up," she soothed, easing him back down again. "You'll bring the fever back. Just lay still for a while. Then I'll fix you a nice hot bath and bring you some clean clothes. If you're gonna be up and around, you gotta be decent," she added with an odd smile.

She looked strange, as if she wanted to cry even though her lips were smiling, but Eric figured he must be mistaken. Sudie wasn't upset. Why should she be? Gently, she laid his hand back down on top of the blanket and turned away from the bed. She closed the door softly behind her when she went out, just the way she always did. So he was right and nothing was wrong.

Except that Adam had married Lori McClintock.

But maybe that wasn't so bad, he decided, as he considered the situation anew. No matter what Eric might have thought when he'd been lonely and facing death, he never would have actually married Lori. Only a fool like Adam would *marry* to get what he wanted from a woman. But since Adam *had* been fool enough to marry her and bring her to live right in his house, now Eric could have her whenever he wanted her.

Lacing his fingers behind his head, he laid back and considered the delightful possibilities. Oh, yes, and wouldn't she be grateful to have a real man again instead of a worthless cripple?

* * *

"What's *she* doing here?" Lori demanded the instant she saw the slave girl Bessie had brought with her.

The girl, whose name she knew was Lucy because she was one of the potential wet nurses Sudie had presented to her weeks ago, had brought her own baby, and now stood uncertainly in the doorway.

"Mr. Ross sent her to feed Matthew," Bessie explained.

"I'm feeding Matthew!" Lori insisted angrily and snatched her baby up from the basket where he'd been lying and hugged him to her, lest someone try to take him away.

"You won't be for long if you don't start eating," Bessie warned. "I told you I'm afraid you'll lose your milk, and then you'll *both* get sick. If you want to make yourself sick, that's your business, but you ain't dragging a poor, helpless baby with you!"

"I'm not sick!" Lori insisted, feeling something suspiciously like panic rising painfully in her chest.

"Not yet, but if you don't start eating—"

"I'll eat! I'll force myself! Adam Ross isn't going to take my baby away from me!"

"Nobody's gonna take him anywhere," Bessie soothed her. "Lucy here's gonna stay with us and—"

"No, she isn't! You send her right back where she came from! We don't need anything from Adam Ross!"

For a moment, Lori was afraid Bessie would point out that they were, in fact, dependent upon him for almost everything, but mercifully, she didn't. Instead, she turned to Lucy. "Why don't you wait outside for a minute while I talk to Miss Lori? Tell the driver not to leave just yet, until we get things settled."

"You might as well tell them both to leave right now," Lori said before Lucy was even out the door. "Because I'm not going to let her nurse my baby!"

"Then I better see you swallow some food, because if I

don't, I'm gonna have that big fella driving the wagon come in here and take Matthew away from you by force!"

"No!" Lori cried, hugging Matthew so tightly he squalled in protest, but Bessie only glared at her, and Lori was very much afraid she would be as good as her word. "All right," she agreed at last. "I'll . . . try."

"Sit down," Bessie commanded her. "We'll start with some mush. That oughta go down easy."

Lori nearly gagged at the mere thought and instinctively laid a hand over the burning ache in her stomach that had prevented her from eating for almost three days, ever since she'd understood just what kind of a man Adam Ross really was.

In a moment, Bessie set a bowl of the yellow goo in front of her. It was still slightly warm from breakfast, but it didn't look the least bit appetizing. Bessie stuck a wooden spoon in it and lifted it to Lori's mouth.

Once again, she felt the urge to gag, but she shifted Matthew into the crook of her left arm and snatched the spoon from Bessie. Giving her stepmother one last, defiant glare, she put the spoon in her mouth and forced herself to swallow the unappetizing glop of mush.

For one awful moment she thought it might come right back up again, but she made herself swallow a second one before that could happen. And when they both stayed down, she swallowed a third and a fourth spoonful. She kept glaring at Bessie who watched her as if she didn't trust her for one instant, until, to Lori's surprise, the bowl was empty.

Only then did Bessie sigh with apparent relief. "Well, now, if I'd knowed all it took was to get you good and mad, I could've done that days ago," she observed and went outside.

She heard Bessie speaking to Lucy and Oscar and, in another moment, heard the wagon driving away.

"How could you have done that?" Lori demanded when Bessie came back inside, alone. "How could you have gone to him behind my back?"

"I had to do something before you starved yourself and that baby to death, didn't I?"

Lori didn't think she'd ever been this furious. "I wasn't starving! Did he think that if he took Matthew, I'd come back to him?"

"I told you, the girl was going to stay here with us. He don't have no expectation you're coming back to him."

"Well, he better not!" Lori fumed, jumping up to pace. She shifted Matthew to her shoulder and began to pat him when he fussed at the change of position. "That . . . that cad!" she exclaimed furiously. "That low life deceiver!"

"You can swear if it'll make you feel better," Bessie said mildly.

"That son of a bitch!" Lori said, just to prove she could, no matter what Bessie thought. "How dare he pretend to be so good and kind and such a perfect gentleman?"

"You think he was pretending?" Bessie asked, taking the seat on the bench that Lori had vacated and watching her pace with apparent interest.

"Of course he was pretending! He wanted me to trust him! He wanted me to believe in him!"

"I expect he wanted you to love him, too."

"Yes, he did!" Lori agreed in outrage. "Because he thought if I loved him, I wouldn't care how he treated me!"

"And he was pretty mean to you, I guess. He beat you and starved you and kept you locked in your room and—"

"There's worse things than that!" Lori insisted, wishing her face didn't feel quite so hot.

"Is there?" Bessie asked. "Like what?"

"You know what! He didn't believe me!"

Bessie nodded sagely. "He thought you was just a silly girl who let herself be seduced by his brother. But he could've thought worse of you, you know. He could've thought you was a cheap little hussy who wasn't worth saving, but he didn't, did he? And he could've thought he was too good for a girl like you, especially one who was already carrying another man's baby. Instead, he married you. Took you for his wife and gave you and your baby his name and a fine home and treated you with as much respect as if you'd been his first choice of a wife."

"Not with *that* much respect!" Lori defended herself. "I told him what really happened, but he didn't believe me! He didn't trust me!"

Bessie shrugged, as if this was of little importance, making Lori even angrier. "So he was wrong. Maybe he was even stupid and foolish. Lots of men is from time to time, Lori. Lots of women, too."

"What does that mean?" Lori asked suspiciously.

"It means *you* was wrong, too, when you figured Adam Ross was perfect. He ain't. He's just a man, like all the rest, and he's gonna be wrong sometimes. He's even gonna hurt the people he loves sometimes, but that don't make him evil or even a little bit bad. That just makes him human."

"He betrayed me!"

"How? Because he made a mistake?"

"He took his brother's word over mine!"

"He's known his brother a whole lot longer than he's known you," Bessie pointed out.

"Then he should know what a liar Eric is!"

"How do he know you ain't a liar, too? And you got more reason to lie about what happened than Eric did, too."

"Stop it, Bessie! Stop being so . . ." She caught herself when she realized she was going to say "reasonable."

"I just figured you needed something else to think about while you was planning ways to murder Adam Ross."

"Bessie!" Lori cried, appalled. "I never—"

"Sure you did," Bessie told her with a grin. "But that's all right. Ain't no wife in the world hasn't given some thought to the matter of doing away with her husband. It can help you through the rough patches, so long as you don't go through with it. I just thought maybe you'd like some reasons *not* to murder him, too. Remembering the good times might help some. If there *was* good times," she added innocently.

"Of course there were!" Lori exclaimed, then caught herself again. She didn't want to defend Adam Ross. She didn't even want to think well of him after what he'd done to her. In spite of her intentions, however, she began to remember. The way he'd been with Matthew, so gentle and tender. The way he'd been with her, so patient and kind when she'd been terrified of his touch. The way he'd presented her to his friends, as if she really had been his first choice of a wife, and not someone he'd taken out of pity and duty.

Bessie was right. He *had* been good to her. Not perfect, perhaps, but then, who could have expected him to be? And when she'd left him, hadn't he come after her? As if he missed her, when another man might have counted his blessings at being rid of a wife he'd never wanted in the first place.

"He wants to come see you," Bessie said.

Once again, Lori felt the panic swelling within her. "Not yet," she pleaded, holding Matthew more tightly to her. "I'm not ready to see him yet."

"Don't make him wait too long," Bessie advised. "He might decide he's better off without all the aggravation."

Unable to concentrate on any one thing, Adam had been wandering aimlessly around the property all afternoon, ever since Oscar and Lucy had returned from the McClintock cabin to report that Lori had refused to allow Lucy to stay and Bessie had sent no message summoning him. He'd been pretending to supervise the various tasks but really just making a general nuisance of himself, harassing his slaves who were only trying to do their work in peace.

Finally, he reluctantly returned to the house where he found Sudie waiting anxiously for him.

"Massa Adam, can I talk to you?" she asked.

Adam couldn't ever recall seeing her like this. She looked shaken and unsure of herself, as if her entire world had suddenly crumbled around her.

"Are you all right?" he asked in concern, instinctively taking her arm. "Is it Eric?" A worse thought occurred to him. "Is it *Lori?* My God, has something happened to her?"

"No," she assured him. "Not that I know of. Please, can we go to your office?"

This must be serious indeed if she needed privacy.

"Certainly." He held onto her arm, convinced somehow that she needed his support as they made their way down the hall to his office door.

"Sit down," he urged her when they were inside, closing the door behind them.

Ordinarily, she would have protested. It wasn't proper for her to sit in her master's presence, but this time she sat without a word, sinking down onto the sofa as if she no longer trusted her legs to hold her.

"What is it, Sudie? Is Eric worse?" She had always been so devoted to his brother, this was the only thing he could imagine that could have upset her so much.

She looked up at him with eyes that seemed to have seen all the suffering in the world. "He ain't sick, if that's what you mean."

"Then what is it?" he asked, sitting down beside her.

She had to swallow before she could speak. "He told me what happened."

"What happened?" Adam echoed in confusion.

"With Miss Lori."

Adam felt as if all the blood in his body had suddenly turned to ice, and he couldn't seem to draw a breath. He didn't want to hear this, he knew he didn't, but he couldn't summon his voice to stop her.

"It was like she said. He forced her." Speaking the words was an agony to her, but hearing them was worse for Adam. Dear God, what had he done?

"He *admitted* that?" Adam asked incredulously when he had finally found his voice again.

Sudie shook her head. "He still don't think he done anything wrong. But from what he said . . ." She lifted a trembling hand to cover her mouth, as if she couldn't bear to repeat the words.

"What did he say?" Adam asked, knowing he didn't really want to know, certain the knowledge would only cause him pain, but equally certain that he deserved to feel it.

"He tricked her."

Adam closed his eyes, remembering how Lori had told him the same thing and knowing now how she must have felt when he didn't believe her. "How did he trick her?"

"Oh, Massa, I can't!" she cried, laying her hand on his arm, as if she could somehow restrain him from making her tell.

Every instinct begged him to do so, but he said, "Tell me, Sudie. I have to know."

Her eyes had filled with tears, and he watched in horrified fascination as one spilled over and slid down her cheek. An ancient memory stirred, one he'd never allowed himself to recall, and he knew that he *had* seen Sudie cry before, very long ago. He'd simply refused to remember because he'd also refused to remember *why* she had been crying.

"He give her a note. Ask her to meet him, except . . ."

"Except *what?*" he prodded as terror tied his insides into knots.

"Except she think the note from you. She had feelings for you, and you was the one she think she gonna meet that day."

He made a strangled sound of anguish, too horrified at first to even comprehend. But his mind was too quick, and before he was ready for the onslaught of guilt, he understood it all. Lori had loved *him*. How many times had she told him that? And how many times had he refused to believe her? But she hadn't told him about the note. Dear God, she could have destroyed him with that, but she hadn't said a word! *Why?* Why had she protected him like that? He had no idea, but for a moment he thought the agony of it would kill him just the same.

And then, mercifully, he felt the rage. The nameless, inchoate fury that rose up inside of him like a red tide until the roaring of it drowned out even the screaming of his own guilt.

"Where you goin'?" Sudie cried in alarm, and only then did he realize he'd risen to his feet.

"I'm going to kill him," he replied, amazed to hear how calm he sounded when inside he was howling with pain and rage.

"No, Massa, no!" she screamed, trying to grab him, but he shook off her hands. He threw open the door and went into the hall and somehow his feet carried him without any conscious direction from Adam, who could think of only one thing: avenging Lori.

Vaguely, he heard Sudie screaming, but that was no longer important. All that was important was finding Eric.

His bedroom door was closed. Adam flung it open. His gaze went immediately to the bed, where he expected to find his brother languishing. But the bed was empty, and when he looked up, he saw Eric was sitting in a chair beside the window, feet propped on the windowsill, fully clothed and obviously enjoying the autumn breeze.

"Well, well, I was beginning to think you weren't going to visit me at all, Brother," Eric said, smiling up at Adam with a grin Adam suddenly realized he despised. "But then, I guess that wife of yours keeps you pretty busy. As I remember, she can really wear a man out, can't she?"

Adam fell on him with a roar, smashing his fist into that awful grin in a desperate attempt to obliterate it completely. The chair fell over beneath them, tumbling them to the floor, but Adam hardly noticed. He was too busy pounding Eric, driving his fists into Eric's solid flesh again and again, wanting to beat him until Eric simply ceased to exist.

Eric threw up his arms instinctively to defend himself and scrambled and struggled to get away, while at the same time trying to strike back. Before either of them could succeed in their purposes, strong hands grabbed Adam from behind and hauled him up to his feet.

"Stop it, Massa! Stop it!" Oscar's voice cried as Oscar's arms restrained him, pinning his arms to his sides and pulling him back. "He still your brother!"

"He raped my wife!" Adam protested.

"Is that what she claims?" Eric demanded, outraged. "That lying little whore!"

Adam kicked out with his good leg, catching Eric in the thigh and making him howl before Oscar dragged him farther back. For his part, Eric scooted in the opposite direction, holding his injured leg.

"You trying to cripple me?" Eric complained, filling Adam with fresh rage for old sins.

But even this rage was no match for Oscar's brute strength, and after a few more minutes, he prevailed, and Adam went limp in surrender, unable to struggle any more.

Still, Oscar did not release him, as if he didn't trust him, which was probably just as well. If Adam did kill Eric, he would have to explain why, and Lori had already suffered enough shame at their hands.

"I want you out of this house. Today," he told Eric.

"Are you crazy? This is my house, too!"

"I might have been crazy, but I'm perfectly sane now. And this *was* your house, but you lost all claim to it when you attacked my wife, and I won't have you here another minute!"

"I'm sick!" Eric complained. "I just got back from fighting a war!"

"I don't care if you're dying!" Adam said brutally. "And if you're still here by . . ." He glanced out the window to judge the time, ". . . by sundown, I *will* kill you, and this time *nobody* will stop me."

He gave Oscar a meaningful glare, and the big slave released him with obvious reluctance. Adam pulled himself up to his full height and straightened his clothes with a jerk. "Do I make myself clear?"

But Eric wasn't intimidated. "This place is half mine, don't forget. You can't send me away with nothing! I'll get the law after you."

Of course, Eric would have his own interests at heart. But with the whole country in chaos from the war, Adam was fairly certain it would be quite a while before the law could deal with such a case. Still, he didn't ever want anymore contact with Eric. This had to be a clean break.

"I'll buy you out then. I have about fifty dollars in gold that I've been saving until——"

"Fifty dollars!" Eric scoffed, pushing himself to his feet with difficulty. Adam was gratified to see that he had hurt him, if only a little. "You've got a hundred thousand dollars worth of slaves out there, not even counting the land! I want half of *everything!"*

"Maybe the slaves were worth that much *before* the war, but you'd be lucky to get fifty dollars in Confederate money for Oscar here, *if* you could find somebody willing to buy him. Face it, Eric. The slaves are worthless, and the land is, too, at least until this war is over."

"And then you'll be rich again, and what will I have?"

"And then the Yankees will own it all!" Adam contradicted him. "You know that as well as I do!"

"We whipped the Yankees!" Eric reminded him.

"In Texas, maybe, but no place else. The South can't hold out much longer, and when they finally give it up, our slaves'll be free, and we'll be no better off than the McClintocks were!" Beside him, he could feel Oscar stiffen in reaction, but he didn't have time to worry about that now. "I'm offering you *gold,* Eric. You can go anyplace with that. Make a new start. It's your only chance, because if you stay here, I'll kill you. I swear it on my mother's grave."

"*Our* mother's grave!" Eric reminded him brutally.

But Eric thought of Lori and felt no guilt at all. He glanced around and saw Sudie hovering in the doorway, her face ashen.

"I'll give Sudie the money to bring to you, and she can help you pack. I'm going to fetch Lori home now. When I get back, you'll be gone, because if you're not . . ."

He let the implied threat hang between them for a moment, and when Eric made no reply, Adam turned and left, forcing Sudie to step aside and let him pass. His bad leg ached, but he welcomed the pain. It cleared his mind and reminded him he was still alive, and that he still had a life worth living.

But only if he could get Lori back. Please God, he prayed as he hurried down the hall to his office safe. He'd only need a minute to get the money out and give it to Sudie. Then he would get the buggy and go to her and beg her to forgive him. He'd go down on his knees if he had to. No humiliation was too great to atone for what he had done to her—if only she would come home.

Eric counted out the gold coins one more time. Forty-seven dollars. How in the hell had Adam managed to accumulate so much? Although he'd pretended to scoff, he'd secretly been shocked to find out Adam had any gold at all. He'd known, of course, that Adam had managed to sell some cotton in Mexico every year since the war had begun, but business had never interested him much. So long as he had spending money, he didn't much care how they were doing, otherwise.

As he pulled the drawstring pouch shut over the coins, another thought occurred to him. Would Adam have offered him *all* the money he had? Of course not! He'd keep some for himself. Which meant there was probably at least this much or more still in the safe.

He glanced up at Sudie who was busy stuffing his few remaining belongings into his saddle bags. "Do you know the combination to the safe?" he asked her. Hell, she knew everything else around here, didn't she?

She froze, and when she turned slowly to face him, he saw with surprise that she was crying. "He give you every penny he gots. Won't do you no good to go lookin' through his safe."

Eric felt a quick flash of anger. He should have known she'd take up for Adam. She always had. "You expect me to believe this is all the money he has in the world?"

"Believe it or not, it the truth." She turned back to her task, pausing only to dash the tears from her cheeks.

What in the hell did *she* have to cry about? *He* was the one being thrown out of his own house. And all because that little tart, Lori McClintock, couldn't keep her legs together. Suddenly, Eric remembered something Adam had said. He'd said he was going to *fetch* Lori, but where had she gone and why?

He glanced at Sudie again and considered his next question carefully. "Uh, where did Adam go? I need to know how much time I've got before he gets back," he added at Sudie's suspicious glance. "He did threaten to kill me, you'll remember." Not that Eric believed for a moment that Adam would have the guts to do so.

"He went down to the McClintock place," Sudie said with obvious reluctance.

"Oh, that's right," Eric said, pretending to remember. "He was going to fetch Lori. But what's she doing down there instead of being here with her loving husband?"

Color suddenly came to Sudie's face, as if she'd just gotten mad or something, although she gave no other sign of it. "When you come home, she took the baby and left," she said, as if she was accusing him of something. "Didn't want to be in the same house as you."

But Eric didn't hear the last part, only the first. *"Baby? What baby?"*

Sudie's eyes grew wide with alarm, but she quickly turned away and resumed her packing. "Does she have a *baby* already?" he asked in amazement, only vaguely aware of Sudie's odd reaction. His brother hadn't wasted any time, had he? When had he said they'd gotten married? April, he thought, although he might've been mistaken. Let's see, that was only . . . six months ago! Not enough time for a baby, at least not unless it got started a lot earlier. Which would, he realized, explain why Adam had married her in the first place. That little whore must've gone after his brother as soon as he'd left! Not one to waste time either, was she?

He counted back to see just how little she had wasted, just for curiosity, and almost ran out of months.

"Your things is all packed," Sudie said with forced brightness, holding up his bags. "You'd best be going. Oscar gots a horse saddled for you. I told him to pick the best one we got so—"

Eric didn't move. "How old is Lori's baby, Sudie?"

He could see the fear in her eyes and felt the glow of satisfaction. "I . . . don't rightly know," she claimed.

"You do know, don't you? You know exactly, and that's why you won't tell me, because you know that *I* know exactly when that baby got in her belly. Because I'm the one who put it there."

"No! He Massa Adam's chile! He look just like him! Anybody can see it!" Sudie insisted frantically, only convincing Eric even more thoroughly that he was right.

"It's a boy, huh? My *son.*" He waited a second, expecting to feel something for the son he hadn't known existed, but all he felt was the burning envy that he'd always felt for his brother. "And Adam was going to take him from me just like he always took everything else! He thought he could take Lori and this place and *my son!* Well, we'll just see about that, won't we?"

"No, Massa Eric, you can't," Sudie cried, dropping the saddle bags and running to stop him when he would have left the room. "It ain't your chile! It ain't! And Massa Adam, he love that boy like his own son! He kill you if you try to take him away!"

"Like his own son?" Eric echoed in triumph, and watched with pleasure as Sudie blanched again with the knowledge that she had confessed the truth at last. He reached out and touched Sudie's face fondly. "If I'd known Adam was buying my son, too, I wouldn't've settled for forty-seven dollars. I think we've got a little more bargaining to do before we're finished."

Fifteen

Lori hadn't realized how weak she had become until she started eating again. Perhaps it was the food or perhaps it was simply the anger she felt at Adam Ross, but whatever the cause, she now had more energy than she knew what to do with. She was sweeping the dirt floor for the second time that day when she heard the sound of a buggy approaching the cabin.

For a second she froze in alarm. *He was coming for her!* But no sooner had that thought formed in her mind than another overtook it. *He wouldn't get her this time!*

Dropping the broom, she ran to where the old shotgun hung on the wall and snatched it down, checking to make sure it was still loaded. Thus armed, she hurried to the door that stood open to the fading sunlight.

But of course, it wasn't Eric, and he wasn't coming for her at all. It was Adam, as she should have known when she heard it was a buggy and not a rider approaching. Adam, the man she hated for all he had done to hurt her. And Adam, the man she still loved in spite of all the pain.

Tears came to her eyes, but she blinked them away furiously. If he was here to get Matthew . . . but she wouldn't give up her child, any more than she would return to Elmhurst. If Adam thought he could force her . . . Her hands tightened instinctively on the shotgun, even though she knew she could never hurt Adam, no matter what he did to her.

But he didn't have to know that, did he? And perhaps the gun would be enough to frighten him away.

She watched as he pulled the buggy to a halt in front of the cabin. She knew he saw her in the doorway. His gaze had found her at once, and he didn't take his eyes off her for more than a second at a time while he tied off the reins and climbed down.

In spite of her anger and her fear, she couldn't help noticing how handsome he looked, even though he was wearing the worn, casual clothes he used when he was working and even though his face looked haggard, as if he hadn't been sleeping any more than she had.

He took a few steps toward her, then stopped, glancing down at the shotgun. "You don't have to be afraid of me, Lori," he told her quietly. "I won't . . . hurt you," he added, and she wondered at the way his voice almost broke. "And I won't make you do anything you don't want to do. I just want to talk to you for a few minutes."

He looked so sad and so defeated that Lori suddenly felt like a fool for pointing a shotgun at him. Hastily, she hoisted it back up to where it normally hung on the wall beside the door and turned back to face him. Her hands felt awkward with nothing to hold, so she locked them together in front of her as she wondered what to do next. Finally, she decided she had to invite him inside.

"Come on in," she said, backing up to allow him to enter because for some reason she didn't feel safe turning her back to him.

But he made no threatening moves. He simply came inside and stopped before her, keeping a proper distance, although she could tell it pained him to do so. Seemingly of their own accord, his hands came up, as if to reach for her, but when she stepped back in alarm, he dropped them to his sides again.

His expression spoke of defeat and a sadness she couldn't even begin to understand. He glanced around the room, as if he were looking for something. "Matthew?" he said anxiously. "Is he . . . ?"

"He's asleep," she told him, gesturing to the bedroom door.

"Is he all right? When Lucy came back—"

"He's *fine,*" she said, instantly angry at the reminder of the way he'd tried to take her baby away.

"I was worried about you both," he explained. "When Bessie said you weren't eating, I thought it might be too much for you to—"

"I'm eating," she told him sharply. If he thought he was going to come in here and tell her—

"Thank God," he said so fervently that Lori's anger evaporated. "Lori, I came to tell you that Eric's gone," he added before she could even get her breath.

"What?"

"I sent him away. I . . . I know what he did to you. I don't know if you can ever forgive me for not believing you before, but that's why I'm here now, to beg you for that forgiveness and to ask you to come home with me."

Lori was sure she must be dreaming because this couldn't really be happening. What could have changed Adam's mind? And why would he have suddenly decided she was telling the truth? She shook her head, trying to clear it, but Adam apparently misinterpreted the gesture.

"Oh, please, Lori, give me another chance!" he pleaded. "I know you must hate me. This is all my fault! If I hadn't been such a fool! If I'd only realized . . . Why didn't you tell me about the note he sent you?"

Lori almost gasped in surprise. "How did you find out about that?"

"Sudie told me. He told her everything that happened."

"He *admitted* it?" she asked incredulously.

But Adam shook his head. "He still doesn't think he did anything wrong, but we do, Lori. We know now that . . ." His voice broke, and to her amazement, Lori saw that he had

ears in his eyes. "I wanted to kill him, Lori. I still do, even
f he *is* my brother, and if he ever shows his face here again,
will!"

"Oh, Adam!" Lori cried, taking hold of his arms as if she
ould restrain him from that violence.

"Why didn't you tell me about the note?" he asked again,
is eyes full of more pain than anyone should have to bear.

She shook her head. "I was so stupid, I was ashamed for
ou to know."

"Ashamed? I'm the one who was stupid! Why didn't I see
ow you felt about me? How could I have been so blind?
Even Eric knew, and he used that, didn't he? He used my
tupidity to hurt you, and it's all my fault!"

"No!" Lori told him angrily. "It's *not* your fault! And it's
ot *my* fault either! It's taken me months to understand that,
and I don't want you torturing yourself over it either! It was
Eric's fault! He's the one—the *only* one—to blame. I couldn't
have stopped him and neither could you. I refuse to feel
guilty any longer, and I won't let you feel guilty, either."

He gazed down at her for a long moment, and in that
moment, in his eyes, she saw how much he loved her and
ow much it would cost him to lose her now. "Can you ever
forgive me for not believing you?" he asked brokenly.

Tears sprang to her eyes, and she didn't even try to blink
hem away. "I think I can."

With a groan, he wrapped his arms around her and crushed
er to his chest. "I'll make it up to you, my darling, I promise
you," he breathed into her hair. "I'll make you the happiest
woman alive!"

She was crying, but that made her smile in spite of her
tears. "I think I already am!" she told him.

He squeezed her more tightly for a moment, then pushed
her slightly away so he could see her face. "Oh, no, you're
not. You don't even know what happiness is yet, but I'll show
you. I'll devote every day of the rest of my life to showing

you!" he vowed with the most beautiful smile Lori had ever seen, and then he kissed her.

He'd kissed her many times in the past few months, but never like this. This time he kissed her as if she were the most precious thing on the earth, as if he were worshiping her with his lips and his hands. And when he was done, he pulled away and asked, "Will you come home with me now? Will you bring our son and come home?"

Lori had truly believed she couldn't be any happier, but when she heard him say "our son," she knew she had been wrong. For a second, she thought her heart might burst with joy, and she smiled through her tears and said, "Yes, I will."

Only when she saw how he closed his eyes and felt the shudder of relief ripple through him did she understand how very much she meant to him and how devastated he would have been if she had refused him. But she hadn't refused him, and he had done everything she had asked of him and more, and for the first time since he had come to this house last spring and asked her to marry him, Lori believed that everything was finally going to be fine. No, not merely fine but *wonderful!*

"I have to tell Bessie," she said.

"No need for that," Bessie informed them from the doorway. She was smiling as proudly as if she were personally responsible for getting them back together again.

They jumped guiltily apart and then laughed because they had nothing at all to feel guilty about.

"I'm going home," Lori told her happily, looking up at Adam who was gazing back down at her with frank adoration.

"That's what I figured," Bessie said. "I come to help you pack. Not that I'm in a hurry to get rid of you or anything," she added with a wink. "I reckon that brother of yours is gone," she said to Adam.

"He's gone for good," Adam confirmed, slipping his arm around Lori's waist *and* pulling her snugly to his side.

"Well, then, what're we waiting for?" Bessie wanted to now.

With their help, Lori had all her and Matthew's things gathered into a bundle in a matter of minutes. The baby was still sleeping in his basket, so Adam picked him up, basket and all.

When Lori saw how he held it, so gently, and how he looked at the sleeping baby, so adoringly, and how he reached out to touch Matthew's satiny cheek with one finger, so tenderly, tears came to her eyes again.

"I think I missed him almost as much as I missed you," Adam told her, his own eyes suspiciously bright. "He really is my son now, and he always will be."

Lori could only nod, not trusting herself to speak because the tears of joy were so close and Adam might not understand if she cried that it was only from happiness.

She followed him out as he carried the baby and basket to the buggy and set them ever so carefully on the floor. Bessie had already placed the bundle of their clothes behind the seat, and she now stood, beaming proudly, ready to see them off.

"Thank you for everything," Lori told her stepmother, giving her a hug.

"Oh, pshaw, I didn't do nothing but put up with you for a few days," Bessie protested, although the tears standing in her eyes betrayed her. "Get along with you now before I embarrass myself!"

Lori allowed Adam to help her into the buggy, then he climbed up, too, and they were off. She glanced down to make sure Matthew was secure and found he was still sleeping soundly, oblivious to the drama that had taken place around him. Then she looked up to find Adam was watching her.

"I love you," he said.

"I love you, too. I always have."

His eyes grew shadowed, and she saw that he still doubted her.

"Why don't you believe that?" she asked.

He smiled or tried to. "I find it difficult to . . . I'm a cripple, Lori, and you're a beautiful young woman."

But Lori shook her head. "Eric is the one who's crippled. His soul is twisted and deformed, and he takes pleasure from hurting others. You're not like that, Adam. You may not be perfect," she said, laying a hand on his damaged thigh, "but you're good inside, where it matters. And *that's* why I love you."

He leaned down and kissed her lightly on the lips, a promise of things to come, and then he said, "You're right, I'm not perfect, and I'm not really good inside, as I think I've already proved, but I'm willing to let you believe that I am," he added when she would have protested, "and I'm more than willing to try to live up to your opinion of me."

Lori leaned her head against his shoulder, perfectly content for the first time since she could remember. The rest of the short trip passed in blissful silence as Lori savored her newfound happiness and contemplated a whole lifetime of it.

She could see the beautiful house up ahead, and the other out buildings, the place she could now truthfully say was her home. She was about to tell Adam how glad she was to be back when she felt him stiffen beside her and heard him make a small sound of alarm.

"What is it? What's the matter?" she asked, looking back and forth between his face and the plantation buildings, trying to figure out what had disturbed him.

Adam tried to tell himself it wasn't possible. Probably, Eric hadn't liked the horse Oscar had saddled for him. Probably, he had demanded another and ridden away on it, which would explain why this one was still standing outside the back door, tethered to the hitching post as it had been when he'd left.

A quick glance at the horizon confirmed that it was officially sundown, even though the sky was still light. He'd
threatened to kill Eric if he was still here when he got back,
and from the rage building in his chest, he knew he would
do just that if his brother had defied him. If Eric upset Lori,
if he said one thing to her . . .

"Adam, is something wrong?" Lori asked him again, and
he tried to smile reassuringly.

"I don't think so," he lied as he pulled back on the reins
and drew the buggy to a halt. Quickly, he set the brake and
tied off the reins. "Wait here for a minute while I check on
something," he said, as he climbed out.

"What is it?" she demanded, but he didn't allow himself
to acknowledge her distress. He was too busy planning what
he would do. He should have carried a gun with him. He
realized that now. Eric would be armed. And if he'd changed
his mind about leaving . . .

Adam froze in horror when he looked up and saw Eric
coming out the back door. He was smiling that impudent
smile that Adam hated so much.

"Well, now, what have we here?" Eric asked.

"I told you to be gone when I got back," Adam reminded
him even as he registered the fact that Eric had a pistol
strapped to his hip.

"There was something you *didn't* tell me, though," Eric
said, strolling across the porch toward Adam as if he didn't
have a care in the world. "You forgot to tell me I've got a
son."

Behind him he heard Lori cry out in horror. Instinctively,
he turned to find her struggling to untie the reins, desperate
to escape his brother.

"Not so fast," Eric warned, jumping down the steps in
one leap. But Adam couldn't let him get to her.

He threw himself against Eric, but this time, his brother
was ready for him, and Eric's fist caught him squarely on
the chin.

Stars exploded before Adam's eyes as the pain ricocheted through his head, and his knees buckled, sending him sprawling to the ground. But Lori's anguished cry galvanized him against the weakness, and he shook his hammering head to clear it.

He came up on all fours to see Eric and Lori struggling. She'd gotten the reins untied, and he was trying to pull them out of her hands.

"You lying bitch!" Eric was saying as he fought with her. "Did you think you'd get away with this?"

The horse was dancing restlessly and the buggy lurched forward, telling Adam the brake had been released. Forcing his protesting body to move, he lunged to his feet, but not before Eric took hold of Lori and dragged her out of the buggy.

She screamed as he threw her to the ground, and Adam roared in rage as he forced his rubbery legs to propel him to Lori's defense.

His cry startled Eric who looked up to see his brother staggering towards him. It was like a nightmare in which everything happens too slowly. Adam's legs were like lead and even though he thought he was running, he wasn't fast enough, because Eric had time to reach for his pistol and pull it out of its holster and point it at Adam's chest.

For one horrible moment, Adam knew he was going to die, but worse than that was the awful knowledge that he wouldn't be able to save Lori and the baby from Eric. In the same instant that this thought formed with crystal clarity in his mind, he saw Eric smile. The same terrible smile he'd worn the other time, when he'd lain in wait to kill the brother who he imagined had stolen everything from him.

But just as Eric's thumb pulled back the hammer, Lori sprang up from the ground and grabbed his arm. The pistol exploded, belching flame and smoke, but the bullet went wild. Glass shattered somewhere behind him just as Adam threw himself against his brother. Frantically, he wrestled the pistol out of his hand.

Eric was still struggling, still fighting, but the sound of Lori's screams and someone else's—Sudie?—drew Adam's attention.

"The baby!" Lori was screaming and pointing and then Adam saw, too. The gunshot had frightened the horse, and it had bolted, dragging the buggy and the baby still inside of it along behind.

Adam drew back his fist and slammed it into Eric's face, and mercifully, Eric went limp beneath him. He forced himself up, taking in the situation with one quick glance. The buggy swayed dangerously from side to side as it bounced behind the horse, and the horse was heading blindly for the fields where the rough ground would surely send the buggy toppling over.

Then he saw the horse that Oscar had saddled, straining against its tether, equally as frightened by the gunshot but unable to escape. Adam ran for it.

He snatched the reins loose, jerking the animal's head down so it wouldn't rear, then jamming his left foot into the stirrup. Ignoring the tearing agony in his damaged leg as he forced it to take his weight, he threw himself up into the saddle. The horse needed no urging to go racing off.

Although Adam hadn't ridden in years, he instinctively remembered how to guide the animal, directing it toward the careening buggy that had now reached the harvested fields. As he watched helplessly, the wheels struck a furrow, and it bounced skyward. Adam lost his breath with terror as it landed, striking the ground with a bone-jarring jolt that sent it crashing over on its side.

"*Matthew!*" he screamed as he urged his horse on then sawed on the reins to bring his mount to a sliding halt beside the other horse that was kicking frantically against the traces in an attempt to rid itself of the dead weight of the buggy so it could truly flee.

Somehow, Adam got hold of the animal's harness and dragged it to a halt. Although he wanted to scream out his own terror—where in God's name was Matthew?—he somehow managed to speak softly and soothingly to the hysterical animal.

Matthew, where are you? he wondered desperately, *and dear God, why aren't you crying?* But all he could hear as he slid down from his saddle was Lori's keening wail as she raced toward him across the field, holding her skirts up with both hands as she ran.

Others were coming behind her, but he took no time to notice who it was. His bad leg had collapsed under him in searing agony when he hit the ground, and he needed all his strength to hold himself upright and keep the frightened horse from bolting again.

"Matthew, can you hear me?" he cried, knowing even as he did so that even if the baby *could* hear him, he wouldn't understand. Dear heaven, if anything had happened to the boy, how would he bear Lori's grief, much less his own?

"Matthew, baby, where are you, sweetheart?" Lori was screaming, nearly hysterical herself as she swooped down on the wreckage of the buggy.

That's when he saw it, the basket Matthew had been in, lying crushed beneath the overturned wheel. His blood went cold and rushed from his head, and for a moment he was afraid he might pass out from the horror of knowing the little body would be just as crushed beneath it.

Lori was trying to lift the buggy, using all her feeble strength. Screaming the baby's name over and over, she was unable to budge it. Instinctively, Adam moved to help her, but his damaged leg refused to carry him, and he fell to his knees in the dirt and had to roll to keep from being trampled by the terrified horse which was still trying frantically to escape.

Then the buggy moved, righting itself, and Adam looked up to find that Oscar had put his considerable strength to the task. Lori scrambled beneath it before it was even upright, lunging for the remains of the basket, lifting it and throwing it aside before Adam could warn her not to look.

Then he heard her cry of anguish and knew he was too late.

"You killed him!" Sudie cried. Adam looked up in surprise. He hadn't known she was there, and then he saw that Eric was with her. His face was flushed from running, and he didn't seem to realize that Sudie had thrown the accusation at *him*.

"You killed your own baby!" Sudie shrieked again, slapping at him again and again with all her might, as if she would beat him to death.

But of course her strength was no match for his. He tried to swat her aside like a pesky fly, but when that didn't work, he grabbed her arms in a brutal grip that made her wince with pain.

"Stop it, old woman!" he shouted into her face.

"You killed him!" she screamed again, defiantly.

"I didn't do any such thing! The horse bolted! It wasn't my fault!"

"Nothing is *ever* your fault, is it?" Sudie replied furiously, even as she struggled fruitlessly to break his grip on her wrists. "You're always the innocent one, aren't you?"

"Shut up!" Eric shook her.

But she didn't shut up. "You're a devil, and it's all my fault!" The tears were streaming down her face. "It was *my* sin! Why did that little baby have to die for *my* sin!"

"Sudie, hush!" Oscar warned, but she didn't appear to hear him, or else she didn't care.

"I should've kept you!" she sobbed into Eric's face. "I thought the worst thing in the world was to be born a slave, but I was wrong! Look at you! You ain't even human!"

Eric pushed her away in disgust. "Stupid bitch! Stupid *nigger* bitch!"

"And if I'm your mother, what does that make *you?*' Sudie cried.

From the corner of his eye, Adam saw Lori reaching for the baby's broken body. He wanted to stop her, but he knew he couldn't reach her in time. Even still, he began to pull himself up, knowing he had to get to her.

"You're crazy!" Eric told Sudie, backing away from her, as if she were a poisonous snake.

"I must be for thinkin' you'd be better off if you was raised a white man!'"

"What are you talking about?" Eric's voice was shrill with a terror that had nothing to do with what had just happened to his child.

Ignoring the tearing agony in his leg, Adam lurched toward Lori, knowing he had to hold her.

"I'm talking about that night when you was born!" Sudie said, her voice even more shrill than Eric's. "There was two babies borned that night, one to me and one to the mistress. My baby was strong and healthy, but hers was dead!"

"No!" Eric shrieked. "I'm alive!"

"That's cause you was *my* baby! The mistress was too sick to know, so I switched them, told her she had a fine, big boy, but her boy was dead."

"No!" Eric was shaking his head frantically. Adam watched in horrified fascination as he half-crawled, half-limped to where Lori knelt in the dirt cradling her dead baby. "I'm white!"

"So am I!" Sudie reminded him, holding out her arm and pulling up her sleeve to reveal an arm even paler than Eric's. "I'm still a slave, though, even though I was whiter than the mistress. But I knowed my baby would be white enough to pass, if I could give him a chance, so I gave him to her and took her dead baby for mine."

Eric's eyes were wild. "Liar! You're a lying bitch!" he cried. "I'm a Ross! Chet Ross's son!"

Sudie's face might have been carved of stone. "Yes, you

is. Chet Ross's son and mine, 'cause he was a rapist just like you. And now everybody'll know that you're a nigger just like me!"

Eric cried out, a horrible sound, as if his soul were being ripped from his chest, and then he turned and ran.

Adam stared after him in horror for a long moment, unable to quite comprehend the story he had just heard on top of everything else. But then he heard Lori sobbing, and none of it even mattered anymore. He threw himself to the ground beside her, hardly even feeling the pain that burned like fire in his ruined leg.

He'd be a cripple now for sure, but that didn't matter. Nothing mattered except Lori and their son. She cradled the small, limp body to her breast as she wept. The little face was so white and still, and Adam could feel his heart breaking in his chest as his own tears began to fall.

He reached out, wrapping his arm around her as he used the other to push himself up, and then he and Lori jumped as another explosion split the stillness. He looked up in the direction of the sound, and he saw his brother back by the house, standing in a cloud of smoke from the shot. Had he fired at them? Was he still trying to kill Adam?

Before he could make sense of it, Eric's body crumpled and fell, and to his horror he understood: Eric had shot *himself.*

Someone cried out in protest, a primal wail that tore at Adam's heart—until he realized the source of it.

"Adam!" Lori screamed, holding up the baby for him to see. The little face was no longer white and still but pinched and purple with rage as Matthew howled out a protest against all the injustice in the world. "Look, he's alive!"

And he *was* alive and screaming like a banshee. But surely that meant he was terribly injured. No one could survive what he had been through.

Forgetting about his brother and everything else, he said, "Let's get him back to the house. I'll send for the doctor right away. *Oscar!*" But when he looked up, Oscar was gone, running after Sudie who was running toward where Eric lay.

And when he looked back at Lori, she was opening her bodice and offering the screaming baby her breast. Matthew was too angry to take it at first, but after a second or two, he decided to accept whatever comfort he could find, and to Adam's everlasting amazement, the baby began to suckle just as greedily as if he hadn't just been as good as dead a moment ago.

Lori looked up at him with tear-filled eyes. "He must've just been stunned!" she guessed, looking pretty stunned herself. She had a streak of dirt across her cheek, and her hair had come loose and was falling down around her shoulders in raven ringlets. With the baby at her breast, Adam thought he had never seen her look more beautiful. "I felt him jump at the shot and . . . Oh, God, the shot! What was it?"

But Adam covered her eyes when she tried to see. "No, don't," he warned her. "Just look at Matthew now."

"Was it Eric?" she demanded. "Did he shoot someone?"

"Himself, I think. It doesn't matter."

She gazed at him with horror-filled eyes, and Adam wanted more than anything in the world to be able to tell her that everything would be all right now. But he couldn't.

"Lori," he said instead, blinking at his own tears, "Matthew might still be badly hurt."

Plainly, she hadn't even considered this possibility. She gazed down at her child in renewed alarm. "He can't be! Look how he's eating!"

Adam had to agree, he seemed perfectly normal. The blanket in which he had been wrapped had fallen away, and now Adam brushed aside his little wrapper to examine the tiny arms and legs. He poked and probed, expecting at any minute for the child to stiffen in pain, but he got no reaction at all until he started exploring the child's soft little belly. Matthew, who had been watching him avidly as he suckled suddenly released Lori's nipple and gave Adam a big, milky, toothless grin.

"My God, did you see that?" Adam asked incredulously.

Lori nodded, speechless with wonder. Then she said, "We should still get him back to the house." Quickly, she fastened her bodice and got to her feet, still clutching Matthew to her bosom. Only when she realized Adam had made no move to get up, did she notice what was wrong.

"Adam, your leg! What have you done?" she cried in renewed horror.

"I think I wrenched it," he lied, knowing it was far worse than that. "Would you call Oscar. I think I'll need some help—"

But Lori was already calling for him. The big man came directly, his dark face grim as he loped across the field toward them. Only then did Adam allow himself to think about what had happened back there in the yard. Sudie was kneeling, holding Eric to her and rocking back and forth, as if she could make him better.

"My brother?" he asked when Oscar stopped before him.

"He dead, Massa."

Lori's cry seemed to come from very far away as the pain in his leg merged with the pain in his heart and rose up in a crimson tide that threatened to drown him. "I'll need a hand here," he managed through his constricted throat. "I've hurt my leg and . . ."

Oscar needed no other instruction. He immediately reached down to help Adam to his feet, but as Adam's weight settled on his injured leg, the crimson tide rose up again and this time overwhelmed him, and he sank almost gratefully into the blissful oblivion of unconsciousness.

Lori didn't know how much more she could stand. On this day of horrors, she'd managed to hold herself together only because she'd had no other choice.

After watching Adam turn chalk white and pass out from the pain in his injured leg, she'd followed Oscar as he'd carried her husband back to the house only to discover Sudie kneeling in the yard, holding Eric's bloody, ruined head to her bosom.

She'd stood frozen for a long moment, watching the macabre sight and wondering why she felt nothing. How many times had she wished Eric dead? And certainly no one deserved it more, after all the pain he had caused. She should have felt triumph or satisfaction or *something,* but she only felt numb.

Then Sudie had looked up at her, her dark eyes full of the same anguish Lori had felt herself when she'd thought Matthew was dead.

"He couldn't help the way he was," Sudie insisted desperately as the tears streamed down her face. "It was my fault! I should've kept him, but I wanted him to have a good life, not be a slave. I wanted him to have the kind of life Massa Adam had! I didn't know what would happen! I didn't know!"

Of course, she didn't know. How could she have?

So many things made sense now. Sudie had been raped by her master and had borne him a son, which was why she understood so clearly the pain that Lori had endured at Eric's hands. The fact that the son conceived by rape had become a rapist himself was an irony she might someday appreciate, but not quite yet. At the moment, she was only aware that she and Sudie were both holding their children to their bosoms. One was dead, but one was, praise God, still alive. And while Matthew appeared to be all right, she couldn't be sure, and most certainly Adam was *not* all right at all.

She started issuing orders, sending one of the slaves for the doctor, even though it would be hours before he could get here, and giving instructions for Adam to be taken to the master bedroom.

She should also decide what to do with Eric's body, but

when she looked at Sudie's ashen face, she knew she couldn't do what she wanted, which was to order it thrown into an unmarked hole and buried without ceremony.

"I'll take care of him, Missy," Sudie told her brokenly, and Lori left her to do so.

The night passed slowly as they waited for the doctor to arrive. Lori sat up through it in a chair beside Adam's bed while Matthew slept in the cradle at her feet. Miraculously, the baby seemed perfectly fine, except for a few bruises, and he'd been awake and alert for a long time after his ordeal before finally falling asleep again.

Lori would doze from time to time, then wake with a start and instantly lean over to check Matthew to be sure he was still breathing. Then she would check Adam who had been sipping brandy through the night to help with the pain. Sometimes he'd be sleeping and sometimes not, and if he wasn't, he would smile at her and tell her he loved her, even though the pain from his leg was excruciating.

The maids kept a steady stream of hot compresses coming, but no one could bring themselves to mention the black lump that had appeared at the site of Adam's old scar. And Lori, at least, could not bring herself to think about what it might mean. Of course, Lori didn't care if Adam had one leg or two. She would love him regardless, but she knew Adam cared very much. But perhaps her love would help him through this time.

It was almost dawn when the doctor finally arrived. He was an old man, too old to go to war, which was the only reason he was still here. His white hair and lined face gave him an air of competence, however, that Lori greatly appreciated.

"Well, well, Master Adam, what have you done to yourself?" he asked cheerfully as he came into the bedroom.

Adam's face was white, his lips bloodless and his eyes red rimmed, but he shook his head. "Look at the baby first," he said in a near whisper. "Make sure he's all right."

The doctor turned to Lori who was holding Matthew in her arms.

"He seems fine now," she told him. "But after the accident, he was all white and still and we thought . . ."

"Let's see him," the doctor said, setting his bag down on the floor by the bed. "Lay him down right here."

Lori laid the sleeping baby down on the bed beside Adam, and the doctor proceeded to undress him. Matthew protested being disturbed, his mewling cry quickly growing into a howl which didn't seem to bother the doctor a bit.

"His lungs seem fine," he remarked cheerfully, as he probed and poked and wiggled and prodded. "Has he been nursing all right?"

"Yes, just like always," Lori reported.

He asked a few more questions as he finished his examination. Then he wrapped Matthew in his blanket and handed him to Lori to soothe. "He seems perfectly fine."

"How can that be?" Adam demanded weakly. "He was thrown from the buggy and it fell over on him and—"

"Yes, your boy told me what happened. This was in the field?"

Lori nodded.

"The ground would still be soft there, which would have helped absorb the shock, and children's bones don't break as easily as ours do. You should watch him closely for a few days, just in case, but he's probably no worse for his experience. Now, let's have a look at his father."

For a second Lori started, thinking he meant Eric, who was most certainly beyond any help, but of course he meant Adam. Adam, who really *was* Matthew's father now.

"I thought I told you not to ride horseback," the doctor said as he folded back the covers to look at Adam's leg.

"This was an emergency," Adam said as an excuse.

Lori watched the doctor's face as he removed the compress and saw the ugly lump, but he didn't seem as alarmed

s Lori had expected. In fact, he seemed simply puzzled
or a moment.

"Good heavens," he exclaimed after he'd probed the area
arefully, making Adam gasp in pain. Lori had to blink at
ears.

"You're not cutting off my leg this time, either," Adam
varned him through gritted teeth, although Lori could see
he fear in his eyes.

"No," the doctor said agreeably, "but I would like to do
little cutting, if you don't mind. Do you know what you've
lone here?" He pointed at the leg.

Adam had propped himself up on his elbows and now he
ooked down at the leg, too. He shook his head.

"You've worked loose the minie ball, the one that's been
n your leg all this time. I couldn't get it out before because
t was in too deep, almost to the bone. But your little esca-
ade last night has forced it out, or almost out, at any rate.
That's it, right there." He pointed to the black lump. "With
your permission, I'd like to make a small incision and remove
t. It's just under the skin now, so it would only take a moment
and—"

"Yes!" Adam cried. "Of course! Take it out!"

"Does that mean Adam's leg would be normal then?" Lori
asked, rocking Matthew gently. He was still whimpering
slightly.

"I can't promise that," the doctor said. "I don't know how
much damage you did to the muscles today, so I can't predict.
But at the very least, I think you should have less pain and
perhaps no pain at all once everything has healed."

Lori saw the hope in Adam's eyes as he said, "What are
you waiting for?"

The doctor turned to Lori. "Mrs. Ross, I'll need three
strong men to help me hold him down. And I think you
should take the baby into another room and nurse him."

"Oh, I couldn't leave Adam!" she protested.

"Lori," Adam said gently. "The doctor doesn't want you in here when he cuts my leg open."

Lori felt the blood rushing from her head and for a second she was afraid she might faint, but she fought the weakness until it passed. And then she knew the doctor was right.

She reached out and took Adam's hand. "You're going to be fine," she told him. His fingers were warm and strong as he squeezed her hand.

"We're *all* going to be fine," he told her back.

Lori gathered the baby's clothes and carried them and him out into the hall. When she had summoned Oscar and sent him to fetch some other men to help the doctor with the operation, she decided to take Matthew to the parlor which, she hoped, would be far enough away so she wouldn't be able to hear Adam if he cried out in pain.

But as she reached the rear parlor, she was surprised to see a light in the room that had nothing to do with the dawn breaking over the horizon.

She stepped through the doors, and what she saw made her gasp in horror. Several candles flickered, casting an eerie light, and at the far end of the room a coffin rested on a makeshift bier. Beside it Sudie sat in a straight backed chair, her hands folded in her lap, her face as white and still as marble.

She looked up when she heard Lori.

"I laid him out, Missy," she said, her voice oddly hollow. "He look real fine."

Lori remembered the blood and the gore and the gaping wound in Eric's head, and knew he couldn't possibly look *fine* at all. "That's very nice, Sudie," she said gently, purposely not making any move to look in the coffin.

"Will you bury him in the family plot?" she asked, rising slowly to her feet. "I know you gots good reason to hate him, and now you know what I did and that he really ain't . . . Well, he ain't who you thought he was, but he *was* Massa Chet's son, and—"

"Of course he was," Lori said, remembering all that Sudie ad done for her, her kindness and her understanding when o one else had understood. Lori owed her a debt she might ever be able to repay. Sudie's only sin had been wanting a etter life for her child, and it was a sin of which Lori had een guilty, too. She couldn't hold Sudie responsible for what ric had become or what he had done to her. If she had earned nothing else from all of this, she knew at least that ric alone was responsible for that. If she no longer blamed erself, she could not blame Sudie, either. And Sudie had uffered enough. "And of course we'll bury him in the family lot." What harm could it do? He was dead now and would ever hurt anyone else again.

She could see Sudie's rigid shoulders sag with relief at er promise. "He couldn't stand the thought that he'd hurt our baby," Sudie said. "That's why he did it. That's why he hot hisself."

Lori didn't allow her surprise to show. She knew, of ourse, that Eric would have felt no guilt at all, even if Mat-hew had died. What had made him blow his brains out was he knowledge that Sudie was his real mother and that, in pite of his white skin, he was colored. Living with such nowledge would have been unbearable for him.

Matthew stirred in her arms, rooting for her breast. She still hadn't dressed him, and as she looked down at him, she suddenly realized the full implications of Sudie's confession. f Eric had been the son of a slave, then Matthew was the grandson of a slave!

"Nobody ever know, Missy," Sudie said urgently. "I never tell, and as far as anybody else know, Massa Adam's Mat-thew's father."

Sudie was right, of course. No one else need ever know. And Lori knew it wouldn't matter to *her,* but what about Adam? Would it matter to him? Would it make a differ-ence?

Just as the horrible doubt formed in her mind, she heard

Adam cry out as the doctor's knife sliced his living flesh. The sound was faint and far away, but unmistakable, and Lori's blood went cold.

Epilogue

Everything was changing. Lori could feel it in the very air around her. The Yankees had apparently been driven out of Texas, but the news from elsewhere was bad. Rumor had it that the Confederate Army was barefooted and nearly always hungry, and everyone was saying the war couldn't go on much longer. Lori should have been relieved, except that what no one was saying, at least out loud, was that the South was going to lose and no one knew what would happen then. Lori was very much afraid things wouldn't get better, at least not for a long time. And if the slaves were freed and Adam didn't have anyone to work the plantation . . . Well, that didn't bear thinking of, either.

Of course, Lori also had more immediate things to worry about. In the week since the doctor had removed the ball from Adam's leg, he had recovered rapidly. He was up and walking within two days, even though the doctor had recommended at least a week of bedrest. But Adam hadn't wanted the leg to stiffen up, so he had worked it every day. Lori knew it hurt him, but he claimed the pain was nothing compared to what he had endured for so many years. And it got better every day.

But nothing else had gotten better, at least not yet, because neither of them had even mentioned the horrible story that Sudie had told, the one that had driven Eric to take his own life. Of course, talking about it might make things worse, too. For Adam to claim his brother's child as his own had been more than enough to ask of any man. To expect him to claim the grandson of a slave, well, that was too much. Lori understood that only too well.

At least he hadn't asked her to leave, not yet, anyway. In fact, he'd been just as kind and affectionate to her as always. Still, she'd been sleeping in his old room while he recovered in the master bedroom and keeping the baby away from him too. And also, Adam had been a bit self-absorbed, concerned as he was with his own recovery. When he was well, she would have to find out for sure. She would have to test him somehow so she would be certain. She couldn't allow Matthew to grow up unwanted and unloved the way Eric had, even if that meant living the rest of her life without Adam.

"Lori?"

Lori looked up in surprise from where she had been sitting sewing in the back parlor, to find Adam standing in the doorway. She smiled at the sight of him. Indeed, he looked more handsome than ever, dressed in a fresh shirt and tan duck trousers. His mere presence warmed her to her very soul, and then he fully returned her smile.

"I'd like to try out my new leg outside, and I was wondering if you'd like to walk with me."

She glanced down at Matthew, who was asleep in his cradle. He looked like a tiny angel.

"I already asked Effie to keep an eye on him," Adam said. "We won't be gone long."

Lori didn't want to go. She knew from the expression on Adam's face that he wanted more than some exercise. He wanted to talk to her, away from the house where no one could overhear them, and when he did, she would know for sure how he felt about Matthew and what he had learned about Eric and how it would change all their lives. She knew instinctively that when she returned everything would be different, and as much as she hated this uncertainty, fearing what he might say to her even more.

But she wasn't going to let her fear control her. If she had earned nothing else from the past few months, she had earned that. Still smiling, as if she anticipated only a pleasant outing, she rose to her feet.

"I'd love to go for a walk," she said and went to him.

She tried not to watch the way he moved as he stepped aside to allow her to pass through the doorway and as he followed her down the hall to the back door. She paused to lift her shawl from the hook beside the door and started when Adam took it from her and laid it around her shoulders.

"Thank you," she said, a little breathless as his hands lingered just a moment too long in a fleeting caress.

"Why are you blushing?" he asked with apparent amusement.

"I'm not blushing," she lied and hurried outside.

To her surprise, he had no trouble at all keeping up with her, though. In fact, as she saw when she looked at him, he was hardly even limping, and he didn't have his cane.

"Your leg doesn't hurt you?" she asked in surprise.

"It's still a little sore, but I've found that the more I walk, the better it feels. Shall we?" he asked, offering her his arm, as if *she* were the one who needed support.

She took it gladly, savoring the feel of his strong arm beneath her hand, and smiled up at him. He smiled back and laid his other hand over hers where it rested on his arm. For a few moments, as they walked in silence, Lori forgot everything except how wonderful it felt to be with him again, just the two of them.

He walked easily, if a bit slowly, and after a while he said, "I'm going to be fine, Lori. I won't be a cripple anymore."

"I never thought you were before," she reminded him.

"But you were worried about how I'd run this place after the war, if the slaves were free."

"I think you were the one who brought that up. I wasn't worried. I've been poor all my life, Adam. I'm not afraid to be poor again, and I'm certainly not afraid of hard work."

His eyes were troubled as he gazed down at her. "I hope

it doesn't come to that, but at least you can be sure that I'll be able to do my share of that work. In a week or two, expect I'll be able to walk behind a plow, if I have to."

Lori almost smiled at that image, but just then she happened to notice the direction in which they were walking. "Where are we going?" she asked in alarm.

Adam stopped. "I want to see where you laid him, Lori."

They'd buried Eric that first morning. Lori hadn't seen any reason to wait, since Adam was in no shape to attend the burial and wouldn't be for several days. Since the Ross family would be expected to feel shame over the fact that Eric had died by his own hand, no one would question her haste or her failure to call their friends and neighbors to gather. She'd simply told Oscar to take care of everything, and the next time she'd gone to the parlor, the awful coffin and its hideous contents had been gone. She certainly hadn't considered visiting his grave, and she wasn't sure she wanted to now.

"You don't have to go with me, but I'd like you to," Adam said. "I didn't want to go alone."

Lori knew what it was like to be alone, and she didn't want Adam to feel that way, not when she loved him so very much. Without a word she started walking again, down the path that led to the small cemetery where the Ross family had buried their dead.

The family plot was surrounded by a wrought iron fence. Inside were the graves of Adam's parents, marked with marble headstones. The flowers that had been planted on them in the spring were fading now and nearly dead. Outside the fence were the graves of the slaves that had died on the plantation. One of them, Lori knew, was the grave of Adam's real brother, the one whom Sudie had claimed was her child, but she tried not to think of that. It was easy when she saw the mound of freshly turned earth that marked Eric's grave.

She had expected to feel some kind of satisfaction at this

proof that Eric had paid the ultimate price for his cruelties to her and Adam. Instead, she simply felt sad.

"You put him in the family plot," Adam said with some surprise.

"I promised Sudie that I would. He was your father's son, after all, but if you want him moved . . ."

"Oh, no," Adam assured her. "I was afraid . . . You've got every reason to hate him. We both do. But he was the only brother I ever knew. I don't think I ever understood how he felt until I found out what he had done to you." Lori looked up at him in surprise, but he was staring at Eric's unmarked grave. "I despised him because he'd taken what I thought was mine, and when I saw him going after you and the baby . . ."

He did look at her then, and his eyes fairly blazed with the memory, "I wanted to kill him, Lori. I wanted to kill him so that I could have what I thought was mine."

"Oh, Adam, you don't have to feel guilty—"

"No, don't you see?" he interrupted her. "That's how he must have felt about *me*. I've been thinking about this a lot while I've been lying in bed these past few days. Our father loved me but not him. It wasn't fair, and it wasn't his fault, and in his twisted way, he must have thought that if he killed me, he could get back what was rightfully his. That's why he shot me years ago . . . And that's why he attacked you."

"What?"

"You told me that you've loved me for a long time, Lori. Well, I had feelings for you, too. They weren't quite that honorable, I'm afraid. I merely wanted you. But I didn't think you were worthy of my attentions. I didn't think you were good enough for a Ross."

His words stung, but Lori could tell by the way his voice broke that they hurt him as much as they did her. "Adam, don't," she begged him.

But he ignored her protest. "If I hadn't been so proud, I would have courted you openly, and then Eric couldn't have tricked you. But because of my stupid pride, Eric was able to—"

"Don't!" she cried. "Stop it! We can't change the past, and we can't take the blame for what Eric did! Lots of people have parents who don't love them, but that's no reason for hurting other people! There's no excuse at all for the things he did to both of us and punishing ourselves won't change that. Adam, the only hope we have is to forget the past and try to go on."

"Can you forget the past?" he challenged.

Lori could almost hear Sudie's warning that she would never really forget what Eric had done to her. "Maybe not completely," she admitted, hurrying on when she saw the despair in his eyes, "but I can make sure it doesn't ruin any chance I have for happiness in the future. I love you, Adam. I loved you before Eric attacked me, and I love you more now. He can't destroy that, unless we let him."

Adam's mouth curved in a smile that was infinitely sad. "I can't believe I ever thought myself too good for you, Lori McClintock. You have more honor than the entire Ross family put together."

Her smile wasn't sad at all. "Have you forgotten? I'm a Ross now, too."

"Perhaps you can save us, then. You may be our last hope."

But she wasn't the *last* hope. "Adam," she began, not at all certain what to say or how to ask him what she needed to know. "What Sudie said, about Eric being her son . . ."

Adam frowned and his gaze drifted over to where the slave graves lay in neat rows, to where the baby that was his real brother lay. "I always wondered why she didn't cry when her baby died. She never shed a tear."

Was it possible? Could he not have thought about what all this meant for Matthew? "Adam, if Eric was Sudie's son, then Matthew is—"

"Matthew is *my* son," he told her fiercely, cutting her off. "Unless *you* don't want him anymore," he added. "Unless you want to send him down to the quarters to be raised with his own kind!"

"*No!*" Lori cried, horrified. "How could you say such a thing!" Only then did she realize how stiffly Adam had been holding himself because suddenly the tension drained out of him and he took her by her shoulders and turned her to face him.

"Are you saying it doesn't matter to you?" he demanded. "That you don't care that Matthew has Negro blood?"

"Of course it doesn't matter! He's my son, and I love him!"

"And he's my son, too, now, because I love him, too."

"Oh, Adam, are you sure?"

"Lori, I know I promised you that I'd be a real father to him because I didn't want him to grow up twisted, the way Eric did, but that was before I knew Matthew. Now I do know him, I know everything about him, and I want to be his father more than ever. So, yes, I'm sure. I'm positive."

Lori threw her arms around him, and he crushed her to him. After a moment, he found her mouth with his and kissed her fiercely, as if he were claiming her for the very first time. When he was finished, he drew away, cupping her face with his hands.

"I want to make love to you, Mrs. Ross, but first I want to see my son."

"I guess we need to go back to the house then," Lori said, so happy she wanted to laugh out loud.

He kissed her again, and then he tucked her hand through his arm once more, and they turned back toward the house. Behind them lay the past, but it was dead and buried now. Ahead of them lay the future. For no particular reason, Lori remembered a part of her marriage vows, a phrase that had seemed somehow important at the time and which she now realized held a particular promise: from this day forward. Not looking back, not held by the shackles of the past, she and Adam would face what lay ahead together, secure in the knowledge that the trials through which they had come had made them strong enough to endure whatever might befall them.

Author's Note

I would like to offer a special note of thanks to Anna Fleck, the director of the Blair County Rape Crisis Program. Anna very generously advised me when I was planning this story, so that I could accurately describe a victim's reaction to rape, and she read the completed manuscript to make sure I had done so. The only thing she asked in return was that I not portray my heroine as making a miraculous and complete recovery from her ordeal after only a few weeks, but rather that I realistically show how Lori's recovery was a gradual process, one she will continue working through for the rest of her life.

Lori McClintock was the victim of what we now call "date rape" or "acquaintance rape." While most people think of a rapist as a perverted monster who leaps out on his victims from the bushes or breaks into their homes in the dark of night and beats them brutally into submission before raping them, the fact is that most rapists appear perfectly normal and function normally, except for their predilection for forcing women they meet or already know to have sex with them whether the women are willing or not. These rapists only use as much force as necessary to subdue their victims and often take no pleasure from hurting them. Their goal is simply to exert their power over women, and they do this by forcing them to have intercourse against their will.

While acquaintance rape is probably most common, it is also the kind of rape least often reported and most difficult to prosecute. The victim typically has no serious injuries to prove she was coerced or that she resisted, and often she was voluntarily in the rapist's company, perhaps even on a date with him. The rapist offers a convincing defense, too, since he truly believes himself to be innocent of wrongdoing because "she asked for it."

But just because a woman knows her attacker and wasn't seriously injured in the attack does not make her any less a victim of rape. In fact, such victims may suffer more because friends and family and law enforcement officials often do not believe the victims or sympathize with them. Like Lori, these victims endure the double humiliation of being somehow blamed for their own attack. Or worse, they are too ashamed to admit what happened and never seek help at all.

If you or someone you know is a victim of acquaintance rape or rape of any kind, do not hesitate to seek help. Most communities have rape crisis programs with trained counselors who will believe you and will help you deal with the trauma. Whether or not you seek to prosecute the rapist, and no matter how much time has passed since the attack, counseling can help.

As a result of researching this book, I have developed a tremendous respect for women who have survived the trauma of rape and for those who help them. I only hope this book will contribute in some small way toward educating the public to recognize acquaintance rape for the crime that it is so that it will no longer be tolerated or misunderstood, as has happened so often in the past.

I love to hear from my readers. If you would like to tell me how you enjoyed this book and would like a newsletter telling you when my next book will be coming out, please send a long self-addressed stamped envelope to:

Victoria Thompson
P.O. Box 134
Duncansville, PA 16635-0134

ROMANCE FROM JANELLE TAYLOR

DANGEROUS GAMES   (0-7860-0270-0, $4.99)
by Amanda Scott

When Nicholas Barrington, eldest son of the Earl of Ul-
combe, first met Melissa Seacort, the desperation he
sensed beneath her well-bred beauty haunted him. He
didn't realize how desperate Melissa really was . . . until
he found her again at a Newmarket gambling club—being auctioned off by her father to the highest bidder. So,
Nick bought himself a wife. With a villain hot on their
heels, and a fortune and their lives at stake, they would
gamble everything on the most dangerous game of all:
love.

A TOUCH OF PARADISE   (0-7860-0271-9, $4.99)
by Alexa Smart

As a confidence man and scam runner in 1880s America,
Malcolm Northrup has amassed a fortune. Now, posing
as the eminent Sir John Abbot—scholar, and possible
discoverer of the lost continent of Atlantis—he's taking
his act on the road with a lecture tour, seeking funds for
a scientific experiment he has no intention of making.
But scholar Halia Davenport is determined to accompany
Malcolm on his "expedition" . . . even if she must kidnap
him!